I0607410

CHANCE

Kate Mac Donald

CHANCE

Kate Mac Donald

Mountain Mouth Press
5980 Wofford Blvd.
Wofford Heights, CA 93285

CHANCE
Copyright © 2019
Kate MacDonald

Published by:

Mountain Mouth Press
5980 Wofford Blvd.
Wofford Heights, CA 93285
themountainmouth@wordpress.com

No part of this book may be reproduced or transmitted in any form or by any means, electronic or mechanical, including photocopying, recording, or by any information storage and retrieval system, without permission in writing from the copyright holder.

Edited by: Gabriella West
Art direction: Kate MacDonald
Cover design: Sarah Aumann, Diane Spencer Hume
Cover painting, author photo, drawing *Chance* on page 298: Kelly McLane
Book design and typesetting: Diane Spencer Hume

Although all reasonable care has been taken in the preparation of this book, neither the author nor the publisher can accept liability for any consequences arising from the information contained herein, or from use thereof.

To My Parents, Rod and Ginny Mac Donald

"You can accomplish anything"

CONTENTS

PROLOGUE

The day the world disappeared, it was a lovely, cold morning, frost glittering and melting on the grass. He had been listening to the wind tickle the sage when a different, ominous sound came from all over all at once, and at once there was panic and everyone was running, running, fast as a storm. Always before, to simply run was to escape all threats; but this time the sound, the overwhelming beating of the sky, chased them, and overtook them, and they ran harder and longer than they ever had, until finally there was a barrier that they could not leap and they were bunched together and sweating and steaming. They circled and fought and screamed, but there was no longer anywhere to go. Their one great defense, their speed, escape, was impossible. They cried and raged; and those who had gotten away screamed too, but they could still run, so reluctantly, with much weeping and calling, they did. And the family was fractured; and the babies' feet were bloodied and the mothers, full with new life, fell down and groaned. And nothing would ever be the same.

His breath came heavy, his shaggy head hung low in shame, and for the first time he did not know what to do. For the first time he shivered not in cold, but in uncertainty, in a deep, chilling fear. Life was over; but he was still purposelessly, disastrously alive.

DESTINY

In the perfect center of the round pen, Destiny becomes an oversized sundial; her shadow draws a lumpy line on the dirt marking the time: a shade past ten in the morning. Circling tirelessly around the perimeter of the enclosure is not the second hand of some giant clock but a snorting, wild-eyed horse, its shining coat darkening with sweat. Destiny sweats too, not in sympathy, but as a new recruit does facing battle. Her heart races; she feels scared and hungry in almost equal measure. Her blue shirt sticks to her back so she can imagine she feels the words printed there: Frontera Women's Correctional Institution. She clutches the cotton rope in her hands like it is a snake she could squeeze to death. Every instruction she has heard that was supposed to prepare her for this moment vanishes from her memory, and she stands rooted to the center of the pen like a rabbit that feels the shadow of a hawk.

"Tubb," yells Varney again. "Swing that rope!"

Swing that rope. The hawk's shadow mercifully passes and Destiny remembers what to do. Her right hand describes a circle and the rope end begins to wobbily revolve. The horse, without slowing, tosses its head and crow-hops, sending a twisting kick Destiny's way. Destiny steps back instinctively, stomach thumping with awe at the animal's quickness, its agility, at its big, hard hooves.

"Get in there, drive him, Tubb," says Varney.

Destiny wants out of this steel pen and away from this sweating, circling monster, but is more afraid of quitting, of losing. She's so tired of being a loser. She keeps swinging the rope and tentatively begins to turn, following the horse in a smaller circle.

"Good, Tubb," says Varney. "Keep at his hip. Just keep at him."

Destiny keeps circling, swinging the rope, and the horse clearly doesn't like it. His head tosses, he bucks and kicks. Keep at him, Varney keeps saying, and Destiny swings the rope until her arm aches but the horse pays her no attention. The horse ignoring her begins to be humiliating. She has been ignored too much already in her short life. This is stupid, she thinks. She can't do this! She wonders what the prison authorities were thinking, to put inmates in charge of wild horses. They probably figured nobody cared if a prisoner or two got tromped to death. Unless it gets on the news.

The horse suddenly stops and faces the fence.

"He's disrespecting you, better get on him," Varney says, and Destiny, only because she has no choice, takes a small step towards the horse and lamely tosses the rope at its flanks. The horse kicks and twists, and Destiny's despair smothers her and she feels a surge of strength, but it is not pure, she moans and throws the rope in frustration, in fear, in rage. The horse rears and clangs frighteningly upon the six-foot pipe rails like it would do anything to escape—and suddenly the terrible feelings subside within her and Destiny realizes: this horse is more scared than I am. He'd do anything to escape. Just like me, like everybody in here. Poor horse probably thinks I'm trying to kill him. She tosses the rope as gracefully as she can, and imagines the horse understanding, responding, and amazingly, it does. It turns off the rail, a change just as abrupt and inexplicable as life itself, and begins to circle again, its head lowered, its paces now rhythmic.

The monstrous white sun and the burning heat are like an interrogation; the inescapable pen and the circles of razor wire on the towering chain-link fences are the perfect symbols and proof of her sentence. The fact of Destiny Tubb in the pen is just like her dreadful crime, the result of another of her stupidities. The circling, sweating monster is like her badness, her guilt: dangerous, out of control. Running in meaningless circles.

Sergeant Varney said most all can all be tamed. Destiny thinks: this horse is wild as crap. It won't allow a touch, much less a rider. It is both beautiful and ugly in its own fear. It isn't large. It is a brown color they call sorrel. Its tail is matted, but held high. The brand is new on its impossibly muscular neck. Its eyes roll, showing white. It snorts deeply, it drums the dirt with steel-hard hooves, ominous and loudly enough to remind everyone its power can be lethal. The sounds alone are enough to stop Destiny's heart. Much less the wild, white rolling eyes! The horse could come at her at any second, and it sure looks like it wants to. Its teeth like steel pincers, flying hooves like bricks, it could kill her before she'd have a second to tell Jesus, "I'ma coming, Lord!..."

"Turn him," barks Varney.

Destiny glances at the cop, hoping, maybe, for reprieve, for mercy, but instead her gaze catches on an inmate from her Block, flashing yet another gang sign she doesn't understand. All of a sudden, death-by-horse doesn't seem so bad. One reluctant step at a time, she moves to intercept the horse at its shoulder. A desperate flip of the rope as the horse comes around towards her. Like magic, the horse snorts mightily, puts on the brakes, and twirls in a ballet-like leap on his rear legs and begins circling in the opposite direction. Destiny is rooted into place, shocked by her own success.

"Good, step back, take the pressure off, so he knows he done right."

So she swirls the rope and the horse continues circling, and a small soap bubble of hope that she might be successful at something rises and pops just as quickly. Just because she can make a horse turn… she's still got her feet on the ground. Getting on it? Riding it? Yeah, right. Like that will ever happen.

* * *

Tonya, who was Destiny's self-appointed tormentor, was all over her about the wild horse program. She demanded to know what Destiny had been thinking and why she thought she wouldn't be gruesomely maimed and killed by a wild horse. Tonya had a brother who was a bull rider and she knew all about wild horses and rodeo. Did Destiny think she could really ride a fucking wild horse?

Destiny shrugged, feeling hot and sick. It was a mistake, just another stupid mistake. She hadn't meant to volunteer for the program. Working in the laundry sucked big time, but it was something to make the time pass; she'd had no intention to do anything more than serve her time and not make enemies, but, as usual, she'd messed up during the assembly when the warden was telling them about "a new opportunity."

Warden Weems had introduced a cop, Sergeant Varney. He had a typical cop's stocky body, his khaki shirt and Kevlar vest squeezing his flesh like a sausage casing. His nose looked like it had been stung by bees, but his voice was calm and smooth, not mean or bossy.

Varney talked about how wild horses were rounded up from the public lands and then adopted by people. If the horses were trained, they were more easily adopted. Destiny had suddenly focused, remembering the old white horse that was pastured next to her Aunt Lacey's house outside Bakersfield. The mare had beautiful, expressive eyes, powder-white eyelashes, and a lovely, soft nose; Destiny all of a sudden remembered picking grass and feeding it to that old horse, and petting that velvet nose with its pink stripe and long, silly whiskers, she could almost smell the green scent of fresh-picked grass… That had been before Aunt Lacey moved to Vegas and got herself killed on some desert highway by a drunk driver…

So this Sergeant Varney had gone on talking and the next thing Destiny knew Warden Weems was talking, so as usual, there was little point in paying attention. A fly was buzzing around Destiny's face. She batted it away. It came back, landed on her nose! Ugh, gross! She could feel the tiny insect feet even after it lifted off—she swatted and tried to decimate the fly, but it spiraled up.

"You volunteering, Tubb?" said Weems.

"Yes ma'am?" yelped Destiny by reflex, frightened at hearing her name called.

"You want in the program?" Weems asked, sounding sarcastic. There was laughing and a current of comments, as indistinguishable as the babbling of a crick.

"Yes ma'am?" said Destiny again, wondering why she didn't say what she meant. The buzzing in her head was louder than a family of disgusting, buzzing flies. Her mouth was stuck. Confusion, hot and suffocating, overwhelmed her.

* * *

"Yes, ma'am," she had stupidly blurted, wanting the laughter to stop, wanting out. And she had done it. Gotten herself involved—again—in something stupid, dangerous, something she had no business with. Story of my life, Destiny now thought bitterly, curled on her bunk, chewing the last bits of a fingernail. She curled towards the wall and pulled her scratchy blanket up over her head; and soon, Tonya shut up, whispered her elaborate prayers, bounced, groaning, until she found comfort, then farted several times, and began snoring.

Immediately, Destiny wished her cellmate had kept on talking; she never knew when the bad memories would come to haunt, taunt, terrify.

Tonight, so far, seemed okay. She had the horses to think about. Destiny could well remember the day the wild mustangs came to the prison.

All thirteen volunteers for the training program were there to see the horses get unloaded from the big stock trailers into the new pipe corrals: green-painted steel rails two inches thick, six feet tall created rows of twenty four foot corrals, with a wide alley in between, and several big round pens. The drivers backed the trailers up to the open gates and then swung open the trailer doors. The horses were loose inside the truck, and there was a lot of banging, kicking, and squealing while the panicked mustangs stumbled, pushed, and jumped out of the big steel trailers.

Destiny was stunned. The mustangs smelled of sage and sweat, their huge eyes were mesmerizing, their immediate, mus-cled, wild strength was as frightening as a tiger's.

They were brown, red, and yellow; they were spotted, splotched, and gray. They surged in wild circles, frantic, futile. Beautiful and tragic. Wildness captured, but unlike Destiny, the horses were presumably innocent. But they surged against their fences and cried more piteously than any virgin.

Then they were all in the corrals, running, kicking, biting each other. Finally, they settled down some, and began eating hay and drinking from the water troughs.

Varney was there, and talked more to them about the program. He said each of the inmates—he called them "cowgirls"—would train at least one horse, they'd get assigned a particular horse. They'd learn to do "ground work" and teach the horse manners. They'd learn to lead it on a rope, pick up its feet, and groom it. And then they'd put the saddle and bridle on it… and then ride it. That's when Destiny thought she'd die, when she imagined having to get on one of these big, wild beasts. She was thinking she'd have to figure out a way to get out of this before that became necessary while Varney showed them how to feed and water the horses and clean up the manure. All the chores plus grooming their horses would be part of their job. All the other inmates complained about that part, but shoveling poop didn't worry Destiny. She was too busy worrying about being killed. Even though she had no particular reason to keep on living.

* * *

The horse is tiring. The exertion of swinging the rope, concentrating on the horse, has its effect on Destiny too. Her panic and fear has abated, leaving her clear-headed, focused, almost light on her feet. She manages to turn the horse several times and is now waiting for the "signs."

"There, his ear's on you, see that?" Varney says.

She did see it. Within seconds, the horse shows other signs of responding. It begins to make chewing motions and then after a few revolutions of the pen, suddenly drops its head, as if sniffing the trail like a hunting dog. These are the signs that the horse is ready to negotiate, Destiny remembers.

"Release the pressure," Varney instructs. Destiny lets the swinging rope end drop to the dirt and stands still. The horse instantly slows to a halt and turns, facing Destiny. It looks right at her and for the first time Destiny realizes, He's beautiful! The horse is breathing heavily but stands calmly.

"Go ahead," she hears. Destiny reaches out a hand, palm down, and steps toward the horse. Its ears, its eyes, are focused completely on her, but otherwise the horse doesn't move. She takes another step closer, then another. Then she is up to the horse, can smell him, his heady sweat, his breath, which is sweet, like flowers or grass. Destiny reaches out, her hand limp, fingers curved inwards, so that her hand looks more or less like a horse's nose. The horse stretches out his neck and slowly, gently, touches her fingers. His breath is hot, his nose impossibly soft.

"Great, now back off," Varney says quietly. "It's all about pressure and release. Pressure and release."

Destiny drops her hand and slowly turns, and as she walks away, the horse follows. The wild, snorting mustang has relaxed, his ears flopped sideways and his eyes no longer showing white. He follows her as if Destiny leads him on a rope, but the only connector is the magic of the training. Destiny walks a few steps, the horse by her shoulder as if he's become her shadow. She can feel his intense curiosity. She knows he can trample her at any second, or bite her with those huge teeth. But magically, the horse seems like the last thing on its mind is hurting her.

Then it's over. Varney tells her to leave the pen, someone opens a gate, she floats through; another gate clangs and the horse trots through, back into the big corral. When the horse drops his head to drink without looking back at her, Destiny feels almost abandoned.

Leaving the sunlight and dry hot air for the cool, clanking cellblock is never more terrible. As she enters her cell to face Tonya's interrogations and insults, she can't believe how different everything is. She can hardly wait for the next time with the horse. Later, after lights out, she lies in her bunk, the itchy, inadequate blanket tucked up under her chin, and for the first time in forever, her prayers are answered, and she doesn't replay scenes from her failures, co-starring Loreen and the kids, Danny and Mitch, and always, Justin. Instead, she sees the horse, his white blaze, his wild mane; his deep brown, wise and wild eyes, that seem to forgive her in advance, for everything.

THE DOCTOR IS IN

This morning: the first edge of sunlight onto my closed eyes is like a slap. I moan and turn over to escape. Later: the beauty of the morning continues its assault. I drag myself from bed, joints clicking and creaking. Coffee. A Vicodin.

The dogs wait unhappily. Finally, I've found slippers and have cup and cigarette in hand and we proceed outside to the porch. Down the path and open the gate so they can run. I should worry about snakes and coyotes but I'm beyond taking the usual precautions. The dogs will return, probably, in a few minutes, for breakfast. I wonder if there is dog food. I can't remember. A bluebird couple flits by, the sunlight is creamy on the sage hillsides, but I'm not moved. There is something eating the roses. In my previous lifetime I would have acted immediately. Now I know, without a doubt, the bugs will eat their way through each closed, sweet, blood-colored bud—and I could care less. I might even enjoy watching them do it. I smoke another Camel and soon the knife pain in my feet and hands subsides, and the idea of staying out of bed for a while seems possible.

There is dog food, fortunately, but not much, and it registers that I am getting dangerously low on supplies, mainly and most critically, wine and tobacco and… what? Oh, dog food. But a trip to town is too monumental to contemplate. I push the thought of it aside for tomorrow. After feeding the dogs, I should go and do the same for the chickens, but it takes another cup of sludgy coffee and a smoke before I feel up to it. The chickens cluck and coo appreciation. There are eight big brown eggs. I add them to the large stash of cartons in the refrigerator, thinking, if only we could live on eggs alone. But even the dogs rebel, eventually, as I have discovered.

I stare at the regiments of cartons of perfect eggs, wondering if I am hungry. After a considerable while, I still can't decide. I turn from the pantry into the kitchen. The tile counter is piled with dirty glasses and dog food cans and empty wine bottles; flies buzz over the repulsive mess.

I decide to clean up at least a little, and pick up an empty bottle. The trash can and recycling bin are both overfull. I have to empty them first, and that defeats me, because, really, who cares? Until there are legions of ants and mice and other vermin invading because of my slovenliness, who cares? The dogs don't judge me—at least on that account... but they do judge me: Teddy, the pathologically jealous dachshund; Freddie, the hyperactive, fun-loving terrier; and Slim, the big, insecure mutt. They wish I were my old self. That we'd go for walks up the canyon, and that they'd get baths, and leftovers from dinner. They miss Hank. And our life. I have little sympathy for the dogs. If I had sympathy for anyone, which I don't anymore, it would be me.

Me, me, me, me, me. I know my mental state is unhealthy, I even know what I should do, but, like the issue of the wine bottles and the recycling, who cares? Who cares, who cares, who cares.

I wander around the hacienda. It was our dream house. Not big, but built for fun and comfort, simplicity and beauty. Adobe walls, tile roof, a simple square with a courtyard in the center. One story; excepting the squat tower that rises from the northwest corner. The fireplace opens both in the courtyard and into the living room.

The sunny dining area—it's an open floor plan—adjoins the kitchen and the living room, overlooking the slate-tiled porch with the trestle table and (now bug-eaten) red climbing roses on the pale yellow adobe walls. Off to the right as you come in the front door is the bedroom with its view of the mountains, and on the opposite wall of the bedroom the pocket doors into my tower and office, which I have barely stepped inside since using it to reply to the condolence cards. All through the house, the rough walls are a pale butter yellow and hung with our art and photos of our travels and relatives. Here is our leather furniture, weathered but still good, our too-expensive rugs and giant bed. Here are our copper pots and pans, electric appliances, and sharp Japanese knives.

I cross the room to Hank's chair and fall into it. I turn my head to the leather, hoping to catch a whiff of him. All I smell is dog. At that, Freddie jumps in my lap, and licks my face. I kiss the top of his head—it's so soft—and close my eyes. The day stretches out in front of me like a desert to be crossed. I will die out there without a canteen and compass. But I am parched, so parched that not even our good well water can help. And my compass is gone.

I sit there until I am completely disgusted by myself, at this pathetic, paralyzed poor excuse for a human that I have become. Hank would be disappointed in me. I push Freddie off my lap, ignoring his growl of complaint. I walk purposefully into the office and find a pad of paper and my lucky pen. I pour another cup of coffee and take everything out to the porch. I settle myself at the table in the dappled shade and unscrew the pen's cap. At the top of a blank page, I write: PROJECTS.

I hesitate as all the things I should do flood my flaccid brain. A drop of ink oozes from the nib, underscoring my indecision.

Wash dishes. Clean kitchen. Sweep entire place and pick up all the clutter. Wash clothes and sheets and towels. Take a bath. Bathe the dogs. Spray the bugs on the roses. Go to town, shopping. Call for propane delivery. Check the batteries and the generators. Take dogs for a walk, take them to get their shots. Get a job or volunteer in town to do something… counsel troubled teens? Work at the Youth Camp? Take old ladies their lunch? I sigh, putting down the pen, staring at the daunting list. I'm an old lady, I think. I wish someone would bring me lunch.

At that exact moment the dogs start barking ferociously. I jump to my feet, heart pounding. Between the yips and yowls I hear a distant car's horn. I clutch up the notebook, then put it down, and then pick it up again and run for the office. I stub my toe going up the stairs to the tower. I had teased Hank when he set up the little telescope pointing down at the gate. But of course we'd used it. From here you can look through the scope down the quarter-mile long drive, and see whoever it is, so close it's like looking over their hood through the windshield. If you wanted them to enter, you pressed the remote control that opened the gate. But despite all this low-tech security, there was never a time we didn't open the gate.

I put my eye to the telescope. I have to blink a few times to get the image to focus, I am trembling, and my heart's still thumping wildly. It's a red pickup truck and the driver is my best-friend-forever.

Fuck. She is here to rescue me. I don't want to be rescued. She is honking her horn and yelling something, right at me, she knows about the telescope. My finger trembles over the remote gate opener. I can't do it. My old self, locked inside me somewhere, desperately wants to see her, to have a friend, to be interested in someone other than myself. I know I should be concerned with her life too, we can surely help each other but fuck, just not right now.

I can't. I just can't. My finger trembles until finally she shakes her head, says something, gives me the finger, and backs her truck around and leaves. Only then can I rise from the scope and clench my hands together to stop the shaking.

Now I'm really around the bend. Now I'm officially acting really, truly crazy. I ought to know, being a doctor of psychology with nineteen years of practice to prove it. I collapse onto the Tibetan rug. I reach for the notebook fallen to the floor. I look at the hopeful list, doubting I can do thing one. It's clear, I'm sick. I need help. If I were my patient, how would I help myself?

How are you feeling, Sara Beth? I automatically ask myself.

Dreadful. Paralyzed. Hopeless. Godless. Meaningless.

Let's take those one at a time. The dreadful feeling. What do you dread?

Today and the next day and the rest of my life.

What can happen today to make it worse?

Good question, I answer admiringly.

So answer it.

I guess… not a hell of a lot. Here I am cowering on the floor, hiding from my best friend.

And tomorrow?

Can't be much worse than today, I admit.

How about the rest of your life?

The worst imaginable thing has already happened. It can't get worse than that. Yep, it's all easy street from here.

Now how do you feel about the dread?

Maybe it's been overrated. Maybe all that's left there is physical dreadfulness.

In what way?

In that, I feel hungry but I can't eat. My muscles are atrophied, my joints are rusted, I stink, and my hair is so dirty it's disgusting. All of that adds up to pretty damn dreadful.

We can do something about all those things. But let's just think about one thing, and forget about the others for now. How about taking a bath? You can do that, right? Just a nice hot bath. Light some candles, relax in the tub, wash your hair?

I guess I can do that, I say. But I bet you're going to make me do something else. And I can't. I bet you're going to make me try to eat something. And I can't!

One thing at a time. Don't worry about food. Let's just take a bath.

Okay, fine, I snarl. All right. I'm going!

I run the water as hot as I can stand. Strip my clothes off in a heap. In the mirror is a skinny old lady: droopy boobs, long, unruly gray-blond hair and crosshatched skin. My eyes are navy blue, not that anyone can see them under my un-lifted eyelids.

I have no emotion regarding my aging reflection. That's one compensation for my extreme mental disarrangement, I decide—there's no point in vanity, or self pity. I call Freddie; he feels left out and whines at the door if I don't let him guard me in the bath. His claws click on the tile floor until he settles with a grunt onto the rug.

I get in the water slowly, crouching at first, then kneeling, then finally lying back. The big slipper-tub is under a window, looking out at the orchard. The trees are all covered in pink and white buds. The last time I remember looking at them, they were bare.

I breathe deeply and I feel the hot water on my skin and smell the expensive aromatherapy candles and try to let my mind rest on the idea of the blossoming fruit trees, plum and apricot and apple and cherry. I haven't sprayed them, or watered them, yet they bloom anyway. The world goes on; spring comes undaunted, even though Hank is gone. I swear I can see him exactly as he looked the day we planted those trees. Old flannel shirt and worn jeans. His straw cowboy hat. His grizzled face and lovely strong hands. We took turns with the posthole digger until we had nice, deep holes, then added fertilizer and then the little bare-root trees. We staked them and watered them and then climbed the hill to admire the little orchard. It was just a neat line of sticks, but we saw tall, verdant trees, heavy with fruit. How sure I'd been that we'd see those trees bear. That we'd pick the apricots and learn how to make jam. I'd bake a cherry pie, Hank's favorite. He never got his pie.

I wish I could believe in heaven; that my Henry is waiting for me there, eating cherry pie in the meantime. Grief is so much harder for those without faith. As a Catholic-raised kid I'd believed in heaven. In my twenties and thirties I'd believed in reincarnation. In my forties I questioned everything, finding no definitive answers; I'd even gone back to church, hoping they could prove God existed. But they didn't want to even open that question, all was answered by "faith" and about how much time and money you could contribute to their bake sales and Casino Night fundraisers. Now, at fifty-four, I seriously doubt there's a hereafter. I don't believe in ghosts or spirits or angels. I do suspect there's life on other planets, just as random and meaningless and tragic as life on earth.

The water's getting cold. I struggle to sit up and wash my hair. I lay back to rinse and do it again. I even condition. Then wash my face, my feet, my crotch. Fuck shaving anything though. Then I stand up and shower quickly. The water in the tub swirls out, quite gray. I do feel somewhat better, wrapped in a big towel, watching my dirt drain from the tub, leaving a ring. I brush out my hair and find clean underwear and clothes. Then I return to the bathroom and scrub the ring from the tub, hang up the towel, gather my smelly clothes from the floor.

Good, says my inner therapist. Now, keep moving. How about a drink of water?

I follow the suggestion into the kitchen and, standing at the sink, drink a glass of water.

Something to eat?

Hah! I yell, startling the dogs, who were following me around as usual—I knew you were going to say that.

So, big deal, I'm you, of course you know what we're going to say. How about an orange? Some toast?

Blueberry pancakes, I say out loud, like somebody's spoiled grandchild.

The dachshund whines hopefully.

Mm, blueberry pancakes! Why not? Sounds delicious.

Quickly, before I can talk myself out of it, I get out the flour and sugar and baking soda, powdered milk, and an egg, and melt some butter in the skillet. I've made pancakes so many times from scratch I don't need to check the cookbook. I get blueberries from the freezer. They are coated with ice crystals. I dump some in a bowl to thaw and throw away the rest of the bag. I mix the dry ingredients then add the melted butter and milk and egg. I mix in the blueberries. I drop the spoonfuls of purpley glop onto the skillet. Soon the tops bubble and I flip them. They smell good and fluff up beautifully. I spatula them onto a plate and add a lot of butter and douse them with maple syrup—the real stuff. I take the plate to the table, all the dogs having meanwhile gathered at the unexpected kitchen activity.

I lift the forkful of syrupy, fluffy bite and stare at it, suddenly doubtful. Seems like an awfully normal thing to do, to make yourself some blueberry pancakes. Seems awfully like something a normal, mentally healthy person would do. And I'm barely alive. I don't know if I can do this. But I keep the fork moving and guess what—I'm eating. The fucking blueberry pancakes are absolutely delicious. I eat another bite, then another, barely pausing to breathe. I clean my plate.

Very sneaky, the way you just got me to eat, I say, but my tone isn't accusatory, it's admiring.

Feeling any better?

A little. "Dissolve paralysis with activity," I know you're thinking that.

Don't worry about what I'm thinking. Let's just focus on that sensation of feeling a little better.

It feels good to be clean.

It's nice that you feel good about that.

I don't feel so nauseated since I ate those blueberry pancakes. My stomach actually feels okay.

Are you still feeling weak?

Not as much, as you know very well.

So do you feel like you could do something else?

I guess, I admit.

Feel like doing some dishes? It might be nice to have your beautiful kitchen clean.

I'd rather have a glass of wine.

How about dishes first, then you can decide if you want to start drinking.

I didn't say start drinking, I said a glass of wine.

Who do you think you're kidding?

Okay, fine. I'll do the damn dishes.

THE MANY SINS OF DESTINY

The trailer stank. Stale smoke of cigarettes and drugs, body odor, dirty diapers, and the ripe kitchen garbage pail.

"Dessie, get us some beers, honey," her mother cooed, her voice phlegmatic.

Destiny did it because Loreen was in a good mood. She thought, as she got the beers, that maybe she'd take the kids to the park before too many cold ones darkened her mother's disposition. "Maybe I'll take the kids to the park," she said.

"Sure," Loreen said. "S'nice day."

Destiny looked down at her mother as anger, dismay, pity and fear battled for emotional dominance. It was not a nice day. It was raining. "Okay," she said, not looking at the naked guy next to Loreen in the messy bed. She backed out of the bedroom and told Leon and Ray and Sue Ann to put their shoes on. They complained until she bribed them with Cokes. They were watching a violent movie; cable TV was one of the things Loreen usually managed to have, along with beer, her drugs, and guys. She didn't bother as much with luxuries like food and kid's shoes. The boys' sneakers barely fit. Destiny dressed the baby without bothering to change her diaper. She grabbed a fresh diaper and stuffed it in her coat pocket. She got Cokes from the opened can on the counter and put them in her backpack. "Let's go, guys," she said and they left the trailer. The rain was slowing to a drizzle and had made the air smell almost good; it smelled almost as good as Heaven must, after the stench of the trailer.

"It's raining!" bitched Ray.

"So what, you ain't going to melt," Destiny said.

"Why we got to go outside?" Leon whined.

"Because bein' inside, glued to the TV, y'all is gonna stunt your growth."

"What's stun my growth mean?" Ray demanded.

"Means you'll stay short, like the little runt you are, and never grow an inch taller."

"You shitting me," Ray said.

Destiny stopped and slapped him. He began to cry.

"Told you not to swear, Ray," Destiny said, already feeling bad. Why'd she have to hit him? she scolded herself. Sue Ann started to cry.

"Aw, shut up, Sue Ann," Destiny said. "Look, I'm sorry, Ray."

"S'okay," Ray said, nose running. He forgave too easily.

"It's not right to hit people," Destiny explained. "Swearing's not good, though, either."

"Momma swears," he pointed out.

"That don't make it right," Destiny said. They reached the park, if you could call it that. They lived in Oildale, a sort-of sub-urb of Bakersfield, California, a sad place of mostly trailer parks and squatty little stucco houses and auto parts stores, psychics and taco stands. In the distance were the oil wells, their repeti-tive up and down dipping like metal dinosaurs feeding. The park was a half-block covered in dead grass with a swing set, monkey bars, a couple of benches, and a few desperate-looking trees at one end.

"Here's your Cokes," Destiny said, handing them out. She popped her own and took a swig. How boring. She wished it was Monday and she was back in school. Even though being a senior in high school was way more difficult and frightening than it was interesting or fun, it was at least something. Better than being stuck in the trailer with all the kids and Loreen and her smelly new boyfriend all weekend. And it was only Friday, the second day of the interminable Thanksgiving weekend. Yesterday they had "celebrated" with Swanson's turkey dinners. Big whoop. When she got her own place, Destiny would cook a real turkey and mashed potatoes and everything and have all the kids over. And she'd invite Loreen, just to show her. Loreen always said Destiny was such a loser.

But just wait until I get my own place, she told herself. Hah. I'm not gonna wait, neither. As soon as I can get me a job and save up some money, I'm so out of here. And I ain't ever quitting school neither. Loreen's sure going to crap her pants when I get myself in college. I ain't going to get knocked up or kicked out of school or flunk out or none of the things everybody expects. I don't give a rat fart that nobody knows or cares that I been working real hard. All except Mrs. Russell, nobody in the world knows. I been working real hard, and I got me some plans, and Jesus is all thumbs up… The kids will be okay, and I'll check on 'em a lot anyway. I wish I could take Sue Ann and the baby though. But I'll have 'em over for sleep overs, anyway. Loreen won't even care when I go except she'll lose her best slave. Let her ugly boyfriends get their own beers and bring home milk and peanut butter and McDonald's and clean up. My place is gonna be so gorgeous. It's gonna have real curtains, not raggity old towels over the windows. It's gonna have a real bed and real sheets and stuff. I'll even get me a matching set of plates and stuff from Walmart. I saw that one set in there. It had little birds flying all around the plates. Wish I could of bought them.

Ray was yelling and Destiny was yanked back to the park. The boys were hitting each other and pulling on each other's jackets.

"Did not!" "Did so!" they were yelling.

"Cut it out!" yelled Destiny. They didn't. She put down her Coke on the arm of the bench and waded into the battle. She yanked the boys apart. "Cut it out," she hollered again. "What y'all fighting about?"

"Ray said - "

"Did not - "

"Shut up - "

"Both a y'all shut up," she said. "Just quit fighting, okay? You're gittn' on my last nerve."

"I hate it here," says Leon. "I wanna go watch TV."

"Me too, me too," Ray said. His cheek was red where she hit him. "I'm hungry," he added.

"Me too, me too," said Leon.

"Me, me, me," said Sue Ann.

Crap, thought Destiny. There wasn't nothing at home except cereal, but no milk, and some tomato soup. Not even any crackers. Her stomach growled. Ray laughed. "You too," he giggled. She hugged him, noticing that his clothes emitted the acrid reek of crystal meth smoke.

"Hey, English Class!" She turned to see a trio of boys she's seen at school emerge around the corner. One of them was in her English class. He sat right across from her. His name was Boyd Carter. He was one of the cute guys that Destiny sometimes fantasized about—not sexually , of course, but romantically. She was shocked, shocked he said hello, and shocked again to realize he was headed her direction. Yet he sauntered up to her like it was the most normal thing ever.

"What's goin' on?" Boyd said.

"Babysitting. In charge of these midgets."

"That sucks, huh? Why don'tcha take 'em to the movies or something? It's raining, you know."

"I noticed." She was trying hard not to grin like a moron.

"Cause we don't got no money, and we're hungry!" Ray blurted.

"Ray!" Destiny yelped. "That ain't true," she lied to the boy.

"Movies are expensive," he remarked.

Destiny didn't know what to say to that. She couldn't even remember the last time she went to the movies. If she had any money she's use it to go to the laundromat and wash the stench of meth smoke from her sister's and brothers' clothes.

"I can make you a loan," he said. "Why don't we go over there and discuss it?" He shrugged towards the line of sad trees.

"No, that's okay," Destiny said. Her face felt hot. Why was he being nice to her?

"Aw, come on, my crew will watch the kiddies."

Destiny found herself following him across the park. Boyd Carter didn't stop at the trees but walked on to the curb and opened a car door.

"My ride," he said. "Get in, let's talk." Destiny looked across, her siblings were laughing on the swings. So she got in, feeling like this was all happening to someone else. The boy got in the other side and put his arm over her shoulder and without prelude, kissed her right on the mouth. Destiny was so shocked that she didn't know if she liked it or not. He pulled his wet mouth away long enough to say, "You're so hot," and then started kissing her some more, his strong arms surrounding her. That felt so delicious. Destiny wished he'd just hold her, warm and close… but his tongue was squirming in her mouth. All of a sudden, his hand was inside her shirt, on her boob, ok, but then he was pinching her nipple, it hurt …

"Oh, God, yeah," he gasped.

"Hey," Destiny managed, suddenly scared. She avoided his mouth and tried to wriggle away. "Cut it out," she said. She reached for the door handle.

"Hang on, hang on," Boyd said. "I thought you wanted that money."

Any excitement she had felt below the waist faded. "I never said that."

"Come on, I'll give you five bucks for a blow job."

"No way!" Destiny said, understanding now: she was not worthy of him.

"Come on, baby. Okay, ten bucks." He grabbed her hand and pressed it down on his crotch, as he leaned in and nuzzled her neck. She shivered, half in fear, half in nerve ends reacting. He whispered in her ear words like I want you so bad. You're so hot. You feel so good.

"Cut it out," Destiny whispered, reeling between embarrassment and desire to believe his compliments. She is fat and has zits, her hair and clothes mark her for a loser.

"C'mon, baby," he said, with intensity. "I want you so bad right now. You feel so, so good. I just want to hold you and kiss you."

Nobody had ever said one tenth of that before. He was so gorgeous. Tentatively, she smiled.

He pulled her closer and nibbled her neck. His touch and moist breath were electric: intense, almost too intense, but good, she guessed: It had been a very long time since anybody has touched her except in anger. Destiny leaned forward and closed her eyes so he would kiss her again and he did. He kissed her a lot, then began moving his hands, and after a while took her hand and helped her touch him through his jeans.

Somehow, she let him press her head down, a zipper was unzipped… she tried to do a good job, but her jaw hurt and she didn't know what to do with her teeth… she couldn't shake the sense that it wasn't real… But he was making encouraging sounds and rubbing the back of her neck. Suddenly it was over. Fortunately, there were unused napkins in a crumpled Burger King bag on the floor of the car.

Destiny hoped he'd kiss her again and hold her and tell her she was his girlfriend. After he wiped up, he reached in his back pocket and pulled ten bucks from a wallet.

"I don't need money," she lied, because all of a sudden she knew: girlfriends don't get money for blow jobs. Whores do.

"Go on, take it. Buy yourself something."

Something pretty, she pretended she heard him say, all the

while thinking about washing the kids' clothes. She took the money and put it in her pocket. A windfall! and a potential boyfriend! She could hardly believe how this previously unremarkable day had turned out. "I might be here tomorrow," she said in a way she hoped was sexy and enigmatic.

"Great," Boyd said, and yawned.

"I'll see you," Destiny said as she got out.

He didn't answer.

* * *

Varney and a couple of wranglers move the horses, and Destiny and the other dozen volunteers go in to clean the corral. There is a lot of shrieking and complaining about the manure, but Destiny's trying to pick out her horse from the herd. She thinks she sees him; then realizes it's not him. Then she does see him. He's the one without any white on his feet, with the big white stripe down his face. She goes over to work on the side of the pen nearest the horses. After she fills the wheelbarrow, she walks over to the dividing fence and looks in. Dang if her horse ain't looking right at her.

"Hey, boy," she says, sticking her hand through the rails, palm up. His ears are pointed at her and his nostrils widen, smelling her. She thinks she hears his breath apart from all the others. "C'mere, boy," Destiny croons. The horses are all surging around the strange pen and as one passes too closely, Destiny's horse lays his ears back and bares his big, square teeth and bites on its neck. She hears the clomp of teeth on hide, and the other horse squeals and dances away. Then her horse tosses his head in victory and strolls over to the pile of hay on the ground. She watches him chew great mouthfuls of hay, the stems disappearing under his loudly grinding teeth an inch at a time.

His mane glints in the sun, not one color, but a mixture: burgundy, cinnamon, silver, and black. His forelock falls over his eyes like a rock star. His muscles are smooth and hard under his dusty coat. His eyelashes are so long it's ridiculous, his eyes rimmed in black, like eyeliner. His glamorous eyes remind Destiny of that old rock star Prince. The dude who changed that his name to a symbol. Destiny knows a little about symbols and metaphors, from paying attention in English class. Her horse does look like a prince compared to all the other horses, they all look downright scruffy compared to him… That's his name: Prince.

"Tubb, you're supposed to be working here, not daydreamin'," says a voice, and it's Varney, who has somehow crept right up on her.

"Sorry, sir," she says, and goes to pick up the wheelbarrow.

"Hang on a minute," Varney says.

She stops, wondering what new punishment she is in for.

"You did good with him yesterday," says Varney.

"Thanks," she mumbles, surprised.

"Have you thought about a name for him?"

"Um, I was thinkin', Prince? Maybe? I don't know." Destiny felt a rush of confusing weirdness at Varney's question. Almost like it was fun, naming a horse, like she used to do with her childhood plastic ponies; but also a jolt of fear: who was she to name this awesome horse? The last thing she needed was to get all attached to some horse and some cop.

"That's a good name. He's a real beauty. I've seen a lot of these mustangs, but this one's something special. I think he might have some Spanish blood in him."

"Huh," Destiny says. She doesn't know what to do with her hands, trapped here.

"You know, the horse evolved here in North America, but then they say it died out with the dinosaurs. Then Columbus and the Spanish conquistadors brought them back to America. The cool thing about the Spanish mustang is that they're the descendants of those very first horses here in America," he says.

"Yeah?" Destiny says, interested despite her fear. It's the first new History thing she's learned since getting locked up.

"Yep," Varney said, staring at her horse.

"And you think, he might be one a them?" she asks.

"I do. He's got that look about him."

"Huh," she says.

"Looks like we're almost finished here," Varney says, looking over the corral. "So, you ready to do some more work with him?"

"Yes, sir," she says doubtfully, knowing she already made her choice.

"Dump that load, then."

She does it, then gathers with the other volunteers at the round pen. One of the wranglers leads a gray mare in. Varney climbs into the pen with the horse and starts it moving around.

"Today we're going to do the exact same thing we did last time. Then, when your horse's responding, we're gonna try touching them, get them used to us a little."

Destiny watches, trying to pay attention so she'll be better at it this time. The mare doesn't take long to start showing signs of cooperation. Varney gets the horse to come to him, then hooks a rope on the halter and starts to walk the horse around. It balks a few times, but Varney tugs until the horse responds. Pretty soon they are circling and stopping together.

"That's all there is to it," Varney says.

Ha, Destiny thinks, easy for you, maybe. A wrangler opens a gate and moves the mare out and brings in Prince. He comes flying down the corridor and races, snorting, hooves thundering, dust flying.

"You're up, Tubb," Varney says as the mustang bursts through the gate.

Destiny goes into the round pen, avoids being run over by the horse, and timidly begins to twirl the rope end. Prince snorts loudly and speeds up, his hooves clanking the metal rails, running so out of control Destiny's afraid he will crash. She swings the rope but nothing feels right, she's just as scared as last time. It's as if the horse had never laid eyes on her before. It turns suddenly and races around in the opposite direction. Now the rope's in her wrong hand and as she clumsily changes hands, the horse pivots again. The rope is tangled, and Destiny feels the horse's contempt, and that of Varney and the rest of the inmates. The horse stops and faces the fence, kicking out towards Destiny with his killer back-hooves.

"Better get it together, Tubb," Varney says calmly. "Get him moving."

"I can't!" she cries. The rope's somehow gotten a knot in it and she tries to work it free while keeping an eye on the horse, racing erratically back and forth. Tears blur her vision and her hands are shaking. Help me, Jesus! she prays, more panic-stricken than pious.

"You're okay, just get that rope moving," Varney says, freaky calm.

Finally, Destiny gets the rope organized as Prince begins to circle at a canter instead of a jerky bucking gallop. Then he even slows to a trot. Varney says then to turn him, and she switches hands but Prince doesn't turn; instead, he faces her and rears up, huge, pawing his hard hooves in the sky towards her. Destiny screams and tries backing up, but trips over her own feet and stumbles and lands in the dirt. She waits for the horse's hooves to smash her skull. But instead, silence. She gets up slowly and then hears laughing and Varney yelling shut up and her tailbone is hurting and she wants it to be over, because, obviously, last time was a fluke and this horse hates her and she'll be lucky to get this over with without being hurt even worse.

"No," she gasps, and throws the rope down and starts out towards the gate. But as she gets there she hears hooves pounding right up behind her, and in one second she thinks he's going to trample her and then the next second the hooves stop and she feels horse breath on the back of her neck. She's standing stock still right in front of the gate and all she wants to do is get out of there but she's scared to take another step.

"Turn around and rub him," Varney says very quietly.

Prince's breath is loud and fast and hot on her neck. She can't move forward for fear of triggering the horse, so she does what Varney said. Prince flinches as she turns and he steps back, but then he stretches out towards her and his ears are pricked forward too. Slowly Destiny reaches up and lets him sniff her hand. She tries to stroke his nose, but at the first movement of her hand, he spins, and lands several feet away.

"Better go get your rope," Varney says. No, Destiny thinks, I don't want to—I can't do it—doesn't he know that?

"I don't think I can," she says, her voice weak and pathetic.

"Yes you can, get in there now and get that rope," Varney says, all stern.

So she moves slowly, butt aching, to the rope and slowly bends and picks it up.

"Now, you're doing fine," Varney says. "This don't happen in one day. Sometimes it seems like we're teaching the same thing over and over. These animals will test us, every day. Because that's what they do with each other, in the herd. So get in there, Tubb, and show him who's boss. You're not leavin' that pen today, until you get that horse to go, and stop, and turn."

And so she does. But it's not like the first day, and it seems like Prince is ignoring her the whole time, she feels stupid and clumsy, and in the end Varney comes in the pen and takes over. He gets Prince to go, stop, and turn almost right away. He makes Destiny limp back in and take the rope, and she does, and is able to direct the sweating mustang around the circle, but all she can feel is her pain and humiliation. Finally Varney says that she's done, and Destiny gets to leave the pen and watch through her tears as the other inmates work their horses, and no one else gets the rope all tangled up or falls on their behind.

* * *

Destiny is dreaming about Justin. As always in her dreams she wants to cry, but her throat is huge and hard and she can't cry and she can't scream, either. Something wakes her up and she lies with her hand on her throat, heart pounding, in the never-black grayness of the cellblock. The sound that woke her was someone moaning and a pounding. Some girl getting raped again? Amid the moans were Spanish words: curses or prayers? Destiny thinks maybe the victim is Delores Sanchez. She is one of the pretty ones who looks mad all the time. Sometimes, Destiny thinks, it pays to be fat and ugly. She prays for Delores until it's over before even trying to fall asleep again. But now she's wide awake. She thinks of Prince, to push Justin away before he can appear to torture her. Thinking about the problem of the horse is a new, and welcome, distraction. Darn that horse, though. Why'd he have to turn out so scary? Just when I think I might actually be able to do something. Maybe I can get out of the program. If they won't let me quit, maybe I can ask for a different horse. But she feels guilty thinking this last thought. In her mind she sees Prince looking at her through the bars of the corral, looking at her like he wants to get to know her. Like she's got something he needs.

Doors Left Open

After doing the dishes, I'm feeling almost human. I've actually eaten and I'm clean. I've even begun to get the kitchen picked up. There is a rack full of well-washed, drying dishes and I'd thrown the clutter from the counter into a garbage bag, which I twist-tie and put on top of the full kitchen garbage pail. I wash my hands and wipe them on a clean towel and stare out the kitchen window at the budding oak trees. How green everything is this year. The chickens are out there pecking and scratching under the oaks. It's going to be too late to plant much of a garden this year if I don't get busy soon. Already it's too late for peas. The thought saddens me. Lost opportunity. Lost days, hundreds of them. I've been frozen in time for I don't know how long; I'm not even sure what month it is, to be honest. I think it's still May but June may well have crept up on me. I want to go check the calendar but I'm suddenly afraid of what it will say. I can't decide what to do next. The garbage bag taunts me, the messy pile of dust-covered magazines and books on the table blatantly accuse me of laziness. I think about my list. I should just focus on the list. I can still get a lot done today. I can get organized here and plan my trip to town. I should do laundry; pull my summer clothes out from the spare closet. No, I should focus on the list…

I find myself reaching for a wine glass and filling it from the bottle on the counter. I take the glass and the bottle into the living room and collapse onto the couch. The dogs gather at my feet and on the couch next to me, settling with resigned sighs. I light a cigarette and sip the wine and think about the list. It's too daunting. I need a shorter list. Streamlined to the essentials. Baby steps. I'll look over that list and make it a little more doable. Right after I finish this glass of wine, just to get motivated.

If you're going to self-medicate, do you think wine is the best choice?

You again. Go away. I don't want to take pills.

You may not want them but they might be helpful.

Ugh. I'm not that depressed. Just grieving. Just having a little wine to take the edge off.

You know where that leads. Do you think you might be able to function a little better on anti-depressants?

I'm not clinically depressed.

Really.

Fuck off.

I turn on the TV and that works—I stare at some talk show until the inner therapist goes away, perhaps off to some expense account lunch. I finish the bottle and then open another and so I endure the perfect spring day.

* * *

Hank and I met over the cucumbers at the Whole Foods market. I was fifty-seven, and had definitively decided to sail solo into my old age without the benefits or disadvantages of a man. (My one significant relationship, with my college boyfriend and later live-in lover, ended after eleven years in a stalemate: I wanted kids and he wasn't "ready" to commit.) But suddenly, over the cukes, I was having a conversation with a handsome stranger, and then later there he was in the next checkout line over, continuing the conversation, not minding or perhaps enjoying the audience of the other shoppers and checkout clerks. He followed me to my car and strangely, I didn't mind. When he asked if I would join him for lunch at the sushi place right next door, I hesitated. It was Saturday and I had no appointments, no clients, and no plans, and nothing to go home to except a nap and a novel. I agreed.

He was tall and lean and his hair was silver and trimmed short. His face was deeply tanned and lined with the ghosts of both his smile and his frown; he had green eyes. He said after we took a table at the sushi bar that he was a fire captain and getting ready to retire. I didn't need to ask questions; he talked freely about himself. He had been divorced six years. There were two children: a son, twenty, and a daughter, twenty-three, already married. His passion was the house he was building in the desert. In time I told him some facts about myself. Then we talked and laughed about a few other things—I wish I could remember every word. I wish

I could remember the exact moment when I slipped from feeling oddly comfortable, having lunch with a stranger, to hoping that we would linger over the tea and that maybe he'd invite me afterwards for a walk on the beach. We were in tune from the first because that is exactly what he did.

I'm shocked, even now, that we went to bed together at the end of that first day, but you can't escape the facts of your past. Of course I felt trepidation, I advised myself to slow down, but the advice was more habit than anything. I was enthralled with him and he was enthralled with me. In mutual enthrallment we fell onto his bed in his house on the hill with the window open to the ocean and we made love; and except for necessities, we were together for the next seven years, two months, and sixteen days.

* * *

I wake to a dark house with the mother of all hangovers.

Instantly, the dogs are all over me, licking me in frenzied relief that I am in fact still alive. I am, barely. Cursing, I push them off and struggle to sit up. My head throbs sickeningly but I force myself up and to the door, and open it to let the dogs out. I lean my head on my hand on the door frame and it is only the sweet cool breath of the desert that saves me from vomiting. I manage to hang there and breathe until I feel strong enough to wobble to the kitchen for a drink of water. And four aspirin. Trembling and lurching from one handhold to another, I accomplish these tasks and even make it to the bathroom and then into my unmade bed. But just in case I haven't suffered enough for ten thousand lifetimes already, instant sleep is not to be my relief and aspirin is slow to take effect. I lie writhing, curling and uncurling like a larvae under a microscope, moaning and whimpering to some god I don't believe in.

* * *

If I'd been looking for a husband, which I am still sure I wasn't, Hank would have been the too-good-to-be-true candidate. (In time, I would, of course, discover all his faults, as he would mine. But they turned out to be faults that we both could live with.) There he was, a tall, handsome fireman. He lived by himself in a beautiful little house three blocks above Hermosa Beach. He liked to read and sail boats and was attentive and even had table manners. I would have been an absolute idiot to not be a bit suspicious. Why on earth was he single?

Like I said, I wasn't looking for a husband. I had thought I'd closed the door was on that option. But I met mine, over the cukes. So the answer to the question seemed to be: he was single for me. I was alone; and he was alone—and we both went into the Whole Foods market on the same day in the same city and we both headed for the vegetables at the same time. We both, at the same time, had a yen for cucumber salad. Our whole lives had led us to this moment, for how could I have been there to meet him if I hadn't left Miami ten years before for LA? If I hadn't spent all those years in school to become a doctor I probably couldn't afford to live in the same pricey beach town, a mere fifteen blocks away from his bungalow. So many choices and it hits me like a hammer that any one wrong choice could have prevented our meeting. The randomness with which I made some of those decisions in my life terrifies me. But every move turned out to be right after all. He appeared in my life and transformed it. Transformed me. I went from a polished professional who drove a low, fast car, to a desert rat who had to have four-wheel drive. I ended up quitting my practice, embracing early retirement without a second thought, and moving with Hank to an improbable paradise.

* * *

The next time I wake up, the terrible headache is gone, but I feel weak and parched. It's too bright in the bedroom; the sun seems to have been up for some time. For once there are no dogs lying on top of me. Just one, under the sheet and too warm against my leg. I throw off the cover and freeze. My heart kicks. Lying next to my leg is not a dog. It is a snake. A big one, as thick as my arm. A Western diamondback, to be exact; I am a woman who knows her venomous reptiles. My body begins trembling violently and the snake stirs. Its wiry tongue flicks out and back. Before I can think too much about the consequences, I lift my arm closest to the snake high over my head and roll away and over and off the bed onto the floor. I jump up, but am tangled in the sheet and am wrestling it off while stumbling backward across the room towards the door, never taking my eyes off the nightmarish invader. It just lies there, hugely, on my bed, its biblically forked tongue sliding in and out. As I reach the door, it slowly coils up into that archetypical position of potential death. It vibrates its tail, the horripilating sound like gas hissing from a leaky valve. I manage to back through the door and slam it shut. I run into the living room and yell for the dogs, the useless self-preserving bastards. Teddy and Slim come galloping, panting, excited at being summoned, I supposed. The world's worst guard dogs.

You bastards, I shout. Where's my gun?

Good question! I answer myself, chidingly. I bet you don't even know if it's loaded.

That's right, I have no idea. Besides, I don't know if I want to shoot a snake in my bed. Think of the mess.

How about opening the door to the courtyard, and shooing him out there?

How do you shoo a fucking rattlesnake?

My inner therapist or schizophrenic voice in my head, or whatever it is, is silent. No handy, guaranteed advice on evicting a large, deadly viper from the bedroom. This is just fucking great. I stomp to the front door and slam it shut. It's all my fault, leaving the front door open—come on in, Mr. Snake, and slither on in to the bedroom. Feel free to curl up under the blanket where it's nice and warm.

Slim is whining, nothing unusual there, but then I realize that one of the dogs isn't looking at me. Freddie is lying on the floor, unmoving. I crouch down next to him, instantly knowing—yet not believing—the worst. He's not breathing. I touch him and he's stiff, hard under my trembling fingers.

Oh no. Oh no. Oh no. I gently turn him over, wincing at the way his little legs stick out. On his other side, on his neck and muzzle, a patch of dried blood. His black and swollen tongue protrudes between his teeth. I don't have to be a vet to diagnose the cause of death. I know when I clean the blood, I'll find puncture marks.

Oh, Freddie, I shriek, gathering his body in my arms. Slim's whine escalates to a crescendo. Tears come, leaking from my useless eyes until the dried blood glistens and begins to run pink down his fur. Freddie. My sweet, funny, adventurous, loyal little dog. He loved to play ball and he taught himself tricks, he would walk on his hind legs or roll over for a dog biscuit. Freddie was only four years old. And I had let him die. He'd been protecting me. But I failed to protect him.

I put Freddie back down on the floor and lurch to my feet, wiping at my eyes. I have some killing to do. I check the front closet. My pistol is not hanging from the hook. I check the dining table, all around the front rooms. It must be in my purse. Where is my purse? In the office, maybe. I go through the doors into the courtyard. Through the window into the bedroom, I can see the snake, no longer coiled, now relaxed on the bed, its body describing an "S" for, I would guess, Snake. It must be at least four feet long. I also notice the door from the bedroom into the office is unfortunately open. I wish it weren't. I don't relish the idea of that snake sneaking up on me. With utmost caution, I ease open the screen door into the office and carefully step in. From here I can't see the snake on my bed, and hate like hell that I can't. I hurry to the desk and sure enough, there's my purse, peeking out from under a pile of mail. I pull it out and grope inside. Yes! My hand closes on the shape of my clip-on holster, the weight of the weapon. I unsnap the holster and draw out the gun. My hands are shaking but I get the cylinder open and make sure it is loaded, then creep towards the bedroom. I go through the doorway. I take one step at a time until I'm right up to the bed. My marksmanship is such that I need every advantage. As I get close, the monster winds itself again into a coil, swiveling its ugly, wedge-shaped head, regarding me with slitted devil eyes. I try to breathe and calm my trembling hands. I aim the gun, supporting my right hand with my left. I can't seem to focus; my vision isn't good in the best of times. Instead of one clear viper there are two blurry ones. I squint to make them merge and, hoping for the best, pull the trigger. The blast is hurtfully loud and the snake jerks and falls over, spraying red onto my pale green sheets. I unload the other rounds into its twitching, writhing body. The gun is empty and the creature is still clenching, squirming, its fangs, poisonous needles, stabbing at a pillow again and again. The dogs are barking frantically and scrabbling on the closed bedroom door. I go back into the office and thank Henry that he insisted on stashing ammunition all over the house. I find a couple boxes of .38 shot in the third drawer of the desk and reload the gun. My hands are shaking less now. I go back into the bedroom and the snake is still squirming sluggishly. I shoot again and again. Finally, the sheets are spattered in a Jackson Pollock of blood, bone, and rattler gore and what's left of the snake is still.

I lower the gun and exhale, long and shaky. My head is pounding fiercely and I feel more than a little nauseated. I really want a drink. But I have things to do. I've got to get rid of the nasty corpse, get this mattress out of here, and get a new one. There's blood on the wall I need to clean before it stains. But first, I need to bury my dog.

Once Upon a Time

After the day in the park, Destiny felt like everything changed. Loreen's boyfriend took off; the heater in the trailer quit working and they didn't have money for a new one. It got so cold and the baby got sick and even though Destiny felt sorry for the kids, the trailer was no place she wanted to be. Outside was no better, though. The neighborhood of hulking trailers, their faded drab paint of every nameless color and their mismatched add-ons for the next and the next unplanned-for kid or grandchild; the proliferation of sad, rusty sheds and broke-down cars and every kind of junk seemed scattered into every yard as randomly as toys discarded by a spoiled child. The trees, slick and black with sodden dark leaves hanging here and there, refusing to let go of the branch even in death, made her want to cry.

She met Boyd at the park and this time he only gave her five bucks, but it was still better than nothing. Then his friends wanted it, too. At that point Destiny felt so low about life in general that she went ahead and obliged them. She prayed real hard about it but God had nothing to say except it was a sin. It was a big one. But she knew she would be forgiven because it seemed unavoidable now that she was already despoiled. She didn't even feel one hundred percent bad about it; sure, she felt dirty and ashamed, but part of the time she felt smug, and if not sexy, well, almost sexy? Sexy-ish? And the money added up, she soon discovered. That helped to ease her aversion to the activity. She never enjoyed doing that, but she loved the money; then she became obsessed by it. Each dollar was religiously divided: fifty cents to Destiny's apartment fund, twenty-five cents to get something for the kids to eat, and a quarter Destiny could spend however she wanted. So, four blow jobs, at five bucks each, equaled twenty bucks. In half an hour, she could add ten bucks to her apartment fund and buy chicken nuggets for the kids and have five bucks left over. Sweet!

After a while, the word got all around school and of course Destiny was considered a slut. The few girlfriends she thought she had became distant—like they were pure! All the judgment from her peers made Destiny rebellious. So I'm a slut, so what? she thought. At least I get money for doing it. Janelle and Trina probably do it for free. It wasn't even sex; and it was only temporary. She certainly wasn't going to become a prostitute! But this... job... had just happened, and she rationalized that it wasn't hurting anybody; the boys wanted it and she needed the money. Maybe she should even start charging more, or let the guys screw her like they always begged her to do. She knew she could get more money for that. But screwing meant you could get pregnant, and Destiny knew that would mess up all her plans. She needed to get out, start her own life, away from Loreen, away from the trailer, even away from her brothers and sister who smothered her with their needs. She had to get out! And once she did, she'd get a real job and quit meeting guys and taking their money. She'd go to church, confess her sins, and start over. But first she had to get out.

She started looking at the apartments for rent in the newspaper and daydreaming about them all the time. She doodled columns of numbers in her school notebook, adding up her potential blow job profits.

She realized she'd been paying less attention to school when she got a shocking D on an English test. She hadn't read the last four assignments and her teacher took her aside after class. Is everything all right at home, Destiny? Oh sure, everything's just fine, Mrs. Russell. She promised to try to catch up on her reading and got out of there as fast as she could. She'd always liked Mrs. Russell, but now her teacher's concern frightened her. She didn't need her teacher questioning the other kids and finding out anything. She'd better do what she promised, and catch up. And she tried, she really did, but lately it was hard to concentrate, even at the library where she went to do her homework. The dark days and darker nights made her mood sag like the fat clouds, heavy with rain. The dead leaves in the gutters were depressing, almost as depressing as the trailer. The only good thing there was to think about was getting out, getting out... By the end of the semester and Christmas break, her report card was a mess of B's and C's but her apartment fund was up to one hundred and eighty dollars.

* * *

"What can I do for you, Tubb?" Varney says. He's got a crummy little office, but there are posters and photographs of horses and people with horses thumbtacked all over the walls. The metal desk is messy with file folders and papers; the fluorescent light hums and flickers. The one high window looks out on the fenced parking lot. It's pretty clear that running the wild horse program doesn't come with a lot of perks.

"I'm sorry, but… okay, well, Sergeant Varney sir, well, I made a mistake, sir," she says.

"How's that?" he asks. Too bad he's nice, she thinks. She has an uncomfortable feeling that he actually cares about her. She doesn't want him to care. She just wants to go back to being invisible.

"I got to get out of the horse program," she says. "I didn't really mean to volunteer, sir. I'm sorry."

"Why do you want to quit?" he asks, using the word she'd carefully avoided.

"I can't do it. I mean, plain as that," she says, becoming a little annoyed with him for making her explain.

"Why do you think you can't do it?" he asks.

"I just can't," she says, the words making her suddenly feel bereft.

"Well, I can't agree with ya," he says. "You think you had a bad day with him yesterday. You think you messed it up. But that horse—Prince—he started out pretty full of himself, didn't he?"

"Yeah."

"By the end, he was nice and quiet, right?"

"Yes sir. I guess."

Varney stands up and calls to the matron who is waiting to escort Destiny back to the cell. "We're going to take a walk," he says.

Amazingly, the matron nods and Destiny follows Varney through the halls and gates all the way outside. Varney talks to the guards and they open another gate and he leads her towards the horse pens. He lights a cigarette and offers her one. She shakes her head.

"There's your guy," Varney says after a few puffs.

She looks. Prince is right there, on the close side of the pen. He's grazing on a few wisps of hay with his hind leg cocked, his tail swishing lazily. Destiny can't help but admire the color of him, the way his coat shines, the way his mane is so long and wind-braided. He looks so calm now, like she could walk right up and kiss his whiskery nose.

"I'll tell you something," Varney says. "Probably I shouldn't ought to be telling you this. Don't spread it around the other volunteers, okay?"

He has no idea that Destiny doesn't talk to anyone anyway, so she just nods.

"This program works," he tells her, "for some crazy reason. But if the higher-ups knew, or even if the volunteers, like you, knew, how hard and difficult and dangerous this really was, it'd be shut down in a heartbeat. None of the officials that decided to implement this have ever been in a round pen with a wild horse, I can guarantee you that."

At that, Destiny felt herself smile. Varney went on telling her about the wild horse program, about how some genius somewhere got the idea, and a few guys randomly hired by the DOJ got to make sure no one gets killed doing it and that those mustangs out there actually learn what they're supposed to. Along the way, Destiny and the other inmates are supposed to gain self-confidence and teamwork and honesty.

"It's damned hard. It don't happen overnight. Every time, you learn a little and the horse learns a little. You've gotta go over and over the lessons with the horse. They will try every trick in the book to get out of doing what you want."

Varney then silently puffed his cigarette long enough to allow Destiny to wonder why he was telling her all this.

"You know, you're doing just fine with this horse. I know, these guys can be scary. But I been working with mustangs for years, and I know for a fact they ain't mean. They just need to be told what to do. They need a leader. Separated from their herd, they need to bond up with somebody. And I think you got a real good chance to bond up with this horse. And when you do, my opinion is, you'll both benefit from it."

Varney drops his cigarette butt to the ground and grinds it out with his boot. Then Destiny can feel him looking at her. She slides her eyes across the dirt and up through the bars to the horse. Prince lifts his head, still chewing. And he looks right at her. And then he whickers. A soft, inquiring sound. It goes straight to Destiny's heart. Like the first time she heard Justin cry. A sound that she knows she must answer; her whole being tells her, answer.

Varney chuckles. "See, he knows ya," he says.

Destiny's throat squeezes and tears come.

"Here," Varney says. He reaches in his pocket and produces some cut-up carrot chunks. "See if he'll come for these."

Destiny takes a chunk and offers it on her open palm through the bars. Prince sniffs and stretches out his neck and sniffs again.

"Talk to him," Varney says.

"Come on, Prince," she whispers thickly.

The horse takes a few steps and then hesitates. "Come on," Destiny says again. "Come on, boy." Prince decisively comes closer and closer. He stops when he is close enough to take the carrot if his neck is stretched as far as it will go. Tentatively he lips up the chunk, then chewing noisily, backs up but doesn't leave. He returns for more, stepping closer. Destiny reaches through the bars and strokes his shoulder. His skin twitches but the horse stays put, even after the carrots are gone.

"Well, I got to get back to work, paperwork, that is," Varney says after a moment.

Destiny strokes Prince one more time and follows Varney back towards the cellblock.

"So ya still want to quit?" Varney asks as they approach the gate. "Or do you think you want another try at that wild beast?"

"I'll try, I guess." Destiny says.

"Good," Varney says, and he says something else, but the clanking gate opening covers his words.

* * *

Feeling flush, Destiny spent some of her apartment fund money on Christmas presents for the kids. And even Loreen. A bottle of perfume, to cover the reek of crystal meth that followed Loreen like a smelly ghost. The vacation days were foggy, wet, and depressing and no one showed up at the park, and Loreen and her boyfriend were either fighting or loaded out of their minds. Destiny thought maybe she preferred it back when they'd been screwing all the time. The boyfriend—Rico—was a stringy, snake- and rooster-tattooed illegal from some unpronounceable hamlet in Mexico. He was always nice enough to Destiny and the kids, but Destiny knew he was a fake. Rico was lazy but not stupid, and he knew that any money Loreen had came from the State for the kids. As long as Loreen kept his habits satisfied, everything was relatively okay. But then, for some reason, the drugs dried up, and things got ugly. When the library closed at nine the last night of the holiday break, and she had absolutely nowhere else to go, Destiny reluctantly returned to the trailer.

Loreen and Rico were having a battle. The kids were all in the back bedroom with the TV on loud and Destiny joined them, but they could still hear the jist of the argument through the vinyl walls. Rico had "borrowed" his cousin's car and smashed it up and he needed money or his cousin was going to "F" him up. He'd be turned in to the *migra* and Loreen would never see him again. He was sure Loreen had more money somewhere. She was holding out on him. She didn't love him. Loreen was yelling and screaming and Destiny could hear Rico slapping her around. She put her hands over the baby's ears. The bedroom door flung open and her mother stomped in, grabbed Destiny's arm, and started shrieking, "Get me that money. I know you got money. Get me that money."

"No," Destiny yelled back, twisting away. "No. It's mine."

"Where'd you get that money anyhow, Destiny? You sellin' drugs? You whorin'? You get me that money, you little slut."

"Don't say that," Destiny said, pulling away. Loreen swung and slapped Destiny hard across the cheek.

"Get me that money. Get me that money." Loreen kept slapping her and clinging on to Destiny's bicep with her claws dug in deep. The slaps hurt, she bit her tongue and tasted blood; but it was the feeling of all hope, all good, and any God being sucked away forever in the tornado of Loreen's madness. All there would ever be was pain, sadness, betrayal, ugliness, poverty, and a bleak chain of days in a stupid, meaningless life.

"No, Mama, please," Destiny sobbed.

Get me that money!

Destiny did.

* * *

The prison library is crummy. There is only one book about horses, The Encyclopedia of the Horse. It is big, however, and full of pictures; Destiny borrows it and reads it cover to cover and then looks again at all the pictures. She learns that horses were first ridden way back before Jesus. There are so many different kinds of horses all throughout the world. Some from countries Destiny had never heard of in Geography class. She learns about different kinds of riding, about jumping and barrel racing and dressage. She daydreams about riding Prince. She can't imagine what that feels like. How do you stay on? None of the riders in the pictures are hanging on for dear life; they look like they are glued to the horses. Looking at pictures of horses clearing gigantic jumps makes her feel woozy. Again, serious doubts assail her. As long as she keeps both feet on the ground around Prince, maybe she can make him do stuff. But getting up there, on top of him, was another thing.

There is one picture that she keeps coming back to: an Arabian mare and colt. The mare looks a lot like the horse that used to live next to her aunt's house. What was that horse's name? Petal. That was it, like the petal of a flower. Petal disappeared that one winter. That winter, so cold and dead, the winter that everything changed; that winter was the beginning of the bad times.

* * *

Once upon a time, they had been a real family. Mama and Daddy and BabyGirl. Daddy was a truck driver and he was gone a lot but when he came home he'd have little presents for his BabyGirl. Daddy would lift Destiny up on his shoulders and she would ride so tall, holding on to his thick brown hair. Destiny had toys and books and sometimes Daddy would read her a bedtime story. They all sat at a round table and ate together. Mama cooked spaghetti, chicken, meatloaf. Daddy grilled steaks on the weekends; Mama took Destiny everywhere in a green car, to the beauty parlor, to the market, to visit Aunt Lacey who had houseplants and a cat named Whiskers and a white horse next door. Aunt Lacey always had Kool-Aid and cookies for Destiny.

But. That one winter, the white horse was gone, "retired," she was told indifferently, and Destiny feared that meant Petal was gone, forever. That happened in movies, but there was always a little baby pony to take the pain away. Petal didn't leave a baby. All she left was her bucket and brush. Destiny wondered why

Petal didn't need her bucket where she was going. Even if she was retired, wouldn't Petal need her bucket for her grain? And she needed to get brushed, no matter where she was going.

The world was suddenly undependable, unsafe; and for the first time Destiny felt a creepy, haunted feeling that didn't go away. It turned out her fears were realistic. Aunt Lacey moved to Vegas, and right away she got killed in an accident. After that, Mama got sad. And it was cold and dark and raining, raining, like the world was crying along with Mama.

And then Daddy quit his job and Mama and Daddy started fighting a lot about money and other stuff Destiny didn't understand. Then Daddy left, and that time, he never came back.

***

After Rico took her money, Destiny tried to earn more. But she really hated it. When one of the boys got mean with her because he wanted to go all the way, and Destiny ended up with bruises on her arms, she decided to call it quits. She wasn't a victim like Loreen. She would never be like Loreen. So she prayed and looked and called until she got a job at a Burger King and was grateful for the nasty polyester uniform that always smelled of French-fry grease no matter how much she washed it.

Destiny was still living in the trailer, but at last her freedom, her future, was close enough to touch. She graduated high school, in a real cap and gown. She was enrolled in two summer school classes and had herself a real job. And right before graduation, a miracle: Destiny was awarded a part-time scholarship at Bakersfield College. In the fall, she'd go to college! Destiny thought maybe she'd like to be a teacher. That was about as respectable a job as there was. Plus, she liked kids. And teachers got lots of vacations. She'd teach first graders, maybe. That would be so fun.

The days were warm and the trees and flowers were all full of buds. A scholarship! A real job! The warmth of success, even more than the welcome sunshine, thawed her depression and hopelessness. The dark humiliation of what she'd done with those boys faded in the brightness of springtime, being young, having a future.

So much was good that Destiny didn't think she was lonely. But she had no friends, no one at home to talk to, and after graduation, didn't even have Mrs. Russell. It was okay, though, because she'd make friends once she got to college. The very last thing on her mind was a boyfriend.

He kept coming to the Burger King drive-through. His name was Danny, and he flirted with her and Destiny could hardly believe it. He was gorgeous. He was a mature, gorgeous man. He drove a big shiny red truck and had a shaggy friendly dog named Blue that rode in the bed. Destiny worked the take-out window and when Danny came, she always had a dog biscuit for Blue. Danny asked her on a date. Destiny had never been asked out on a date. She said yes.

She spent money on a new dress even though she was supposed to save every cent for college. She changed in the bathroom at work and Danny picked her up without Blue in the truck. He took her to play miniature golf. They had a blast. Danny let her win. After, they went to a real restaurant, a Mexican restaurant. They both had beers—nobody asked for her ID. Then they went driving, all the way out of town, past grape fields and orchards, and into a canyon and down a road that followed the twisting, frothing river. Danny pulled over at a turn out and they walked down a little path and sat on some rocks above the river. Danny had bought a six-pack and they drank beers and talked. Danny had a real job: he installed cable TV. He'd grown up in Bakersfield too. He told Destiny he was twenty-three. That he loved football and fishing and hunting. He kept interrupting his stories with corny little jokes.

"What did the bride give her husband after their honeymoon? A head start."

He told Destiny that her intelligence was one of the things he found attractive about her. Emboldened, she asked him what else. Your hair, your eyes, your personality, he'd answered. When he kissed her, it was completely different. It was really different when you kissed somebody and you were falling in love with them.

ALL IN

Out back, overlooking the apple trees. The little hole gapes, a wound in the earth. The digging has exhausted me; the hard-baked soil grudging every shovelful. I stand over the grave dreading the next thing. While digging I'd been able to empty my mind and focus on forcing my weak, ineffective arms to scrape and poke at the ground. But now the hole's finally deep enough. I take a big shaky breath and go back to the house.

I clean the dried blood from Freddie's muzzle and neck. I wrap him in his blanket and gather his bowl, his favorite ball, his leash. I take him and his stuff out to the orchard, I kneel to place him in the grave. I lay him down gently. I stare at his stiff form, his face frozen in a rictus of pain. That's when I lose it. I wail. I moan, and scream. I didn't think there was enough left of my broken heart to feel this much pain—but I was so wrong. Poor little Freddie. He loved life, exuberantly. Each morning, he'd wriggle in delight at the miracle of waking to a new day. He'd yawn luxuriantly, swipe my chin with a quick good morning kiss, then chase his tail, excited to be going outside. My lap was going to be so empty now. He didn't deserve to die so young. And it is all my fault, I wasn't paying attention—to the one important thing—.

"I'm so sorry, I'm so sorry, Freddie," I sob, as I stagger to my feet and take the shovel and scoop up some dirt. The pain of my guilt and grief is so intense it's not bearable. "Aw, shit, fuck!" I scream as I dump the shovel of dirt over Freddie. The horrible finality of that. I curse and gibber as I cover him as fast as I can. I make a neat mound then I fall to my knees and smooth the dirt with my hands, and now I really cry.

* * *

"I'd better come clean about something," he said, two weeks after the cucumbers. We were in bed, his arm around me; I was stroking his hair, Letterman on the TV.

My stomach lurched. I had known it was too good to be true. There was someone else! —even though he'd said otherwise. "What's that? I managed to say lightly.

"I've been neglecting something. You're a pretty big distraction."

"A distraction, am I?" I was still stroking his hair as he rubbed back against my hand like a cat.

"Yep."

"So what have you been neglecting?"

"My house."

"Looks pretty clean to me," I said.

"Not this house, my desert house."

"Oh, right," I said.

"So, want to go up there this weekend? I warn you, though, it's not going to be lying around eating bonbons. I have to work. And you're going to help me."

"Is that so?"

"Only if you want to, of course, my queen."

I giggled like a high schooler and of course, I agreed to go. I couldn't wait to see this other side of Hank. I knew the Hank that kicked back in his lovely bungalow after work, barbecuing tuna steaks on the deck, barefoot, wearing only board shorts. I knew the Hank that dressed in crisp shirts and took me to the expensive beach restaurants and comedy clubs. I knew the Hank whose touch melted and ignited me. I'd met the Hank that played beach volleyball like a madman and the one that wore the uniform of a fire captain. So naturally I was curious about what else there was.

The drive itself was an adventure. We left hideously early, in the gray predawn, and were out of the city before it was fully light. We had good coffee and croissants and music as the urban sprawl gave way to hillsides dotted with wildflowers. A few hours later over a mountain pass the edges of the desert appeared: scrubby pines, sage and prickly-pear cactus, bare-rock mountains. It was pristine and beautiful. A tiny hamlet—a couple dozen homes, one stop-sign, a grocery store, and a post office—was the last outpost of civilization, according to Hank. Then a steep, winding dirt road that ended at a heavy iron gate. The drive curved upwards, and

I could see the house, perched way above. This is it, he said, as he got out and opened the gate lock. Leaving the gate open, we bumped up the drive to the house.

"Well, this is it," Hank said. I realized he was nervous about my response. I considered teasing him then quickly changed my mind. I answered honestly.

"It's gorgeous here," I acknowledged. The view was pristine: miles of rolling hills, a violet mountain range in the distance. Pine forests and meadows. No roads, no houses. "Where is everybody?" I asked.

"It's a couple hundred acres," he said. "It goes up to the government land. So, not too many neighbors. The closest are over that hill, there, can't see their house, but if you look there's their water tower, just left of that Ponderosa pine. The nearest stores are back in Canyon City. Seven miles. Slow miles." He chuckled contentedly as if being that far from a pack of cigarettes was a good thing.

"My God," I said. "And the house…?" I turned and studied the house. It looked like a pueblo with a squat tower rising from the back. The exterior walls appeared to be gray cement. The roof was supported by massive round beams. There were windows, a lovely carved door. "My goodness," I said. "It's unusual."

"It's not done," he replied. "You just wait. Come on." We went up four steps to a wide flagstone patio and crossed to the door. "Welcome home," he said, unlocking the door.

Inside it was light and spacious, the rooms flowing in a circle. French doors opened to an interior courtyard filled with plants and sunlight. But the rest was bizarre. The walls were unfinished, and bristly looking. The floor was dirt. There were no cabinets or appliances in the kitchen.

"Told you it's not finished," he said, laughing.

"What on earth is this stuff?" I asked, moving closer to the bristly wall.

"Straw bales," he said. "They have an insulation value of R52."

"Huh," I said. "So do you leave them like this?"

"You wish," he said, laughing again.

An hour later I was wearing the old shorts and t-shirt Hank had advised me to pack, and in my left hand held a scoop of plaster. In my right I held a trowel. "Don't be scared, slap it on there," he said. With his own scoop, he demonstrated. He flung it on to

the straw, and in a continuous motion, smoothed it with the trowel.
I copied him on my section of wall. The plaster was heavier than it
looked and quite a bit ended up on the floor before I got any onto
the wall. Laughing, I kept on, getting more determined to show
Hank I was not a wimp, or one of those women who never do anything to endanger their manicures, and so never do anything.

"It's fun," I admitted, about ten minutes before I realized my
arm was already beginning to burn at the use of long-ignored
muscle groups. But now my competitive nature had overtaken
my good sense and so we finished a whole wall before, famished,
we gobbled sandwiches and guzzled beers outside at a rickety
table set in the shade of a leaning oak tree. All I wanted was a
nap, but I followed him like a puppy back to the work zone and
we completed another damn wall. By the time we were finished
the sun was dipping towards the mountains and I was sure I'd
never regain the use of my arms. We were sweaty and dotted with
plaster. Hank finished washing the tools and then grabbed me in
a hug.

"You were magnificent," he said. "Ready for a sun shower?"

"A whatever shower," I said. He led me outside to a big black
bag with a nozzle hanging from a hook. A weathered board shelf
held shampoo, soap, and towels. He stripped and tossed his
clothes on a bush. He began to douse himself with the nozzle
and I tripped getting out of my shorts, unable to take my eyes
off him. I stepped towards him and he turned the spray on my
body. It was the perfect temperature. He wetted me thoroughly
then soaped me methodically while I stood with my eyes closed,
concentrating on his hands on my body. I have never been completely comfortable in my body, but Hank somehow changed that
in me. He made me believe he saw me as beautiful: everything
about me: my no-longer tight skin, my beginning-to-gray hair, my
once-tiny facial wrinkles that were resolutely growing more insistent. But he worshipped me with his eyes, his hands, his words,
and so I was able, by that point, to accept, enjoy, even savor, the
still-absurd notion of getting naked, falling in love, ripping your
emotions out, and flinging them on the poker table, all in.

He dried me with a towel and led me back inside to the bedroom to his bed, a mattress on the floor, and we made love over
and over until finally falling back on the sheets to let the breeze
dry our sweat. He reached over and took my hand and kissed it

and we lay there, not speaking. And it was one of those moments. I knew right then that I was having a perfect moment. One that you never want to end, that you want to go on savoring forever. Perfect, as in: complete. Being entirely without flaw; faultless, immaculate, picture-perfect, and seamless. If there is a meaning to life, it is this, this moment, I thought. Living boils down to moments, and if you're lucky enough to get a perfect one, to pay attention. Pay great attention.

* * *

It is while I'm lying on the prickly ground, my stiff fingers clutching the dirt of Freddie's grave, that the miracle happens. I hear Hank's voice, clear and distinct, in the center of my brain as if I am wearing headphones.

Sara. It'll be okay. It'll be okay.

That's what he would say every time I needed to hear it. Meaningless words, but filled with his confidence, they were magic. And everything would be okay. Well, was, as long as he was around. I'd given up on anything being okay, ever again, when he died. How could anything ever be okay? But was that really him, telling me the words I couldn't believe, but needed to believe?

"Hank?" I croak through my tear-thickened throat. Only silence, if the mountain wind through the pines and the layered chittering of multitudes of birds and insects is silence. "Please," I whisper, longing for the miracle to repeat itself. I'd gladly be insane if it would mean I could hear him again. If we could have a conversation. Because I need him. I need him so badly. I need him to tell me it will all be okay. To tell me anything, everything. But, sadly, it appears I'm not able to hallucinate at will. My pleas are answered with silence.

It's up to me. I may not deserve it, but I'm still alive. Life continues, the planet reliably revolves and day determinedly still follows night. I breathe, my shattered heart still pumps blood. The unavoidable truth confronts me, as horribly real as Freddie's grave: I have a responsibility to life. As long as I breathe, I must live. Start living again. Start taking care of my dogs, my home, myself.

I push myself off the dirt and sit up. I wipe my hands on my jeans and stare at the mountains. It is all so beautiful. The tumbled boulders and trees, so random, impossible, and magnificent. The spiny yuccas with dramatic white blossom-covered spikes; the digger pine's baby cones, the color of a cut lime; the pair of ravens, swooping above the ridge, their drunkard's croaks, glossy feathers black like spilled ink, like a hole in the flawless blue sky. The sun on my face like a warm hand, like a benediction. Life. That's the miracle, not the voice of my dead husband. Life. If there is a way to live without my love, I have to find it. I promise Hank, and my dogs, and myself. Time to get it together.

THE MEAT MAN

His fingers drummed the wheel as Hank Two raged on about lawyers, guns, and money. No shit. You're screwed if you don't have that holy trifecta in your back pocket, right? The semi cab jolted monotonously as the highway miles swept past. He had his stereo cranked; a triple Americano and a fifth of Jack, a half carton of Camels, and a delivery to make that would net almost four grand. Sure, it was crap compared to the old days. But it was a living.

He fucking loved to drive. It got him away from the incessant demands of the world and to a jealously guarded haven of solitude. He could always set his phone so it appeared to simply be out of range, and ta-dah! The entire world can go fuck itself.

The clanging from the trailer he hauled crescendoed. For many miles, with the help of the music, he'd been able to tune it out. But this sounded like a hell of a mess. God damn fuckers. He cranked up the volume as far as he dared—didn't want to blow the Jensen speakers—and lit another smoke. Eventually the shit back there would resolve itself. Or not. There was no way he was going to stop and try to intervene. If they killed a few of each other, so be it. It might cut into his profit but not by much. He grinned, checked his grin in the rear view. He smiled wider. God damn, Randall Pennant was one handsome motherfucker. Those new teeth were worth every penny. Made people like you, good teeth...

Hell yes, mas tequila, he remembered saying, before the blackout.

As always: He was golden. He was stardust. He woke to a gentle, barely there rain and sweet fog, and it accompanied him; it hugged him down the cobbled street to the bodega... He might have slept or had a meal or a fuck. That part was a little hazy, but mostly because of the torturous humdrum boring repetitive sameness… so many trips, the thrumming of miles, the monotonous desert landscape, slipping by anonymously, the beers and tequila shots and greasy Mexican food and the hard whores and the smell of shit and blood…

So he hailed a cab and got to his rig and paid the bribe and went on his way, north, back across the border with the damn trailer beautifully empty, his pocket beautifully full; on his way home.

But home was never what he wanted it to be. Margie had started out voluptuous but turned fat. Fucking fat. Her bouncy, blonde hair turned out to be the result of weekly visits to an expensive salon run by faggots. Her sexy nails. Same thing. Fake. And that fucking kid? Yeah. Mine. Right. Fucking cunt.

Don't forget sweetheart, we aren't married and there is nothing to keep me from waltzing out that door right now, he'd say. So try to please shut the fuck up. That usually worked but sometimes he had to smack her around, it was the only way. He loved feeling his fist smash her spongy face, but after, he had to figure out how to keep the cops off his ass. It wasn't worth it. That was the only good thing about fucking Mexico. Those putas take a lickin' and keep on tickin'.

Margie had made some slop involving hamburger, American cheese, and crap from a box. Smelled like dog puke. "Yum, Yum!" he said, just to fuck with her. Her smile was so pathetic. Encouraged, she nattered on and on about random bullshit until he had to tell her enough. "I was fucking with you, babe. I come home after three days on the road, and this is your idea of fucking food? Really? Put a lot of thought into it, huh? Really went way the fuck out of your way for me. Right?"

He turned the volume way up on the TV and chewed with enthusiasm. "Mmm, mmm! This sure beats steak!" He kept on, shoveling big forkfuls and chewing loudly, with his mouth open, letting half-chewed food drop back onto the plate. Stupid Margie started to cry.

Phone went off just as he was considering whether to hit her, or just go to bed. It was old Wallace telling him about a government contract. The way Wallace explained it he could make ten times as much doing the same thing they been doing. Bids out to the public, but that means a select few got the heads-up. Maybe my luck's about to change, he thought. It made him benevolent. Ten times the money. Damn.

"Come over here, baby. Get sexy on your old man."

Margie plopped onto his lap like a giant bag of flour dough. She was fake-crying; it made her tits bounce. She felt sad, he guessed, because she knew she was pathetic: cheap, ordinary, and practically middle-aged. He made a hobby of interpreting emotion-based behavior. You might say, this ability had gotten him where he was today.

SEEDS

The changes were so slow to happen it was like hair growing, Destiny thought. Usually. But then every so often, there would be a big jump forward. She didn't even think much anymore of the fact that Prince would come up to her in the corral, and lower his head for the halter. Just weeks ago she'd have to chase him for hours sometimes, in the scary small pen. Now, she could brush him with the rubber curry and a soft bristle brush, and even work on untangling his tail. Sometimes he was quiet and as tractable as a sleepy kitten; but still some days he was impatient, scary. When he got mad at her, he'd try to nip, or switch his tail, trying to hit her in the face with it, and sometimes succeeded. But he never kicked out at her like some of the other horses did, and other times, he leaned his head gently into her body, his half-closed eyes soft. Then Destiny would kiss him on the nose, and Prince would breathe out, and wait for Destiny to breathe back into his nostrils. They'd breathe back and forth a couple of times. When this happened, Destiny felt like she was in love. His smell was indescribable. His strength, fearfully unimaginable. Yet his nose was soft as a newborn's skin. His breath, tentatively beginning to trust... The big wild animal, when calm, morphed into a scared, young soul, in a hostile world, imprisoned without having broken any laws. The irony of it stung her heart.

* * *

Destiny didn't even think twice about refusing sex with Danny on their first date. Right there next to the river, as the twilight wrapped them in privacy, Destiny kissed her technical virginity goodbye. Danny was gentle and full of whispered compliments and unlike the boys Destiny had known, wasn't in a hurry. She told him she was a virgin, omitting any mention of blow jobs for money. He made a big deal about her virginity, asking her over and over again if she was sure. She was sure. That part was over quickly and was pretty disappointing. When a little later they were making out and Danny put his hand on the back of her head and began guiding her down, she smiled. Here was something she knew she was good at.

They held hands all the way back to Bakersfield and Destiny just knew Danny was feeling the same way about her as she felt about him. Everything was different, everything would be different. She waited for him to ask her to come home with him, but when Danny took the Union Street exit towards Loreen's, she had to ask him.

"Take me home with you," she said.

"Oh, honey, I would but I've got a cousin staying with me. From out of town."

"Oh."

"From Texas. He's real religious."

"Oh, okay."

"But I'll see you tomorrow."

For the first time in memory, Destiny went to bed excited about tomorrow.

Danny worked a lot of overtime hours at the cable company. The cousin from Texas turned out to be staying with Danny all summer. So Danny picked Destiny up after her shift; they'd drive somewhere deserted and jump in the back seat of his truck and make love. Then he'd drop her off at the library except on the nights it was closed. It was a hot June and kept getting hotter and Destiny made a little camp out back from Loreen's trailer. There was a nook behind a rusted utility shed where the weeds were overgrown and trash blew up against the fence from the freeway, but at least it was private. A shedding cottonwood tree gave shade but covered everything with its fuzzy pods. She'd scored a rusty lawn chaise from the curb on trash day, and brought out her sheets and pillow, made a night stand made from milk crates and with an extension cord brought out a reading lamp. She slept out there just to be as far from Loreen and Rico as possible. She hung out there and read in the mornings before her shift at work. She lay on the lawn chair dazed with sweat and heat and swatted flies and daydreamed about Danny, and sometimes she touched herself... She couldn't wait for the end of summer when the cousin would go back to Texas and she'd turn eighteen and be in college. She just knew Danny would ask her to move in with him.

Fourth of July. Flags were everywhere, limp in the windless day; red, white, and blue. Blue: Danny's blue eyes, Loreen's bruised face, banner-blue sky, blazing hot. White: Danny's white t-shirt, pure white; Destiny's no-longer-virginal but still white panties. Red: red roses, emblems of love. Blood red, blood filling Danny's penis, flushing his skin with the rose of lust. Red blood, missing. Not a drop of red blood staining Destiny's snowy-white underpants.

Destiny knew right away. She woke up one day in late June knowing. She waited a week then bought a pregnancy test that confirmed what she already knew. She greeted the knowledge with about a million different emotions. She felt like a Madonna, blessed. She knew just what her baby would look like, a boy, soft blond hair and big blue eyes. But the next moment he was a monster, an alien succubus, ruining her life, her plans. Her body seesawed along with her feelings. She'd puke, and the next moment, feel great, full of light and energy. She kept waiting for Danny to notice, hoping he'd notice so she wouldn't have to tell him. He'd be so happy. They'd have a wedding, nothing too fancy, but she'd wear a white dress and he'd wear a suit and maybe they'd go to Disneyland on their honeymoon. Then she'd fix up Danny's apartment (which she still hadn't seen but could picture perfectly) and turn the second bedroom into a nursery. But maybe he wouldn't be happy. It had happened pretty quick. Maybe Danny wasn't quite ready for a family. Maybe he'd be mad. Maybe he'd want her to… Destiny always abandoned this scary line of conjecture.

She decided that if he didn't figure it out by the Fourth of July she'd tell him then. But he was late picking her up after work and she got tired waiting for him and without having anywhere else to go, took the bus back to Loreen's and stripped down to her snowy-white underwear and bra and lay on the lawn chair trying to nap through the heat and the cracks of firecrackers. She woke to a touch on her behind. It was dark—she had slept for hours and felt thick, her tongue fuzzy. She rolled over to see Danny, his white shirt gleaming like the moon. He leaned over to kiss her and Destiny turned her head away because she was worried about her breath but put his hand on her bra to show him it didn't mean she wasn't interested. They started making out and Danny entered her while she sat on the lawn chair and he knelt in the dirt. Afterwards he pulled up his pants and sat on a milk crate and lit a cigarette.

I have to tell him, she told herself fiercely. Firecrackers still punctuated the night like slaps.

"Danny. I have to tell you something." He looked up so slowly with blank eyes that she felt a stab of fear.

"Here it comes," he said, his voice as blank as his expression.

"I'm pregnant," she said, before she could chicken out. She expected declarations of love or anger; mentally, she was prepared for either. But his silence was something she'd not imagined.

"Aren't you going to say anything?" she finally asked.

"What do you want me to say, Destiny?" His voice was low and flat.

"I don't know."

"There you go," he said. "Well, see ya." He stood up and pocketed his cigarettes.

"Wait," she said.

"What?"

"Well, I mean, what are we gonna do?"

"Do whatever you want, Destiny."

"What do you want?" Destiny persisted desperately.

"I don't give a fuck, Destiny. But don't think you're getting any money from me. Whose is it, anyway?"

"What do you mean?" she cried, knowing exactly what he meant.

"Go ahead and try to prove it's mine. But you still won't get anything. If I was you, I'd get rid of it quick."

"Danny," Destiny pled, and began to cry, messily.

"Oh, shut up," he said. "You little girls are always pulling this shit. Fucking white trash. Ever heard of birth control?"

"We used condoms most of the time," she sobbed.

"Yeah well," he said.

"Danny, please," she managed to say.

"Please what?"

"Help me," she said, wiping her nose.

"Okay look, I'm being an asshole. Maybe I can get you some money. There's a clinic down on Chester."

"I don't want that!" she said.

"Well, you're on your own, then. I gotta go." And he turned to leave.

"Can't we get married?" she begged.

"Married? Destiny, I'm already married. As far as I know, it's still against the law in California to have more than one wife."

"You're married?"

He shrugged. "You never asked," he said. "I got three kids, too. That's plenty. Believe me."

She lurched away and ran down the block, still in her underwear. By the time she realized it, and reluctantly returned, Danny was gone.

* * *

With a little grunt of effort Destiny lifts the heavy saddle up and onto Prince's back. Her heart is galloping and she feels like she can't breathe. She tries unsuccessfully, to calm down, knowing Prince can sense her unease. She drops the offside stirrup, and he flinches but stands still. Then she reaches down under his belly for the cinch, but Prince abruptly begins to back up and the saddle begins to slip, and even though she grabs the horn it's too late, the saddle thuds into the dirt—again! and Prince dances away to the end of the lead rope, snorting, his eyes wide.

"No sir! I ain't doin' that!" came a comment and laughter from the inevitable audience of the other inmates. That Landris girl always had something to say.

"No, mommy, I don't want that nasty ol' saddle," added Swit. "Y'all can't make me neither."

Destiny wants to throw down the rope and run away. She wants to whip the crap out of Landris and Swit. She wants to cry. This is the third time in a row the horse has dumped the saddle.

"You know what to do," Varney drawls. He sounds bored.

Destiny takes a deep, shaky breath and twirls the rope end, sending Prince off around the round pen. He tosses his head in protest but then begins to trot calmly. He thinks he's winning, she thinks. Her frustration lifts as she watches him move, she finds herself smiling at how easy this part has become, how much Prince has learned and how much she has learned about him. Like how stubborn he seemed sometimes; but he wasn't really

stubborn. He just got mad and embarrassed when he didn't understand what she wanted him to do. Once he learned something,
he seemed happy to do it, perfectly, over and over. He was a big
show-off, really.

She turns him easily and sends him clockwise. His ear is on her
like a bird dog on a covey. She makes the kissing noise, and Prince
instantly changes gait to a lope. She lets him eat a mile or so then
slows him, turns him, and makes him lope the other direction.
Finally, she brings him down to a walk, then come to her, halt. He
stands like a statue, not even breathing hard, while she rubs his
neck and then moves to pick up the saddle. She loops the off-side
stirrup and with a grunt, heaves the saddle up over one arm, and
with the lead rope in the other, she steps casually up to Prince's
side. He doesn't budge a muscle. As she swings the saddle up and
over, he doesn't flinch. She drops the off stirrup. This time she's
ready for his antics. She reaches under his belly and as he begins
to back up she snaps his lead rope sharply. He freezes for an instant, surprised at her retaliation, and in that instant she grabs the
cinch and smoothly threads the leather twice through the ring on
the saddle like she's practiced in the metal shed that served for a
tack room. She smoothly tightens the cinch just enough to hold it
if he jumps around. She motions the command to step over, and
the horse does, so she is on his right side, where she checks that
the saddle is lying okay and then asks him to step back, he does;
and it feels like a dance.

"Real nice, Tubb," Varney says, not sounding bored anymore.
"Send him around."

Destiny sends Prince in both directions, to let him get used
to the feel and sound of the saddle. It's a triumph, but naturally
Destiny doesn't get to savor the feeling because for the next half-
hour, she has to saddle him over and over until she is positive she
can't lift that darned saddle one more time. Finally, Varney tells
her it's enough and he comes in and takes the saddle and even
shakes her hand.

"Nice job," he says.

Destiny's arms are so wobbly that she can barely lift them to
take off Prince's halter back in the corral. She rubs his forehead
and scratches under his chin, and he yawns, hugely. She grins.

"I know," she says, "me too." The horse yawns again and then
closes his eyes as she scratches him some more. An emotion so

long unfelt courses through Destiny as strongly as an opened fire-plug. Pure and fierce and sweet, a feeling Destiny had long ago reserved for Justin, only Justin.

"I love you," Destiny whispers, and kisses Prince on his hairy, so-soft nose.

A Leg Up

I drag myself up from the dirt and trudge back to the house. I put the shovel away instead of just leaning it on the wall of the shed. I go inside the house and hug and kiss my remaining dogs. Their bowls are empty. I fill up their water, scramble a dozen eggs and feed them, and as they eat, I begin to clean my house.

Getting the poisoned, bloodstained mattress out and into my truck is almost impossible until I utilize tie-down straps and a pulley... Mrs. McGuyver. That's me. Then, garbed in the plastic suit, gloves, and booties Hank had stashed in the case of biological warfare (don't ask!), I scrub the blood spatters off the wall. I reload my gun. I check the oil in the generator and fire it up and then gather together all the dirty laundry, start a load. It will take days to catch up on the laundry. I feed and water the chickens and collect another basket of eggs. I vacuum the rugs, I attack everything with my feather duster and then I mop. I'm getting tired and my back's beginning to ache badly, but instead of stopping, or popping a few Vicodin or a shot from the last bottle of whiskey, I drink two glasses of water. Then I start washing the windows. I don't stop until the sun dips over the ridge and I'm weak with hunger and badly need a cigarette.

Smoke... wine, my brain suggests, but I resist. Instead I pour leftover coffee into a tall glass and add ice and some sugar and sit at the kitchen table to admire my clean house. I've shut down the generator and absence of its roar is sweet. Through the window I watch the hummingbirds buzz around the empty feeder. Something else to attend to; but I've done enough for today. Yeah. Too much. That was always my cycle, mild to medium bi-polar: rush of energy, sustainable for days, weeks, but then a crash. When I was mentally healthy, I would simply sleep in; take it easy for a day or so. But this last crash has left only smoking wreckage, and gone on for so many months. Yes, I am sick of it. I am ready to at least pretend that I am living a life.

I finish my smoke and light a few kerosene lanterns. I go into the office and find my notebook, bring it back to the kitchen, and start a shopping list. Tomorrow I'll go to town, dump the mattress, and grocery shop. Maybe even get a haircut.

After another cigarette I get up and heat up a cup of instant vegan mushroom soup, and don't have to force myself to eat it. I walk the dogs in the last of the day's light; I take a shower. My house and I are clean and I'm pleasantly exhausted. I get out a sleeping bag, a pillow from the guest couch in the office, and throw it on the couch. I make sure all the doors are closed!—and check the screens on all the windows and blow out the lantern and candles carefully. No more mistakes: I can at least try to avoid the preventable tragedies. I fall onto the couch and the dogs settle around me and I don't think about missing Hank or Freddie or my tragic stupidities; my mind's a tamed, tired thing for a change, and I drift off just as if all's right with the world.

Teddy, the dachshund, wakes me at sunrise and my first impulse is to push him away and roll over and go back to sleep. But I don't. I play with him a little and Slim jumps on the couch, and now I'm fairly awake. I get up and throw on clean clothes and get my gun and we go outside. The sun is just coming over the mountain. The rooster's crowing like mad and the hens are gurgling and pecking bugs and the light has a hazy blue quality. I breathe deep and cough my smoker's cough and breathe again. I think about going into town and start to get scared. It's no big deal, I tell myself. Truthfully, if I didn't have to get rid of the mattress, I'd probably blow the trip off. But the blood could draw a bear or coyotes, just what I don't need. Plus, there it is, already in the back of my truck, perforated with bullet holes and spattered with blackish dried blood, looking like a prop from a horror movie. The sun's rays, mote-filled searchlights, poke over the mountain, coloring the day, and I turn back inside.

One thing at a time.

Right. I'm going to make coffee. Feed the dogs and chickens. Load up the trash. Go to town.

Leaving the house is wrenching, but finally I'm in the truck and bumping down the drive. Locking the gate behind me and winding down into the canyon. At the bottom the seasonal creek is still running and I surprise a doe drinking in a little pool. I stop the truck and watch her watch me, water dripping from her muzzle. A few seconds, then she makes up her mind, bolts, and leaps up the bank like she's jumping a series of invisible fences, and disappears into the trees. I drive on. A few miles down is my mailbox, at the intersection—if you can call it that—of the dirt and paved roads. My oversized mailbox is stuffed full. It takes several armloads to dump it all on the passenger seat. A truck passes, and I wave—it's George Watley, a neighbor, who gives a casual wave back with his cigarette hand. I am somewhat shocked that he doesn't stop and scream, "You're alive!" then remember that I'm only the center of my own universe, not anyone else's. This thought calms me. Maybe I can anonymously drive on into town and do my business.

So I do. A few curving, climbing miles later I come up onto the view of the town and lake. A haze lies over the valley but the road is bordered by an outrageous display of purple and white lupine. I wind down and through town to the dump. The dump employees are surly as ever and don't even make a comment about the bloodstained mattress. Do they see this sort of thing everyday— or will they call the cops as soon as I've left? I wonder, driving away with my empty truck, feeling cleansed.

My shopping list is a full page long. I park at the supermarket and get a cart and begin cruising the aisles. All the people... all the brightly colored products... the muzak... I immediately start to feel like I've taken a hit of real strong pot. I wander a few aisles just spacing out before I remember my list. I start over, at the end, the bread aisle. I try to focus. Whole wheat bread. Onion bagels. Beer, ooh, look. Sam Adams on sale. Some cheese. I have an idea about making enchiladas with black beans and corn. Now I am getting somewhere. I am tossing stuff into the cart like a regular person, one with errands to do and meals to make and a life to live. The tightness in my throat is subsiding, and the only thing in the world I'm thinking about is the merits between corn and flour tortillas when I hear, "Hey, Siggy!"

Lee calls me Siggy, for Sigmund Freud, and my heart jolts like I've been caught shoplifting, but she's hugging me and I'm hugging back.

"Where the fuck have you been, I've been calling—" she says.

"I know. I'm sorry..."

"I came by… "

"I know."

"Hey, it's okay—"

"No it's not, Lee, I'm so sorry."

"Forget it, I'm just glad to see you. Bitch."

We stop and grin at each other.

"So here you are, out of your castle," she finally says.

"Apparently," I admit.

"Wanta get some lunch at the Shady?"

"Sure," I say, surrendering to the inevitable. So we make plans to meet up at the bar across the street in a half hour and I finish up my shopping and load up the truck and cooler with groceries and meet her in the cool darkness of the Shady Tree.

"The usual?" asks Linda the bartender, putting two tap beers down on little napkins in front of us.

"I'm not hungry," I say. Linda puts an ashtray in front of us on the bar between the beers. It is illegal to smoke, but at the Shady everyone conspires. Linda has a dragon tattoo that disappears down her shirt onto her large bosom and rings on all but one finger. I wonder briefly about that ringless finger.

"I'll have the dragon burger," Lee says. "Have something to eat," she says when I remain silent except for the lighting of a cigarette. "You're too skinny."

"No… no thanks," I say, "I'm not hungry," and slug down half my beer.

"Try the fish sandwich," Linda says.

"Fish sandwich?"

"Yeah, it's pretty good," Linda says. "Plus, we got some killer homemade cold slaw that comes with it."

"Okay," I say, surrendering again, wondering how it is I live in a place where the slaw is "cold" and not cole. We wait for the food and Lee and I exchange preliminaries. Her girls are fine but her six-year-old has an ear infection. Her husband, Charlie, is swamped at work. Her mare foaled a paint colt two months ago.

"So what the fuck has been going on with you?" she finally says. "I've been so worried about you."

Without planning, I suddenly confess. "It's been pretty bad, Lee."

"What can I do?" she presses.

"I don't know. You know, yes, I'd love to ask for help. But I don't know. I'm just trying to… you know, start functioning a little. I was thinking I should just get involved in something. Volunteer, or something. I just don't know what."

"That's a good idea. The right opportunity will present, now that you've put out for it."

"You think?"

"I know. Why don't you come on down tomorrow and we'll go for a ride."

"I guess could do that," I say, the beer making me agreeable.

"Promise?"

"Sure."

"Really, Sara Beth," Lee says forcefully. "Don't you dare go back up there to your castle and blow me off and ignore my phone calls. I mean it. You better show up tomorrow or I'll come up there and kick your skinny old ass."

"I promise," I say, and this time I do mean it, simply because I can't come up with a reasonable excuse.

"Here ya go, ladies," says Linda, setting down two loaded plates.

We finish lunch (and I actually eat the entire thing—it is greasy and quite wonderful) and I promise again to meet Lee the next morning at her place. She peels out of the parking lot and I head to the bank—my dreaded next move. I haven't checked in with my financial reality in so long I truly don't know what to expect. I look up my balance outside at the ATM, not wanting to face any of the tellers inside, in case I'm thousands of dollars overdrawn. The little slip of paper spits out and I look at it and my heart jumps. There is over one million, twenty thousand dollars in my checking account. I count the digits again to make sure. What the hell? It has to be a bank error… I do a quick mental review.

The land—two hundred acres—is all paid for. Ditto, the house: Hank always insisted on avoiding lenders. That's why it took twelve years to complete the building; he was a big believer in "pay as you go." A month after his death, I began to get his pension deposited into my account, which was plenty to cover the bills and more. But how in holy hell could those deposits could have added up to a million bucks? I went inside and sat down with Lisa the branch manager. She gently reminded me that I'd set up automatic bill-paying—all my bills were current. And a check for a tad over nine hundred thousand dollars had been electronically transferred four months ago. From an insurance company. I hadn't even known Hank owned life insurance, although after the funeral, my meeting with the lawyer involved signing papers, but I had not been able to listen as he droned on about money. Maybe he had told me then. I stare at Lisa. I might be frightening her. My face is frozen, but I'm just trying not to burst out in hysterical tears. Hank! Goddamn, the sweetest man on the planet, my guardian angel, my hero. If only I could trade this fucking million dollars to have you back. My Hank.

I mumble thanks, and lurch to the door while she is saying something about interest-bearing accounts.

That night, my good intentions of reform are not enough to stop me from succumbing to a fresh tide of grief. A million dollars, a million dollars! Hank is still taking care of me even though he's dead. As if I didn't already miss him enough, this new evidence of his generosity overwhelms me and I fall onto the bed in a frenzy of tears. How can I feel so desperately, horribly hopeless when my life is what most people only dream of? I'm retired and don't have to do a damn thing. My house is paid for, so is the truck; the property taxes are low. I have everything I need—clothes for town and work and summer and winter (even though they are a few sizes too large)—every appliance, all the housewares from blender to vacuum. I've got free electricity from my solar panels and water from the well. The income from Hank's pension, my Social Security, and portfolio is more than enough for food, firewood, propane, gas, insurance. What am I supposed to do with a million dollars?

He was just taking care of you.

He did. I am. I'm already taken care of.

Then maybe use it to take care of somebody else.

Like who?

Just like Lee said: it will come.

I try to not drink but lose the brief battle with myself. A bottle and a half of wine later, I stagger to bed, blessedly stupid and numb. Vaguely, I know I should take a couple aspirins and drink a quart of water but I'm too tired, and I just don't care enough. My inner therapist doesn't even put up an argument; maybe she's exhausted too.

In the morning, naturally, I'm hung over. But it's not too bad; I've definitely experienced worse. I take some aspirin and water and go back to bed for an hour until the pounding subsides. As soon as I pull covers over my head I remember promising Lee we would go horseback riding. Today. Fuck! I call her and try to tell her to forget about it. But she won't accept my excuses and takes advantage of my weakened state to force me to agree to come down to her place after all. By the time I hang up, I'm smiling and realize my headache is almost gone anyway. I braid my hair and change into jeans and boots and get my cowboy hat and head out before I can talk myself out of it again.

It is another perfect spring day, the wildflowers are dots of paint from a drunken artist's brush, the birds frenetically chirping away in a sweet cacophony.

When I get to Lee's, she is already saddling the horses. She rides a big paint mare and I ride her sweet old buckskin quarter horse named Buddy. He's tall, and I'm old and creaky, so Lee gives me a leg up and we head down the dusty, empty road into the hills. Buddy clomps along calmly; all I have to do is enjoy the ride. Buddy's a "bomb-proof" horse, meaning a complete idiot would be safe upon him—even Lee's four-year-old rides him. Which is all good, because I'm not the best rider. But do I love it. Hank and I used to come down and ride with Lee often, and we even built corrals and a barn and stalls and fenced a pasture up at our place, planning to get some horses of our own. I hadn't even thought of my empty barn in a long time. I inhale the smell of horse sweat and leather, loving the measured clop-clops of their hooves on the dirt, the exhilaration of a swift canter down the flat roads through the canyon. I love the entire gestalt; but what I love most are the individual horses: so insanely beautiful, so compelling in their mysterious silence and their unfathomable desire to cooperate with us humans.

We're riding side by side, the horses' steps are in sync. Lee roots around her saddlebag and produces a battered silver flask.

"Shot?" she offers. She grins and I notice how beautiful she is. She wears only pale lip gloss, her skin's brown and weathered like mine, but of course not as disastrously —after all, she's fifteen years younger. Her hair's all tucked away under a battered straw cowboy hat. She wears a white man's undershirt and a purple sports bra with straps showing that enhances her substantial cleavage, camouflage pants with the top button undone; her belly pooches out a little above the waistband. What a great smile she has; what a gorgeous day. What a miraculous planet.

"Surely," I say, and take it and slug down a sip of rum, hand it back. "Thanks for making me come, Lee. It's nice."

"I'm proud of you. I know it wasn't easy. I'm sure all you want to do is hide out."

"True."

"But you can't, sweetie. You can't go on isolating yourself forever. It's been over six months."

"I know."

"I know you miss him like mad, but you got to go on living."

"I know."

"We miss him too," she says. "Henry was a really great guy."

I instantly get a big lump in my throat. Lee senses this and becomes aggressive.

"Look, Siggy. It's over. Your mourning period is officially done, hear me? You're gonna get yourself a project or a hundred and keep busy. Believe me, girl, I know. It's the only way."

I suddenly remember that Lee lost a baby, when he was only six months old, her second. Her only boy. And a beloved aunt, to breast cancer. This was all before we met; but still, I feel like a complete shit for having forgotten those facts, even for a moment.

"I know you're right," I say, the lump gone. I think of the million dollars. I say, "Maybe I should check out being a foster parent."

"I thought you were happy not having kids."

"I never said that—" I blurt, defensive. Then I know that if now isn't the time for truth, it never will be. "Children do make me a bit nervous," I confess. This admission makes me feel awful: I am a selfish, mean-spirited woman.

"It's okay, Sara Beth. Not everyone has to like kids. Hell, most days I don't even like kids, and I'm stuck with four of 'em. Consider yourself lucky. You can do anything you want. Trust me, girl. Your mission—it will come."

I might as well grasp Lee's hope, held out like an offering of toasted marshmallow on a stick. Why not choose to hope, for a change? No matter how sweet and sticky.

GIT 'ER DONE

Danny disappeared. Destiny didn't know where he lived, so she couldn't take the bus there and stalk him from behind the bushes like she wanted to. His cell number had been disconnected with no forwarding number; there was no Daniel McNally listed in the phone book and needless to say he never again came to the Burger King. It was as if he had never existed. Except for the inescapable fact of the little souvenir he had left behind: a child, smaller than a peanut, for sure, but still, undeniably and just as incredibly, an actual child, growing away inside Destiny's belly, which was already feeling different and pooched out like she had a chronic, bad case of gas.

If I was smart, I'd get an abortion, she told herself endlessly, but to no point, because she could never do it. It was killing; it was baby murder. She'd go to Hell, for sure. So there was no point to thinking about options; there were no options. Her life, so carefully planned, was never going to happen. There would be no college. How could she go to college and work to pay for everything and raise a baby? Leaving her baby with Loreen, even to go to college, was not ever happening, no way would her baby be subjected to that environment. So, a sacrifice would have to be made. Maybe, once the baby was in pre-school, Destiny would get to go to college. She'd lose her scholarship, meanwhile, so she'd have to pay for it herself, but maybe she could do it in a few years or so. Part-time or something. And make a really good life for me and the baby. In the meantime, I'll just have to figure it out, she resolved.

She got busy and scoured the Help Wanted until she found a second job—cleaning houses and offices for an agency. They gave her an apron with the logo on it and a pail of cleaning implements but she had to find her own transportation to the job sites where there would sometimes be another girl. It was difficult and embarrassing riding the buses with her pail of mop and broom and scrubbers and bottles of Windex and Mr. Clean. It was humiliating to scrub stranger's scum from toilets and the bending and stretching was exhausting. But she made eight dollars an hour and they gave her as much work as she wanted because she always showed up and was never late and worked hard and did a good job. Destiny's windows never had streaks and when she vacuumed, the lines in the carpet were straight.

Her pregnancy had become a constant, overwhelming reality. She spent a lot of time throwing up in strangers' toilets. Between her two jobs she was putting in over sixty hours a week and the money was adding up—just in time, because the weather was turning cooler and eventually it would be impossible to continue sleeping outside behind Loreen's trailer. Now Destiny was scouring the Apartments for Rent instead of the Help Wanted's. Most places in her price range were trailers and Destiny was never again going to live in a trailer, but there were some available apartments. She used the pay phone outside the library to make some appointments and went to go see them.

The first place was in a faded, once bubblegum-pink duplex with six half-junk cars crowding the driveway and broken toys and crap filling the yard and two howling and barking pit bulls behind a chain link fence that encircled the house. Destiny didn't bother looking inside, not that she would have dared trying to get past the dogs. Another long bus ride. The next turned out to be a room in an old hotel in the downtown section. The hotel had been nice, then seedy, now it was nice again, but it was surrounded on both sides by taverns and the rest of the block was filled out by pawn shops and tattoo parlors. No place to raise a baby.

The next was in a residential neighborhood of low bungalows and smallish newer condos and duplexes with reasonably neat yards and a reasonable number of cars per house. There were a couple of dogs that barked as she walked slowly down the sidewalk, but they were little dogs, secured behind good fences, and their yaps were amusing instead of frightening. The houses were nicely kept and the yards were neat and there were trees shading the sidewalks. She walked three blocks and came to the address. It was a small, brick modern-style apartment building with a manicured lawn and two big trees with brick-circled flower beds surrounding their trunks. There was a driveway that went along the side and a multi-car garage back there, and a big yard in the back, with more trees. And a little iron bench sat under one of them. Destiny could see herself on that bench holding her baby. Reading to it from a book of nursery rhymes. She went back around to the front of the building and rang the bell for the manager and saw the apartment but her mind was already made up and not altered by the apartment itself, even though it was on the basement level, with only small windows high up. It was roomy and there were two bedrooms and a kitchen with gleaming white appliances, and there were big closets and the bathroom gleamed too and the carpets smelled new and it was perfect.

* * *

Her dreams are full of horses. They gallop through a misty meadow, the air saturated with the smell of their sweet grass breath. Destiny is not one of them but she is not apart from them either; in her dreams, she is connected to them somehow. They are all colors, all sizes, and Prince is always there, larger than the others, more beautiful, commanding, leading, a gentle tyrant. She moves with them, effortlessly, as they gallop over fields and through rivers, through vast vivid pastures guarded by tall mountains of incomparable beauty. It always hurts to wake to the dull gray cell, to Tonya's snoring and the clanking and bells and cursing. She feels like Dorothy in The Wizard of Oz. One world is Technicolor and the other gray and black. But unlike Dorothy, she doesn't believe that there was "no place like home." Destiny doesn't have a home to long for. Even if her parole is granted, at her hearing in two months, she would probably be on probation, and she'd have to work some crummy job and try to prove that she was rehabilitated before she could even think about getting her life going again. She isn't sure that she is even ready for that. The last thing she wants to do is let Justin down again. Maybe she should just stay away from him. Some days, as much as she hates prison, Destiny wishes she could stay inside forever. Here, you didn't have to try so hard. They fed you and you didn't have to worry about getting money to buy food. They told you what to do and all you had to do was obey. That, and keep your head down. Unlike in the men's prisons, here you didn't have to join a gang. The women were grouped into families instead. Sure, some of them were mean or sick, mentally sick. But if you stayed a loner, the women seemed to mostly respect that. Still, there was violence and rape and stealing and fighting. Lots of fighting, with screeching curses, hair yanking, and fingernails clawing.

Destiny really didn't want a prison "family," she didn't think she deserved one; she deserved to be alone, lonely. At first, she'd had to fight for her right to not join any group. But after winning all her fights and losing only a tooth, she earned her respect. There were those who tried to do their time without trouble, and it was always the same ones that got into trouble over and over. Tonya belonged to a family consisting of seven other white girls, and weirdly, all of them were fat like Tonya. Other families were more diverse. One Mexican family had a grandmother, several "aunts," and teenage daughters just like it would be in real life.

She waits her turn to lift weights in the yard, because the physical pain makes her mind a blank, gives temporary relief from her morbid thoughts.

Prison. The runny, nasty food, the chill grayness, the noise and smells and the very fact of being behind bars, is all a dull torture. Every dull day is a torture like a bad toothache, being here. But it feels right to Destiny. It's her punishment, one she has earned. She absolutely deserves every tragic, wasted moment of it. But, now, unforeseen, like a plot twist in a book, the grayness has been suddenly relieved by the blessed mornings, Technicolor mornings. The horse program.

The time she spends with Prince is like coming to the surface for a gulp of air. The sunlight and the horse smells and the sheer physical and mental exertion of the training are like an injection of anti-prison. She has moments where she fills up with hope, so much hope that it felt like she's overflowing with bubbles, enough to float her right over the razor fence and on to those vivid pastures… somewhere beyond the rainbow. She'd think, maybe I could get a decent job when I get out. Something she could be proud of, that Justin would be proud of. Not just cleaning houses, maybe work that meant something… But the bubbles always burst when she'd remind herself no one was likely to hire a felon for any decent job. Her mistakes would never be erased; they'd always be there, the past tainting the present and making the future impossible. It was a heck of a thing to ruin your life: get yourself sent to prison, when you were nineteen and a half. Every time, her thoughts ended up there, and every time they did, Destiny longed for some drugs. She longed so much to not remember, not think, not care.

* * *

She had thought long and hard about it and decided to not tell her mother she was pregnant.

"Ma, I'm moving out," she said. Loreen was alone in the trailer, having sent the younger kids outside ("Get out there now or I'll whip ya"), the baby was sleeping, the boyfriend absent.

"You ain't doing no such thing," Loreen replied. She was twitchy, not stoned. Maybe it was not the best time for this conversation, but when was a good time? —Never. So Destiny plowed on.

"Yeah, I am. I've already rented an apartment."

"I'll call the cops. You're too young. I need you here, besides."

"You're gonna have to try and find me."

"Go then, you little bitch. Get on out, right now. Don't plan on crawling back, neither." Loreen lit a cigarette, pointed the remote until the TV was blaring, and exhaled a yellowish cloud that encircled her in the stagnant atmosphere like toxic halo.

"Okey-dokey," Destiny said, trying to stay calm. She was nervous about leaving Loreen in charge of the kids, she almost wished she were eighteen and could get guardianship of them... but that was just dreaming; maybe someday, eventually; but for now, one softball-sized baby was more than enough to worry about. It was time for Destiny to take care of herself.

Destiny didn't have anything to pack; her clothes were already in two cardboard boxes on the curb and her other stuff in her backpack. She was more than ready to go. She checked her pocket for her cash, rubbed the folded, soft bills between her trembling fingertips. The cab she'd called came rolling up to the curb. "Bye, Ma," she said, and went out back and kissed the kids and then got in the cab with her boxes, and as it drove away she didn't want to look back, but she did anyway, all the way down the block until they turned the corner and the trailer could be no longer seen.

* * *

The heat wave breaks with a big thunderstorm that turns the pen and corrals into mud so the training is cancelled for two days, but as if to compensate, there's good news for the horse program. A rich family, friends of the warden's, donated a bunch of new fencing: enough pipe corrals for each of the thirteen horses to have their own, twenty-by-twenty-foot corral. The corrals are set up in two long rows, six adjoining squares on each side. When the ground dries up they move the horses into their new homes. Each horse has their own water tank and a tractor tire on the ground to hold their hay. With the new corrals comes a new method. Now the girls can each work their horse in their own area and not have to wait for the round pen. Along with the pens, the people had donated a dozen pair of boots and safety helmets and Destiny got a barely used pair of doe-colored Justin Roper boots that, as soon as she puts them on, fit her perfectly and makes her feel more capable, more cowgirl-like; authentic, even. The first day with the new setup begins to resemble a three-ring circus. Everywhere Destiny looks a horse is going in a different direction. She and some of the others who are doing good with their horses, like Landris, and Freeman and Young, take them out of the corrals and trot them up and down the new aisles. There's a lot of laughing and experimentation. Varney stands, arms crossed comfortably, a faint smile on his pulpy face. He offers occasional advice but mostly just sits atop his old gelding, one hand crossed over the other, reins looped over the saddle horn, as his horse stands so relaxed he looks ready to fall over, but never does.

"Tubb, Freeman," he says as they leave to go back to the yard at the end of the morning. "Let's have you two git on them ponies tomorrow."

Fear taps Destiny's shoulder and she has to dumbly ask, "Tomorrow?"

"Don't want ya'll getting bored," Varney says.

Destiny has dreamed and worried about it for so long, that now that she is actually about to do it, it feels unreal. But here she is, and here is Prince, saddled up like an old pro. Here she is, putting her foot in the stirrup.

Prince turns his head and sniffs her boot. Destiny is holding his lead rope, which has been doubled into a set of reins, and a big hunk of his mane in her left hand. Her right hand is on the cantle of the saddle. She hops lightly up and down a few times and Prince stands as he has been taught. She wiggles the saddle so Prince won't be surprised by it moving when she gets up. She takes her foot back out of the stirrup and checks the girth again, then grasps the mane and the cantle again. She puts her foot back in the stirrup, and hops a few more times.

Varney chuckles, says, "Any time now."

"Yeah, Tubby, any year now!" calls Shondra Freeman, but her tone's encouraging.

"Git 'er done, Tubb," yells Landris.

"Git 'er done," Destiny repeats to herself, and takes a deep breath and with a bigger hop, hauls herself until she's up and leaning over the saddle. Prince steps backwards and sideways and Destiny tugs on the rein until he circles, and then he stops and she releases the pressure on the rein.

"Put your leg over, nice an' easy," Varney says.

She does, careful to swing it high so as not to kick Prince in the butt. And she slowly settles into the saddle. Prince twitches his skin but stands. Destiny knows she's to try and keep calm but her heart's thundering like a wild horse herd, her hands are shaking. She can't stop worrying about Prince suddenly going berserk, and bucking and galloping madly, as she's seen some of the horses do. Prince himself has done plenty of bucking himself, in the early days when Destiny drove him around the pen. But right now he seems calmer than she feels.

"Pet him," Varney suggests. She transfers the reins to one hand and pets his shoulder, then scratches up his mane. "Hey, good boy, that's my good boy," she says softly, for her horse's ears only.

"Don't forget the rest of him."

Destiny smiles and reaches back, stroking Prince's rump.

"Remind him you're up there and get him to turn his head for ya." Destiny lightly tugs one rein then the other, getting Prince to yield his head all the way to his shoulder, several times, both sides.

"Move him on out a little," Varney says. "Lift up them reins and lean a little forward."

Destiny gingerly lifts the reins, clucks.

Prince's ears go crazy, swiveling in all directions, and then he makes a little shudder and then he takes two lurching steps and then abruptly stops. "Walk on," Destiny says, clucks some more, and squeezes with her legs, and with a little jolt, Prince begins to circle the pen at a walk. Varney chuckles, a reassuring sound if there ever was one.

Destiny's thundering heart changes tempo from fear to nervous elation.

"Woah! I'm riding him," she hears herself say, in a clear voice that doesn't sound like her own.

"You sure as hell are, Tubb. Doing fine. Now let him take a few more steps, then double him, back the other way, nice and easy."

Destiny rides Prince around the pen a few times in each direction. Varney is telling her to relax her back, keep her hands low and all that, but telling someone to relax, and having that person, who is riding a horse for the first time in her life—and a wild horse at that—having that person relax, is not so easy. But she tries, and for a brief moment, maybe four or five of Prince's steps, she begins to feel the way her back is supposed to give and when she does, her butt kind of melts into the saddle and she can feel his legs, his back; his movements are hers and they're one, she's like that myth of half-man, half-horse, the centaur… and it's easy, it feels so easy, but then she remembers that she doesn't know how to do this, she's not good at anything; and what if Prince suddenly rears or starts bucking? —and she clenches up and her fists close and Prince's head jerks up and he starts to trot, and Destiny realizes that she must have been squeezing with her legs and she stops doing that and pulls on the reins, but Prince's head stiffens, his nostrils wide and eyes rolling, he's trotting faster and she's bouncing all over heck, and one foot's coming out of the stirrup.

Varney's saying something but it's drowned out by the pounding hooves, creaking leather, flopping stirrups, Prince's snorting breath, and Destiny's heart, now thundering like Seabiscuit on the home stretch. Easy, she thinks somewhat desperately. She lowers her hands and unclenches her fingers, and Prince drops his head and slows, just a little, and suddenly Destiny feels the rhythm of his trot and she goes with it, she knows about posting to the trot and now it makes sense; she lets Prince's back legs push her out of the saddle and then she comes back down and then is pushed up again. Her foot magically slips back in the stirrup and she's posting, and Prince is trotting a nice, slow trot, no longer snorting, and his neck is curved and his ears are forward and her hands on the reins are light, and she's moving not just on him, but with him, effortlessly, just like in her dreams.

He Was in Heaven

This gig was too beautiful; he only wished he'd known about it years ago. Who knew?—The goddamn government rounded up thousands of mustangs every year. All those useless fucking nags had to get hauled someplace. Oh, yes indeed.

The roundup that busted his cherry was full of the thrill of loud engines and screams of terrified horses. Dust and flying ropes and helicopters hovering like alien birds, whipping up tornadoes of dust. He couldn't believe how badass the pilots were, coming in low enough to bump a slow nag with his sled rails! The wranglers with their horses and hats and boots and shit—it was like being inside a movie. The stupid horses ran from the helicopter and then actually followed a tame horse—that was trained to be the "Judas"—damn, he loved that part. The doomed mustangs follows the Judas into a trap, and when they realized it, too late! They jumped around and made noise like crazy. Tough luck, suckers, he thought, watching them leap and kick, eyes wide and white. He'd never heard a horse scream before. To be honest, the whole thing gave him a woody.

The best part was to come, when thirty-eight of the fuckers were loaded into his rig. Twenty-four hours later each one would bring a sweet thirty-five bucks a pound in good old Guadalajara.

He'd dumped fucking Margie. Found a sexy whore, brown, but so what?—she did what he wanted, and the sweet part was, she did it for cheap-ass crystal. That was all she wanted, she'd literally let him fuck her every sick-assed way he could think of, just for a pipeful. I'm a king, he realized. Cleansing the deserts of those fucking ugly-assed nags, and at the same time, setting himself up a sweet damn savings account in Switzerland. Yeah, he was no dummy. America the Beautiful was going to hell. Best to tuck the stash elsewhere. America—fuck! What a disaster. Diluted, polluted.

Yeah, he would strike while the iron was hot, so to say. Stuff away the cabbage. Each run with horses to Mexico was netting him over seven grand. Cha-ching, fuckers. He ground his jaw as he thought these words, though the identity of said fuckers remained vague.

He was hungry. A nice, bloody steak, garlic bread, and a couple Jack and Cokes. He could have it. He could have it every night if he wanted. He was getting hard again. Maybe a quick blow job before dinner.

SPECIAL TO THE COURIER

That horseback ride made me feel better than I had in weeks—no, months. I was filled with energy when I arrived home and flew into action. I washed more windows, cleaned closets, and even returned phone calls and correspondence. Painfully, over the next few days, I even talked to Hank's mother and his kids. We reassured each other that we were all okay. I even got outside and watered and fertilized the fruit trees and worked in the garden. It still wasn't too late to plant beans, corn, squash, tomatoes.

Kneeling in the dirt is as close to church as I get. As I poke the little, promise-filled seeds into the dirt, I pause to look up as a falcon wings over, screeching a threat to the chickens. The sky is cloudless blue, the trees sway and whisper. The yard is filled with purple mariposa poppies encased in a sea of tall green grass that will turn brown in a matter of weeks. I should mow the entire yard because snakes could be hiding in the grass, but the poppies are too magnificent. I will play viper roulette until they go to seed. I take a moment to appreciate my life. A lovely house, surrounded by all this wild beauty. My two dogs—my constant companions, my entourage, my posse. The sweet hens, delivering eggs faithfully. I water the seed beds. The smell of wet earth is intoxicating.

I've started to eat three meals a day, even if they are my own weird menu: a poached egg on toast, cut up as if for a child. A bowl of chocolate ice cream. Albacore tuna from the can. Five Granny Smith apples. Egg salad and root beer.

A couple weeks pass, and my windows are gleaming, my laundry's all done, the house is clean. All of a sudden as I am putting away the Windex, I ponder, what next? The house is so new there is no painting or maintenance to do. I've caught up on my mail, on the yard, the dogs, the chickens, the orchard. I have been focused and sober, so much so that my Inner Therapist has been mollified to silence. But. Now what?

Honestly, a wave of panic overtakes me. I was out of it for so long, I'd thought it would forever to catch up. But I'm caught up already. Then, just like in a movie, the phone rings. Saved by the bell. It's Lee.

We exchange preliminaries, I assure her I'm doing so much better. She then comes right to the point.

"Didn't you tell me you used to write for your college paper?"

"A little," I confess. "It was a column, a humor column. I gave joke advice to made-up letters."

She seems to think that suffices as credentials. She tells me her husband needs help at the paper. Charlie is the editor-in-chief of the local weekly.

"But…"

"He's desperate for some new writers, please, Sigs. Why don't you give it a shot? It might be fun. It pays shit, but I just thought, I don't know, it might be fun for you."

"What kind of writing is he looking for?" I ask skeptically.

"Honestly, I don't know for sure, but talk to Charlie, he's in the office all the time. Do it for me, for us. Pleeeease."

"Well. When you put it that way."

I stop by the newspaper office the next day when I go in to buy to-mato plants and rent a carpet cleaner for my rugs. Charlie is there, piles and stacks of paper on his desk and surrounding the room, a half-eaten Whopper perched precariously atop a paper mountain. Charlie jumps up and gives me a big hug. Lee's husband is a tall, skinny, blue-eyed, political liberal with a background in journal-ism, which landed him this low paying, demanding job. But when you are in the sticks, any profession requiring creativity is as rare as a summer downpour. So the job at the paper fits Charlie to a T.

"How are you," he asks, but casually, not with that glum sym-pathy that I hate.

"Better," I say. "You?"

"Not bad, can't complain. Except, I'm swamped here. Corpo-rate cut our budget, can you believe that, even with our ad reve-nues up? I had to let my assistant go and now I'm too busy to do any of the writing myself. The last few weeks the paper's been freaking pathetic. Have you seen it?"

I nodded, of course I'd checked out the paper before coming. It had indeed been thin on articles.

"Hell, I doubt anybody reads the articles anyway. They just clip the coupons and read the obituaries. It's pathetic. My life's a waste."

"Charlie! That's not true. Everybody reads the paper."

"You think so? So then you'll help me out, right? I need you to concentrate on crime."

"Crime?" I giggle, assuming he's joking.

"Well, yeah. There's that serial child molester on the loose, and I want to follow up on that gang killing from last year, and I want to do a series on meth. There are so many addicts around here. There's a lot of spousal abuse, kid abuse. The Mexican cartel's growing pot in the forests. There's a lot going on."

"You're kidding me."

"No."

My god. Here I'd thought I'd moved to Shangri-La and left all that behind. "A child molester?" I ask, uneasily.

"He shows up in little girls' bedrooms in the middle of the night wearing a Halloween mask," Charlie says. "So, you'll do it?"

"No, no, I'm not qualified…"

"Come on, Sara Beth. You can write a sentence, I know you can. Give it a try. We pay twenty-five bucks a story. How can you turn that down?"

I sigh. "How do I even start?"

He tells me he'll give me his notes and the numbers of the D.A. and the sheriff. Says to just ask them the questions that come to mind. It's not the New York Times, he adds, telling me not to "stress out" over it. All I have to do is write up three or four pages and e-mail him the files; deadlines are Mondays.

"Oh, and any pictures pay extra," Charlie says. "Five bucks each."

"My god, I'll be rich," I joke, then remember that bizarrely, I already am rich. The money isn't the point. What the point is remains to be seen.

"Good luck," says Charlie.

I am tortured by doubts the entire way home. I don't know a thing about newspaper reporting. I have no idea how to even begin. I don't want to let Charlie and Lee down; but even more, my pride is at stake. What if I'm a lousy writer? My hands get sweaty on the wheel, and I find I'm driving too fast and chewing the inside of my cheek.

Relax. It might be fun.

Oh, sure. Easy for you to say, you don't have to perform. You just criticize.

No, I just support.

Hah. How am I supposed to pull this off?

You'll figure it out. Like Charlie said, it's not the New York Times. Don't you think it will be good to have a project?

That's the general opinion.

Well then. Just have some fun.

But I don't even know how to start!

Yes you do. Read Charlie's notes. Think up some questions for the cops. Then call them.

One step at a time.

There you go.

So when I get home, I unload my goodies from town, walk the dogs and feed the chickens, collect eggs and water the garden. Then I head back inside to my office. I get out my lucky pen and a fresh spiral-bound notebook. I read Charlie's notes and transcribe the basics into the notebook along with the names and phone numbers of the district attorney and the local sheriff. Then I pick up the phone.

***

"Serial Sex Predator Strikes Again"
Sara Beth Corcoran
Special to the Canyon Courier

"The Canyon County Sheriff's Department is intensifying the search for the sex predator that has terrorized several female children in incidents dating back to October.

On June 3, a knife-wielding man unlawfully entered a home in the Topaz Mine subdivision. A 10-year-old girl awoke at approximately 3 a.m. to find a male intruder wearing a Halloween mask, standing next to the child's bed, holding a hunting knife. The child screamed and fought with the intruder. Her screams awoke a male resident who joined in the fight. During the struggle, the suspect escaped.

There are four other related incidents being investigated..."

The day I sent off that first story I got an e-mail back from Charlie. He said the story was "fine" and wanted more. A local had seen two men stop on the road through Road-runner Wash, load up three newborn calves in the back of their pickup, and drive off. Charlie asked, would I investigate?

"Cattle Rustling Not a Relic of the Past"
Sara Beth Corcoran
Special to the Courier

"'$3500 Reward for information leading to the arrest and conviction of CATTLE THIEVES stealing longhorn calves from Canyon Creek Area.'

It sounds like an advertisement that might have been nailed to a fence post at the turn of the century. But this seeming relic from the past was in fact posted on Canyon County fence posts just this week. The reward is being offered by several local ranchers who have suffered losses due to cattle rustling.

'Cattle rustling is alive and well. It's still going on,' said Sergeant Shawn Vale of the Canyon County Sheriff Department's Rural Crimes unit.

Unlike in the days of the Old West, today stealing cattle is no longer a hanging offense. 'But it is a felony, punishable by incarceration in state prison,' Vale said. 'The reality is, all the cases are looked at by the courts on an individual basis. There is always an attempt to get restitution.' The attempts for court-ordered restitution are almost 100% successful, he said. 'But of course, the rustlers have to get caught first...'"

Reporting that story was surprisingly interesting: meeting the local ranchers and brand inspectors and the deputy in charge, a Rural Crimes Specialist. Next was a story on the new hair stylist in town. Then Charlie got the idea for some profiles on the local cops and the firemen, so I did "ride-alongs" with a couple of the deputies. Then I interviewed firefighters—of course, I had a special thing for firefighters, and these guys were something special: wildland firefighters, Hotshots. They could drop from a helicopter into a raging forest fire and fight it with chain saws and shovels and courage. I asked them whatever came to mind, and later at home tried to reconstruct our conversations from messy scribbled notes. I read and re-read the style guide Charlie had sent in an e-mail, which turned out to be rules on grammar and capitalization particular to the newspaper realm.

I decided, why do anything halfway? I handed out my new business card, and asked everyone I met to call me if there was anything newsworthy going on. I had determined not to worry if they considered me a nuisance or a freak. But apparently, at least some of them didn't, because just a few weeks after my first story I got a call from one of the Forest Service cops I had met, asking whether I wanted to go along on a pot bust in the forest.

I agreed, thinking I was cool as hell.

"Then meet us tomorrow morning, at zero dark early."

"Uh, what actual time is that?"

"Five a.m."

"Ugh. Where?…"

The next morning I arise at three-thirty and make a thermos of coffee and get in the truck and drive an hour and a half up to Green Mountain Summit. I sit for thirty minutes, drinking coffee and smoking in the dark, wondering if I am the victim of a mean joke. But then, headlights, followed by more, and six anonymous sport utility vehicles and trucks pull around me and park. I get out and am surprised to find I'm the only reporter. The Forest Service cop who'd called me gives me a camouflage jacket and explains we will be hiking way up into the forest and preparing an ambush for the pot growers that they have located. I'm excited, but also a little in shock. They are taking me—an old lady, bogus reporter—into the forest to arrest a bunch of armed, cartel pot growers?

"Let's go," says the handsome Forest Service cop, and about a dozen SWAT team guys wearing camouflage and jungle face paint and high tech radios and guns start hiking up a lovely little creek. I fall into line, feeling rather out of place and even more midget-like than usual. Three hours later of mostly uphill, narrow, slippery, bug-infested trail, I want to kill them all. I am trying so hard to keep up. To not cough my smoker's cough. To not fall on the guy in front of me while I'm trying to take a picture, to not think about how bad I have to pee after that thermos of coffee. Finally, we stop and are motioned to stay down. I crouch under a cedar tree and am afraid to move a muscle. Cute Forest Service cop whispers that another team that has hiked in earlier from the opposite side of the forest will flush the growers from their camp toward us. The guys all draw weapons and melt into the brush.

At first, my heart's thumping, I am imagining a bunch of desperadoes leaping from the forest, guns and rifles spitting fire. It is exciting for maybe the first twenty minutes, then the sun begins to remind me I have barely slept four hours, and I begin to realize I'm hungry, and my bladder begins to proclaim urgency. I dig as quietly as I can in my backpack for my notebook. I get it out and take some notes on the mission thus far. Then I sketch a butterfly flitting nearby. Finally I write in big block letters on a fresh page: WHERE ARE THE CATERERS? I "psst" discreetly to get the attention of the nearest cop and hold up the notebook. He grins when he reads the message. He tosses me a Power Bar. I take it with a mouthed "thanks" and write a new message: I AM GOING TO PEE. He shrugs and elaborately turns his gaze uphill. I slide down to hide behind a brushy manzanita and do so and it is hard not to groan loudly in relief. But I manage. Then I pull up my jeans and crawl carefully back uphill to my post and wait another hour or so. Finally, we get the word to continue and to the dismay of my aching legs, hike another couple of miles. Then I smell it, but it is not the sweet skunk smell of weed, but a stomach-lurching stench of death. A bit later we come upon the growers' camp. Rotting fly-covered bones of a deer carcass, explaining the death smell. Porn magazines and human shit and nasty wads of toilet paper scattered about. A crude shelter made of pine branches knee-deep inside with trash. The cops already have a suspect in custody and are questioning him in Spanish.

I take some notes and pictures while the cops search around for the rest of the plants. Then they handcuff the suspect with a cable tie and we start the hike back down. The cops have caught both growers and found over a thousand plants and they are happy. And right there on that path, crossing a stream with butterflies everywhere, I realize, I'm feeling good too. Maybe it's the result of all this extra oxygen flooding my brain from the unaccustomed exercise. Or maybe it's that sense of the surreal—like I've been transported into an Oliver Stone movie. Maybe it's the rush these cops and firemen feel—which is partly why they chose such a dangerous job. Maybe it's my pride of being chosen to come along and having not too terribly embarrassed myself.

Whatever. I finally feel almost… alive.

HARD HISTORY

The first night in her new apartment, Destiny slept on the floor with her denim jacket as a blanket. The next day, her shopping spree began. She went right after her shift at work and bought a blow-up bed, sheets, a pillow, and a yellow and green striped comforter. She spent over four hundred dollars that first week; ruling out a couch as way too expensive, but she bought a wicker rocking chair, a crib and everything she could think of to furnish a nursery and a kitchen. She didn't need a TV or stereo, but she did find a cheap radio so she could listen to music and the news. She knew she could get stuff at yard sales and thrift stores and the Salvation Army store, but there was no way. She wanted everything new. Nobody's used junk was going to make its way into her clean, new apartment. It was fun setting up her bed and kitchen. The first meal at home was macaroni and canned fruit salad for dessert. Destiny was thinking about nutrition for the baby. She fixed the macaroni in her new pot and served herself on her new plate. She sat at her new table and sipped milk from a new glass. Afterwards she carefully washed the dishes and put them away. She turned on the radio and rocked in her new wicker chair and gazed happily around. Her apartment. She put her hand on her belly and wondered how long it would be before she felt the baby move. Then, like a sudden rain cloud on a perfect day, some uninvited thoughts assailed her. She needed to go see a doctor. She should probably be taking special vitamins for the baby or something. How much did doctors cost? How much would the vitamins be? What about the actual delivery and everything? How bad was it going to hurt? She was scared of the pain. The idea that a whole, grown baby was going to push its way out of her you-know-what frightened her half to death. And what if something went wrong?

And how long was it going to take before she could go back to work after, and who was she going to get to watch the baby while she worked? What would that cost? She knew that there were government programs and stuff. But she was never going on welfare. She didn't believe in that. She was going to be independent, and have a real life. Once you started taking money from the government, it was like drugs, you could never stop doing it. And then you'd become just like Loreen. No ambition. No goals. No thoughts of making life better. You'd just coast along and pretty soon you'd coast right on down into a deep old hole.

But it was hard, so hard! She was so alone. Why did Danny have to be married? It would be so different if he were helping her, if he was here with her, if this apartment were theirs together. Darn him! Darn him anyway, she thought, and stinging tears accompanied these thoughts. He had said he loved her. He had said she was pretty. And she felt pretty and smart and thin when they had been together. It could have been so perfect. How come he had even dated her, made love to her, if he was married? How could he have walked away like that after she'd told him about their baby? When her baby was born, she'd never tell him—or her—about Danny. She'd tell her baby that its daddy had died. She'd invent a lovely, tragic death. Maybe he was a soldier. He had died fighting for our country. And one day, Destiny might meet a guy, a nice, honest guy, who would love her and her baby. It could happen. "Dear Jesus," she prayed. "Dear God…" but she didn't know what to pray for, she needed so much. A healthy baby. A way to take care of it. A husband. Hope. Happiness. "Dear Jesus, help me," she ended up praying. Her tears had stopped. She got up to blow her nose and then poured another glass of milk and turned her radio to the country music station. She'd listen for a little while but then was going to bed. Tomorrow she had to get up at five and had a twelve-hour day ahead. She wanted to make sure she'd get enough sleep for the baby.

* * *

The very first thing that Destiny learned working with the wild horse was that repetition was key. Consistency. You can't expect a wild thing to change its ways overnight. "Just because I did it yesterday doesn't mean I'm doing it today," she used to imagine Prince sassing her in the round pen. But this day, Destiny is full of delicious thoughts about last time, her very first time, on Prince's back and that first lesson from horse to human is the farthest thing from her mind. A hot, grit-gusting wind whips Prince's mane all around and he's bouncy, he doesn't want to stand still, and so Destiny drives him around and around the pen, hoping he'll calm down. But Prince is a mustang. Varney has said that in the wild, the herds will travel thirty miles—on a slow day—to forage grass and water. A hundred circles around this dinky pen doesn't even faze him. Prince circles, a fast trot, but keeps breaking into fits of bucking or galloping and fighting Destiny when she tries to turn him. It's like he's regressed, completely forgetting the last weeks and weeks of training. Destiny is getting hot and out of breath and more than a little frustrated. She's using up more than her allotted time in the round pen, but Varney makes her stay and Destiny knows, though Varney doesn't, that this will make the other girls mad and they might try to take it out on her. But she is stuck with Prince until she rides him again and she knows it. Eventually Varney says to go ahead and saddle him up, and so she does. Prince jumps around when she tightens the cinch and the saddle almost slides off. Destiny jerks his lead rope hard and hisses, "Cut it out!" He rolls his eyes at her and sidles away. Destiny is more mad than scared, this time, when she puts her boot into the stirrup. She swings up into the saddle, wincing at how sore her leg muscles are. Prince starts moving before she gets settled and she tries to circle him left but her rein's too loose and he charges ahead into a jagged trot and as Destiny reaches for the rein she loses her other stirrup and now she's bouncing hard, off balance, and Prince's head comes up and he trots faster and then breaks into a gallop and it's all Destiny can do to grab onto the saddle horn and try to stay on. Varney is saying something and the girls are all yelling and Destiny tries to settle into the rhythm but there's no rhythm, and then Prince's head points down and he kicks out with his back legs, he's bucking and twisting, and Destiny catapults into the air and into the dirt with a sickening, cracking thud.

* * *

Destiny and another Pro-Kleen girl named Valencia got a full-time assignment cleaning a K-Mart store at night. They arrived at ten at night and were locked inside by the security guard, a mostly silent, looming black man whose name tag read Duwayne.

The dark parking lot with its little group of inexplicably left-over cars, the humming of the buildings' many machines, and the dark corners were all creepy, but all that was nothing to the claustrophobia of being locked in. And the creepiest of all were the red eyes of the security cameras positioned to observe their every gesture.

Valencia operated the floor polisher and Destiny wielded a big feather duster and the glass cleaner. Then she had to do the employee bathrooms. They were both always finished before the shift was over and Duwayne would let them out into the raw dawn. During the last hour, Destiny and Val started to hang out in the employee lounge at the table underneath the camera, in its blind spot. They drank sodas from the machines and ate chips and candy and Val smoked, and they'd talk.

Val was from San Diego. She'd moved to LA instead of finishing high school, with a boyfriend who wanted to be an actor. The boyfriend was long gone and the closest thing to acting he'd ever done, as far as Val knew, consisted of dressing as a giant wiener and handing out Woody's Hot Dog flyers. Since then Val had waitressed and washed dishes and even picked grapes and oranges in the San Joaquin Valley.

"I hate this fucking job," Val said every night.

"At least it's something," Destiny would offer, encouragingly.

"Fuck it, I'm thinking of getting a job stripping, down near the airport," Val said one night.

Destiny regarded Val dubiously. She was short and bony. Her skin was light brown, rough and kind of mottled looking, with irregular patches of acne. Her eyes were small and mud brown and she practically had a unibrow. Her hair was so curly it was nappy like a black girl's, but Val was Argentinian. Or so she said. She wore her kinky hair in sloppy braids. She had small breasts and a round belly. Destiny couldn't imagine anyone paying to see Val naked. Still, the discontented and mysterious Val had become, in Destiny's mind, her best friend.

"I would hate that, having men stare at me," Destiny said.

"I wouldn't give a shit," Val said, popping gum. "Pays real good."

"Can you... don't you have to know how to dance?" Destiny asked, hoping Val might reconsider.

"Aw, no, you just get up there and grind it. It ain't the ballet."

Destiny didn't want to ask how Val has acquired her knowledge of strip clubs. "Do you ever think of going back to school?" she asked.

"Shit, no, I hate school. I just wanta make as much jack in as little time as I can. This cleaning shit sucks."

Destiny sighed. She too knows it sucks but she also thinks she's lucky to have this job. She wishes Val weren't so negative all the time. "Brad Pitt has a new DVD out, I saw it on the shelf," Destiny said to change the subject. "It looks like a cowboy movie. Did you see it?"

"Brad Pitt sucks," Val replied. "Now, Denzel. He's got him a fine ass."

"I know what you mean," Destiny said, feeling let down. "Denzel is pretty hot," she added, trying for a point of reference.

"For a nigger, anyways," Val said.

Destiny sighed again. She looked across at the big clock on the wall that ruled their nights. Seven minutes to go. It could as well be seven days. She's so tired. She doesn't even know how she will make it home without falling asleep on the bus. She lives in terror of missing her stop and ending up back in the old neighborhood. She had been thinking of asking Val to go see a movie on their day off, Sunday. But now she was kind of afraid Val might say the N word in public or something.

"Want to come have dinner at my place sometime?" she asked instead. "I'm learning to cook." She giggled apologetically.

Val narrowed her eyes at Destiny through a cloud of hanging cigarette smoke. "You a dyke?" she asked in an accusing tone.

"No, no, I mean, I'm pregnant!" Destiny said.

"No husband, boyfriend, though."

"No."

"So you're scared of bein' by yourself."

"No, no, I'm not scared. I just thought, you know, it would be nice."

"No husband, no boyfriend, no friends. That's the only reason you're askin' me to come to dinner."

"Well, I guess you could put it that way. But I like you, Val." Although Destiny wasn't one hundred percent sure of this, in fact, Val made her mostly uncomfortable, but she thought everybody deserved a chance; and she was trying to make a normal life, in which having friends over to dinner seemed to be a part.

Val's eyes flitted from Destiny to the clock and back and there was a second in which they both knew Val was right, it was a desperation move.

"Sure, whatever," Val finally answered, shocking Destiny. "When?"

"Sunday?" Destiny squeaked.

"Sure, okay." Val said. "Just don't get too experimenting on my ass, Dessy. No Eyetalian or Chink food or none of that shit. I got IBS."

"What's that?"

"Irritable bowel."

"Wow, I'm sorry."

"Anyway. Gimme your phone number. Where'd you live, anyway?"

"I don't have a phone," Destiny said. "But here's my address."

Val read the scrap of paper. "Huh, I never been up there. I dunno."

"Well, you can let me know tomorrow," Destiny offered, already regretting the invitation.

"Okay, whatever."

They sat in silence until the clock's second hand clicked onto the hour then stood up and shrugged into their coats. "Another night, another dollar," Destiny said with an effort at cheerfulness.

"Yeah, whoop dee doo," Val said. Duwayne loomed up the aisle and shined his flashlight in Destiny's face as usual.

"Y'all redah?" he droned.

"Yeah, yeah. Let us the hell outta this craphole," Val snapped.

* * *

"Val?" Destiny opens her eyes and through the fog of pain, sees those small brown eyes, that unibrow. Was she back at the K-Mart?

"Relax, you're okay," says a smooth, accented voice, completely unlike Val's bored, nasally monotone.

Destiny tries to sit up and is rewarded with searing pain in her shoulder, her entire side. She moans, squeezing her eyes shut against the glaring pain.

"Relax, you're in the infirmary," the voice says.

Prison. Prince. I fell, Destiny realizes in that order.

"What happened," she manages to mumble.

"The horse bucked you off and you got a little banged up. You were lucky, there's nothing broken. You have to rest right here tonight though. Once the doctor checks you out, maybe we can give you something for the pain."

"Hurry… please," Destiny grunts.

The doctor comes a few minutes later and shines a light in her eyes and prescribes Vicodin. The sweet-voiced nurse gives one to Destiny and she swallows it like a Communion wafer, with reverence. The pill works and Destiny drifts off, but before she does her last thought is, I am so done with that dang horse!

The next day she is so sore that she can barely lift her arm or walk, but she's sent back to her cell and on the way she requests to see Varney. The warden says, I'll let you know. Two days of boredom, of pain only temporarily relieved with the stingy pill she's allotted with meals. She tries to read, but the dull throbbing is all-consuming. She dozes and stares at a few books and limps around and it's a struggle to sit or turn over in her bunk. And the whole time she gets madder and madder, at Prince, at Varney, at the prison that put her in a pen with a wild horse in the first place. She could have broken her back or her neck and gotten paralyzed or even killed. By the time the guard tells her it's time to see Varney, she's been mad so long, she's calm.

"How are you feeling?" He asks, his face wrinkled in a concerned look.

"I feel like crap, actually," Destiny grumbles.

"That was quite a fall."

She waits for him to go on and apologize but he doesn't add anything.

"I'm quitting," Destiny says.

He nods like he was expecting it. "Your first name's Destiny, ain't it, Tubb?" he finally says.

"Yes sir," she says, thinking "stupid name," as she always does.

"That's a nice name," Varney says, his cabbage face in a smile.

Destiny snorts like a horse. She knows what he's doing. It's not like she's never been manipulated by a man.

"I'm just thinking, maybe this horse's destiny involves you, personally," Varney says. "Do you know about the history of these American mustangs?"

"Just what you already told me, about Christopher Columbus and the Spanish guys bringin' 'em," she answered, feeling decent about remembering, like when she got a good grade in school.

"Right," Varney said. "Well, those horses and the ones that came after with all the people comin' to America—some of 'em got loose and pretty soon there was a hundred thousand wild horses roamin' the ranges. Whenever anybody needed a horse—pioneer, Indian, miner, soldier—they'd just go on and rope one and break it and they were set. It worked out pretty good, for a while. But ranchers started feelin' like the horses were over-running the range. And then the dog food business came along and they was rounded up by the hundreds. The mustangers would chase 'em down in planes and trucks and on horseback. When they got close they'd rope 'em with the other end tied to a big old truck tire. The horses would run for miles draggin' that tire until they stopped from exhaustion. Then they'd get loaded up and trucked to the slaughterhouses: stallions, pregnant mares, foals. It didn't matter to the hunters, the horses to them was just hard-won profit. So much per pound, that's what they was to 'em."

Destiny shakes her head and thinks about the prison herd, the horses she's come to know better than her fellow inmates. Chewbacca and Tommy-Hawk and Lupe and Brave Spirit and Harley and her Prince. She thought of them running with a tire tied to their neck, being chased by monsters in the sky. Being killed for no good reason.

"That's really messed up," she admits.

"Well, there's more to the story," Varney says. "In the nineteen-seventies, the wild horses got protected by Congress. They still rounded up the excess horses but they got adopted out, or went to a sanctuary. But then a few months ago, Congress took some of that protection away from them, so now the mustangs older than ten years and ones that've been to the adoptions three times have to be offered at public auction.

That's where the horsemeat buyers can get ahold of 'em. These days, though, they don't sell the meat for dog food, they can get more money for it for human food."

Destiny gasps in disgust. "People eat horses?"

"Yep," Varney says, relentlessly grim now. "They eat it in some places like France, Mexico, Japan. Here's somethin' I printed out about what's going on. Its hard, but I think you should know."

He hands her a few pages stapled together. A newspaper article about the new Burns Amendment that made the new terrible threat to the mustangs. Another article with a picture of horses being killed in a slaughterhouse. She stares at the horrible image numbly.

"Listen up, Tubb. This guy, Prince. He's barely four years old, and could have a useful, long life. Make somebody a real nice trail horse, or a kid's horse, or a workin' ranch horse. But he's been to the adoptions two times already. He's got two strikes against him. If he don't get adopted this time, that's it, he goes to auction. This is his last rodeo. Next stop, dinner for some Frenchy."

Destiny is dizzy and feeling sick from all this information. Varney waits awhile like she's supposed to say something. But she doesn't. What in heaven is she supposed to do about it? She can't save all the wild horses; she can't save Prince, she can't even save herself. She couldn't even keep her own baby.

"So," Varney finally says, "if we can get Prince to trailer load and pick up his feet nice, if we get him to accept a rider and not send them airborne, he'll go to a good home. No question. The trained ones get adopted, but the untrained ones can fall through the cracks. Now, I know you think I'm puttin' a lot of pressure on you. That you can either work with this horse and get him trained right and give him a chance at a life, or not. But it ain't me being harsh on you. It's just the way it is. It's just hard history and hard present reality."

"Maybe somebody else can finish him," Destiny finally says.

Varney shakes his head sadly. "It took time for him to trust you, Tubb. We'd have to start him over in the next group, that means he'd be sittin' around for months and have to start over. I'm not even sure I can get him in the next group. My supervisors might look at this little fall you had and decide he's a little too dangerous. I don't know for sure, but my gut feelin' is, this here's his last chance."

Destiny doesn't even know when she starts crying. But in her mind, she sees Prince, the way he looks at her sometimes, so calm and friendly, and then thinks of him being sold by the pound, being on a truck and so scared, she imagines how they would all be crammed in, the stallions fighting, the foals getting trampled, then, frantic, thirsty, hungry, hurt, Prince, her Prince, prodded with electric poles and an iron bolt shoved through his brain then hung by his hoofs and then his throat being slashed while he is still alive… and her horse faces his death not bravely, but scared, frightened out of his mind, and betrayed, bewildered; wondering why? Why the humans who he tried to get along with have hurt him so badly—killed him, even, and finally aren't even watching or caring as his life's blood pumps to the stained concrete floor. Maybe, in those last moments, he thinks about her, Destiny! Maybe he wonders why she lets them do this.

"Okay," she says with tears and snot choking her words. "I'll try."

"Okay. Good." he says quietly. Destiny is crying so hard herself that she doesn't see the tears like tiny rivers flowing down the topography of Varney's weathered face.

THE WEDDING ALBUM

"Sex Predator gets 95-year Sentence"
Sara Beth Corcoran
Special to the Courier

*"The serial child predator that terrorized the Canyon City com-
munity was sentenced Thursday to a total of 95 years behind
bars. Louis Leroy Lange, 35, received three 25-year, one 14-
year sentence, and one 9-year sentence, making him eligible for
parole in 49 years. The Canyon County Superior Court jury
found Lange, also of Canyon City, guilty of all felony counts of
burglary, attempted child molestation, child molestation, sexual
assault with a foreign object, assault with a deadly weapon, and
sexual battery.*

*Deputy District Attorney Judith Meyer explained that some
of the sentencing in the case is set by statute. 'My goal was to
make sure he had a life sentence to meet,' she said. Because of the
threat posed by Lange to the safety of the public, Meyer said she
was pleased with the sentence. 'Of main concern was taking him
out of the population,' she said..."*

My stories start to end up on the front page and most of them as
the lead. I keep a copy of the A section each week and soon the file
drawer fills up and I start another. I'm writing about two stories
a week on average.

I go on several more pot raids, though none involving quite
as much hiking. (Was it a test?) I'm invited by the sheriff's commander to a methamphetamine lab bust, and watch as two un-
speakably filthy children are led away by a Child Services worker.
That inspires a four-part series on methamphetamine which I research on the internet and by interviewing several ex- and current
addicts, the cops, the probation department head, and drug coun-
selors.

I had been naïve about small-town life. The cities have no monopoly on tragedy, senseless acts, poverty, desperation, insanity. A father and son suicide. Fourteen peacocks shot to death. An elderly woman's wheelchair stolen—while she napped on a park bench! Two ten-year-old boys start a fire for fun and burn down two of their neighbors' homes. A mother high on speed breaks her daughter's arm. And, since it is summer, someone drowns almost every other week in the river and there are lots of minor boating accidents and drunk drivers arrested. I never have to look far for a story. So much for Shangri-La.

The sumptuous spring has long since given way to the relentless oven of midsummer. Searing dry winds blow dust devils twisting into the white sky. I reset the automatic watering system to keep the garden from wilting. The hens pant and hold their wings away from their bodies; the dogs spend their days asleep, flattened on the tile floors inside. I begin thinking about putting in a swimming pool—I can certainly afford it. It is either stay busy all the time or succumb to the heat, so I keep doubly busy, both consciously occupying my mind and my body with mindless tasks. I think about lots of trivial things these days. About the stories I am working on, of course. About the people I've met while researching the stories. About improvements I could make to the house and the garden and hen house. I redecorate the bedroom; I buy a new bed frame and have the one Hank and I shared hauled to the dump where I'm sure someone will nab it. I paint over the yellow-gold walls in a new light celery green and buy purple saris on e-bay and make them into curtains. I hang netting over the new virgin bed so it looks like a sheik's tent and then add a new rug and dresser, and when I am done I can walk in there and not think, immediately and constantly, about Hank. Once a week I take several dozen of the hens' eggs, beautiful, brown delicious things, plus my extra garden produce, to the abused woman's shelter. There is always a lot to do in the garden and another room to redecorate and another dozen phone call interviews I have to make and the subsequent stories to write. I make a few drives upriver and cautiously wade in the icy water of the Kern, drinking in the beauty: sparkling water, lush riverbanks, and distant rough mountains.

Each day is full, too full for my old standbys: pointless reminiscing, wallowing in grief, drinking to oblivion, zombie-eyed television viewing, and long coma-like naps. But even so, I am far from happy. There is a clichéd, big gaping emptiness at the center of all the activity. Almost like being a cocaine addict, each task completed gives me a little rush, but the high is transitory and unsatisfying and followed by a craving for more. I know if I start wallowing and drinking again, it will be the beginning of the end; pulling myself out of the grave once is one thing. But I seriously doubt I have the fortitude to do it twice.

Although I have forbidden myself pointless reminiscing, one stifling Thursday in August I am in the middle of reorganizing my office, which has become frighteningly cluttered with junk mail and notebooks and folders of story drafts and piles of newspapers. I decide to make some room by weeding out a big old steamer trunk covered in peeling travel decals. It is a mistake. Inside, among old tax records and a messy stack of psychiatric journals—now there's something I can toss—are our photo albums. I haven't looked at them since Hank has been gone. I reach in and take out the big silk-bound one. Our wedding album.

Are you sure you want to look at that?

No, I answer myself, but then my hand opens the cover anyway. Our wedding invitation is on the first page; underneath it, a picture of us on the day he asked and I said yes.

* * *

We were here on the mountain, working on the house. We had dinner outside, on a blanket under a big oak tree. Smoked Kern river trout, a Spanish cheese, home-baked baguette, and white wine. The picture—we used the self-timer on the camera—captures his arm around me, the tree behind us, the hillside covered with purple lupine and the sky just deepening. We both wear jeans and white t-shirts and are both darkly tanned. My hand is extended to the camera, showing off the ring. My face in a delirious smile and Hank's is more formal, as if he's pondering the seriousness of the moment.

A few weekends later we went to Catalina with James, Hank's longtime friend, and his wife Kendall. James used to work at Hank's station and had since transferred, but still kept his boat at King Harbor. It was a lovely, big sailboat, and we had sailed with them a few times before; but this was my first trip to Catalina. It was chilly on the sail over despite the clear sky. Halfway across, a pod of dolphins zoomed up to the boat and accompanied us for a few miles, speeding just under the transparent bow spray, and leaping in smooth arcs out of the water, entering without a splash. After the dolphins disappeared, Kendall and I went below and we drank wine and played gin rummy until we were coasting into the harbor and were summoned above by the yells of our men. The harbor was postcard-perfect: sailboats and yachts bobbing at moorings, a crescent beach with a half-dozen striped umbrellas shading beachgoers and a group of kids and some dogs playing in the gentle surf. The bars and restaurants, all quaint, the streets spotless, the golf carts were cute and even the other tourists mellow and strolling in the buttery sunshine. We explored the town, shopped, had some drinks in a pub, devoured a gigantic Mexican dinner, and then putted back to the boat for music and drinks and a game of poker. The berth where Hank and I slept was shaped like a wedge of pie but was large and covered with a goose-down comforter and the rocking of the boat was like a baby's cradle. We made love silently and then slept in exquisite comfort.

The next day we lifted the anchor and motored north alongside the island's rocky cliffs. The going was choppy, the spray salty and cold, and I was getting queasy and very anxious to reach our destination. When we did I decided the trip had been worth it. Tiny Two Harbors was even more engaging, to my eye, than Avalon. The town was not big enough to earn the name. It was a handful of ramshackle cottages flung on a hilly isthmus; a tiny beach and one dock. A dive shop. A small market-tourist shop and two restaurants, one for breakfast and lunch; the other for drinking and overpriced steaks and fish. I was enchanted and that was before we went ashore and hiked the little way across the wasp waist of the isthmus to Cat Harbor where the hills above were shaped in a precise crouching feline that gave the place its name. The beach was edged with palm trees; a few sailboats floated motionlessly at anchor in the cove. Pelicans bobbed and puffy clouds promenaded, far off on the western ocean. We picnicked on a hillside decorated with orange poppies and cactus.

James poured the last of the second bottle of wine into my glass.

"I don't know about you youngsters, but a nap on the boat is looming big on my agenda," he said.

Hank looked a question at me. "I'd like to look around some more," I said.

"I guess we're not sleepy," Hank said, mock-stifling a fake yawn.

"Take Sara Beth to see the Banning house," Kendall suggested.

"What is it?" I asked.

"Oh, it's a little hotel, just up over there, it's cute."

"Oh, goody, let's go see it," I said to Hank.

He imitated, perfectly, the sound of a whip cracking and got to his feet, held out a hand to me.

"That's not funny," I said, embarrassed, hurt.

"Take it easy," he said, hauling me to my feet. "A joke."

"Not funny," I insisted.

"Lighten up, you lovebirds," James said.

"I'm sorry. I request the privilege of accompanying you, my love, to the Banning House," Hank said.

"You can bite me," I said, though without conviction.

"Come on, baby," he murmured in my ear.

"I don't want to anymore," I whispered childishly.

"Yes you do. Please."

"Okay. Let's go," I said, suddenly inarticulate, strangled by this, our first public—or private—disagreement.

We all murmured "see you later" and Hank struck off down the hill. I followed him, feeling Kendall's eyes on my back, all the way down the hill, down the road and into the trees. I was about to yell, "Wait for me, asshole," when at that instant he stopped, turned back to me, and as I got nearer I saw tears in his eyes.

"I'm an asshole," he said.

"It's okay."

"I'm sorry."

I fell against him and we hugged hard. I love you, we said. We kissed and the smell of eucalyptus and salt and the cries of seagulls became part of the kiss. We walked slowly, hand in hand, up the hill under the delicious smelling trees.

"If you ever met my dad, you'd understand why I am... the way I am," he said.

"Tell me more about him."

"An Irish cop in Boston, right? It's a whole world. He was a tough guy and had hundreds of friends and this huge family. He was the funniest guy. But it was his way or the highway. If you didn't do what he said he'd beat the crap out of you."

He was quiet then and I couldn't think of how to comment. I had never heard that particular fact.

Then he said, "I fucking worshipped him."

"It's difficult, when someone dies and there are painful, unresolved issues," I ventured.

"Don't analyze me, okay, Sara? You don't know, you can't imagine what it's like, never being able to measure up. To worship somebody, always trying to win some god-damn faint word of praise. To get whipped for not eating your peas or getting a C on a report card, or missing a catch at a softball game. Being afraid all the time. Not being able to protect your little brothers. Or mother."

"No, I don't know. Oh, babe. I'm so sorry."

"Don't feel sorry for me either," he said, roughly. "I just want you to know, I'm not always a nice guy."

"To me you are," I said with feeling.

"Then I'm the luckiest son of a bitch going," he said. "Here's your Banning House."

I wanted to pursue the conversation about his father, it felt incomplete—I had failed to respond adequately, and there was more he wanted to tell me. But we were approaching the fieldstone steps to the porch of the hotel. It was like the town: not too congruent but deeply charming. Huge palm trees framed the white pillared porches. Inside there was a Mission feel, even a fireplace and unfortunate animal heads on the walls above. As Hank studied a brochure, a young woman hurried down a hallway to greet us. She was smartly dressed for an island where flip-flops were standard.

"I'm so sorry, I got tied up on the phone," she said. "You're here to see about a wedding?"

I opened my mouth to explain she had us mistaken for another couple, when Hank, to my utmost surprise, said, "Yes. We sure are."

I looked at him, waiting for the punchline. He just smiled and put his arm around me. The woman introduced herself as Diane and opened a notebook. "And you're interested in an August wedding?"

"That's it, right, honey?" Hank said.

"Excuse us a minute," I said to Diane, and steered Hank back onto the porch.

"Well?" I demanded.

"Well, what? Seems like a great place, doesn't it? We can put up family right here. It's cute, isn't it?"

"It's great," I admitted.

"Well, did you have someplace else in mind? You don't want a church wedding, do you?"

"Heavens, no," I said.

"Look, sorry if I jumped the gun. I love this place and I love you. I want to tie the knot quick before you change your mind about marrying me."

What was a girl to do? It took a nanosecond, after that little speech, for me to agree: let's get married here. We went back inside and made all the arrangements with Diane and her notebook. The other couple who'd made the appointment never showed up and we took their August 15th date. A Saturday, just two months away.

✳ ✳ ✳

Maybe the Universe intervened when the phone rang just as I was about to turn the album page to the wedding pictures. After all, I had forbade myself indulgent reminiscing. So I didn't look at my sexy antique wedding dress or our amazing four-tiered cake bedecked in blue violets made of icing. I didn't review the photos of our friends, Hank's family, the one of Hank feeding me cake, or dancing with my aunt. Or my favorite, the one of the two of us on the patio, Cat Harbor behind us, a canvas of cactus and blue skies and silvery sea, me on my new husband's lap, and us looking at each other with delighted expressions.

But whether it was divine intervention or pure chance, the phone did ring, and I got up off the floor and answered it, only after closing the photograph album and putting it back into the chest. And shutting the chest's lid, and turning the lock.

It was Charlie calling from the newspaper office.

"Want to do a story on a wild horse adoption?"

BIRTH DAY

Destiny's baby grew as fast as her bank account. The baby was active and huge. It kicked and squirmed as Destiny polished and mopped. She found a doctor and toured the birthing center at the hospital; she took vitamins and checked out books from the library on childbirth and infant care. She worked every day available, which was usually six or seven days a week, and it was a good thing because it left her so exhausted that she couldn't think about how lonesome she was and how terrified she could become at the looming prospects of childbirth and parental responsibilities.

She rode the brightly lit bus through the night on her way home, thinking about dinner. For the first time in her life, she didn't feel guilty about eating. Of course, her diet had changed. Salad, and fruit, lean chicken, even whole wheat bread: good things. No more fast food. Tonight she was having a chicken breast and spinach. And chocolate-mint-chip ice cream for dessert. She smiled and even her weariness felt good. She put her hands, fingers interlaced, over her mountainous belly. She didn't need an X-ray to tell that her hands were on her baby's forehead. She had gotten so used to having him-or-her being in there, it was bizarre to think about him-or-her being out, separated from her, in her arms instead of inside her. And it would be so soon. In the beginning nine months had seemed an eternity. Now eight and a half of those months have passed and she could, in actuality, easily have this baby right now. She prayed she was ready; she tried to feel ready, she hoped she was.

* * *

The chaos, the mortifying embarrassment, the unfairness, the nightmare events of the day Destiny gave birth were memorable enough, but she still could precisely remember the pain, the pain so consuming it dwarfed even the tragic turn of fate that was obvious even amid the chaos. For she knew that her life would never be the same. She knew that in this one awful day, her dreams were being ripped from her just as painfully as the child, who felt like he was bursting her right open. But that pain of shattered hopes she could face later. As she struggled to give birth, it was the physical pain that stared her in the face like an opponent in a fight-to-the-death match.

* * *

Since that day, Destiny has not felt comparable physical agony. Until now. Varney and the prison doctor tried to get her to wait before she rides Prince again. But for once, Destiny, usually so meek and mouselike, speaks up. She demands her right to "get back up on the horse" and argues that Prince's training must continue so he will be ready to graduate with the rest of the class. To her surprise, Varney and the doctors capitulate.

It's one thing to stand up for your principles but it's another thing, sometimes, to just stand up, she thinks, as she tries to walk without limping towards the corrals, leg cringing, arm burning, neck stiff, wrist on fire. Prince neighs loudly, shrilly, when he sees her, not his usual low rumble. As if he's demanding to know where the heck I've been, she thinks. Varney opens the gate and Prince trots up and Destiny halters him and rubs his neck and scratches under his jaw. He stretches his head up and out in obvious enjoyment. When she stops scratching, he lowers his head and presses gently against her thigh. Destiny strokes his mane, plays with its multicolored strands. Prince sighs, a deep sigh. Destiny sighs too, burdened with the knowledge that soon, whether she's able to ride him or not, they will be parted, forever. What will Prince feel? Will his new owners know how much he likes the underside of his neck scratched, will they be gentle with the reins and not hurt his mouth? Will they realize how hard he tries, how fast he learns? Will he get the right food and have room to run and play, and other horses for company? Will he gaze down the road at his new home, waiting for Destiny to appear?

"I hope you get to go to a huge ranch, with lots of other horses, and some of them are mustangs," she tells him silently. "I hope there's lots of green, green grass, and a rushing creek to drink from. And a nice warm barn for winter. I hope a really nice person gets you, but only if they're a good rider. I hope they treat you really well, and groom you and love on you. I know you're going to be a great horse. You'll be so steady on the trail. A deer jumping out or even a bear or a jet plane won't faze you. You'll cross rivers and bridges without flicking an ear. You'll never get tired or barn sour, you'll never buck or bite or kick. Little babies will be able to crawl around your feet and kids will be able to ride you bareback. But you'll be that one person's horse and they won't ride any other but you, and you love it best when the two of you get to go up and up some beautiful trail and gallop like the wind in some mountain meadow."

It is hard not to burst into tears at these thoughts, but Varney is right there and so are the other girls. Wiping her eyes surreptitiously, she tries to focus. Mechanically, she leads Prince to the rail and grooms him and picks out his feet. She is eager to ride, fatalistic about whether she will fall again or not. Physical pain is nothing compared to mental anguish; Destiny knows this well. Losing what you love more than anything hurts even worse than childbirth. If I break my neck on this horse, so be it.

"Let's do it, kiddo," Varney says, and Destiny leads Prince into the round pen.

The pen is no longer a symbol of Destiny's imprisonment. These days, it's a place of freedom, the one place Destiny is free to succeed or not, free at least to try. The horse no longer represents her badness. He's become the opposite: her ticket to redemption. Here is a chance to risk herself for this creature's life; this formerly wild horse that knows her and trusts her. If she can't salvage her own life at least maybe she can help Prince create his future.

"I've got to trust you too, buddy," she whispers in his furry ear before stepping back and sending him around. He circles like a pro and soon she's saddling him. He stands quietly, swishing his tail as if his only concern is the fly buzzing his flanks. He opens his mouth for the bit like the cold steel was a piece of licorice. He gazes back into Destiny's eyes calmly; in fact, he looks like he's practically falling asleep.

Lifting her leg all the way up in the stirrup had been worrying her for days. She can barely bend her knee much less lift her black and yellow leg up that far. But as she prepares to try, suddenly there is Varney, down on one knee and making a stirrup of his hands down low. "Step on up," he says gruffly.

Hesitantly Destiny does and he lifts her smoothly up, and she swings her good leg over and they lower together and she's in the saddle. Varney puts her foot in the stirrup and pats her boot.

"Just take it nice and easy, Tubb."

Destiny nods and finds the other stirrup with her toe. She settles slightly and picks up the reins. She clucks and before she can even squeeze with her legs, Prince moves off in a slow walk. Destiny immediately forgets to be afraid because there's nothing scary about it. In fact, Prince's smooth stride is soothing. His head bobs in time to his steps. She forgets her leg and her shoulder and wrist are whimpering in pain. She feels it, for sure, but it's just not that important. It even hurts less the more she goes limp, letting her legs bump along, riding like a drunk sack of potatoes. But she keeps a light contact with the reins, remembering her fatal mistake last time. One circle around, then Destiny turns Prince inside. There's not the slightest resistance; in fact, it seems like all Destiny has to do is look the direction she wants to go.

The ride begins to feel like floating on angel wings. Destiny and Prince are like one being. Varney doesn't say a thing the whole time; he and the girls (for once) are silent, just watching. Destiny lifts the reins and Prince smoothly picks up a trot. Circles. The other way. Patterns within circles within the sacred round of the pen. Then back on the outside of the circle Destiny gives the cue and Prince surges into a slow, smooth lope. Around and around. Prince's ears forward, his mane flowing, hooves drumming a deliberate dance. Destiny knows he will do anything for her, and in a wild and completely uncharacteristic move, checks Prince and sits back, and together they execute an almost perfect sliding stop. Prince stands like a statue except for his heaving sides. Destiny, still shamelessly showing off, backs him ten paces in a perfectly straight line and then comes to a standstill in the center of the circle. Varney and the inmates explode in applause.

"Hard to believe this is only the third time this horse has had a rider," Varney says. "That was a pretty good job."

Destiny sits on Prince and smiles calmly, like a queen. This is not the best moment in her life, but it is a close runner-up.

***

A full moon night at the K-Mart. Destiny dusted distractedly. She'd had a backache all day. She knew this could be a sign of labor, but nothing else had happened and so she reported for work as usual. Val was wearing white jeans with swirling patterns of multicolored sequins and a low-cut fuzzy sweater.

"New outfit?" Destiny asked as they put on their Pro-Kleen aprons.

"Yeah, you like?" Val asked in her abrasive voice. She popped her chewing gum loudly.

"Yeah, cute," Destiny lied politely.

"Check this out," Val said, holding out her arm. A wide gold bracelet glitters harshly in the fluorescent light of the break room.

"Wow, looks expensive."

"Better believe it," Val said.

"So are you still comin' to dinner tonight? I got some steaks, rib-eye steaks."

"Yeah, sure," Val said like she was doing Destiny a favor.

The night dragged on and Destiny's backache got worse and she felt like she weighed a thousand pounds. Kneeling over the toilets with the cleanser, she felt the first twinge. It started as a twinge, then raced into a flame of pain, then subsided.

"Huh," she said. She tried to step up her pace in the bathroom in case she had to go to the hospital. She didn't want to lose her pay for the shift, even if she was going into labor.

The twinge repeated itself once or twice but it didn't seem to be worth becoming alarmed about. Finally she finished the mirrors and gave a final swipe to everything with the Windex. She collected all her tools in the bucket and hauled them to the break room.

Val was sitting, smoking. Destiny collapsed into the chair opposite and moaned in relief.

"You okay?" Val asked.

"Gosh, just tired, I guess."

"Who ain't." They sat, without conversation, Destiny too weary and Val too disinterested. Eventually Duwayne's flashlight preceded him down the hall.

"Ya'll readah?"

"Fuck yeah." Val was already on her feet. Duwayne helped Destiny with her bucket of tools as he had been doing for the last few weeks.

"Thank you, Duwayne."

"Ya'll have a good night, now," he basso-profundoed.

They exited into the moonlit parking lot.

"So, I got to run home first, so I'll see ya later," Val said.

"Oh… okay." Destiny has assumed they'd go to her apartment in Val's car; she'd been looking forwards to a ride.

"Hasta la vista," Val replied. She clicked her way across the parking lot to her beat-up sedan. As she reached for her keys, the doors of a van parked nearby slid open and four dark suited men jumped out.

"Hold it right there, Miss," said one. "Police."

"What you want with me, man," Val wailed, and Destiny turned to see, and two of the police officers were hurrying in her direction and said, "Stop! Miss!" and "Put down your bag, put your hands in the air!"

"What's going on?" Destiny whispered, frightened.

One of the cops flipped a badge. "CCSD," he said curtly. "We need to see your bag right now."

Numbly, Destiny extended her purse. Val was wailing loudly but Destiny couldn't focus on her words. The cop grabbed her bag and opened it. Said something in a monotone to the other and they both peered inside like it contained the secrets to the universe. Then to her horror, the first cop opened a hole in the lining and drew out a handful of watches and jewelry. Price tags still attached.

"These yours?"

Destiny's jaw dropped and she shook her head dumbly.

It was a blur and as she was handcuffed and hustled into a squad car and listened to her Miranda rights, the twinges began again. Before they arrived at the police station, the twinges were becoming insistent, and regular, and no longer anything that should be ignored.

But she was afraid to say anything; she didn't want to have her baby in a crummy, vomit-smelling squad car or a nasty police substation. As soon as they got there, she'd tell them it was all a mistake and they'd let her go and she could take a cab to the hospital. And if it was false labor, so much for the better. She still hadn't packed a hospital bag or put away the last bag of purchases into the nursery: baby powder, lotion, more diapers, a cute dinosaur pacifier.

The substation was worse than she'd pictured. Instead of grimy, it was sterile, too sterile. Like a cancer ward. She was escorted immediately to a small, naked room by herself and left alone for five torturous minutes. There were three chairs and a table. Gray industrial carpeting. That was it. She was ready to scream when the door opened and a woman cop came in.

"I'm Deputy Farmer," she said. She was a small, neat black woman, with a small, neat smile.

"I'm here totally by mistake. I didn't do anything."

"How did the watches and jewelry get in your bag, Miss Tubb?"

"I don't know!"

"Well, come on, we both know that's not believable."

"It's true!" Destiny wailed, and a twinge turned into a thrust and she moaned and doubled over.

"Are you all right?" the cop asked quickly.

"I'm fine," Destiny grunted.

"When is your baby due?"

"Not for two weeks," she said, sitting up.

"Are you having contractions?"

"No, I'm fine, just a kick," Destiny lied, and smiled—an effort.

"Miss Tubb, I'm afraid it doesn't look good for you. You were caught red-handed, so to speak. You'll have to spend the night here, sometime tomorrow you'll be transported to court for arraignment. Then you might get bail."

"You gotta be kidding," Destiny said. "I can't stay in jail. I'm gonna have a baby. I didn't do nothing. I'm innocent. You have to let me out of here. I didn't do nothing!"

"Can you explain how that merchandise got into your purse?"

"No ma'am," Destiny admitted. Hoping the truth will set her free.

"Then I'm sorry, Destiny. Let's go."

Down a carpeted hall that ended in bars. Deputy Farmer opened the bars and they sounded just like they did in the movies. The cell was small and clean. There were four of them in a row. Destiny was the only—prisoner; the other cells were empty. Two bunks and a metal toilet and sink. Navy blue wool blankets and flat pillows on the bunks. There was a smell of air freshener and the hum of air conditioning. There were no windows. But Destiny could see down the hall, to a bunch of closed doors.

The pains were like the ocean. Relentless; just when she thought she might be able to catch her breath and get ready, it was too late, it was upon her already, and she was losing strength. Too much pain, too much, she could drown in the surf. The fluorescent lights hummed. Destiny might as well be giving birth in hell. She knew it was too late, but she began to scream. "Help! Help! My baby's coming!"

It didn't take long. Deputy Farmer and other cops rushed in and a few minutes later she was lifted onto a gurney and outside and into a waiting ambulance and a few minutes later, sirens screaming, to an Emergency entrance with the green walls and the painful bright lights and the looming doctors, and all the time, the cop there, watching, watching, waiting.

Herd Animals

"Wild horse adoption? Sure!" I say to Charlie's question. "When, where?" I ask, fumbling for a pen on my cluttered desk.

"Sunday the seventeenth. In Ridgecrest. At the BLM facility there."

"BLM?" I ask.

"Bureau of Land Management. Check it out online. They do these mustang adoptions periodically. It might be neat to give some background on the wild horse program and then when you go, get a couple personal stories from the folks that adopt. Have they always wanted to adopt a wild horse, that sort of thing. Good photo op too."

"Okay," I say, scribbling notes.

"Well, I gotta go. Thanks for doing the story, on a freakin' Sunday and everything."

"No problem, Charlie. I've intended to thank you for the job. It's been—good for me."

"Are you kidding? We're getting more letters-to-the-editor than ever. Lots of compliments."

"Well, good."

"You're a good writer, Scoop, and you work your ass off on these stories."

"Aw shucks, Chuck," I say, embarrassed.

"Anyway. Gotta run, you know where to find me."

"Bye, Charlie."

Wild horses! Just the words on my notepad conjure up an ancient emotion. I fire up the computer and go online to the BLM website to read about the Wild Horse and Burro adoption program. I surf a little more and am surprised to find what seem like hundreds of websites relating to wild horses and wild horse rescue and the like. I print out some information and contacts and stare at the pages spitting out without focusing. Instead I'm seeing pictures in a book, I am holding the book, I am on my window seat in my blue bedroom; I am eleven. The book was Mustang, Wild Spirit of the West, written by my absolute favorite author of those days, Marguerite Henry. My hardback copy, a birthday present from Aunt Stella, had even been autographed, and Mrs. Henry had drawn a little horseshoe next to her beautifully penned name.

The book's heroine, Wild Horse Annie, is based on a real person, Velma Johnston, who has an epiphany one day driving down a highway in Nevada. A truck filled with mustangs is just ahead; the horses are in terrible shape. She follows the truck to a slaughter-house and finds out what is happening to the wild horses: rounded up and slaughtered for dog food. She spends the rest of her life fighting to protect the herds; and succeeded with a Congressional Act back in the sixties. The wild horse adoptions, the BLM program, all of it, were in place mostly because of her efforts. She began a letter-writing campaign to support the bill, and I was one of those millions of kids who wrote Congress. It was the first time I had done anything like that. Somewhere, in one of these trunks, there is a forty-year-old letter from the real Wild Horse Annie, thanking me for my letter.

I'm getting excited about going to this adoption. I can't wait to see the wild horses.

I go to the window and look down past the garden to the horse barn and corrals Hank and I built. There are stalls in the barn, a tiny apartment above, and in the tack room, even a brand-new saddle, a Christmas present from Hank. That gorgeous saddle just as empty as the promise that we would ride up the canyon on our horses. Maybe I should adopt one of these mustangs, I think, feeling abruptly happy at the idea. But no. I can't train a wild horse. The last thing a person in their sixties should be doing is bronc riding. The thought of getting bucked off or kicked makes me literally shudder: in my young, horse-crazy days, I experienced both, and have absolutely no desire to risk it again. Oh, well. It will still be fun to see the mustangs. I go to my desk and write the event on the calendar. The dogs mill around, begin whining, reminding me it's their dinnertime. Obediently I head them towards the kitchen.

Filling their bowls, I think again of the wild horses, and that letter from Wild Horse Annie. I wonder which trunk it's in. Which leads to thinking about the other trunk, and the wedding album.

Ah, shit. That was such a great day.

***

The boats had streamed in bearing white and red pennants with our initials. Friends of Hank's, the boat owners, from the fire stations. Then his relatives arrived on the ferry, and were checked in to their rooms at the Banning House. Then my girlfriends Suzette and Mary Lynn from Miami. And from Milwaukee, my Uncle Dan and Aunt Stella, the only relatives I had left. Everyone loved the island, everyone loved the perfect weather, just barely hot with sea breezes, they loved the California poppies watercoloring the tawny hillsides with dots of brilliant orange. Everyone loved everyone else with the glaring exception of Hank's mother and eldest sister. They were barely cordial to me. He took me to our room and explained that they had never forgiven him for getting a divorce. Catholic and all.

"Then why are they here?" I asked, feeling susceptible to an ugly crying fit.

"Because I asked them to come. I begged them to come. It was probably stupid."

"Definitely stupid. If you knew how they felt."

"It'll be okay, they'll behave."

"I can't stand that there will be people at our wedding who don't want to see us get married," I said with childish stridency.

He was silent for a moment then said, "I said I was sorry."

I realized there was not much for me to do but get over it. I was certainly not about to ask them to leave. Maybe I could charm his family into liking me. Or at least tolerating me.

"Once they get to know you, they'll love you," he said then. "If they don't, I'll just disown them."

"Good," I said. "Kiss me, then get out of here. It's time to change into my bridal attire."

He did kiss me, a thoroughly memorable kiss. Said, "Thank you for marrying me."

So a few hours later we stood on the patio and got married. Music and earnest poetic words, tears and then applause. Then we promenaded through the grounds and took photos and then went inside for champagne and the customary festivities.

I don't have to look inside that album to see the pictures because they're branded into my memory. They give shape to the overwhelming, emotional blur that is my memory of the real event. I have some vignettes, though, snatches remembered, that accompany the photos. There's Suzette, Mary Lynn and I at one of the tables, leaning in towards one another, faces animated yet serious: They were asking me if I was happy.

"Completely," I had answered in all honesty.

The picture of me dancing with Uncle Dan: "He seems to be a fine man, Sara Beth. And as you know I'm an excellent judge of character."

And there's one of Aunt Stella and I in a hug, comical since she barely comes up to my shoulder: "I'm so happy for you, darling," she had been saying.

And there are the dozens of pictures of Hank and me, because we were practically joined at the hip the whole evening. Dancing. Laughing. Kissing.

Like I said, it was such a great day. I wonder if I'll ever achieve a state in which I can be purely grateful for having had, in my life, such a great day, without feeling tortured because it's all over, like it never happened, the promises were broken; I'm here alone. I wonder when all this healing that my Inner Therapist has promised is going to occur.

Do you think it's possible you're being a little hard on yourself? that annoying voice butts in.

You again. Can't a poor widow have any peace?

Peace, huh? Is that what you were experiencing?

Oh bugger off.... hard on myself, how?

You're doing just fine. Healing is a slow process. In time you'll find joy in those memories, and it won't be all painful. In time you'll find your present reality isn't such a bad place to be.

In time.

Yes, but healing is going on right now. You're getting better. You're coping really well. And soon you'll find something that will help.

What is this, a Tarot reading?

When someone is in the process of change, of healing, often they'll find things that help them. Usually it's a hobby or a new interest.

Hobby? Are you kidding me?

Or new interest.

Jesus Christ, I say disgustedly. I suck at this, should have re-tired long ago. I feel sorry for every patient I ever had.

There's no answer; perhaps I offended her again.

I'm sitting outside under the pergola on the patio. The ros-es are doing better, I've sprayed the aphids into extinction and the new buds are unsullied. Four chickens have dug themselves holes in the dirt up against the adobe wall and are lined up in them like soldiers in a foxhole. A few other hens peck under an oak tree, making that soft, silly noise like a kazoo band. The dogs are dispersed, attending to their bathroom duties. A pair of doves land among the pecking chickens. From far away I hear then watch a small plane pass over in the deepening sky. I pour myself another glass of green tea. I decide to go inside and do some computer shopping. I want to order that book, *Mustang,* and read it again.

PART TIME. PAYS GREAT.

It was a boy. Justin Andrew Tubb. Destiny wished she could do better for a last name, but that was one of her least disappointments. Because she was still under arrest, a woman from Child Services actually took tiny Justin from the hospital before Destiny woke the next morning. She couldn't believe it. When she found out Destiny went berserk. That horrible cop held her down in the bed until the doctor came and gave her a shot. Destiny was drugged to the gills that whole day and then transferred to the city jail.

Aching down there, breasts aching, in a cell alone, awaiting her hearing. Wanting Justin, needing him. It was an amputation without anesthetic. Destiny whimpered and sobbed, tossed and turned. Why was this happening? What had she done to deserve this?

It just got worse. At the hearing the evidence was presented, it was over quickly, Destiny was guilty, guilty of grand theft, but since it was her first offense she was given time served plus thirty days.

Thirty days! Thirty days without her baby. Destiny sobbed and had to be dragged out of court.

Having grown up with Loreen for a mother, Destiny had been long familiar with all types of seedy characters, but they were model citizens compared to her fellow inmates at Lerdo Correctional Facility. They scared her to death.

When they asked her what she was in for she told them she was innocent. They laughed and said they were all innocent too; their lawyers were crooked, the jury was racist. She made no friends but it seemed everyone had enemies. She was slapped around in the shower and tripped in the dining hall, landing in her tray of food and knocking loose a tooth. It wasn't a pleasure cruise. But worse than the fear was the humiliation, and the worst of all was the awful, aching void where her baby ought to be. She cried every time she used the breast pump but kept at it, so she'd have milk for Justin.

Interminably, the thirty days crawled by but finally it was over and she was released, blinking like a veal calf in the sunlight. She was shocked when that cop lady was there waiting for her with a police cruiser and took her to get Justin and then to her apartment.

Justin was at a private home in one of the nice parts of town. Destiny had to stay in the cruiser while the cop and a Child Services woman who had met them there went up a flower-lined walk to the house. Destiny slumped down in the seat, pretending not to look. The lady that answered the door was pretty and she was crying. She kissed Justin about ten times before the Child Services officer finally pried him away from her. At last they were coming down the sidewalk and the cop opened the door and Justin was placed in Destiny's arms. He was screaming his head off.

"Oh, baby, oh, shush, it's okay, Mommy's here," Destiny cooed, but Justin wrenched his head away and howled. Like Destiny was a big bad monster. He screamed all the way home.

"Good luck," said the women at her door.

"That would be nice for a change," Destiny said, shutting the door in their faces.

Justin screamed interminably. She tried everything. He refused to even look at her and if he did by mistake, his eyes went wide and scared and he screamed anew. Finally though, he fell asleep, after a bout of sobbing hiccups. Destiny walked with him awhile, and for the very first time was able to appreciate his yeasty, lovely smell, his fine reddish hair, his translucent fingernails. She eventually laid him in his brand-new crib, with its lovingly washed tiny sheets and blanket. Ever so gently she laid him down and drew up the snowy covers. His cheeks were red and his fists slowly uncurled. He breathed softly. Destiny stood over him for the longest time, despite her fatigue. Then she pulled up the rocking chair close to the crib and watched him sleep until her head fell on her shoulder and her soft snores joined his.

She woke with a start—someone was watching her. She was entirely disoriented, wondering where in the world she was. Then his eyes caught hers and she remembered everything. His eyes were wide but no longer afraid. They were wide in a kind of wonder. She spoke to him softly and said his name. Justin's eyes went wider, then he smiled.

"Hi, baby," she said.

He waved his hands and made a gurgling sound. He had dimples. His eyes were gray. His skin was a perfect peach. He was sturdy yet delicate. He was beautiful. She reached out her arms. He reached out his too, though they waved like his joints were made of Jello. She cautiously scooped him up. Close up, his perfection was unmarred, unlike everyone Destiny had ever known. My baby, she said. One of his waving hands caught her cheek in a moth-like caress. She lifted her shirt and pointed her heavy breast to him. His eyes closed. His head turned. He clamped down with a force that made her gasp. Tears of gratitude slid down her cheeks, then dried. Then her mouth curled in a contented, peaceful smile.

Bliss, it was bliss, lying in bed with Justin, dozing away the chill of prison and the wound of their separation. It was as if he'd never screamed when they were reunited. He smiled, he grinned, he cooed and dimpled. He nursed with religious fervor and belched with smacking, masculine appreciation that made his mother laugh with pure delight. Destiny indulged herself with fresh food and milk, lots of milk and ice cream. She'd tuck in bed with Justin and a bowl of ice cream and listen to melancholy country tunes and watch her baby sleep. Her clean, quiet apartment was a heavenly cloud pillow after the gray cell. The luxury of a candy bar, of being able to choose the radio or silence, was acute. The trees were budding, the air was warming, tomorrow she'd take Justin on his first walk outside in the stroller.

Destiny reviewed her finances and it wasn't all bad. She'd been appointed a public defender so the nightmare had only cost her future, not any actual cash. She had enough in her bank account to live for at least another two months without working. So they whiled away the days in bed, on the couch, strolling slowly down the even sidewalks. Every few days, a bus ride to the grocery and back. Justin loved the bus, he nodded his loosey-goosey neck and grinned at everyone. Destiny even got familiar with a few bus regulars; Justin was great for ice-breaking. At the market, the checkout women smiled at Destiny, called her ma'am as she presented her cash money, Justin clean and quiet and cute in the child seat in the grocery cart. Some days, they would go farther in the stroller, to the little park, so manicured, grass as green and even as a golf course. So different to the park Destiny remembered, the park where she began her fall from grace.

She put it off and put it off, but more and more she knew she needed to get a job, and line up daycare for Justin. There was a home visit from Child Services, a different woman, Chinese, with black shiny eyes in a broad, noncommittal face. Justin and her apartment passed approval and the woman, Mrs. Fong, left behind a bunch of papers about finding a job and taking care of babies and food stamp applications and AFDC forms. But still Destiny put it off until she realized as she wrote her rent check that she didn't have enough money left for next month. She had just enough for a couple of trips to the market and that was it.

It was almost like Justin knew what she was planning because he turned uncharacteristically cranky during job interviews and screamed his head off the whole time she was visiting a day care. It was hard enough to get a decent job with only fast food wrapping and cleaning as job skills. Harder still when they find out you were in jail. Impossible when your baby's there, screaming his head off and spitting up on your blouse. She interviewed at a coffee shop, at a restaurant supply store for a cashier's job, at a Dunkin' Donuts. She visited another day care but all they spoke was Spanish. She wondered how normal moms found a babysitter: not some dope-smoking teenager but a sweet, grandmother type. There was a "Nanny Service" listed in the phone book, but she nearly dropped the phone when she heard the rates. It cost more per hour than Destiny had ever made! The situation began to look desperate. She lowered her standards and began trying to get a job at a fast food place. The answers were the same—we'll let you know. But they never did. She'd have to call again and again, only to hear that the "position had been filled." Destiny hated Val even more than she had every thirty days of her incarceration. Because she knew Val had put the stuff in her purse. She'd figured out Val must have lifted the stuff right in front of the security cameras and then put it in Destiny's purse while in the camera's blind spot, planning to get it back later when she came for dinner. Since Val had none of the loot, she'd been let go; no charges even filed. It was Destiny's life that was ruined.

Well, almost ruined. At least she had Justin. But how was she supposed to provide for him? With distaste she dug out the forms the caseworker had left. She qualified for food stamps and a check from the state. They might give her enough to get by on. A sleepless night, tossing and grinding her teeth. In the morning, she stared at the papers with tired eyes and sighed a great exhalation of defeat. She picked up a pen, and while Justin drained her right breast, she began to neatly fill out the forms.

The problem with depending on public services, Destiny thought, wasn't the humiliating waits in the crummy rooms for the inevitably short, impersonal meeting with some gray-faced caseworker. It wasn't the embarrassment of enduring the judgmental stares as you counted out the food stamps at the grocery. It wasn't the fact that your freedom disappeared—because you could only buy certain things. The worst thing was the boredom. Deprived of working, all she had to do every day was take care of Justin. And although he was vastly entertaining, after a year slid by, she was ready to go out of her mind. She'd had to move from her nice apartment. The checks just weren't enough to cover the rent and utilities and the stuff Justin needed. The new place had come furnished, which had been a good thing for one reason—she couldn't afford a mover. Leaving all her new furniture behind, she and Justin and their clothes and stuff packed in liquor boxes moved to the new place in a taxi. And that expense meant she'd be eating Top Ramen and oatmeal until the end of the month. But the furniture in the new place was shabby, stained, and smelled of cigarettes. There was no crib for Justin, so she made him a bed in one of the dresser drawers. It would be too small for him soon and she didn't know what she would do then. There was not enough money for a phone or a TV. These days, Destiny wanted a TV, anything, to keep her occupied. The new apartment was carpeted in a brown, textured wall-to-wall that had worn traffic patterns. The vinyl floor in the tiny dark kitchen was made to look like brick. But it wouldn't fool anybody. It was a depressing place, no matter how much Destiny cleaned and scrubbed. The window in her bedroom looked out on the space between the duplex and the next house and was filled with trash cans that were always overflowing and other junk: half a bicycle, some bare car tires, a headless doll that made Destiny sad. There was no park nearby, and the neighborhood was treeless and in the yards were the ubiquitous pit bulls, barking hoarsely when Destiny walked down the street pushing Justin in his stroller. There was just nothing to do.

One cold, gray day, she bundled up Justin and rode two busses to the library. But by the time they finally got to the library, Justin was cranky, having fallen asleep on the second bus. He was fussing and pulling her hair as she wandered the familiar stacks. Eventually she selected a few books, a couple mystery novels, a book on careers and one called How To Come To Your Own Rescue. Then she found out her student library ID was long expired. She had to fill out a form to get a library card. But there was a hitch. She didn't have a driver's license—Loreen had refused to sign her up for Driver's Education. If she didn't have a license to prove her address, she'd have to bring in a utility bill.

"My landlord pays the utilities," she said, feeling anger rise and grip her throat.

"Then a rent receipt will be okay, as long as it shows your address," the pimpled librarian said.

Destiny shifted Justin on her hip and left, leaving the books stacked neatly on the librarian's counter.

Down the stone steps and putting Justin into his stroller, trudging on to the bus stop, she felt like crying; she felt like screaming. She felt like going back in there and ripping all the stupid books off the shelves. Why was the whole world against her? The wind shoved its way down the street like a school bully, blowing plastic bags and rolling an empty beer can down the sidewalk. Justin whimpered steadily and squirmed in the stroller.

"Quit it!" she screamed at him. He looked up, startled, then began to cry, noisily. He cried as the bus rolled up and fought her while she took him from the stroller and clumsily shoved it up the bus steps. The driver stared at her disgustedly while she struggled to find the bus fare while wrestling with Justin. As if to punish her for being poor and fat and husbandless, the driver started the bus before she'd found a seat. She lurched and almost fell, grabbing a seat back just in time.

"Here," said a guy, getting up, gesturing an offer of his seat.

"Thanks." Destiny collapsed into the hard seat. The bus groaned to a stop at a light. Destiny looked blankly out the scratched plastic window, trying to ignore Justin's sobbing. The guy who'd given up his seat stood over her, she could feel him looking at her.

"He's cute," the guy said.

"Thanks," Destiny said again, not meeting his eyes.

"I bet I can guess his name."

Destiny was stuck. She couldn't just ignore this guy, since he gave up his seat and all.

"I doubt it," she said, but with a small smile. The guy wasn't creepy-looking: tall and skinny, longish hair, wavy brown, clean jeans, nice shirt, nice smile.

"Okay, we'll see about that. Okay, um, Franklin."

"No."

"Milton."

"Nope."

"Elmer."

"No," Destiny said, giggling a little. Justin's wails died to a hiccough-laced whimper.

"Moe. Larry. Curly."

"No, no, no."

"Mortimer."

"Sorry."

"I give up."

"Justin," she said.

Hey, that's a cool name. My favorite boots."

"Yeah, well."

"And what's yours?"

"Destiny."

"I'm Greg. My car's in the shop, thus the bus," Greg said.

"Huh."

"Yeah, I'm getting a new stereo, satellite radio, Bose speakers, the works."

"Oh, that's nice," Destiny said.

"Yeah, I love music. I was almost a classical pianist."

"Oh, wow."

"Yeah. But I decided I didn't want to play concerts around the world like a trained monkey. So now I just play for fun."

"Wow."

"Yep, I work in the technology side of the business, too."

"Well, this here's my stop, coming up," she said with relief and a twinge of regret. Adult conversation. Wow indeed.

"Yeah, mine too," he said, surprising her.

The bus lurched to a stop, the doors wheezed open. Greg carried and unfolded the stroller and Destiny strapped Justin in.

"I have an associate that lives right around the block, that's where I was going," he said. "But I have time to walk you home."

"That's okay," she said, being cautious.

"I'm not a rapist or anything. Promise."

"Oh, of course not, but still. I'm okay."

"Okay, if you're sure."

"I'm sure! Well, bye then," Destiny said, backing away. "Thanks again."

"My pleasure, Destiny and Justin. Nice meeting you," he said, tipping an imaginary hat; he turned and began strolling down the street.

Destiny shook her head, feeling too late that he was harmless; and turned the opposite direction, feeling lonelier than usual.

At home, depression overtook her again. What was she going to do? She had to make some money and get off the welfare. It was sucking her spirit dry, just as she knew it would. Justin picked up on her mood and began fretting. She fed him lunch but he wouldn't go down for his nap. The shabby apartment was so dark. It began to feel just like her prison cell, like there wasn't enough air, like she could suffocate. She'd hoped to come home with at least a book to read. She paced around and finally put Justin's coat back on.

"We're going for a walk," she told him.

The neighborhood was nasty but she wasn't ready to face another bus ride: wrestling with the stroller, the mean looks. She wrapped her scarf around Justin's head so just his eyes peeped out and stuck him back in the stroller and headed into the wind towards the freeway underpass. The underpass smelled like a toilet and it was littered with cans and bottles. But once through, the neighborhood was marginally better. Here the sidewalks were in better shape and the dogs were regular dogs, not pit bulls. The chill and the exercise began to make her feel a little better. Something would work out, she decided. It just had to. She had to pray more and think positive.

She turned the corner and there was the guy from the bus, walking in their direction. She almost did an about-face, but knew he'd seen her, she couldn't run away.

"Hi, Destiny and Justin, so we meet again," he said.

"Hi, Greg," she said, stopping reluctantly.

"Can't get enough of this lovely weather, huh?"

"I just felt all cooped up," she explained. Then wished she'd said she had somewhere to go.

"I totally understand the feeling. Humans were not meant to live in little boxes of isolation. We should all go back to the communal cave."

"I don't think I'd like that," she said.

"Why not? Warm fire, nice furry skins to sleep in, lovely dinosaur bones to chew."

"Yuck, no thanks," she said, but she was smiling.

"Well, civilization does have its advantages," he said. "One is, restaurants. Want to grab a bite? I'm thinking about a burger and a beer. My treat. We could head over to Wally's. It's just a few blocks up."

"I don't drink," she said. She was stalling for time, trying to decide.

"A burger and a Coke, then. C'mon. I hate eating alone. Please."

"All right," Destiny said, shocking herself. But what could happen, she thought, in a diner, in the daytime?

They got a booth in the mostly empty restaurant. Since Greg was buying, Destiny went ahead and ordered a huge burger with bacon and cheese and a side of fries and a chocolate milkshake. Justin was quietly gumming a cracker and looking at Greg with wide eyes and Destiny began enjoying herself. Greg was kind of cute in his hippie way, and certainly interesting. Brainy. He kept up a steady stream of talk and didn't eat much. Destiny ended up eating most of his fries when he pushed the plate towards her. He told her about the different things he'd done. He'd traveled all over, to Alaska and the Rocky Mountains and New York City and even Mexico. He talked about a book he was reading. It was something about society, and corporations, and capitalism.

"The average Joe can barely make ends meet," he explained. "Meanwhile the corporate fat cats are lapping up all the cream."

"Don't I know it," she said.

"You just get screwed working for the Man. That's why I'm an entrepreneur."

"Wow."

"That means, I work for myself."

"Oh, what kind of work do you do?" she asked, to be polite.

"Electronics, stuff for recording studios. Hey, you wouldn't be looking for some part-time employment, would you? It pays great."

Destiny couldn't believe her ears. "Doing what?" she asked.

"Piece-work. Making microphones, wiring cables."

"Oh, I don't know anything about that stuff," she said, unable to keep from sounding disappointed.

"It's easy to learn, you just need a little manual dexterity. We can teach you. At least come by and I'll show you the ropes."

"Maybe I could do that," she said.

"Here's my beeper number," he said, and scrawled it on a napkin. "You'd be doing me a favor, we're really swamped."

"I'll think about it," she said, already deciding she'd call.

Justin was waking up and making noises like he wanted to nurse.

"I've got to get home," she said. "Thanks for the burger and everything, Greg."

"No problem. Call me."

"I'll think about it," she said again.

Back home she nursed Justin and put him down for his nap. She was feeling optimistic. Part time. Pays great. They were magic words.

* * *

The adoption is looming, just a week away. It is all she can think about. It is unthinkable that Prince is going to be adopted and she'll never see him again. The moments with him are painful and exquisite. They're practicing loading the horses into trailers, practicing riding, and going over and over all the old lessons. Varney is all proud of himself that he'd gotten permission for Destiny and the three other girls who'd managed to ride their horses to go for a trail ride outside the prison gates. The four horses including Prince are the stars of the program and will be featured at the adoption in a separate blind auction as being "saddle trained" while the rest are "halter trained." It is a success for Varney and the prison and the training program. But for Destiny, it is hard to feel good about it. She simply can't imagine him gone from her life.

Destiny brings Prince up and lunges him in a few circles in front of the trailer ramp. Then she stands back by the side of the ramp and points inside, clucks, and Prince climbs right in the trailer and stands quietly.

"That's how it's done, ladies," says Varney.

Today they are actually going outside, outside the round pen, outside the arena. Through the gates and into the fields and along the access road. Destiny saddles Prince and they warm up in the arena. Then off they go, accompanied by Varney on his big roan mare, and an escort of two trucks with armed guards. Like any of them would actually try escaping prison on horseback!—Destiny thinks with a shake of her head.

As soon as they walk the horses through the first big gate, Prince's head comes up and his ears stiffen. He looks around at everything. She had been nervous about this ride. She didn't want to fall again, and all she could think of was Prince spooking at a flock of birds, a motorcycle, a jet plane. She wouldn't be in control of everything like she was in the round pen. But now that they are out here, instead of feeling like she has to protect Prince, he seems to be protecting her. He is steady and careful where he puts his hooves. They walk to the turn in the road and come to a big ditch. One of the other horses, the black mare Spirit, refuses to cross it—wheeling and backing up and hopping sideways. Linda Oliver is her trainer, one of the older inmates, with a creased face and droopy eyes. She's in for writing bad checks, fraud. Spirit is always afraid of something, but Linda never loses her temper.

"Okay," Varney says. "Tubb, you go, and Oliver, follow right on their behinds."

Destiny points Prince into the ditch and he slowly steps down, his hooves biting the soil. At the bottom she makes sure he has plenty of rein and he gathers his hindquarters and leaps out in two mighty bounds. They trot on a few steps then stop. Spirit and Linda are right there. Linda's face is alive and she's laughing.

"That was great," Oliver says, smiling right at Destiny.

"Yeah!" Destiny agrees, stroking Prince's neck. She hopes Varney will let them do it again. He does, so they all cross the ditch several times, then single-file down the road some more at a walk and a trot. Destiny has lost her fear and is having a blast. Prince responds softly to her legs and the reins. He moves forward easily and slows just as effortlessly at Destiny's cues. Riding out is so different than the round pen. Instead of training it feels like she and Prince are having an adventure together. The only bummer—and it is a big one—is the fact that they're both prisoners. If only they were riding on their own, on a meandering trail through a beautiful woods. If only she could get to keep Prince once she gets out. But of course that's impossible. He's going to the adoption and he is sure to be chosen. At least he'll be safe from the killer buyers. But after that, she'll never see him again. It is awful to think of not being around him; it is the only thing she looks forward to in life, and the times with Prince are the only times she feels adult, competent, hopeful. Not stupid and hopeless and doomed—her normal state of mind.

She could be released soon. Her parole hearing is coming up right after the adoption. She has no idea what she is supposed to do if she is released. It is easier not to think about it. If only there was someone to talk to. Just then, like he has read her mind, Varney trots up and falls alongside.

"Doin' good, Tubb," he says.

"Thanks, sir," she grins.

"Ready for a little gallop?"

"No way," she says, meaning, do you mean it?

"Yes way. Just keep a light rein, but let him go. I'll be right with you."

"Okay."

Varney yells back to the wranglers to hold back, then turns in his saddle back to Destiny.

"Ready, Tubb?"

"Yes sir!"

Varney clucks to his roan and she surges into a lope. Destiny follows and Prince's lope has never felt more fluid. Then Varney lifts his reins and leans forward and the roan changes gears and Destiny mirrors him and Prince is galloping, the easy rhythm is replaced with an exciting staccato pounding; the wind streams tears from her eyes. Destiny urges Prince though he doesn't need it. His muscles surge and his massively strong legs pound the dirt and Destiny is over his shoulders as they fly down the road like they are in a real horse race. All too soon Varney pulls up his horse and Destiny reluctantly does the same. Her heart is still galloping and Prince snorts and pulls on the bit.

"Circles," Varney suggests. Destiny guides Prince in a few circles until he is easy on the bit again. They walk the horses on, slowly.

"How'd you like that?" he says.

"It was great! I'm sure going to miss him," she blurts. And is instantly horrified at having made such a personal statement.

"I know, it is, it's real hard," he says. "But we just got to focus on the fact that he's goin' to a good home now that he's started so nice."

She wants to demand, You promise? But she knows he can't promise. She just nods, like she believes it. She sure wants to believe it. As much as it makes her painfully jealous to think it, she hopes that whoever gets Prince will realize he's special. She knows it, Varney knows it, even the other cowgirls all think Prince is so cool. Whoever gets him sure better know it. They sure better not ever be mean to him either. It drives her crazy that she won't know what will happen to him.

It seems a good time to ask Varney about what she should do if her parole is granted, but she doesn't. The clip-clop of the horses' hooves seems conversation enough.

CONVERGENCE

The book *Mustang, Wild Spirit of the West* arrives the afternoon before the wild horse adoption. I pick it up from my mailbox on my way back from town.

I'd been interviewing an old guy who had been arrested for the pot plants in his backyard. He claimed the plants were perfectly legal under the state's medical marijuana laws; the deputies, on the other hand, didn't care what the California law said. Pot was pot and it was illegal under federal law; if you were growing it in your backyard, you were busted. He was a bearded Jerry Garcia look-alike, the sole minister of the Church of Peace, Love and Forgiveness. That day, driving from his ramshackle trailer, I couldn't know the outcome of the trial he faced, but I was pretty sure he'd win based on what I'd heard. The Commander and deputies I'd interviewed had come off badly and I was mulling over how to write the story in a neutral manner as I wound the truck through the yellowing hills and graying sage.

The book in my mailbox is a welcome diversion. I sneak looks at it in its brown box as I bump up the dusty drive, and put it on the dining room table when I get home. I walk and feed the dogs, feed the chickens and water the garden, collect some beans, lettuce, and tomatoes and fifteen eggs.

Finally I step back inside as the sun drops low and the light outside turns lavender. I rinse the lettuce, dump it in a bowl, smother it in ranch dressing, get a beer. Light the lamp, grab a fork, and attack the book's wrapping with more greed than I utilize invading the salad. With my trusty reading glasses in place, the dogs snoring at my feet and moths making kamikaze runs at the propane flame, I gobble greens and re-read the story of Velma Johnston and the mustangs.

The American mustangs were perhaps just years away from becoming wiped out when Velma Bronn Johnston, "Wild Horse Annie" as she's called in Marguerite Henry's book, intervened. Annie's destiny is interwoven with mustangs even before her birth—her own father was saved by the milk of a mustang mare as his parents made the pioneer crossing west. Annie rode and fell off a mustang when she was three; but she got back up and from that moment spent her life atop or around the horses on her family's ranch. Her "Pa" ran a mustang-powered shipping company over the mountains to Reno. But at five, her childhood was overnight changed from an idyll to hell; she contracted polio and ultimately ended up imprisoned in a body cast, isolated in a sanatorium. During that time, a certain painting on a wall inside the hospital, depicting wild mustangs galloping free, kept her sane, reminding her of the horses at home and the wild ones, with their freedom that was the farthest thing from her current reality. Finally released from the cast, she went happily home, and later married her Charley. They took over the family's ranch and operated a children's dude ranch, and briefly, all was bliss until the day Annie was driving to work and saw the truck, packed with dying horses. She was so outraged at finding out they were being tortured and annihilated she attacked in every way she could think of and more, until the bill was passed by Congress protecting the wild horses.

By the time I finish the slender book, I had cried a few times. I try to imagine Velma's life: her commitment, her courage, her sorrows. Imagine devoting your life to saving wild horses. My imagination fires up. I rinse my plate and pour a big glass of wine. What if she hadn't fought so hard? Would the wild horses now be a thing of the past, relegated to history texts? All of a sudden this story I am supposed to write becomes a lot bigger. This new legislation. All the wild horse advocates are up in arms about it. I can't believe that I'd looked it over with a shrug. Now I gallop to my office and dump piles of folders on the floor until I find the print-outs. In January, the President, "W", (or as I call him, "Slimy Ratfucking Puppet of the Illuminati") had signed the Appropriations Bill, and hidden within was a change to the law regarding the wild horses and burros. Now the rounded-up mustangs and donkeys could be sold at auction, if they met certain conditions: ten years old or older, or having been offered at a public adoption three times. I read that this could mean the slaughter of twenty thousand mustangs under the authority of the BLM. I bet Velma is flipping over in her grave, I think, as I read on. I go online and get as much information as I can process. By midnight I've printed out a fat folder. I was planning to get up at four to get to the adoption early; but even so, I tuck into bed with the folder and read myself to uneasy dreams haunted by frightened horses and a weeping Wild Horse Annie.

The alarm shrills in the dark. Monstrously early, it seems like I've just fallen asleep—but I shove off the dogs and struggle from the bed. Shuffle to the kitchen, light some lamps and make coffee. Mechanically shower while the water boils. By the time I'm dressed, slurping espresso-thick coffee, I am raring to go. Camera, notebook, pens, pencils, camera, spare batteries, check. Thermos of coffee, an apple, my faded pink cowgirl hat, check. Dogs have been fed and run outside. I grab my lucky denim jacket and a burlap bag of garden carrots. I get in the truck and drive through the pre-dawn. So many rabbits on the road! I drive slower, despite the caffeine, my racing thoughts. I am so excited to see the mustangs. I think about the article I will write. I'm going to do what I can to help overturn this new bill. The power of the pen. Yee-haw. Winding down the hill towards town, the streets eerily empty—it is still too early for anyone going to work. I cruise through, breaking the speed limit. The only lights on in town are at the donut shop, the gas station. Three blocks later I'm back on the highway. Eighties music and a to-go cup of java, the straight road. The sky lightens from violet to coral. Falling-down barns, cattle grazing alongside the road, prickly pear cactus. Cottonwood trees and a stop by the side of the deserted desert road. I pee and listen to the birds, quail and finch and scrub jay, welcoming the first strike of sunlight over the mountains. Back in the truck, I eat the apple and begin to climb a steep pass with stark and awesome views; on the downside the sun is suddenly bright and warm. Outside Ridgecrest, the BLM facility is easy to find. I follow the signs with mounting excitement. When I spot it, it's because of the line of cars. I check my dashboard clock: it's just 6 a.m.; the gates won't open until seven. And there are already four cars parked ahead of me at the gate. I see pillows and sleeping bags and realize they have been here all night to have first pick of the horses. There is no movement from the cars and trucks at the gate, so I light a cigarette and wait.

* * *

My first horse bore the unimaginative name of Whitey. He was fat, and yes, he was mostly white; sure to never win an equine beauty contest. My parents paid one hundred dollars for him when I was eleven and Whitey was fourteen. He had one blue eye and one brown. His mane and tail alternated colors: yellowish white and dull blue. His coat was splotched meaninglessly with faded blue spots, his muzzle and hooves were pink, his back swayed like a fifty-year-old mattress. But to me, he was perfect. I rode bareback, fearlessly. When I tumbled off, Whitey stopped dead, looked down at me with concern, and let me lead him to the nearest log or rock to remount. We galloped gravel lanes and swam ponds and wandered through thousand-acre cornfields. Eventually, sadly, I "outgrew" Whitey, when I was fifteen—which was horse-crazy girl jargon for, "I am ready for a better horse." Sapphire was a Thoroughbred-cross mare, big and imperious. She was a dappled palomino and I eagerly sold off old faithful Whitey in the thrall of my new infatuation. Atop Sapphire I cleared bigger jumps and accomplished flying lead changes, diagonals, and other esoterica of the craft of riding. We went to horse shows and won some ribbons. But when I was ready for college, I had to let Sapphire go. I was to be a scholar, not a debutante, and there was no money to board my horse at school.

When Hank had heard this story he'd declared I would have a horse again. And he would get one too, and we'd ride the arroyos and canyons together. So we built the barn and corrals, and the little apartment above for a ranch hand. But, as they say, shit happens.

❋ ❋ ❋

There is movement in the van just ahead of me, people are getting out of the cars and trucks and stretching, peering through the BLM gate. One little girl holds a giant bag of carrots. I get out with my notebook, deciding to get some interviews before the gates open.

I introduce myself to the girl and her older sister and the mom. They are the Wilsons from Paso Robles. Mom is Jen, the girls are Shelley and Laurie. Laurie is the ten year old and she's the one getting a horse. She plans to adopt a yearling.

"I'm going to train her by myself," Laurie tells me.

"Have you ever trained horses before?"

"I ride my sister's gelding and he's only green broke," she says, all confidence and big teeth.

I ask some more questions and get them to agree to a photo once they have picked out their horse.

"Are you getting a horse too?" asks Laurie.

"Oh, no, I wasn't planning on it," I say, suddenly, perversely, considering it.

"You should!" Laurie says forcefully. "Oh, you really, really should. If you can afford it and all, I mean."

"It's a huge commitment," I say, not knowing if I'm warning Laurie or myself.

"Yeah, that's true, but it's oh, so totally worth it!"

"How's that?" I smile.

"Horses are just the best! You can groom them and ride them and love on them. They're the most beautiful of all animals. Even God loves them best, it says so in the Bible. And they are always teaching you something new, you know? And besides, do you know that the law was changed and now some of them might go to the auctions? And if they go to auction, they could get bought by the slaughterhouses? They eat horses in France! Isn't that just the grossest thing you can think of?"

Laurie's face is red and angry, her eyes narrowed to mean slits. She stares at me defiantly.

"It is horrible." I do know it, although I just learned about it yesterday.

"Yeah, well, I get the BLM newsletter online and I visit all these wild horse websites and stuff," she says. "I've known all about it since January. I've been writing letters to the Congress and stuff. I've loved the mustangs since I was little."

"Good for you, Laurie," I say, in real admiration. Kids are amazing sometimes—like now, when this one was making me feel stupid, small, and selfish.

"Anyway, you should! You should totally adopt a horse! Or more, if you've got room! And we can be e-pals and we can e-mail each other about how the training's going and stuff!" Her anger gone, her smile is huge, her excitement infectious.

"Well, maybe you're right, Laurie," I surrender, smiling back.

Thinking if I told her about my empty barn and my million bucks, she'd have me adopt every last one.

"Oh my gahd, they're opening the gates! Momma!" Laurie yells, ear-piercingly.

"Go on ahead, kiddo, I'll get our number," her mother calls.

"See you later," Laurie yells as she sprints for the gate.

"Good luck!" I call, but she is gone, racing to the corrals to find her horse. I am smiling as I get back in my truck, drive up in line, and take a number, just for the hell of it. It doesn't mean I am going to adopt a horse. But my number is number 5, the adoption is on the basis of first-come-first served; and behind, there are now at least a dozen more vehicles. That means I'd have a good chance of getting whichever horse I pick. If I did decide to get one. Which I really wasn't planning on. I should really think about it for a while, adopting a horse is a gigantic commitment and one you should definitely not make impetuously...

I park, get my hat, get out. Amble towards the pens, thinking I'd just have a peek at the horses before doing more interviews.

They are in groups in smallish pens of tall steel pipe. They are separated by age and gender. There are four donkeys in the first pen. They look like cartoons come to fuzzy life. I wander along and spend some time at a pen filled with mustang mares. They are all types of brown—bay, sorrel, chestnut, and there are three black ones. One is very pretty with four long white socks that remind me of my schoolgirl uniform knee-socks. The mare has a luxuriant glossy mane and a snip of white on her nose. She stays toward the back, using the other mares to shield her from the people leaning over the fence. She rolls her eyes as she's nudged aside by another mare. I keep watching her and suddenly I am picturing her in my barn. I grin at my susceptibility and move on. Pen after pen of gorgeous animals. Whoever thinks mustangs are scrawny and ugly should see this bunch. They're not muscled like quarter horses, but their stocky bodies with strong hindquarters and big, straight-nosed faces look just right to me. I stop at a pen of geldings and stallions, mesmerized by a flashy bay stud. He trots back and forth and the others fall out of his way like he's the king at court. The stallion's flanks are battle-scarred. His shiny mahogany coat is accented by black tail and mane and legs, over which are white socks.

"He's fulla piss and vinegar," says a voice, and I turn and nod at the cowboy leaning on the fence.

"He's gorgeous," I say. "But too much horse for me. That's for sure."

"Too much for me too, ma'am. What are you lookin' for?"

"Oh, no," I say. "I wouldn't know where to start, training one of these."

"Well then, you'll be checking out the saddle trained. They're showing 'em purty soon. I'm heading over. Y'all coming?"

"Sure," I say. I keep quiet on the fact I still am not here for a horse. I ask permission for an interview and he agrees and I ask the usual questions as we walk to a big arena. His name's LeRoy and he works on various ranches and rides rodeo sometimes. He does something called team penning and roping. He's here for a couple yearlings. He's trained seven mustangs and they are the best for cow work in his opinion. He made a nice profit on a buckskin mustang he trained for three years then sold to a lady in Onyx.

By the time we take auction paddles and seats on the bleachers overlooking the combed sand of the arena, LeRoy has given me enough great material for two articles. He's pausing in his narrative to stuff a wad of tobacco in his cheek and I think about doing a series of articles on real cowboys.

"Welcome, Ladies, Kids, and Gents," a voice on the loudspeaker system says. The speakers whine briefly and a volume adjustment is made.

"I'm Sergeant John Varney and I work for the California penal system and through our partnership with the Bureau of Land Management, I'm real pleased to show you this morning, some real nice horses. They've all been through a twelve-week trainin' program at Fontana State Penitentiary, administered by yours truly. These are all BLM mustangs and were green as a blade a grass when they arrived. They've all come a long ways in the training; we use resistant-free training. That means, no bribes, no beatin's. They are ground-trained and will let ya work on their feet and they'll trailer load. Three of 'em have been doing beginnin' work under saddle. Now, the proceeds from these adoption-auctions goes right back into the program to help get more horses and burros adopted. So let's see some good prices for these good horses!"

There is appreciative laughter and applause for Varney's speech. An auctioneer takes over.

The faultlessly groomed mustangs are brought out one-by-one, by women in identical blue jeans and boots and blue shirts. Anonymous in big safety helmets.

"Them's the inmates," LeRoy whispers, tobacco-scented information.

"Wow, really?" I whisper back. This is way more fun and interesting than I'd imagined. Who knew female prisoners train mustangs? Another great story! I watch, delighted, while the first few horses are put through their paces by the inmates. They lead them, lunge them in circles at varying paces, back them up, and demonstrate picking up their feet.

"They been doin' good with 'em," LeRoy opines. I agree. The halter-trained horses bring some surprisingly brisk bidding, and decent prices, from five hundred to a thousand dollars apiece. The auctioneer announces the first of the saddle-trained mustangs: a bay gelding, tall and rangy, which brings nineteen hundred. The next horse is introduced. A sorrel gelding. Three years old.

"Well, lookit here now," LeRoy says. He seems to grow as he leans forward, staring intently into the arena.

A fat girl riding a nice little liver-brown gelding. But as I watch for a moment, I too, lean forward. The horse is stocky and muscular and gleaming. Faint dapples on his belly—and are those stripes on his legs? His face is arresting: a wide, even white stripe down his nose, big, intelligent calm eyes. His thick mane and tail are of indeterminate color; mixed strands of silver, burgundy, copper. But it's his movement that is mesmerizing—high stepping, flowing. The girl seems fused to his back. As one they surge into a rocking-chair lope, execute a flying lead change in the dead center of a figure eight, then come to a sliding stop. The girl strokes the horse's arched neck. The horse's neck curves even more, he lowers his head, chews the bit calmly. He's grace incarnate. It is almost as if he wears an aura of light. He emits a gravitational pull like the moon.

"This here's the one," LeRoy says, turning to me, speaking low. "How much you got to spend?"

I can barely tear my eyes away from the horse.

"Whatever it takes," I hear myself say. I hand my paddle to LeRoy. "Get him for me," I say. "Whatever it takes."

* * *

Destiny strokes Prince's neck. This is the last time for us, she says to him in her mind. I hope you understand, I'm not deserting you.

She can't, she just won't!—cry in front of this big crowd and she takes a deep breath and banishes the tightness of her throat with a force of sheer will. Lifts the reins and trots Prince around while the bidding starts. She tries hard to excel, wanting the people to see what a great horse Prince is. What he can do. She collects Prince on the bit and he tucks his chin and she urges him ever so lightly and his feet extend in the trot. His rhythm is so strong, posting is effortless. She urges a little more and feels his stride stretch out. She moves him towards the center, drops in the saddle for one step in the epicenter of the arena and resumes posting on the new diagonal. The fact that she has become a decent—if not even good—rider over the last two months is of no concern or comfort whatsoever. But the fact that Prince has gone from a wild and wary outlaw to this calm, cooperative athlete, is a comfort. Even though it is ending with the tragedy of his loss, having trained Prince is still the one actual, above-average thing she has ever done.

Varney motions to her and she brings Prince to the end of the arena under the auctioneer's stand. Now that she's not in motion, the auctioneer's voice is loud, unavoidable.

"That's fifteen-hunnert, fifteen, and there's sixteen, there's seventeen, I see ya, seven, eighteen hunnert. Eighteen hunnert, do I got nineteen? Nineteen? This here's an insult to this here horse, he's a fine mover and will make a real nice cow pony or trail horse, that's right, nineteen, twenty, twenty two, three, twenty three hunnert… twenty three. Twenty three. There you go, twenty four, five, six. Three thousand, now there we go, folks. That's right. Are you going to let this little lady get this here horse? Will you give me thirty-one? No sir, he says. That's three thousand dollars, three thousand, going, once, twice, three thousand dollars… Gone! And sold to the lady in the pink hat. Nice hat, ma'am, and you got yourself a real nice mustang. Now, we got a pretty filly next folks, Spirit is her name and spirit is her game. Let's start her off at five hunnert dollars. Who's a going to give me five?"

Destiny didn't want to look at the "lady in the pink hat." Well, she did, but she wouldn't. She wouldn't be able to stand to see her smiling; see her happiness, the lust in her eyes under the pink brim of her stupid hat as she looked at Prince, who was now hers. Destiny kept her head down until the applause died and Oliver was riding in on Spirit. Destiny lifted the reins and tried to ride proudly from the arena, but she felt like she was dying. Her throat closed for good this time, and fat, hot tears were oozing from her eyes. She cried the whole time walking Prince back to the holding area, the whole time she unsaddled him and rubbed him down and while gave him water and some alfalfa hay. She felt Varney coming up behind her as she was brushing Prince's tail, which didn't need more brushing in the least.

"You did real good, Tubb," he said.

"Is it all over?"

"Yep, all done. Y'all done real good. That price we got for this guy is a record!"

"That's good," she said bitterly. She knew it wasn't fair but she felt that Varney was a traitor.

"I just wanted to thank ya, Tubb, it was a pleasure working with ya and a pleasure knowin' ya. Good luck. I know you'll do real fine when you get your release."

In her all-consuming grief of losing Prince, Destiny hadn't given any thought to the fact that now Varney would no longer be in her life either. A stab of new pain that was both loss and shame ground into her belly.

"Oh… crap, she said. I hate this!"

"I know. I'm sorry."

Destiny longed for him to hug her despite prison protocol and her own unworthiness and fearful reserve. But he didn't.

"Well, finish on up here, we're getting on the bus in ten minutes."

"Don't you want me to load him in the trailer?"

"No, the wranglers'll do it. Some of 'em will be shipped today but not all, prob'ly. So … say your goodbyes."

"Yes, sir."

As soon as Varney was gone she put her arms around Prince's neck. He didn't stop chewing, but swiveled his head so he could look at her.

"Goodbye, buddy," she whispered, tears starting fresh. "Goodbye." She sobbed louder and louder and didn't even care who could hear. In fact, she didn't care about anything at all any more.

* * *

Randall Pennant spat derisively when the sorrel mustang brought three grand. A lot of money for a mustang! Old skank in the pink hat didn't look like she could afford it. He never would figure out women—who fucking cared, anyway. The tobacco juice hit the sawdust of the back corrals but he imagined it landing instead on the little fat prison bitch's face. The way she rode that horse was both annoying and provoking. She looked like she could use a good fucking with a lot of ass slapping. Fuck, she had been in prison, she must be fucking horny as shit. He could do anything to a sad-faced little fat bitch like her. He wrenched his mind onto business before he became too distracted by the cute fat ass jiggling in the saddle. Soon they'd be selling the wild ones. He eyed the crowd, hoping he was the only meat man.

Sure enough, he grabbed up ten horses for seven hundred bucks. Ten times about eight hundred pounds per, eight grand maybe if he was lucky. Even minus the road expenses, it was a sweet profit. Finding out which crossings had crooked brand inspectors wasn't hard. The bribe for a truckload of horses was surprisingly affordable, especially for return customers. He planned on becoming a very good customer.

Meet the Family

I can't believe it. I just adopted a horse! I am stunned by the suddenness of it as I float into the office to write my check and arrange for shipping and collect the horses' dossier. It isn't until I do all that, and find Laurie and her new horse, and take her picture, and exchange e-mail addresses, and say goodbye to LeRoy, before the shock wears off, replaced by child-like excitement.

The horse is back in the pens. I pick him out right away—that white-blazed face is unmistakable—I don't need to check the number on the tag around his neck. I lean over the corral rail and offer him a carrot. He strides right over, nosing the other mustangs out of his way. He accepts the carrot and I touch his neck. He is warm, slightly damp from the riding. His neck is solid muscle. There are tufts of hair behind his striped knees. His eyelashes are thick and cinnamon colored. He looks at me calmly with bittersweet chocolate eyes, and lips my palm, wanting another carrot. I oblige.

"You're going to be living with me," I tell him. "Your ass is mine."

I can hardly stand to leave but there is no point in staying. He'll be delivered tomorrow. I have to get ready for him: buy hay, and grooming tools, a watering tank. I have to get home and write my article, the newspaper deadline is tomorrow evening as well. I pull out my camera and take his picture until the memory chip is full. I tell him goodbye. As I walk away, he watches me, and whinnies as I leave his sight. The sound pulls at me, like the cry of her baby pulls at mama's milk. I can't wait to get him home.

The next day the truck hauling the horse trailer pulls up to the corral. The wranglers—a rotund mom and her skinny teenage son—open the back and lead my horse down the ramp and through the corral gate. They untie the lead rope, leaving the halter on. I tip them twenty bucks each and they accept a glass of lemonade and then are gone, without a word of advice.

The horse—my horse!—goes directly to the hay manger and begins to eat. I watch him, my elbows on the fence rails. After a while, he investigates the water tank, then drinks, his ears twitching with each big swallow. Then finally, he takes stock of his surroundings. He looks at me, he noses all around the corral. Then he slowly kneels, then flops over, and rolls over and over in the dirt. Then stands up and shakes like a dog after a bath, raising a cloud of dust. He snorts and groans, a sound of pleasure. Then he meanders over to me at the fence.

"Hi, beautiful," I say. I reach out a hand. He snuffles it, and nibbles gently.

"You're home," I inform him.

I am a little afraid, but I open the gate and step into the corral. He clops right over. I touch his neck. He doesn't object, and so I begin running my hands over his coat, smooth as expensive Egyptian cotton sheets. I touch him all over. I step back out and retrieve a currycomb, hoof pick, and brush; I let him sniff the tools and begin to groom him. He stands perfectly still, seeming to enjoy the treatment. I begin to feel less cautious and bend down, within brain-injury distance, to pick up his front foot. As I run my hand down his shoulder, he lifts his hoof for me. The potentially lethal foot lies lightly in my palm. I clean it with a hoof pick, then do the others. He knows the routine perfectly.

"Good boy," I say, as proud as if I'd trained him myself. It is hard to believe this horse was a wild stallion just a few months ago. He is three years old, according to the paperwork I'd received at the adoption. He's from Nevada, the Humboldt Herd Area, in the Jackson Mountains range, far north in the state. All this identification is recorded within the freeze brand on his neck, a tattoo of white hieroglyphics on the glossy brown coat. His name, according to the auctioneer, is "Prince." A dumb name for such an unusual horse, I think. He needs a better name.

Now that he is here, he is mine, you would think that I'd be champing at the bit to get on and ride. But I feel timid. It's been so many years since I have done any serious riding. And even though he'd seemed perfectly trained at the adoption, the fact remains that he is green-broke; quite recently a one-hundred-percent wild horse. I rationalize: it's best to let him chill out for a day or two before I as much as try to work him in the round pen.

I take off his halter and leave the corral, chaining the gate closed. I go up to the house and bring down a lawn chair and a small table. Another trip for my old laptop and solar charger. I put the charger out in the sun, then set everything else up under the shade of an oak tree next to the corral. I sit down to work on my article about the adoption, taking too-frequent breaks to watch my horse. He doesn't do much, just stands under the same oak-tree shade, one hind leg cocked, swishing his tail now and again. He yawns, once, a big, comical grimace. But nevertheless, he is infinitely fascinating. I finally manage to pull my attention from the horse to the computer. I realize, as I look through my note-book and the files on the BLM legislation that I should write two stories, one a feel-good piece on the adoptions, and an accompa-nying story about the scary new law. That one would take more research: I should do some interviews with the BLM people and the horse advocates… I need to find a local angle. So I turn my attention to the adoption piece first. I finish a first draft then look at the photos I downloaded last night and pick one to send with the story—one of Laurie and her new horse. It's terrific: Laurie smiling wide, the big bag of carrots in her arms and behind her, the filly, a red roan with a sweet, speckled face, looking gravely at the camera through the fence rails. Last night Laurie had al-ready sent me an e-mail and I had replied. As I re-read her cute story about how her new filly had been introduced to the Wilsons' other horses, I started worrying. It's true, I can worry and stress even in the midst of happiness. It seems that I am incapable of just being happy.

So what exactly is so stressful?

Now that I have this horse, I don't know if I'm ready.

Well you've got him, so you better be ready.

I didn't think about the fact that he might be lonely up here, being the only horse. They're herd animals. The herd is every-thing to them.

You'll be his herd.

I guess.

Feeling better?

I guess.

So get another horse, if you're so worried about it. You've got the room, the money. You have the time.

Another horse! I don't know about that.

Think about all those BLM horses going to auction. You could save a couple, at least.

Jesus! The guilt. I can't solve that problem. At least I'm going to write about it.

You could do more. And it would solve your other problem.

Yeah, yeah. On one hand it makes sense. On the other hand, it seems awfully impetuous.

What's so impetuous? Didn't you build these corrals, this barn, intending to have horses?

Of course. But that was Before.

And now it's After. But you're still living your life. What comes After but Next? And what's Next, Sara Beth? Do something wonderful.

I guess.

That night, I call Charlie and Lee. She answers.

"You'll never believe what I did."

"You adopted a mustang!"

"How did you know?" I cry, disappointed at being robbed of my surprise.

"I just knew, when Charlie said you were going up there."

"But I didn't even know."

"Who's yo' mama? I'm so excited! Tell me all about him."

So I lavishly describe my horse. I admit I'm trepidatious about riding him or even working him in the round pen.

"You be careful, Siggy! Those mustangs can be dangerous. The flight instinct is real strong in them."

"Right," I say, feeling instantly scared. "Do you want to come see him?" I ask. "We can take him into the round pen together."

"Sure," she says. "Tomorrow?"

"Around ten?"

"I'll be there!"

"Thanks, chica," I say, hanging up feeling relieved. With Lee here, I won't be so afraid to take the horse out of the corral. In fact I'm looking forward to tomorrow. It takes three glasses of wine before I can finally think about going to bed. Before I do, I take a flashlight and go down to the corrals one last time. He's standing quietly; his eyes gleam amber in the beam of light. He clomps up to the rail. I pet him on the white stripe. I lean over and put my nose up to his big nostrils. That intoxicating horse scent overwhelms me, surprising me every time. I breathe in his sweet grassy breath. He breathes in mine. The first inhale tentative, the second, more curious. It feels like he is accepting me, almost welcoming me. As I stand up and pat him one more time, he chews, a sign of cooperation. I walk away and he nickers, clearly saying, come back! It makes me want to bring out a sleeping bag so he won't be alone. But that's silly. He'll be fine. But my heart drags as I close the front door.

Keep this up and the fucking horse'll be sleeping in the bedroom, I scold myself.

* * *

Destiny is riding Prince across a green meadow speckled with purple wildflowers in her dream. Yet the whole time she is dreaming, she's aware it isn't real; she is in prison, Prince is gone forever. It makes the dream bittersweet to say the least. She fights against waking but the farts issuing from Tonya's bunk are insistent, as is the rustling, clinking, complaining layers of morning noise in prison.

And I thought my life was crap before, is Destiny's first waking thought.

No Prince, no Varney. No more smells of leather and horse sweat and horse breath. No more the incredible sensation of—freedom? Destiny isn't sure how to name the feeling of riding Prince, of just being with Prince. She is sure about one thing though. Losing Prince is almost as bad as losing Justin. All during the wonderful (at least after the beginning) experience of the horse training she had been able to bear—for the first time—the loss of her baby. But now that is all over and the pain comes crashing back, worse than the agony of childbirth itself. Hurts to get them, hurts worse to lose them, she decides. So deep in misery, she is a shell, a zombie, a ghost. If there is something in all of life to look forward to, she can't imagine what it is.

Ghosts know nothing of time, and so Destiny is surprised when she's reminded her parole hearing is due. In the dread and anticipation of the adoption, Destiny had almost forgotten her hearing is scheduled for the following week. She's been incarcerated over six years. If she isn't paroled this time, her sentence could go on and on. She might not get out until she is thirty-eight years old. The difference between being her present age of twenty-four and thirty-eight is vast. But she doesn't care as passionately as she should. She has no vision of what her life could be outside. She should try to get Justin back. But he might hate her—if he even remembered her. The difference between twenty-four and thirty-eight is nothing compared to Justin's reality. He had been only eighteen months old when it happened. Now he'd be almost eight. His whole babyhood, gone. He'd be in second grade. He'd have brothers and sisters and friends and maybe a dog. A school and clothes and toys. A whole life. And Destiny is supposed to swoop in and uproot him and take him—where? No way would she make his life any speck less than what it was. No crummy hotels or busses instead of a car, no neighborhoods with trash and pit bulls and mean gangster kids.

The idea of all she'd have to accomplish in order to even deserve thinking about getting him back is overpowering, like being smothered in a wet sleeping bag. As she walks into the office to face the parole board, Destiny isn't even sure that she wants to be released.

They were four: the square and stern Mrs. Fong from Social Services. Matron Davenport, beige as her uniform. The prison administrator—a dark, intimidating-looking man in a suit—she doesn't know him at all. And a guy from the Probation Department with a thick body like a wrestler.

First, they talk about her crime. The Probation guy asks her something she's never been asked, in all the interrogations, the entire trial, no one had ever asked it.

"In the time before your arrest, are there any choices that you made that you'd now make differently?"

"You mean, where'd I go wrong?" she asks with a ghost of a smile.

"That's another way of putting it," he says smiling back.

"Yes sir," she says, "I know right where I went wrong."

* * *

"Hey, Destiny! Welcome to the beehive," Greg said, through the intercom. He buzzed the lock and she shifted Justin to her other hip and pushed the door open. Inside it was a big open warehouse space. Big but clean, open, and brightly lit even though there were no windows whatsoever. Metal benches and shelving with boxes of all sizes and rolls of mul-ticolored wires. There was loud, invigorating rock music playing on a huge speakers like at a concert. Greg came hurrying over and to her surprise, hugged her, Justin and all. Greg was grinning ear to ear.

"So glad you made it! Is it still raining?"

"Raining?" Destiny didn't think it had rained since yesterday. "No, sun's out," she said.

"Ah, well, like we'd even recognize it," he said, but sounded happy about it. He asked her if she wanted a cappuccino, espresso, or a soda. She agreed to a Coke. He went to a dispensing machine and opened it with a key and handed her a can. Next to the soda machine was a refrigerator and a counter with a shiny sink, an espresso machine, and neat stacks of china cups, plates, silverware. Across the big room were worktables and people bent over them.

The grand tour, Greg said, leading her through a labyrinth of cartons and shelves. He introduced Destiny to the others. Louisa, June, Eric, Josefina. They all smiled and greeted her and cooed over Justin.

"Meet the Bees," Greg said.

"B's? "Destiny wondered aloud.

"We call ourselves the Bees, like in worker bees," Louisa laughed. "Cause all we ever do is work."

"And buzz, buzz, buzz," giggled Josephina.

"A happy hive," Greg said.

The Bees were all young and skinny and wore cool, hip clothes and jewelry. Destiny felt outclassed but tried to stay calm. She reminded herself to smile.

"Louisa's making mic cables, microphone cables," Greg said. "Show her, Lou." Destiny watched as Louisa bent her curly dark head over the bench and wielded a smoking tool on an electric cord. Greg explained that was the soldering iron. Louisa had a coil of small silver wire and she touched it to the end of a length of cable that was flayed out into wires of different colors. With a little puff of smoke, Lou attached one of the wires to a prong on a silver plug. Then she neatly connected the other wires. Then she screwed the top over the plug.

"That's it, now the other end," Louisa said, deftly flipping over the coiled bundle.

"Simple, huh?" said Greg.

"It doesn't look too complicated," Destiny admitted.

"I'll set you up to give it a try."

"Right now?"

"Sure." Greg led her to a spare table. Patiently, he showed her every step while Justin played happily on the clean floor with an empty cardboard carton. It was hard at first, way harder than it looked when Louisa had done it. But finally Destiny managed to finish a cable.

"So, for cables like these, you get a buck each. You can make more the faster you can do them. Louisa does about twenty-five an hour. I pay cash, no taxes or anything," Greg told her, and slurped his cappuccino.

Even she could do that math. Twenty-five dollars an hour! Destiny was stunned.

"Sometimes other jobs pay more per piece, then we can really rake it in," he added. "What do you think?"

"I'll try," Destiny said.

"Want to get started right now?"

"But I have Justin."

No problem, we love the little guy. We can make him a play-pen out of some cartons.

So they did, and Destiny put his toys inside and gave him a bottle of juice. She got a bench and a chair and a lamp and a sol-dering iron and little pair of pliers. A toolbox with rolls of solder and a jar of flux. A big pile of raw cables and a box of plugs. And she went to work. Louisa and the others worked steadily except for quick bathroom breaks and so Destiny tried to do the same.

Hours later, Justin was fussing and her back was aching and her foot was asleep but she'd made eighteen cables. Greg had been on the phone in his "office," a partially enclosed room near the kitchen. He emerged yelling, "Coffee break, you maniacs!" Grate-fully, Destiny stood and stretched. Picked up Justin and joined the others in the kitchen area. Greg worked the hissing machine and handed around little cups with frothy white foam. Destiny decided to try it, watching the others to see if they used sugar. She stirred in a bunch of sugar and then sipped. It was good. Sweet and dark-tasting at once. She pretended she always drank cappuccino. The talk was quick and funny. Everyone was smoking but Destiny didn't mind. She was laboriously doing math in her mind. Eight bucks an hour wasn't bad at all. And she'd get a lot faster. Eventually she could afford a babysitter and then work a lot and make some real money.

"So do you dig it?" Greg asked her.

"Yeah, it's fun," she said.

"Hah, fun! You need to get out more," June teased.

"That's for sure." Destiny smiled. "I have to get Justin home pretty soon for his dinner, though."

"No problem," Greg said. "Can you come back tomorrow?"

"I… yeah, if I can bring Justin?"

"No problem. That's great! Destiny's going to be joining the party, kids."

They all toasted Destiny with their cappuccinos, and as she gathered up Justin's things they headed back to their benches and the irons began smoking.

"What time should I come?" she asked Greg.

"Come in around ten, we'll be here all night."

Destiny promised to return in the morning.

She did make money and got a babysitter and worked with the others late into the nights. The money piled up. She made enough in the first month to move to a nice place. Then, enough for new clothes for Justin and good food and books and toys. Enough, even, for new clothes for herself, and new furniture. For late night dinners of pasta and sushi and other fancy food; she was even shopping for a car. But the work was hard and seemed to get harder. Bending over the bench, her back, her shoulders, her neck, ached. Her legs got numb. Her eyes burned in the solder fumes. The cappuccinos were all that kept her going. Until she found out what it was that kept the others going.

* * *

"I guess it was when I started doing the crystal, sir," Destiny admits. "But I ain't never touching it again. Never."

It doesn't take the parole board long to make a decision. They say her record is good. Her voluntary participation in the wild horse program tips the scales. Destiny's release is approved;

though she is to be on probation for one year. The day after to-morrow, she'll be free. Whatever that means.

* * *

"Meet the family," said the social worker, and four-year-old Randall Pennant stared up at the strangers. The low double-wide trailer smelled like burnt popcorn and pee. Randall knew enough to be afraid. He had loved his last foster mom but she had died. Her heart attacked her. Randall knew then it was a good idea to make sure your heart was hard so it would never attack itself.

His new foster brothers and sisters—all eight of them—were loud, selfish, full of weird habits, and largely unsupervised. The Foster Mom, Mrs. Weldon, was gone a lot from the house. Then the kids would follow the dirt alley to a swampy area and catch frogs, and blow them up with fireworks. If it was hot it was fun to start fires with a magnifying glass and burn up an anthill. They incessantly teased Albert, who was autistic. It was easy to make him scream and rock back and forth. Fat Mary was fun to pinch and kick. She was so fat she couldn't get out of the way. When she cried, her face became disgustingly blotchy, which made Randall begin to hate her. All the kids were covered in scrapes and bruises from fighting and being picked on, but nobody ever noticed. The food was ramen, canned spaghetti, Hot Pockets, peanut butter. Naked hot dogs or milk and cereal were a rare treat. The refrigerator was protected from snacking with a chain and padlock. Randall was always hungry and it made him indifferent to the suffering of his housemates.

One rainy day they found a nest of kittens in a dumpster in the alley, and brought them home. In the garage, the kids fought over them. An orange kitten was adopted and protected by the girls, but the black kittens were bad luck. Eventually, after discussion and experimentation, they hung one of them with an electric cord, and the other one was drowned in a trash bin.

A Bad Ride

Lee comes over the next morning. We have coffee and fruit on the terrace. I am only half listening to her news; I'm eager to show off my horse. Finally Lee grinds out her cigarette and says, "Let's go see this mustang."

We walk down to the corrals. The mustang is in his usual spot, head over the fence, looking down the driveway. I call him and he looks at us with disinterest until I produce a carrot. Then he ambles over.

"Wow," Lee says. "Just, wow, he's gorgeous. He's no mustang!"

"Yeah he is," I correct. "See his brand?"

"I mean, he doesn't look like a mustang. Nice conformation. Good legs. Good feet. Look at those stripes and feathers on his legs! Cool."

"I know," I say with undeserved pride.

"His head's nice too. Those eyes."

"Isn't he nice?"

"Real nice. And he's saddle trained?"

"Yep. He's awesome under saddle. He was trained by prison inmates. Women."

"Right? That's so cool. What's his name?"

"I don't know yet."

"Well, let's take him down to the round pen."

I retrieve the halter and rope and go into the pen. The horse lowers his head, he practically halters himself. I lead him to the gate, Lee opens it. We head on down the dirt lane. The horse looks around, but curiously, calmly. The thousand-pound horse feels like a feather on the end of the rope. At the round pen, Lee opens the gate and I lead the horse through.

I step into the center of the circle, point, and flick the end of my lariat. The horse tosses his head and regards me with startled, white-rimmed eyes. He snorts and shakes his head, clearly saying, I don't think so. I repeat the cue, snapping the rope closer to his flanks. He stands death-still, then explodes into motion as if he's reached a sudden decision, one he's not too happy about. He swerves, twirls, flings his head, and bucks in one complicated, intimidating motion, like he's Nijinsky in a horse body—then an instant later he's trotting around to my cue. I have him circle five times, then begin to change hands to cue him to change direction, but before I've even got the rope and lariat exchanged, he's already turning and circling in the other direction. I cluck for a canter, and he changes gaits easily. A circle later I slow him—with the slightest tug on the lead line he falls into a steady trot. And so it goes, like the horse is reading my mind. I barely have to think of what I want him to do: walk, trot, canter, change, stop, back up; he does it without the slightest resistance. I bring him to the center of the pen, back him, lift all his feet. Let him rest.

I reach to pet him but he jerks his head away like a diva with an unwelcome fan.

"Jesus H," Lee says. "He looks damn good."

"I know, huh?" I say, flushed with exertion, exhilaration, and pride.

"Gonna get on him?"

"Thinking about it."

"I'll go get your saddle."

"Okay."

She hurries off and returns with the saddle, blanket, and bridle.

She brings them into the pen and pets my horse on the neck. His skin flinches.

"You're a gorgeous, good boy, you are," she tells him. And holds the lead while I saddle and bridle him. Then makes a cup from her hands to help me mount.

"Here goes," I say.

I step into her hand and swing into the saddle. Carefully lower my old self down. The horse doesn't flinch, doesn't budge.

"Okay?" Lee asks.

"I think so," I murmur. My heart is racing. I take an unsuccessful breath to relax.

Lee backs away outside the perimeter fence. I pick up the reins and squeeze gently with my legs to cue the horse to walk. His head comes up and he grabs the bit in his teeth and in a mighty tug, jerks the reins from my hands. Flustered, I gather them back up. Take a deep breath. Urge again with my legs, this time pushing with my pelvis at the same time. His head comes up again, and instead of going forward, he backs up. I bump him with my legs and he backs faster, in a twisting circle. I lean forward and try some more and finally he lurches forward, but not into a nice walk, instead, to a jerky trot. Now I try to slow him, which produces more head-tossing and bit-grabbing. The ride is like bad sex, when you just can't get into a rhythm, there's an inordinate amount of painful bumping, and you wonder what you're doing in bed with this creature in the first place. I finally manage to get him to respond a little, trot, walk, stop. But it's a struggle the whole way, and I'm quickly exhausted. After only ten minutes I halt him and rather hastily, ungracefully, slither to the heavenly ground.

"You okay?" Lee asks, as I limp to the rail, dragging the horse behind me.

"Sure," I pant.

"Three grand, huh?"

"He'll be fine," I gasp. "Just needs a little more work. New rider and all."

"Sure. I mean, I'm sure you're right."

She opens the gate and I lead the horse out and to his corral. I take off the saddle and bridle and decide I'll put them away later. Need a beer. Now.

"It wasn't that long a ride. Do I have to brush him out?" I ask Lee.

"He'll be okay," she says. I know Lee always grooms her horses after working them, whether or not they need it. But I'm pissed. At myself? or the poor horse?

"Well, he needs work," I review, over the beers back at the house.

"Just be careful, Sara."

"I will. Maybe I'll stick to groundwork for a while."

"Good idea," she says.

After Lee leaves, I have another beer, and think about my bumpy ride. I remember the fat girl riding him during the adoption— then he was like a different horse, a perfect horse. He has that in him, I tell myself. He is awesome. He knows how to do it all so much better. It must be me, I decide. After all, I'm rusty. My legs are weak, my spine's stiff, my hands no doubt clumsy with more than a touch of arthritis. I just need to start doing some yoga, sit-ups, take some joint supplements, calcium… I want to ride him like that inmate—fluidly, effortlessly, floatingly. I know I could get a different horse, an easier horse, but the idea repulses me. There's something about this horse. Something I need, suddenly and just as urgently. Like I just smoked some crack, I want another hit right away.

I spend most of the afternoon down in the corral with him. I want to get on him again and try to do it better, but I'm afraid it will be worse. In the end I just groom him from head to tail. I give him a scoop of oats with chopped carrots in a bucket, and while he munches I start with the rubber curry-comb, working it in circles over his body, raising all the dust and loose hair. Then the body brush, then the soft brush, and finally I wipe him down with a damp towel until his body gleams. With my fingers and a comb I separate every hair of his mane and tail, then dunk his tail in a bucket and soap it, rinse it, then comb it again. I dampen a clean towel and gently wipe his eyelids, his nostrils, the insides of his ears, and even his anus and sheath. I clean his hooves and paste on a hoof dressing. I use every brush and grooming aid and can't think of a spot I've missed. He looks great and my arms are pleasantly exhausted. So I remove his halter and watch in rueful amusement as he wanders around, picks the dustiest spot in the corral, kneels gracefully, and rolls and rolls until every bit of my grooming is obliterated. He grunts to his feet and shakes all over like a wet dog, literally disappearing into a cloud of dust. When the cloud clears, there is my horse, no longer gleaming, but look-ing immensely satisfied with himself. He groans loudly, snorts, farts, then investigates the hay rick and busies himself chewing a few wisps.

"You're a scoundrel," I scold, grinning. Still, I'm reluctant to leave. All afternoon, working on the horse, I've finally relaxed into a Zen state of calm emptiness, free of guilt, sadness, grief, loneliness. But the sun is dropping; the dogs and chickens need their dinner. The garden is wilting from inattention and I ha-ven't eaten all day. So I tear myself from the corral and do the chores, then make an omelette and eat ravenously, glad I'm alone to gobble shamelessly. Full and calm, I pour a glass of wine and smoke a cigarette, thinking with surprise that I haven't lit up since this morning, or even craved one. I smoke and drink on the front porch, watching the sky go dark and the bats appear. But my mind's on my horse, and the mustangs, and Wild Horse Annie. This horse is a revelation. He is no scrub, no cayuse. He's smart and gorgeous and I hope one day, he will be the best ride of my life. I'd take a horse like him over any pedigreed Quarter or Arab, or any breed, I think. It is true of my dogs, too. The mutts always have the most amusing personalities and higher survival IQs; their health is better and they are more independent than the purebreds I've known. I want to know more, I think, more about my horse, his habitat, his ancestors; I suddenly have a wild hair to know everything there is to know about the mustangs.

I head inside to the office and finish reading the files on the wild horse legislation. One of the websites is published by a couple who operate a ranch and wild horse sanctuary. The website is full of photos and links and lots of information on training and adoptions and fencing and shoeing and wild horse history and of course, the new legislation. The story is big. As I read I become convinced that the lawmakers are condoning unnecessary slaughter of perfectly nice horses not to solve a problem of "overpopulation" of the wild horses, or even to save taxpayer's money, but simply on the whim of a senator from Montana. The budget for the wild horse program is a pittance, and I easily find out that the lion's share is eaten up by administration, not by the horses themselves. As far as the so-called problem of overpopulation—it turns out that the population of the wild horses might not be what the government claims. Horse advocates were claiming that the horses aren't actually counted; the BLM's herd counts instead are derived from statistical formulas. The whole raison d'être of the government program hinges on the premise that the horse herds breed incessantly and if unchecked, the horses would overrun the ranges in no time. Thus, herd areas were mapped, and target herd sizes decided upon. Thus the herds must be culled; the excess horses rounded up and adopted by people like me and Laurie. I had certainly believed on first glance that the herds needed "management". But now I am not so sure. Why can't they just be left alone? But they hadn't been left alone, they'd been rounded up by the thousands and now this legislation had created within them a subset, over eight thousand horses deemed "unadoptable." Over ten years old. Offered for adoption three times. I wonder if my horse had been previously offered for adoption. His papers had no information on that. And what if he were ten? He'll only be an even better horse, of that I'm sure. This law makes no sense! It's obscene.

I go online and checked a website, Wild Tails. There on the home page is a flashing message, Wild Horse Slaughter Alert. Frowning, I click on and read the newest developments. The BLM has begun sending horses to public auctions as mandated by the new law. And this morning the first mustangs ended up at a slaughterhouse. I do an internet search and find the story is already being picked up by the national media. I stay up late and get up early and by ten the next morning I've finished my own story. I've talked to the folks at Wild Tails, and a local couple who'd adopter four mustangs, and a frightened BLM spokesperson.

"*Wild Horse Legislation Results in Slaughter*
Sara Beth Corcoran
Special to the Courier

In January, wild horse advocates went on the warpath against new legislation which removed protection for some wild horses and burros gathered from public lands, warning that the bill would result in some animals being sent to slaughter. The Burns Bill stated that the mustangs and burros would be, for the first time since they were protected by Congress, subject to being sold at public auction. Horses and burros over ten years old or those that have been offered at adoptions three times would be subject to the sale authority. At that time, 8,500 animals housed in BLM facilities met those conditions.

Horse advocates objected to the method of the bill's passage; it was slipped at the eleventh hour into the 1,100 page Appropriations Bill, avoiding public debate. But they are also fearful of the consequences of the animals being sold at auction. The bill stipulated that the animals be sold "without limitations", meaning they could be sold by the pound to horsemeat brokers. There are three foreign-owned slaughterhouses in the US; horsemeat is then exported to France, Belgium, and Japan, where it is considered a delicacy.

And yesterday, the horse advocates fears were realized. A hundred and five horses were bought by the Rosebud Sioux Indians in South Dakota for a dollar apiece. Of those, 87 were sold to a horse broker, who in turn sold 51 to Cavel International in DeKalb, Illinois, where they were slaughtered. A worker there was said to have called the BLM upon noticing the mustang's distinct freeze brands.

'We feared this would happen, but we prayed that it would not,' said Congressman Nick Rahall, a Democrat from West Virginia, at a press conference. 'Those involved in the slaughter of wild horses and burros have blood on their hands, and what has transpired is a wake-up call to the Congress.'

The issue is a hot one for horse advocates across the country as well as here in Canyon County. Juliette and Nathan of Cottonwood Creek have four mustangs. 'We didn't take these guys in to sit back while horses are slaughtered,' she said. 'We're not going to rest until horse slaughter is outlawed. Mustangs helped build this country and they're a beautiful living symbol of the thing that's great about America, freedom. Killing them for meat is just so wrong.'"

I send the story to Charlie, feeling good about it, glad to have met the articulate and impassioned Juliette. But I don't feel good otherwise. I am haunted by the specter of my own horse's alternate destiny. Only by a twist of fate, he is here with me, instead of on a plate surrounded by pommes frites. By a twist of fate he was given a chance. Chance. There was his name! My Chance. I shut down the computer and run down to the corral. I can't wait to see him, touch him, and smell him with my arms around his neck.

* * *

The sky, the people, the air, the noise; the noise of traffic and civilization. No Tonya and no bars on the windows and nobody telling her what to do. Despite her depression, despite her frighteningly obscure future, not to mention present, Destiny is kind of excited to be Out. At first.

She meets with her probation officer, a sleepy fat man of indeterminate age. His collars are too wide even for his huge jowly neck and his tie is too short. He does not inspire confidence. Nor does he offer much help. Just Xeroxed copies of lists of organizations and regulations. She is supposed to let him know everything, where she is living, what job she gets, et cetera. She tries to ask him how she is supposed to get a job. He hands her another paper listing job counseling services.

And then it is just like she thought it would be. A crummy room in a fleabag hotel that they called a rooming house. The job counseling is lame. Just stupid advice on resumes, like you were applying to be a bank vice president or something. And more Xeroxes of more organizations, and temporary work businesses. She goes to those and fills out the applications. Despite being on the probation department's lists they never seem too thrilled to find out she is an ex-con. After too many embarrassing, frustrating interviews she is finally offered a job: for minimum wage, on an assembly line, packing cosmetics into boxes.

It is excruciating. She is the only white girl. All the other assembly line workers are Latino—Mexican, she guesses. They never speak to Destiny and barely look at her. The noise in the warehouse is constant and punishing. The conveyor belt trundling along with its cargo of creams and lotions, polishes and lipsticks, is unceasing. Except at noon when it stops for a blessed half hour. Unfortunately there is a huge clock on the wall opposite where Destiny stands on the assembly line. It makes it impossible to stop thinking about the time. The clock moves too slowly, desperately slowly. The hours on the line are mind-numbing, foot-aching, spirit-breaking. Every box she packs disappears instantly, replaced by another empty, hungry one. There is no sense of accomplishment; no sense that it will ever end. The boxes will never be satisfied. They will come on and on, towards you, little monsters hungry for another bite of your soul.

But she can stand it. She has to stand it. She has to have a job or else she'll be in the gutter in no time. At least it is that, a safety jacket, keeping her from drowning. After her shifts she usually goes right back to the hotel and takes a bath and crawls into bed exhausted. But she wakes up in the dark first hours of the morning, still tired but wide awake, relentlessly awake. There is nothing to do but toss on the squeaking bed and think. And that thinking is often too sad. Too sad to bear. She keeps trying to think creatively, positively. How to improve her life. How to get Justin. How to deserve to keep him. But every idea seems to have a catch. She'd love to go back to school, she'd love to get trained for a good job; but those things take money, time, and commitment. She doesn't have a spare dime or the time. Well, maybe she could make the time, but the money is still the obstacle. She even goes to the library after work to look up information on scholarships. But they all seem to be for ethnic kids. No scholarships being offered for ex-drug addicted, single-mother felons on probation.

There is no one to talk to. Everyone from her ex-life is as good as dead. She isn't allowed to consort with the Bees, because of the drugs. Loreen would be no help, as always. And Loreen's kids— thinking about her brothers and sister makes Destiny weepily frustrated. She goes to a pay phone once, to call Varney. Just to hear his voice, the voice of somebody who actually cared about her. But at the last second, she chickens out. She wants to be able to tell him something positive. She wants to prove worthy of the faith he'd had in her. But at this point, she just can't. She hangs up the receiver having wasted three whole quarters.

* * *

"Want a bump?" asked Louisa, coming into the two-stall bathroom.

"A what?" Destiny said, washing her face, trying to wipe away her exhaustion. It was the fifth day in a row of fifteen-hour days. They had a big order to fill and had been working until one, two in the morning, starting up again at ten. Justin spent the mornings and afternoons at a nice day care then Destiny left work at three, picked him up, grabbed to-go food for her and the Bees, and raced back to work, where Justin had his own playpen and toys, even a high chair. He'd nap and Destiny could get back to work until it was time to feed him, then he played mostly happily until his bedtime. Then she'd tuck him in, surrounded by pillows, on the couch in Greg's office. It had been a grueling five days but she kept herself going by doing the math over and over in her head as she wired the circuit boards. She was averaging eighteen bucks an hour. She'd made about two hundred and seventy dollars a day. So far this week she'd made over thirteen hundred dollars. But she was so tired, her shoulder muscles cramped and pinching, her eyes dry and sore.

Louisa, in answer, was unfolding a little folded paper packet, and tapping out some whitish powder onto her compact mirror. She produced a rolled up five-dollar bill and snorted up each nostril. Handed the green tube towards Destiny.

"Oh, no, no thanks," Destiny said, backing up instinctively.

"Trust me, girl, it'll keep ya going," Louisa said. "Shit, we're all doing it. How do you think we can stand these hours?"

"What is it?" Destiny said, just to be polite.

"Crystal. It's not cocaine, don't worry!"

"But…" (what is it?) Destiny wanted to say, but didn't want to sound uncool.

"Have a little tootski, see if you like it," Louisa suggested reasonably.

Destiny actually found herself considering it. She was so tired… but she needed to keep working, and if it would make her less tired… But her mother did drugs. She didn't want to end up like Loreen. Especially now she was finally making a success of things. But Lou said this wasn't cocaine. One try certainly couldn't hurt anything. And if they all were doing it, it must be okay! Greg and the Bees were the coolest—they were what she longed to be. Smart. Rich. They had futures. They had fun. Destiny took the five-dollar tube and gingerly inserted an end to her nose and sniffed.

It was a magic key unlocking a door, like the one Dorothy opened to the Technicolor magnificence of MunchkinLand. The door behind which Destiny had always and forever lived her dull, black and white, dingy, uneducated, loser life. She had so much energy it felt like she could float. The work became fascinating and easy and her piece per hour went up by fifty percent. Her brain kicked into high gear and she found she had things to say. At last she was one of the Bees and could even make them laugh sometimes with the stuff she'd say. For the first time in her life, she was smart and even funny. And she didn't need to eat, either. A total bonus was that she started losing weight.

She'd felt bad about asking Lou for bump after bump and was happy to find out that Greg could sell her some. It was cheap considering that extra work output. And Destiny only used a tiny bit, just when she began to feel tired. She didn't make nearly as many trips to the bathroom as did Lou and Josie, she noticed. Eric apparently was the only one who didn't "indulge," as Greg called it. Eric was Japanese with a sweet, wide moon face and scant, tufty eyebrows like bird down. He was just as talkative as the others but there was an inner seriousness to him. Lou and Josie definitely indulged, as did Greg. Josie was beautiful: she had luxurious black hair in a thick braid and pouty lips, and cappuccino-colored eyes that slanted like a cat's. Lou was the loudest, and the ringleader. She took Destiny clothes-shopping when they finished three big jobs in a row and all got paid in wonderful big handfuls of cash. Destiny was stunned to find out she was a size eight. Lou insisted Destiny get her hair cut and find a babysitter for Justin. Lou's boyfriend had deserted her by joining the Army and she was in the market for a new one.

Destiny found the babysitter and although she was nervous about leaving Justin with a stranger, she was excited too. She took a long shower and put on her new skinny jeans and a silk blouse in a jungle print, with shoulder pads which made her look like she had good posture. She put on makeup and gave the sitter—a blank-faced teenager named Miranda—a long list of instructions. Then she kissed Justin goodbye until he complained and left in her new—well, used, but new to her—car, a gray Toyota. She met the Bees at a sushi restaurant. They all sat at the bar and drank sake and made lots of loud toasts. Two by two they went off to the bathroom for a bump. Destiny felt quite sophisticated drinking the strange, biting, hot wine. The green mustard burned her nostrils pleasantly, just like the drugs. The food was perfect, it sat lightly. After dinner they went to a club. And danced and drank and laughed and had a hilarious time. Destiny had to get home, but it was hard to leave while everyone was having so much fun. She said her goodbyes and somehow managed to drive home without getting in a wreck. She parked carefully at the curb, which was difficult because everything kept spinning. Success. She opened the car door, lost her balance getting out, and fell. She staggered back to her feet, feeling no pain. But her pants were ripped at the knee, and she was bleeding. Crap, my new pants, she thought as she tried to walk without lurching up to her door.

Even though the sitter saw her bedraggled condition and adopted an openly contemptuous tone, and the rest of the night was spent pacing, wired, gnashing her teeth, and drinking everything she had in the apartment (a half bottle of red wine, a six-pack of beer, and a glass of flat champagne), and then next morning she finally fell asleep just as Justin awoke and began to cry, crying his anger at being left with a stranger; even though that morning was pure torture, what with the worst hangover of her life and a twisting, screaming angry baby, even though she had to call in sick for two days following, despite all that, as soon as she felt better, she returned to work and called Miranda to watch Justin and they all went out to party.

New Hobbies

Chance stands at the far corner of the corral, next to the gate. He is facing away from the barn, facing out towards the drive. It has become his customary spot. He stands there for hours sometimes, ears pricked, just looking intently down the dirt driveway. As if he is waiting for someone.

I made a big mistake with him this morning. He was standing there, staring down the road when I came into the corral with the halter and lead, and brushes in the other hand. I called to him softly as I approached but he was entranced in his vigil. I was almost to his shoulder before he noticed me and exploded. He wheeled away, snorting loudly, and galloped, bucking and twisting, to the opposite corner of the corral. He paced there, with white-rolling eyes, full of mistrust and fear. He breathed heavily and ran back and forth while I stood there frightened and dismayed, ashamed at myself and awed by him. He was a wild mustang, pacing along the fence line, tail flagged high, sides heaving, nostrils red. He was scary, magnificent. With shame I realized I had just taken several steps back in our relationship. He didn't know me yet, there was no basis for trust. And I had just given him reason to mistrust me, sneaking up on him like that. Horses are prey animals, and humans, with our front-set eyes, are predators. That's one of the essential things to keep in mind when dealing with them, especially the wild ones. I knew that from my research. Now I had to start over, convince Chance that I was not going to eat him.

I waited patiently for him to calm down. Then I left the corral for some carrots. I was going to resort to bribery to break the ice. It worked. I fed him carrots from my hand, and although his skin quivered with the first touch, he let me stroke him all over, and eventually I started in with the currycomb. All seemed well until I haltered him and began to lead him to the gate, intending to take him to the round pen. At the gate he backed up and then refused to go through. I tugged and cajoled and he dug in his hooves and stiffened his neck. He stared off into the distance as if confronting me with his body, but ignoring me with his gaze. I tapped him with my training crop and he bolted through, too fast, and at the end of the lead, spun around facing me. This was not going too well. I knew I should make him go back and forth through the gate until he did it calmly. I clumsily tugged on the lead, towards the opening and waved the crop, but instead of going forward he backed up. A couple more replays of this I was panting and my heart was racing and I gave up, deciding it might be easier to get him into the round pen. I managed to get him pointed in the right direction down the drive. His ears pricked up and he walked along eagerly, a little too fast. I tugged his lead and he'd slow but then surge forward again in a few steps, crowding me. At the turn he stopped. The round pen was to the right, the drive continued to the left. He wanted to go left. He planted roots and stood like a bronze tribute to the stubborn horse. To get him moving I went to his flank and guided his nose towards me and tapped his hind-quarters. He obediently stepped over, the inside hind crossing over the outside. I spun him in circles this way in both directions then assertively started towards the right fork. He followed, but lagging behind now. I tried to get him up to my shoulder—I didn't like his head where I couldn't see it, behind me. But instead of like a feather, he felt heavy on the lead rope.

I know what happened. I lost his respect. Up till now, he'd given me the chance to prove I am worthy, dependable. But I seem to be failing him at every turn. It kills me. He's an awesome horse; he has power, smoothness, sensitivity, beauty, willingness, and intelligence. But these are gifts he can choose not to bestow. Chance has to want to be with me, choose to be with me. I have to gain his respect or it will be all over. He isn't tall but he weighs almost a thousand pounds and could kill me in an instant if he chose; without his respect I won't even be safe around him. It is not a game. But I am already passionately in love with this horse. I can't bear failure, or the thought that he won't love me back. So we continue to the round pen, and through its gate, and I untie the lead rope and make him circle the pen. I am going to win him over. It doesn't matter how long it takes. I am happy to spend all day, every day with Chance. As he begins to respond to me in the round pen, my confidence returns and euphoria with it. Chance flows to my cues and I think: there is nothing that this horse can't do. I have more to learn than he does. I just have to make myself worthy.

I am a woman obsessed. Everyday I rush through my chores to be with Chance. I muck his corral and change his water and then groom him and take him to the round pen, or for walks around the property. I am not quite ready to ride him again. When I relayed this lack of progress to Lee, she said she thought it was smart; and reiterated her belief that mustangs were never quite as dependable as other horses and even though Chance seemed docile, you just never knew. So with that in mind, I am contented to slow my calendar of goals: trail riding, training him to harness, riding in the Fourth of July parade. But it is okay, more than okay; the walks with Chance through the arroyos and hills are exquisite. He follows gently, stepping carefully. If we find a patch of still-green grass under a tree, I perch on a boulder and let him graze. I walk him over sage so it tickles his belly and under tree branches that graze his head. We surprise a family of deer and flush quail, and Chance never loses his wits. Meanwhile I keep working with him in the round pen on ground exercises. Over obstacles, dragging objects, waving plastic bags and lariats. Letting the dogs run around his feet.

When I'm not with Chance, I am on the phone or the computer, delving into the world of horses, especially the wild ones. The political firestorm set off by the slaughter of the BLM mustangs is blazing. I get e-mails and calls from people who have read my articles in the paper. Soon I have a circle of horse people, new friends and fellow zealots. We trade information and I begin another article. One of the people I talk to is a wild horse and burro specialist with the BLM. He tells me of an urgent need for a home for sixty horses at the BLM facility in Ridgecrest. These sixty mares, geldings, and four stallions—some were from Chance's herd—were headed for the auction block. I decide to drive up there and to take pictures and do an article—maybe someone will read it and rescue some of the horses.

    I get up an hour earlier and spend an hour with Chance. As I rub him goodbye I tell him I am going to go see his family and that I'm going to try to help save them. He yawns.

    Driving through the desert I let my mind wander. I think about Chance and imagine riding him through the sage. I am ready—

we are ready—to do it soon. I picture that first gallop down the straight part of the road, and taking him to the pond for a drink. And I think about the mustangs I am about to see. What a travesty if they are bought by the killers. Why can't someone just take them all, and turn them loose on pasture? Somebody should, I fume. Somebody with money, and land…

I feel like God just slapped me upside the face. I have money. And land. I had mouthed off in print that these horses deserve saving. Instantly, I know what I will do. I will fence the upper hundred acres, dig a new well, excavate a pond, put up shelters. There is some grazing and plenty of trees for shade, a spring. It is hilly and rocky but there are flat saddlebacks and canyon bottoms and it is perfect terrain for a wild horse herd. I can see it already. I am grinning and driving too fast. I can't wait to get there and whip out my checkbook and buy every horse that needs a home.

Thank you, Hank, I say, and I can just see him, smiling. He is happy with my decision. He'd made sure I had money not just for essentials, but for some craziness as well. It will be hideously expensive—not buying the horses, but fencing a hundred acres and installing gates and shelters, which means road-building and ground moving. Feeding troughs and watering fountains; unimaginable amounts of hay to be constantly supplied, and vet care and the farrier… but what am I going to do with all that money anyway?

Don't start having second thoughts. It's a grand idea.

Aha… is this my new hobby?

Perhaps it's a vocation.

I just love the idea.

Then go for it.

But maybe it's selfish. Maybe I should use the money to help orphans, or something.

Oh, please.

Yeah. I am going to do it. Hank would have loved this idea.

Yes. He wanted you to be happy.

I get it. With sixty-one horses, I won't have time to fall back into depression. That's the plan, right?

Caring for others allows you to be gentle. Maybe some of the gentleness will rub off on yourself.

Gentleness. For some reason, that word, if it is a word, makes me cry. I feel baptized with each tear. A dark heaviness falls from my center, leaving a clean emptiness, warm and buoyant. If this is healing, it doesn't feel half bad. I speed on through the cactus-spiked landscape, towards sixty wild horses.

I am in luck; the BLM guy, Dave, is there when I arrive. He looks like an extra in a cowboy movie: probably in his mid-sixties, he is short, slightly bow-legged, and wears an ancient sunburned hat with a wide brim and a silver mustache that curls up at the ends. His eyes though, and his grin when I see it, are years younger than the rest of him.

He thanks me for writing the articles on the wild horse legislation. I thank him for his articulate contribution. When I'd interviewed him on the phone, he'd told me that he personally had adopted five mustangs. He had talked to me about the nature of the wild horses, saying they were exceptionally curious, smart, and bonded strongly with their humans. Now that I had Chance, I agreed.

I don't blurt out my intentions right away. We go to look at the horses. They are held in a bare, fenced area.

We look over the mares and geldings, the stallions separated by huge metal fences. The youngest among them are a few three year-olds, the rest are older. They are in almost all colors. There are sorrels, like Chance, and black ones, grey ones, buckskins, roans, and paints.

They're all from Nevada, from five different herd areas, Dave informs me. He pointed as he named them: "That bunch are from Calico Mountains, that band there from Buck Bald. Over there, the Maverick- Medicine herd, and these here from the Jackson Mountain range."

"That's where my horse is from," I say, excited.

"How do you like him?" Dave asks.

"He's just awesome."

"That's real good. Yeah, those inmates do a good job of training."

"Yes, they surely do," I answered automatically, thinking about the fat girl. Wishing again I could ride like her. But not about to admit any of this to Dave.

It seemed to be as good a time as any to launch into my proposition.

"You want to take all of 'em?" he says when I finish, his eyebrows shooting under his hat brim.

"Yes. All of them. I would need some time to set up the facilities."

"Uh-huh. Now, you know most of these here ain't the pick of the litter so to speak. We got a blind one, coupla more blind in one eye, a half-dozen are lame, one has a broken windpipe, and a bunch of 'em are past twenty. And most of 'em are just plain ordinary."

"That's all perfectly okay," I say, with conviction. I look at the horses again. There are a bunch of younger ones, good-looking ones. The old ones, with sunken eye sockets and swayed backs, are in the minority. Surely Dave knows there are a lot of good horses here too. Besides, that doesn't matter. Saving their sweet lives. That matters. My heart lifted.

"I want them all," I say again.

"Then we'd best go on up to the office and chat," he says.

* * *

"Destiny, would you be into helping me and Lou and Josie do some work in a studio down on Chester? It's a recording studio of a friend of mine. He's replacing his board and so we'll be wiring it up for him."

"It'll be fun," Lou called, grinning through a twist of blue solder-smoke.

"It should take a week or so, after that you can have some time off, I promise."

"No problem," Destiny replied.

It was fun. The recording studio was like an ongoing party. Musicians drifted in and out, there was always music, and booze, cigarettes and pot, and lots of drugs. Lou and Josie and Destiny took to doing their bumps openly, and on occasion took a toke if a joint was passed their way. Still, the work got done, somehow.

The second day a band dropped in, four guys with tattoos and piercings and crazy hair. One of them, Destiny thought was cute. He had long, dark hair and a soul patch, snakes and thorns on his arms, but beautiful brown eyes and a sweet smile. Almost every time Destiny glanced up from her work, he was looking at her. She sat straighter, and when she went to the bathroom to pee, she brushed her hair and put on lipstick. After a while, he came over and stood next to her.

"Nice work," he said, touching the newly soldered joints with a slender finger. He wore heavy rings, one was a skull, one a dark, flashing stone, one of twisted silver.

"Thank you."

"I'm Mitch."

"Destiny."

"It could be," he said, grinning widely.

"No, I mean, that's my name," she said, feeling a blush of embarrassment, or excitement, heat her cheeks.

"Yeah, I knew that." he said, smiling that sweet smile. They chatted a while about the new studio. Then he invited her to come hear his band play.

"Sure! We'll come," Lou called, butting in as usual.

So that Saturday they all went to a club, the Kennel. Mitch had put them on the guest list. The club was dark and smelled of beer. The first band was deafeningly loud and the lyrics were unintelligible, and when Mitch's band, Frenzy, appeared, it was more of the same. But the beat was there, and they all danced until they were sweaty and then drank and danced some more. Destiny could swear that Mitch looked at her while they were playing. He played the guitar, and although Destiny couldn't tell if the music was any good or not, she was very sure that Mitch looked very sexy on stage, with his skinny but muscled arms and his tight leather pants. Each time Frenzy finished a song and the crowd applauded and whistled, Destiny felt proud. After the set, Mitch and two of the other band members came and sat with Destiny and the Bees. Mitch sat next to her, and right off the bat put his arm over her shoulders. The live music had been replaced by recordings, but the volume was still intense, and when Mitch spoke, he had to put his mouth right up too Destiny's ear. She could feel his breath on her neck and it made her shiver. The band got up to play another set, and Greg and Josie got up to leave but Lou said she would stay. She had her eye on the band's singer.

After the second set, it was late, the club was closing and Destiny knew she should get home to Justin. But when Mitch asked her to come with him just for a while to the after-party, she found herself saying, just for a little while. As long as Lou was coming too, it would be okay, and stupid Michelle could just put up with Destiny being a little late for a change. So they all piled in the van, crowded with amplifiers and guitar cases and the drum set. Drove a few blocks to the warehouse where the band had its rehearsal space. It was a big open loft, with battered, stained couches and a giant wooden spool for a table. A fridge and a stereo rounded out the décor. There was loud music and strong pot and bottles of imported beer and vodka. All of a sudden, Destiny realized she was quite drunk and then Mitch kissed her right there on the couch in front of everybody. It was a good kiss, not too wet or anything but it made Destiny dizzy.

"Gotta go," she said, and staggered up.

"Hang on there, I'll take you home, "Mitch said.

"But… Lou," Destiny managed to say.

Lou came over and said, "I'll come with you. If you want."

"I'll get her home all right," Mitch said.

"Iss okay," Destiny said. Lou looked sharply at Mitch and said you better take good care of her.

"Cross my heart and hope to die," he said.

Mitch and Destiny went outside and got into a different car and she was able to give him semi-coherent directions to her apartment. On the way, with the window rolled down and the air rushing at her face, Destiny sobered up somewhat. When they got home, she'd do a bump and feel okay, she thought.

Michelle was openly mad at being kept so late. It was two hours after the time Destiny had promised to be home. So she gave her an extra twenty bucks and was relieved when the sitter left looking a bit mollified. She went to Justin's room and peeked in. He was sleeping on his side, his thumb in his mouth. His cheeks sucked in and out. Destiny tiptoed over, trying very hard to keep her balance, and gently pulled his thumb out. She leaned over and kissed him, careful not to fall over and crush him. She turned to leave and Mitch was leaning in the doorway.

"Beautiful kid," he whispered. Destiny smiled and closed Justin's door and they went down the hall. She got them beers and they went to the living room. Destiny fished her little bottle of crystal from her purse and prepared a bump. Offered a rolled up bill to Mitch. He didn't decline. Next Destiny had her hit, and she was right, it made her feel instantly better. The dizziness went away and she was actually ready for another beer. They talked and talked and then he began telling her that she was beautiful and kissed her some more. His hands moved slowly over her. He unbuttoned her blouse and undid her bra and kissed her breasts and said more things about how she was soft and sexy. Destiny was overcome with emotion; it felt so good to be touched, to be acknowledged. The next thing she knew they were making love on the couch. It got faster and faster and he rubbed her in the right place and she was almost having an orgasm, but couldn't, and it seemed Mitch might be experiencing something similar because they went on and on until all Destiny felt was sore and numb at the same time.

Finally they stopped without reaching a conclusion, and Mitch turned away and fell asleep. Destiny was wide-awake though, and wrestled her arm from under him, got up, paced, drank and thought about Mitch and what it would be like to be his girlfriend. Being with Mitch—that meant she was cool, sexy. He was, after all, very gorgeous and the ultimate in cool—a musician! She envisioned making him breakfast in the morning, spending Sundays with him, they'd take Justin to the park maybe. Evenings when he didn't have a gig, they could watch TV like a regular couple. She imagined him coming in the door, saying, "Hey baby, I'm home." He'd serenade her with his guitar after they'd made love. She admitted to herself that she had been lonely. She was kind of getting tired of all the late nights and partying with the Bees. The drugs were starting to be a necessity instead of a welcome indulgence. It would be good to settle down a little, have a relationship. The fact that Mitch drank a lot, and took drugs and dreamed of being a big rock star, that he had snakes and thorn tattoos, didn't seem at all at odds with her fantasies.

WILD HORSES

The total peace of my hacienda is a thing of the past. Every day at sunrise, trucks come roaring up the drive, overfilled with fence posts, lumber, and the workers I've hired. A giant backhoe, like a yellow mechanical dinosaur, rests at night in my drive. A chemical toilet has been installed next to the barn, doing little to improve my view from the terrace. All day the sounds of the backhoe, trucks, and men shouting and hammering drive my dogs crazy and they spend the days barking impotently inside the house. It's impossible to write and so I asked Charlie for a couple of weeks off. I feel useless, and on the third day I simply demand the foreman to put me to work. His name's Len. He has a handlebar mustache and a beer belly, but his reputation is good: he works his crew hard and charges fairly. You want to work? he asks me dubiously. I say yes. I know he thinks about liability and whether I'm going to ask for a discount. I know he'd rather I limit my contribution to bringing lemonade and cookies and signing checks.

"Well, I guess you can help set posts," he said.

Wild horse enclosures are supposed to be six feet tall, made of sturdy iron pipe or wood. But I'm fencing such a large area—one hundred acres—that BLM Dave advised me I can use woven wire fencing, supported and topped by thick wooden posts. In addition, I have planned for another two acres to be cross-fenced with corrals. Each will have a shelter and there will be four additional large shelters scattered around the big pasture. To construct these, roads have to engineered and then sculpted with the backhoe. And as everything began to take shape, I balanced my checkbook one night and realized I would spend about three hundred thousand dollars. It was daunting but I was still in good shape financially. Dave had called to remind me that some of the mares— about a dozen—were pregnant. My herd would increase, come spring. But it had occurred to me that since this was a sale, not an adoption, that I was free to sell any of the horses in the future. I had visions of training some of the prettier ones, and maybe selling them for good prices to good homes, thus off-setting some costs in the future.

Len drove me down the newly cut road. The backhoe had carved a swath through the sage in a fairly straight line running east to west. The workers were spread in small groups. Half were out of sight down another new road, building shelters. Ahead was a slowly driving pickup. One guy was in the back, tossing out posts every ten feet. Two other guys followed, driving a small tractor hauling a noisy cement mixer. One guy held the post in a pre-drilled hole, the other poured the concrete.

"Doc Corcoran here wants to work," Len yelled as we rolled up next to the pickup. Both trucks stopped and we got out. I greeted Frank and TJ.

TJ said, "Well, we don't need three..."

"Then come on, Frank," Len said, sounding weary at all the commotion I was causing.

So Frank went off in the truck with Len. I pulled on my gloves and said, "Show me what to do."

"Shoot," TJ said. He was so skinny he'd disappear if he turned sideways. Otherwise he was a good-looking young fellow in a big, new-looking cowboy hat. "You sure you want to be doin' this?" he said.

"If I can't keep up, you can send me packing."

He shrugged and spat tobacco juice into the dust. "You got it," he said.

It was simple. All I had to do was pick up a post and heave it into the hole, try to hold it level. TJ shoveled the wet cement. It was strangely intimate—as I held the posts in place, and he shoveled, our faces were less than a foot apart. TJ kept his eyes on the posts. After the first dozen though, he seemed to relax. Apparently he felt I could cut the mustard.

A few more posts and suddenly they get a lot heavier. I grunt, struggling to pick them up. TJ waits impatiently, his jaw working over the cud in his cheek. I begin to wish it were lunchtime. Just when I think I might have to ask to stop for a while, TJ says, "Taking a break after this one."

"Thank god," I mutter under my breath, collapsing onto the ground. It feels blissful, even the pine needle poking my ass.

"So you're gettin' some horses?" he says, squatting on a log in the shade of an oak tree.

"Mustangs."

"Huh."

"Do you ride?"

"Well, yup, I do a little ropin'."

"Have you had any experience with mustangs?"

"Naw," he says, his tone making it clear he didn't think he'd missed anything.

"You're more of a quarter-horse person."

"Yes ma'am."

"Call me Sara Beth."

"Yes ma'am."

"Did you see my horse down at the barn?"

"Yep."

"He's a mustang."

"No kiddin'. He's a nice lookin' colt."

"Thanks."

There is a slightly uncomfortable pause. "We best be getting back to work," TJ says. "Don't want to make the boss lady mad."

"That's for sure," I agree.

That night I have cause to regret my impulsive participation in the fencing project. Bending and lifting the posts all day results in a spinal agony and I can't lift my arms over my head. Fortunately, I find an old prescription from the dentist. I take a pill and a hot shower and fall into an instant sleep on Hank's side of the bed.

There are too many horses and not enough fence. There is a gap as wide as a barn and if the horses get out they could fall over the cliff. Hank appears in the truck. I'll get more posts, he says. The horses are galloping towards the gap. Don't go, I say, don't go. I can do it. I spread my arms to fill the gap, to ward off the galloping herd. It works! They swerve off, flowing away, back into the safety of the pasture. When I look back, Hank is disappearing in the truck. Don't go, I yell. Hank!

As if I am an eagle flying above, I see his truck zoom down the paved road towards town, then he is suddenly on the highway. The sky darkens and it begins to rain.

No! I scream as an approaching car begins its swerve into his lane. But I can do nothing to change what happens and I see it all, just like I've imagined it a thousand times: the car smashing, the metal screeching, the truck rolling, and my poor Hank mauled like he is in the grip of a giant pit bull until he is bloody, limp, and still.

I jolt awake, drooling and sweating, my throat aching with unvoiced screams.

I unclench my fingers from the crumpled pillow and tell myself it was a dream. The problem with that is, this dream is real. As if it has just happened, fresh horror and shock of losing Hank hits me like a mule kick. Time doesn't heal shit, I think. Tears and sobs overtake me and I weakly sit up, mechanically shuffle to the bathroom, and stand, holding on to the sink, and cry until my nose is so clogged I can't breathe. I try to blow and splash water on my face. If Hank were here to put his arms around me. If I could just hear his voice. See his face. I stagger back to the bedroom and get dressed, and leaving the dogs inside, go out into the night. I go down to the corral and call to Chance as I approach. He's at his corner, staring down the drive. He turns his head and whickers softly.

"Hey Beautiful, hey Chance." I unlock the gate and go to him. He regards me calmly. I see the moon in his eyes. His silk-smooth coat is cool on his back, warm under his belly. I put my arms around his neck. His sweet grass breath slowly blows away the smog of my pain.

* * *

One day, no different, no more tedious or boring than any other, Destiny wigs out. Her feet ache, standing on the line, but they always did. The boxes move along just like they always do, it wasn't like anyone made the line move faster or anything. It is ten forty-three on the big clock and Destiny is thinking about how long it is until lunch, and after lunch how long until the blessed quitting time and suddenly she quite simply has had enough. She stands still and lets some boxes pass without packing them, causing Marciella on her left to swear in Spanish. Everyone begins staring meanly at her and she backs up, a silly, apologetic grin on her face, and then turns and runs out, slamming through the door to the hall to the lockers; with trembling fingers she works the combination and opens the metal door and grabs her purse. Now she hears yelling and someone walking rapidly towards her. She almost, for a second, reconsiders and thinks about going back, apologizing profusely and taking her place on the line. But she doesn't. She turns and runs, out the back door into the parking lot and keeps going, running three blocks looking over her shoulder as if they would actually bother coming after her.

Destiny slows to a walk, breathing hard. It takes another whole block before her heartbeat returns to normal. She feels elated and frightened all at once. What has she done? Without the job from hell there is no money, there will be no place to live; her next residence will be a cardboard box. But that job was killing her. If that is all there is to life she might just as well kill herself. Seriously. She almost starts crying, feeling intensely sorry for herself. None of this is her fault. Oh, sure, she's made some bad choices. Okay, a lot of bad choices, more than most people seemed to make. But shoot, it isn't like she comes from a privileged home or anything. And she didn't deserve jail the first time, but that fact had sure made a difference when she was in front of the judge the second time. That judge looked at Destiny's record, convicted of grand theft, and the fact that she'd had her baby taken away for thirty days and saw: a loser. A career criminal. A really bad mother. So why not take her kid? Why not throw her in prison for six whole years of her life?

Snap out of it, she tells herself. What's past is past. I got to be worrying about right now.

She has nowhere to go. The last place she wants to be is alone, in that crummy room. If she goes back there right now, she just might kill herself for real. She opens her purse and counts her money. Great. A whole seven dollars and twenty-eight cents. She stops at the corner, unable to decide whether to cross the street, or turn right. Then she realizes where she is. She's walked all the way downtown. She is only two blocks from the library. She has her social security card and her rent receipt in her wallet; those are enough to get her a library card.

She gets the card without any problem and spends some time browsing the magazines. They are brand-new, not all wrinkled and nasty like the ones in prison. Then she notices some people—even a little kid—working on some computers. She wanders over and reads a sign that says using the computers was free and you could ask for help. So she goes back to the desk and shyly asks if somebody could show her what to do. A hippie-looking guy, in a Hawaiian shirt and longish, gray hair says he'll show her. "It's easy, don't worry," he says.

At first it isn't, he uses a lot of words and acronyms that are totally new. But then, all of a sudden, she does see that it's easy. She says, thanks, I think I got it. The guy smiles and casually pats her on the shoulders like she is in kindergarten or something. It makes her want to cry again; it is such a sweet, innocent touch. He leaves to go back behind the desk and Destiny takes a deep breath and begins to click.

She clicks on the internet and types in, one cautious letter at a time: WILD HORSES.

She finds a lot of "websites." She browses delightedly, reading about different people who have adopted mustangs. She studies the pictures. Destiny is looking for Prince, of course, but she doesn't admit it to herself. She is just looking, learning. Then she finds a "link" to a newspaper story, and reads it. She can't believe that some mustangs have actually been slaughtered for human food! Varney had told her it could happen, and it had happened. Now she doesn't want to cry. She's mad. Kill those creeps that would buy a mustang—any horse—and send it to be slaughtered. The story grips her unlike anything she's ever read in a newspaper. It is written differently, too, more like reading a book, not like reading a regular newspaper story. Destiny does something she's never done—she scans back to the top of the page to read the writer's name. Sara Beth Corcoran, Special to the Courier, it says. A woman, that figures, Destiny thinks. It would take a woman to write so sensitively about the mustangs. She reads the story all over again, and then stares a long time at the pictures. One is of wild horses grazing in some big meadow, with blue mountains behind them. One is of a little palomino colt, looking straight at the camera. And one is of a silhouette of a horse in a big corral with part of a fancy barn showing. Destiny leans in and squints. That horse. It sure looks like Prince. The caption reads "One of the lucky ones, this BLM mustang enjoys his adopted home." Is it really him? It is impossible to say. He stands in profile, so she can't see his blaze. The silhouetting makes it impossible to tell his color or see the stripes on his legs. But it looks enough like her Prince that Destiny prints out the whole story even though it will cost her a dollar for each color page. Three whole dollars.

When it finishes printing she gathers up the pages and decides to write a letter. She exits the internet and brings up the writing program.

Dear Sargent Varney, (she writes, one letter at a time)

It is Destiny Tubb here writing. I hope you are doing good. I wanted to thank you for everything. I loved working with the horses. I am doing okay sinse my release from Frontera. Today I quit my job tho. I cant find a desent job. I am willing to work very hard. I have a question. If you were me, what would you do?

Thank You for Everything,

Destiny Tubb

She adds in her address, and because she doesn't know about the spell-checking option, prints it out knowing there are spelling mistakes. She feels optimistic until she holds the printed letter in her hands. What does she expect Varney to do? He won't be able to help her. But she wants him to read the thank-you part anyway. She thinks about rewriting it but here the hippie guy is, coming up to her.

"Sorry, but there are people waiting to use the computer. You can work indefinitely as long as no one's waiting. But if there are we have to limit your time. You've been on for two hours," he says, looking truly regretful.

"That's okay, I'm done."

"Here, I'll help you log off," he says.

Destiny doesn't bother watching what he is doing. "Thanks," she says, gathering up her purse and the documents. "Do I pay you for these now?"

"At the desk," he answers. She follows him over.

"So did you find what you were looking for?" The hippie asks as he takes her three dollars and twenty-five cents.

What had she been looking for? Prince? A connection, if virtual, to horses? A reason to keep breathing? Destiny smiles bitterly and shakes her head. "No," she says. "But it was interesting. Thanks."

"Come back and try again."

"Yeah, maybe," Destiny says. But she doubts she'll be back. He looks so sorry for her that she asks him for an envelope and he gives her one. She thanks him again and leaves the library. The post office is just down the block. She'll mail the letter to Varney before she changes her mind.

* * *

The days whiz by and finally the acreage is fully fenced, the shelters are completed in the pasture, and the pond filled. The backhoe is gone, the crew left yesterday, happy with their bonuses for finishing on time; and peace has returned to my ranch. Writing all the checks only made me feel terrific.

Excited and anxious, I barely sleep the night before the horses are to arrive. Still I bolt awake at five, wanting to walk the fence lines one more time. I set off with the dogs just as the sky begins to lighten. The new roads already look like they belong. The fence is taut and straight, as straight as the crazy terrain allows. The pasture isn't bare. Beyond the swath cut for the fence line there is sage, oat grass, saw grass, live oak, juniper, foxtail, yucca, and trees, plenty of trees: gnarly oaks, many-branched pinion, and graceful long-needle pines. Even the occasional lone Ponderosa. There are open spaces too, where the trees thin and the shrubs grow low and sparse, places where a nice gallop could be arranged. The spring-fed pond is almost an acre wide, and has a nice sandy approach along the dry creek bed. I detour down one of the roads winding through to a shelter. I could have put all the shelters on the side closest to my house; it would undoubtedly be more convenient. But I want the horses to have as much freedom of choice as possible, which is why I scattered the shelters around the whole of the pasture. How would I know where a mustang would want to be in the snow or during a drenching rain or a terrific windstorm? So some shelters are on high ground, some under trees, one up against a rock monolith. I would use the connecting roads to deliver hay and feed to different areas. I reach the first shelter and it looks good. Three-sided, a roll-shingle roof and heavy plywood sides covered with redwood paneling. I circumnavigate, looking for nails on the ground. Am reassured when I don't find any.

I retrace my way back to the fence line and by walking fast, work my way all around by eight o'clock. I have barely finished wolfing down some toast and coffee when I hear the gate alarm. The horses are here!

I buzz the gate open and run outside. A caravan labors up the long drive, six big diesel trucks hauling long stock trailers. Lee and Charlie bring up the rear, their red truck dwarfed by the others. I'd been on the phone daily with Lee who was as excited about the project as I. Charlie wanted me to write a story about it, and he was bringing his fancy camera to take the pictures.

The caravan wheezes to a stop. In the silence of the stilled engines, I hear Chance whinny, high and loud, imperiously—demanding to know who has intruded upon his territory. The door of the first truck swings open and BLM Dave hops out, followed by another BLM employee, Carol. We say our hellos.

From inside the trailer comes the banging of impatient hooves striking metal. A shrill whinny, answered from within another trailer.

"Look here, Doc," Dave says, handing me a thick clipboard. "We got 'em all on this list, and Carol took pictures of each of 'em to attach to their files. 'Cause reading those brands can be hard at first. Thisaway you'll be able to tell who's who."

I realize I have been thinking of the horses as a group. Sixty mustangs. But they aren't. As much as a horse—any horse—is a herd animal, they are all individuals. Each mare or gelding or stallion has its unique history, its own opinions and prejudices, fears and favorite things. I hadn't even thought about the importance of figuring out "who was who." How embarrassing. I thank Carol profusely. She looks pleased with herself.

"Let's get these boys unloaded before they punch a hole," suggests Dave.

He directs the driver until the first trailer is backed up to the gate of the holding corral, ten thousand square feet—which in turn opens, through a wide gate, into the big pasture.

"Git your camera ready," says Dave. Charlie answers that he is all set.

Dave calls to Carol and the driver. They stand on both sides of the trailer doors and slide big bolt locks free. "Here they come," Dave says, and simultaneously the ramps are swung down. For a moment, the horses all blink at the opening without moving. Then it seems like they all move at once—leaping, stumbling, sliding—from the trailer into the enclosure. I have been holding my breath but let it out when the dust clears and there are ten horses, all on their feet and none seeming the worse for wear. They surge around the corral a few times then head for a pile of hay in the center of the pen and fall to eating.

We discuss how to proceed. I wonder if we should let them into the big pasture in groups or all at once.

"They already know each other," Dave points out. "I think we can keep putting 'em in here then later you can turn 'em loose. You want to keep the stallions separate until you decide who to cut and who you want out there makin' babies."

I agree, grateful there is someone who seems to know what to do. So the process is repeated until the first five trailers are empty and fifty-six horses fill the corral. Then the stallions are unloaded one at a time into the cross-fenced corrals. The first is a light gray, almost white fellow, with a proud line to his neck and a silver mane and tail. The second is his opposite: a black stallion with a narrow white-strip blaze. He has feathery feet and a profusion of black mane, shiny like a raven's wing. His tail sweeps the ground and his forelock hides his eyes.

"He's pretty, but quick as a snake so be careful," Carol advises. I nod, wide-eyed, at the stallion as he paces his corral, whinnying and snorting. The next is a golden dun, smaller than the others. He has a distinct stripe down his back like Chance's. The last stallion is a paint, chestnut and white. He is well put together and just darn pretty.

"We call him Piute," said Carol.

That's a good name, I say. I'll keep it. What about the others?"

"I call that black devil Pirate," Dave says. "The others don't got no names." He laughs, a rusty sound. "You'll have quite a time naming fifty-eight horses, huh? Well, you're a writer, so it'll be easy."

"I don't know about that," I laugh. "I had a hard time naming my dogs."

"We could do a contest," Charlie suggests. "In the paper. We can print a few pictures a week and get the public to suggest names."

I say I love the idea. I ask if anyone wanted a cup of coffee, and they all do. The drivers join us and I bring coffee and cups and bagels and fixings out to the terrace. I ask Dave all the questions I'd thought of since my impulsive horse-buying trip. Is alfalfa hay best? What other feeds do they need? When is the vet due? How do you round them up for shots and such?

Dave explains all about the different hays and grains, and feed supplements which are unnecessary unless the horses are being worked hard or for babies and the old ones over twenty or so, and then only in winter. All the horses are current on their shots so they won't need more until spring. By then I should be able to catch them, halter them for the vet and farrier; if not, I'll need wranglers to drive the horses, one at a time, into a restraining chute.

"Once you get 'em into that big old pasture, they'll think they're back in the wild," he added. "So if you're gonna be gentling 'em, you'd best get on it soon, and every day. They got to be used to seeing you and bein' around you. Cut a few out at a time, work with those in your cross-fence. You got some help, dontcha?"

"Um, well, not yet," I say, distracted by all the information, suddenly feeling inadequate. I am trying to remember what he said about feeding bran... was it "be careful not to use too much water"? Or "make sure you use enough water"...

Carol snorts. "You ain't thinking you can do all these yourself," she says bluntly.

"Well, I... yes, I was going to hire somebody part-time," I lie. (Until now the thought has not occurred to me. Now it seems elementary.)

Carol and Dave exchange glances.

Lee speaks up. "I'll come up in the meantime, until you get somebody."

"Put an ad in The Western Horse," Carol says, a command, not a suggestion.

I'd seen the magazine, one of those free ones you could pick up at the feed stores. "Good idea," I say mildly. Carol is just being protective of these horses, so recently in her care. She probably thinks I'm an idiot, in way over my head. She is probably right.

Help Wanted

Later it occurs to Destiny that she could probably find out almost anything using that computer. For instance, she could find out about how to petition the court for custody of Justin. Or at least, how to get the right to visit him. But she knows that she'll have to improve her circumstances first, they would hardly give her Justin if she was living on the street. On the street. The idea makes her literally sick with fear. She hopes that she can still get her check from the factory tomorrow. Even though she'd walked off, she still had worked three days since her last check. All that remains of that paycheck is forty bucks, hidden in a Tampax box in the bathroom. But she should get almost one hundred twenty for the three days. So she'll have one hundred sixty dollars to her name. One hundred and sixty. The hotel was seventy five a week. That meant she'd be out on her butt in two weeks unless she got another job… and if she could stretch ten bucks into two weeks worth of food somehow… and not go anywhere on the bus, which was impossible if she expected to find a job. So, one week then. Here at Hotel Cockroach, you had to pay for at least a week in advance: "no day at a time shit, this ain't no ho house" as the manager had put it. Her heart beats faster as the wolves of hunger and homelessness howled their threats. Desperate ideas begin to form. She could go to Loreen's. But there'd be drugs there, and probably some ex-felon boyfriend. If she was caught in the vicinity of either, it would be go directly to jail, do not pass go, do not collect two hundred dollars. Besides, she wouldn't be welcomed with open arms. Her mother had visited her in prison exactly once, when she'd cried and cursed Destiny's stupidity, then said prison was too depressing and left. After that Loreen hadn't written a single letter or sent a card on Destiny's birthdays or even Christmas. Going back to the trailer would really be not much different than sleeping in a cardboard box, Destiny decides. At this point she was ready to risk going to Greg or Lou, begging for work, or a loan. But she had looked for their numbers in the phone book and found neither; these days everybody had cell phones. Justin's dad had disappeared off the face of the planet long ago. And Mitch was dead, just as dead as the guy that they had killed.

She has to face it; she is all alone, there isn't a single person in the world that would help her. Nobody at all gives a crap about her.

What do you do when you have no job, no food, no prospects?

Destiny finds out. You sleep a lot, and in between, you drink a lot of instant coffee, eat dry popcorn, and hang around places where you can get a free newspaper. (She gets banned from the coffee shop on the corner when she went in to take the leftover want ads two days in a row without buying anything.) You walk the streets hoping to see a Help Wanted sign. Like a wino, you park your butt on a bench and watch the buses pass because you have nowhere better to go. You count and re-count your dwindling stash of money. You feel sick each time you have to put coins in the telephone, each time you shell out bus fare, all on another fruitless attempt at employment. You count and re-count the days left before you are out on the street.

* * *

Lee stays after Dave and the caravan of trucks and trailers leave. Dave would drop Charlie back at his place on the way out of the canyon. I top off our coffee cups.

"You look good, Sara," she comments. "I do believe you're coming back to life.

"I've been working a lot outside."

"Bullshit. You're better, I can tell."

"If I'm better, it's due to Chance. I love that guy."

As if answering, Chance whinnies. An answering, challenging trumpet from the black stallion. We smile.

"I can't wait to see how he reacts when he sees his new buddies," she says.

"There are some here from his herd. I wonder if he'll know them?"

"It's just amazing, what you've done, saving all these horses, Siggy. So cool! That Carol chick was right though. You will need help. "

"I guess you're right."

"I wish I could think of someone. A nice, cute young cowboy."

I snort my disinterest in the young and cute part.

"But all the reliable ones have jobs," she shrugs. "The rest are a bunch of tweakers and users."

"I guess I'll have to take out an ad."

"You can do it online, that's how I sold my old saddle."

"Yeah, I will. Thanks."

"So, when are you gonna let them into the big pasture?"

"Now?" I shrug and grin.

"Yeah! Let's do it," Lee says, jamming her straw cowboy hat on her head. We stroll down to the holding corral and lean over the fence. The horses are calm, some grazing on hay, some drinking, most just standing around. My eyes and brain are insufficient to the task of appreciating them all as individuals. Amongst the plentitude, a few, though, catch my eye: a triplet of startlingly blue roan mares; a small, perfectly marked bay with a shining red mahogany coat; a tall chestnut gelding; a silver dun. A big, chunky buckskin, a pale palomino mare, obviously pregnant. A sorrel paint with a bald face. I look for the ones that were from Chance's herd. I see one that looks a little like him: an old mare with bony hips and a back swayed like a well-used couch is the same color as Chance, that red-tinged sorrel color. Her head has that same chiseled shape. Her mane and tail are flaxen like his, too.

"They're not all that bad looking," Lee says. "I mean, a few of 'em are older than the hills. But you got some pretty ones too." She pointed out the buckskin and the chestnut gelding, and a few others. "You could do something with those," she adds.

I tell her of my idea to train a few for sale.

"Yeah, you could, but your place is so cool, and now you've got all these horses. You could open a dude ranch or a camp for kids, too. Or do trail rides…"

I shudder at those ideas. Inviting a bunch of strangers onto my property was the last thing I thought I needed, and tell her so.

"Whatever. Your life," Lee says, without taking umbrage. "Come on, let's let 'em go. Want me to get the gate?"

I say sure.

She slips through the corral rails and fearlessly walks through the milling horses, parting them like Moses did the Red Sea.

Reaching the opposite end, she unhooks the chain and swings the gate to the pasture open.

"Come on, you scrub puppies!" she calls. "Gee up!"

The group nearest the open gate eyes it suspiciously. They begin inching towards it, then cautiously edge through. They sniff the ground and taste some dry grass. The apparent leader, that old sorrel mare, tosses her head and begins trotting, nosing and pushing the others farther into the pasture. Then all hell breaks loose. Suddenly the rest of the horses realize something like freedom is just on the other side of the open gate, and through it they surge, snorting, bucking, twisting. They gallop down the fence line and disappear out of sight. Like a mirage, all that remains is a huge cloud of dust and the diminishing sound of hooves pounding the earth.

"Come on!" yells Lee. I climb through the rails and we take off following the hoof prints. We are both panting when we finally catch up with them at the pond. A few stand knee-deep in the water, drinking. Some are rolling on the ground, sweeping dust over their bodies with their tails. Others are grazing and farther off, a group is playing. That is the only word for it—they'd gallop a short distance, then neck-wrestle, kick at each other, and rear up, pawing at the air.

Lee takes some photos with Charlie's camera. We perch on a big flat rock and watch them a long time, entranced. Finally, Lee says in a strange voice, "You did a good thing, girl."

I tear my eyes from the horses and look at Lee. Her eyes are shiny. She wipes a tear with her wrist. "They look so happy," she explains.

I throw my arm around her shoulder and we hug, content to not say much more.

Eventually the horses begin to explore, small groups wandering off into the trees. We follow some, watching them taste everything: pine needles, oak leaves, the grasses; we even see one licking a rock. After reaching an open, south-facing slope, they begin seriously grazing, and some lie down to doze in the sun.

Lee says she could watch the horses all day but has to get home to pick up her girls from the school bus. I can't believe it is two o'clock already. Guiltily, I realize my dogs haven't even gotten breakfast. I know I am in for some deserved dirty looks. At least I'd fed Chance. Poor Chance. He is probably curious as hell about what is going on, feeling left out, abandoned.

We hustle back to the house, say our goodbyes. As soon as Lee is headed down the drive, I go to Chance's corral. He stands at his usual corner, looking after Lee's disappearing truck. I call to him and he cocks an ear but doesn't even look at me. I let myself into the corral. I stroke his neck and he turns his head, nosing my hand with gentle lips.

"Don't worry, buddy. You're still Number One Mustang around here," I tell him.

Prove it, Chance seems to say as he nudges me. Where's my carrot?

That afternoon, reality and I come face to face. Feeding sixty-one horses is a chore. A big chore. A horse should receive a little over two pounds of forage for each ten pounds of body weight. That meant my mustangs, at a nine hundred pound average, should get eighteen pounds of feed a day, split into at least two feedings. But right now, many of the mustangs were still underweight from their time on the range. The forage in the pasture was sparse this time of year (in winter and spring, with the rain, the grass would provide most of their feed). So I decided to count the forage in the pasture as about twenty percent, and to feed them sixteen pounds a day per horse. Sixty horses times sixteen pounds was nine hundred and sixty pounds. That worked out to seven and half bales. The hay bales weighed one hundred and thirty pounds each. That was more than I did.

At least I'd had the foresight to buy the tractor and trailer. I pull up alongside the giant mountain of hay. I set an extension ladder and climb to the top of the pile. Slapping the hay hook into one of the topmost bales, I tug. It barely moves. I tug again, putting everything into it and am rewarded by an inch more movement. The spiky bales stick to each other as if they are made from some kind of Super-Velcro. Grunting and cursing, I heave and shove an inch at a time until the first of the damn things is poised over the edge. I give a mighty shove and it tumbles down. I'd planned to drop the bales right inside the trailer, but the bale has other ideas and misses the trailer entirely, bouncing first off the seat of my brand-new tractor, covering it in alfalfa buds, then hitting the ground, bouncing some more, and ending up a good ten feet from the trailer.

Lovely, I say. I climb down the ladder to move the tractor out of the line of fire. If I don't want the tractor crushed I'll obviously have to dump the bales on the ground, then load them in a separate operation. I wipe off the alfalfa debris and start up the tractor; moving it well away. Then climb the ladder again. I am already exhausted. With a lot of grunting which rapidly becomes cussing, I manage to drop three more bales over the edge. They are scattered all over hell. I climb down, leaving the ladder in place. Then I realize I've left the hay hook up top. So back up the ladder I go, retrieve the damn thing, down. Move the tractor. I try to back up to the bales but the trailer insists on going off in the wrong direction. Finally I go forward and down the drive, turn around, then circle back. Park close to the first bale. Open the trailer doors. Get the hook and drag the bale closer. Then with a mighty effort lift one end up to the trailer bed. Lift the other end and push. Grudgingly it slides into the trailer. Success. I stand, panting, and put my hand to my lower back which is firing pain. I eye the remaining three bales balefully. Is that where that word comes from?

By the time I load the bales and crawl back into the tractor seat, I am whimpering. Drive down to the pasture fence. Get out, open the gate. Drive through, lock the gate behind me. Then cut open a bale—at least I'd thought to bring my pocketknife! I flake off about half the bale and throw the flakes in the hay rick. Get back on the tractor and drive down the pond road. A group of horses are at the pond. They eye my noisy conveyance warily, and move away as I come closer. But as soon as I start tossing the hay into the feeder they stop and turn to watch, ears pricked with interest. I dump the rest of that bale and half of the next. Drive off and as I look back the horses are already jockeying for positions on the hay. So it goes until I've distributed the hay in the other feeders, hoping everybody will be able to claim their share.

I drive back to the house trying to ignore my back, shrieking in pain. I still have to feed Chance and the stallions then the chickens and dogs (and the garden needs watering, badly). I have phone calls to make for the story I was writing for the paper. The housework—my floors were dusty and the fridge was gross, not to mention the piles of dirty laundry and a funky bathroom... I'd get around to it. Maybe tomorrow.

I rarely regret getting older. What I regret is doing it alone, without Hank. But now I wish desperately that I was in my twenties. Hell, I'll take early forties. But time has done its number on me. My joints ache, my back is marginally functional, especially up here without a decent chiropractor—and arthritis is getting a grip on my hands, which often loose their grip. I'm fairly strong for a sixty-four year old. But I am a shrimp, barely one-ten on a five-foot-three-inch frame, and I have to admit that I'm challenged by a one hundred-thirty-pound hay bale. But feeding the horses isn't optional, nor is cleaning up the corrals. I just have to make time for the good stuff: working on riding Chance, watching the horses, getting to know each and every one, playing with them, training them. I can do it, I think. It's all a matter of time management.

Three days later I still haven't gotten around to the housework. But I'd managed to keep all the animals fed, the garden watered, and I'd finished the story and sent it to Charlie. But I feel guilty about Chance, having abandoned our walks since the arrival of the new horses. So in the afternoon, instead of attacking the laundry, I head down to his corral.

He is in his usual spot, and when he doesn't come up when I call, I go to him. He stands while I halter him, but resists when I start to lead him to the gate. I back him and circle him and eventually he comes along, and I open the gate and lead him out. His head comes up and he whinnies as soon as we're through the gate. I start towards the round pen and he makes it clear that's not his choice of direction. He starts whirling, pulling back on the rope. My heart rate doubles and adrenaline pricks my armpits. I tug sharply on his halter, cooing, "Easy, boy, easy…" I get us to the round pen and exhale in relief as I close that gate.

Chance knows the routine and he goes in the direction I indicate, but his attention isn't on me, he's whinnying and listening to the answering calls from the stallions behind the barn. I give up and lead him back to his corral, which is even worse than the way out. He's practically dragging me. By the time I get him inside, and his halter off, I'm sweaty and completely out of breath, discouraged and pissed off.

I head to the barn for the afternoon feeding, wondering what went wrong. Sure, Chance was distracted by the new horses. He wants to see them, to try to beat them up, probably. But I still should be able to control him. It's suddenly clear that Chance doesn't completely—if at all—accept me as his leader. He doesn't respect me yet. I sigh, not knowing what to do differently. I reach the barn, mechanically climb the ladder, heave the bales to the ground.

On the way down the ladder my foot slips. I tip backwards, loose my grip, flail wildly for a terrifying moment, then manage to grab the ladder. It's too late, I am already falling. I fly backwards towards the cement barn floor, pulling the ladder down on top of me.

* * *

Destiny applies for jobs as dishwasher at a pancake house, house cleaner for a rich woman way out on Stockbridge, clerk at a discount tobacco store, clerk at a gas station-convenience store, janitor at an office building, ticket-taker at a movie six-plex. Nobody hires her. Maybe it is because of her address at the Hotel Cockroach, and the fact she doesn't have a phone. Maybe it is because she's fat. Or maybe she bears the stench of prison and the look of failure. She is coming to the end of her money. She has no more for rent and only two days left at the hotel before she'll have to pay up or get out. That morning she leaves early as usual, to find a newspaper and keep looking. As usual it is a frustrating, fruitless day. Her stomach is clenched against its emptiness as she walks back to the hotel a little before five o'clock. She hopes to scurry through the lobby avoiding contact with the desk clerk, who always seems to eye her with disapproval. But as she passes by the desk, he pulls his gaze from the little black and white TV tuned to Wheel of Fortune.

Hey, girlie. Mail call. He waves a big yellow envelope.

For her? It must be a mistake, she thinks, but approaches him and takes the envelope. Sure enough, it has her name on it. The return address has a box number and the address of the prison that used to be her home.

Got yourself a pen pal? the desk clerk leers.

Destiny shakes her head and retreats. "Thank you," she calls as she starts up the creaky stairs. She goes up them as fast as she can. Inside her room, she doesn't bother to sit or even catch her breath. Who could be writing her? Is she somehow in trouble?

It is from Varney. There is a letter, badly typed, and two magazines, horse-themed magazines. And folded within the letter, are ten twenty-dollar bills. Two hundred dollars!

Dear Miss Tubb,
Thanks for your letter. It's nice to know you learned to like working with horses. I always like to hear how you girls are doing when you get out. Sorry to hear you had to quit your job. I know it is not easy for some people being out. So here's a little just in case you need it. Don't worry about paying it back. It is not a loan it is a gift. Also here are some magazines and you might want to check them out.
Your friend,
Sgt. J. Varney.

She could hardly believe it. She was saved—at least for another two whole weeks.

* * *

It is pure chance that I have my cell phone in my vest pocket. When I regain consciousness, there on the barn floor, my first reaction is surprise that I'm alive. I think I dial 911 before the pain really hits. Then it comes like a tsunami—pain and fear. Am I permanently disabled? Am I going to die of some internal injury? The fear and pain is only surpassed by anger at my own carelessness. In one second everything can change. A second ago I'd been preoccupied with my trivial difficulties of having too much to do. Now the question is, will I ever be able to do any of the things I love ever again? I lie there moaning, overwhelmed with the breakers of pain rolling from my ankle to my hip to my arm. Waiting for that ambulance is the longest hour of my life.

It isn't as bad as it might have been. The doctors even say I am lucky. I am lucky to have procrastinated sweeping the barn—the cement was covered in a deep litter of hay that softened my fall. I have a fractured ankle (twisted in the ladder as I fell), a cracked elbow, purple-black bruises from knee to hip, and a good concussion. I have to stay in the hospital two days, then am released with a cast from above my toes to my shin.

Lee comes to drive me home.

"Thanks so much for looking after everything," I tell her.

"Always here for you, girl," she says.

"I owe you big time."

"You sure do," Lee laughs. "But I'm worried about ya. We have got to get you some help."

"I know, I realize that."

"Me and Charlie'll cover you in the meantime," she soothes, a true-blue friend.

✳✳✳

The euphoria of Varney's gift fades as quick as the money is sure to do. A reprieve—that's all it is. Like the lawyers when they get some poor guy on Death Row another couple of days, but then they go ahead and execute him anyway. Destiny just knows, here at the Hotel Cockroach, that her last darn meal will be popcorn since that is all she dares to eat. It is the absolute cheapest thing. Though she wishes over and over that it had butter. She doesn't even care that she must be losing weight. She's just hungry.

She is lying on the squeaky bed, popcorn bowl balanced on her stomach, flipping through one of the horse magazines Varney sent. There aren't any stories, just stuff about horse shows and who won what. But the advertisements are hypnotizing. Big beautiful barns, horse trailers with bedrooms, bathrooms, and microwaves! Silver-inlaid saddles and bridles and cool, cool boots and cowgirl clothes. And real estate ads for "horse properties". But the best ads are about the horses. The stallions whose sperms are worth hundreds of dollars! Wide-nostrilled, muscular, with arching necks and flying tails. And the horses for sale, some of those are photo ads. Destiny reads every one of them, then reads them all again. She pretends she's rich and can have any horse she wants. But it is so hard to decide! There is a beautiful pinto mare, for three thousand dollars: "6 yrs, excellent trail horse, has speed and does it all" and there is a silver dun mustang! "Green broke, loads, clips, ties, $900." A half-draft palomino mare looks real good too: "Awesome, sweet disp., English, Western, harness, show prospect, $7500."

Maybe I'm so rich, I don't have to choose, Destiny imagines, her brow frowning in concentration. I'll just get all three of them.

Heck, I'll get as many as I want, a whole herd of them! But she can't concentrate for long. Because to have horses you'd need a ranch, with a house or at least a trailer—but, wait, she swore she'd never live in a trailer again—anyway you'd need all that and a barn and fences and stuff. And she'll never be rich. She'll never be able to have a horse; she'll be lucky to afford her next bag of popcorn. Suddenly she is furious. Mad at life, mad at herself. Mad at Mitch. Mad at baby-daddy Danny; and of course, mad at Loreen. Mad at the California judicial system; and mad at Varney. What is he thinking?—to send her these magazines, full of unattainable dreams? She slams the magazine down in frustration. She covers her eyes with her hands and squeezes back tears. Even crying doesn't help. It just stuffs up her nose. Oh crap. Help me, she cries silently, to no one in particular. Then she makes it specific. "Dear Jesus. Please help me. I know I been stupid. But I want to do better. I want to live a good life. Please, I just want one more chance."

She doesn't expect any answer. She slumps down onto the stinky pillow, throws her arm over her eyes against the dull light from the skuzzy window, and falls into a defeated sleep.

The sound of winos shattering bottles in the alley below jolts her from a deathlike sleep hours later. The light is dim; the sun must be going down. Her eyes are crusty and her cheek is glued to the magazine. She sits up and rubs her eyes. Looks around the bleak room, so bleak that even the mellow setting sun's rays do nothing to improve it. Looks down at the stupid magazine. It is open to a dog-eared page of ads, not picture ads. A few ads have been circled in pencil. Destiny scans to the top of the column. HELP WANTED.

HELP WANTED: HORSE TRAINER/
BARN MANAGER/CARETAKER.
Live-in position available caring for 61 horses. Feeding, mucking, grooming, halter breaking, and saddle-training. Experience with horses a must. Also light housework required. Start immediately.

   Nice apartment over barn with own bath, kitchen and entrance, plus salary, neg.
980-421-9867
Box 238 Little Canyon, CA 93518

* * *

The day the ad comes out the phone rings off the hook. I screen out the obvious losers and end up making appointments to meet three applicants over the next couple of days.

By now, a week after my release from the hospital, I am painfully hobbling around on crutches, despite the prescription drugs. I'm practically useless. I can't carry much or go far. Lee and or Charlie were up twice a day to feed and do essential chores but with each visit my guilt increased. I hoped I would find someone to help right away before my friends decided they hated me and my sixty-one horses.

The first to show up is an eager-voiced person named Ned. He sounded okay on the phone, but in the morning when he arrives, I am instantly uneasy. It isn't just the fact that he looks like a troll. He is very short, almost dwarflike, and his hair is greasy, his face a caricature somewhere between Wallace Shawn and the kid who played the banjo in Deliverance. It isn't his repulsive physical appearance that puts me off, nor his halitosis which is unavoidable from my distance of about three feet. It is his manner; an arrogant, pushy demeanor and the assumption that he'd already won the job. A few things he says convince me that he doesn't even know shit about horses. I get more nervous the more he compliments my ranch, the house, the barn, the garden; he even compliments the chickens. It feels like he is casing the joint.

"Okay, I am meeting a few other people, but I'll let you know within a few days," I say, finally having to interrupt him in mid-sentence. His jaw hangs open for a minute, then he croaks, "Aw, you don't need to go through all that, I can start tomorrow."

"No, that's okay," I say firmly. "I'll let you know."

"Don't bother," he sputters. "I'll call you!"

I felt a melting relief as he drives away in his rusty little car.

The next applicant is a lanky, laconic cowboy named Walt. He seems to know horses at least. He inspects the apartment, the barn, the stallions in their pens. He nods approval.

"Thing is, I got me a family down in Lone Pine, so I don't need to live here or nothin'," he drawls just as my hopes are rising.

"Well how many days a week could you work?"

"Maybe four-five," he said.

"Let me think about it," I say. We shake hands and he drives off. He's a definite candidate, I think. Maybe I'll have to hire a whole damn squad.

The next hopeful shows up thirty minutes later. It is a girl. A very young-looking girl. She comes up the road not in a vehicle, but on a huge buckskin mare followed by three hound dogs. She is riding bareback. As I stump across the yard on my crutches, I am impressed but confused. Close up, she looks about twelve years old.

"Hey, I'm Amanda," she chirps, sliding to the ground. Her hound dogs sit obediently. "Here about the job," she adds.

Momentarily, I am stunned into silence. There is no beating around the bush, no matter if she does ride horseback like a centaur. "How old are you?" I ask, my voice sounding unnecessarily school-marmish.

"Um, seventeen," she mumbles, reaching into her battered jeans jacket and withdrawing a folded piece of paper. "Here's my resume."

I tuck both crutches under one armpit and I unfold the paper. It is done on a computer and there are no spelling mistakes. She lists school achievements, FFA and 4-H participation. Claims ribbons and trophies at gymkhanas, horse shows, and rodeos. She claims to be an expert horse trainer.

"Well, you seem to be very qualified," I say. "But can you lift a bale of hay?"

"No problem, I help my dad deliver hay all the time. I can stack hay all day long." She grins engagingly. She has blond hair in long skinny braids, wears a faded cheap cowboy hat, jeans, scuffed boots. Her eyes are amber. She is pretty. And very young.

"Okay, Amanda. On the level. You're not seventeen. How old are you?"

Her face turns red as fast as a curtain falling. "Fourteen," she mumbles.

"I thought so. Aren't you in school?"

She sighs. "Yeah, sort of. But I thought... I could work before and after school, and as late as I have to, I have a lot of energy. That's no problem!"

"What about your parents, Amanda? Aren't you living at home?"

"Yes, but I hate it."

"I can't get in between you and your family life, dear. You can understand that?"

"Maybe, if I had a job, they'd let me move out…"

I sighed. "I hope you don't mind me asking, Amanda. Is there anything bad going on at home?"

"No, there's just too many of us kids, I don't even have my own room…" Amanda trails off and her face is redder than ever. She wrings her tiny hands, tanned with bitten nails.

"Well. Look. Is all this stuff on your resume for real?"

"Yes! Yes, ma'am. I know horses. I really do. It's what I love. It's what I want to do."

"Well, maybe we can work out something part time in the future, okay? Right now, as you can see, I hurt my ankle, I need full-time help. And you need to stay in school. I'm sorry."

"That's okay," she says morosely.

"But we can be friends, and you're welcome up here."

"Really?"

"Yes."

"Cool. That's pretty cool! Thanks, Ms. Corcoran."

"Call me Sara."

"Okay, Sara. I'll definitely see ya!"

I was smiling as she rode away. But two days later the smile is long gone. I lie to the Troll, telling him I've hired someone else. When I try to reach Walt, though, all I get is an answering machine. He never calls back. As much as I like Amanda, she has a teenage life going on and her fantasies of being a full-time horse trainer will just have to wait. The calls have dwindled. I am getting desperate.

HERE IS YOUR CHANCE

Destiny reads the HELP WANTED ads in the horse magazines Varney sent. The first one she calls is a racetrack and they say they are only looking for experienced track grooms. The next is at a horse breeding farm but it's way down near San Diego. She calls anyway and they tell her to fax her resume. So she walks all the way to the library and writes a resume with the help of the hippie. She doesn't want to lie and so unfortunately it is obvious that her only experience with horses has been in prison. She isn't even sure how to describe what she'd done with Greg and ends up calling it "Electronics Assembly." It sounds vague. Before that had been the cleaning job from which she'd been, of course, fired. And before that, the Burger King. It looks pretty lame. Anyway, it is true, at least, and she faxes it to the phone number. The other job that Varney has circled is a live-in job caring for sixty-one horses. It isn't as far away, about fifty miles—she uses the map at the library to locate the desert town. She calls and there is an answering machine, so she is glad she's prepared what she will say. My name is Destiny Tubb and I am interested in the caretaker job, she says carefully. I have trained mustangs and love working with horses. I don't have a phone but you can reach me at (she gives the address of the Hotel Cockroach).

Then she waits. Two days later she calls both numbers back. The horse breeding farm says they already hired someone else. The caretaker job number is the answering machine again. She hesitates, not wanting to sound desperate. But when the beep sounds, she says, "Hi, this is Destiny Tubb, again, and I was just wondering if you got my other message about the—"

"Hello?" A voice comes on, sounding all out of breath.

"Oh, hi—this is Destiny—"

"You called about the job?" the woman interrupts.

"Yes ma'am…"

"When can you come?"

"Oh—um, when ever is convenient for you," Destiny says—a good answer, she thinks.

"As soon as possible," the woman says.

Gee, she is kind of rude-sounding, Destiny thinks, but says, "Okay, I can come tomorrow?" despite having no idea how she can get there.

"Fine, that's good, say ten o'clock in the morning?"

Destiny agrees and the woman gives her directions from the town. It is seven miles, "up a gnarly dirt road."

As she hangs up the pay phone, Destiny is elated, and overwhelmed. How in heck is she going to get there? She mentally counts her money from Varney. She still has one hundred and fourteen dollars. Seventy-five has to be saved for next week's rent in case she doesn't get the job. She hopes there is a bus she can take, and that she can afford the fare. She thumbs through the phone book for the Greyhound. She calls and finds out there is a bus. It is nineteen dollars, each way. Well, that would leave her four whole dollars for food and everything. Should she risk it?

But then, what choice does she have? She walks to the bus station—seventeen blocks—and buys a one-way ticket. Maybe she will hitchhike back and save the fare although she is afraid of getting picked up by a pervert. There is a bus that leaves at 7 a.m. It will take about an hour to get there. Two hours should be enough time to walk seven miles to the lady's house, right?

She doesn't sleep much, she is too afraid she will fail to wake up in time. So she watches the clock from three until four until five, when she finally gets up. She takes a long shower, until the water turns cold. Dresses, fixes her hair, makes some instant coffee; takes her spare resume and her money and is at the bus station forty minutes before the departure time.

The bus ride winds along the river for a while then up over some hills and then along a bunch of farms and open land. There are cows grazing the hillsides. The little town of Canyon City isn't much. Two stoplights, two food markets, two gas stations, a sprinkling of other businesses. Trailer parks on the edges of town, neighborhoods behind the main streets She disembarks the bus and consults the directions. Wishes she could afford to splurge on one of the glazed donuts from the gas station. But she is afraid to spend the money. So she starts walking, ignoring the rumbling of her hungry stomach.

The woman hadn't bothered to tell her it was seven miles up-hill. Destiny is sweating and huffing and has no idea how much farther it is. The road is dusty and she passes few houses. Some of them have horses. She would like to stop and pet them but is worried she'll be late. So she just admires them as she huffs by. Gradually there are trees all around and it seems she is in the middle of nowhere. She begins to worry about wild animals. Out here there could be all kinds of things: bears, snakes, mountain lions even. She jumps every time she hears a rustling in the bushes. She tries to see what is causing the noise and it is mostly birds. But sometimes she hears something but can't see anything and it is entirely possible there's a lion in there getting ready to jump on her. She begins walking as fast as she can, jogging a little. Her feet hurt in her cheap shoes. She is so hungry and now, and getting terribly thirsty, too. She passes a little stream that runs through a culvert under the road and she was so thirsty she's tempted to drink from it. But she is afraid of bacteria and things. So she stops only long enough to splash some on her face.

It seems like she walks forever through that scary forest. She knows she's late.

Finally, she reaches a big red iron gate. With relief she reads the sign, Corcoran. The lady had told her to press the buzzer inside the box at the side of the gate. A voice comes on an intercom.

"Yes?"

"It's Destiny Tubb, ma'am," Destiny gasps into the metal box. In answer the gate buzzes, startling her. She pushes it open just in time. Geez. A driveway that stretches forever. She trudges up and up. Then she finally sees a house and barn at the top of the hill. It takes another forever to get there. At last, she rounds a curve and she's there. Log-fenced corrals run next to the driveway and connect to a nice big barn. There is a horse in the corral, just one. It stands with the rising sun behind it and Destiny puts her hand like a visor above her eyes. As she does, the horse whinnies, loud. Destiny stops still, staring.

She doesn't even remember closing the distance to the corral rails. She must have run. Miraculously, unbelievably, it's him. Her horse. Prince!

She puts her hand out, through the rails, palm up. He noses her hand and whickers, that deep soft sound that always melts her heart. She squeezes through the rails and throws her arms around him. It is really, really him. She'd know him anywhere, and he knows her too. She can tell he does. She is crying, crying in happiness. She never thought she would see him again. Never. Yet here he is. Just as gorgeous as always. Smells just as wonderful. Feels just as smooth and warm and strong as she'd remembered.

She stands back to make sure he looks healthy, and he does; if anything, he's a little fat. He doesn't take his eyes off her.

"Miss Tubb?"

Destiny startles. She's forgotten the reason she is here. She turns to see a little old lady limping towards her on crutches. She has long gray hair in braids. She is skinny and her face is all tanned and wrinkled with tiny wrinkles, but you can tell she used to be pretty. She wears dirty jeans, a stained cowboy hat, work gloves, and a sleeveless t-shirt, with no bra! And a big gun on a belt around her waist.

"Yes, ma'am," Destiny says, her heart thumping like she's been caught doing something bad.

"I'm Sara Beth, and I see you've met Chance."

"Chance? Oh—yeah. He's beautiful," Destiny says. Some instinct tells her to keep the fact that she knows this horse—that she's trained him—to herself, at least for now.

"He's my sweetie pie," the woman says casually.

Destiny nods, too stunned at this coincidence and suddenly jealous to speak.

"So, let's go up to the house, I was just going to have some breakfast. Did you eat?"

"No ma'am," Destiny says with utter truth, and her stomach grumbles loudly as if to prove it. But the woman pretends not to hear it.

"Where's your car?"

"I took the bus. And walked."

"You walked? From—from town?"

"Yes ma'am."

"Call me Sara. Jesus Christ! That's a pretty good hike."

Destiny smiles, hoping her tiredness doesn't show. "It was a pretty walk," she says diplomatically.

"You don't have a car?"

"No ma'am—I mean, Sara."

"But can you drive?"

"Yes, well, I mean, yes." She tries to figure out how to say her license has been revoked, but can't think of any way to explain it without ending this interview before it even starts. In her moment of indecision, the lady starts crutching away.

"Okay, good, come on, I'm starving," Sara said, and slowly leads the way up to the house.

Destiny strokes Prince one more time, then follows the strange old woman, hoping, hoping, hoping. She has to get this job!

* * *

When the girl doesn't show up on time, I think, Perfect. I'll never find anyone to help. I start crying. It might have been a huge mistake getting all these horses, I think, feeling foolish and scared. I simply can't keep depending on Lee and Charlie. If I don't get help, I'll have no choice. I'll have to get rid of them. What a disaster!

I am in the middle of a big guilt-fest when the buzzer sounds. Maybe it is her!

It is.

She is down in Chance's corral. He is acting like he'd just been reunited with a long-lost friend. Because he's mad at me, I think. What an exceptionally smart horse, able to manipulate someone's feelings better than most humans.

The girl is chubby and tall, dwarfing me. But it does look like she can handle a bale of hay. At that point my original high expectations have taken a dive. Now all I want is someone who would show up and do the work. I could care less if they entertain the troops in their spare time.

She has dark blond hair tied back in a cloth-covered elastic band. She wears jeans that are too tight and old boots. A western shirt that looks like polyester, straining a bit over her substantial bust. There is a stain on the front. She has a purse with frayed edges under her arm. She smells a little of sweat. She has wide, innocent-looking brown eyes, dark lashes. If she lost about forty pounds, she'd be pretty, I think, not too kindly. I ask her up to the house—I'm suddenly starving.

Hopping around on one foot and with the girl's help, I scramble some eggs and on impulse make pancakes too. Some raspberries from my vines and a cantaloupe from the garden. I have her set it all out on the table with my good silver and Desert Rose china. A fresh pot of coffee is already in the carafe and I add cream and sugar and syrup to the table. While we are doing all this, I interrogate her.

"Tell me about yourself," I say.

"I've got a resume," she says, gesturing to her purse hooked on the back of a chair.

"Why don't you just tell me what it says?"

"Well, I'm from Oildale," she says. "I'm twenty-four. I went to Bakersfield High School and graduated with an A-average. I, um, got some experience with horses. But I got into some trouble, you know, but I paid my debt and I work hard. I don't do no drugs and I don't drink no more. I'll work real hard."

Paid my debt? My heart sinks. Is she really saying what I think? And her language is terrible. I'd go crazy listening to those double negatives and that Dolly Parton twang.

"Where did you get your experience with horses?" I ask, deciding to save the hard questions for the moment. She is staring at the food like she hasn't eaten in a month. Her stomach growls, so loudly that one of the dogs growls back. At my innocent question, the girl flushes darkly. Her face contorts into an ugly, self-deprecating sneer.

"Well, to tell you God's truth, it was in prison, ma'am."

"Ah. Do you mind me asking why were in prison?"

"Vehicular manslaughter, ma'am. But it was an accident, really."

She pronounced it vee-hic-i-ler. I feel sick to my stomach. She'd killed someone with her car. And there had been criminal negligence or else she would not have gone to prison. Some selfish, illiterate moron just like her had killed Hank.

There is nothing about this girl I like. I want to say, "Get the hell out of my house." But I think about the horses, and where they might end up if I can't keep them, and I hear myself say, "Why don't we eat?"

I drink coffee and pick at a pancake while she gorges herself. She eats and eats, her fork and mouth in steady motion. Four pancakes, a big pile of eggs. Three pieces of toast. She cleans her plate. I can tell she wants more. I urge seconds on her but she refuses even while looking longingly at the fruit platter.

I light a cigarette, offer her one, she refuses.

I consider whether to send her on her way without further ado. The idea of a felon living in my barn is totally repugnant. This girl will probably vanish with her first paycheck, taking everything that isn't nailed down. Hell, I know I'm not being fair. She'd obviously been disadvantaged. But I can't get over that "vee-hic-i-ler" manslaughter. If only she'd been in prison for kiting checks or prostitution, I could get over those things.

But I need help and here she is. Wanting the job bad enough to have walked all the way from town. I sigh, grind out the spent cigarette, and light another.

"So tell me about this horse experience," I sigh.

She tells me all about the WHIP, Wild Horse Inmate Program. Her face becomes animated and she says that she has been one of only three from her group of twenty that had trained their wild horse all the way to accept a saddle and rider.

"That's quite a coincidence, that's where I got Chance," I say. "He was trained by inmates, also."

"Huh! No kidding," she says, in a weirdly high voice. She clears her throat and adds, "Would you be wanting me, um, I mean whoever you get, would you be wanting them to ride him? Until your ankle heals up and all?"

"No, I'll be training Chance. But you'd be feeding him of course, and cleaning the corrals."

She nods, as if disappointed but expecting it.

"I recently bought sixty BLM mustangs to save them from being sold at auction," I say. "If they go to auction they're in danger of being bought by slaughterhouses."

"I heard about that," the girl says. "I read an article about it."

"Another coincidence," I laugh lightly. "I've written a few. For the local paper."

"Oh! Are you that writer? It is you! I read your story!" She seems stunned, like she's just realized she is in the presence of a major celebrity. "You're a good writer!" she declares.

"Thanks," I say, amused.

"You bought them to save them? That's so cool," she enthuses. "I love mustangs. I didn't know you had all mustangs. I think they're just, like, the best horses! Another coincidence."

I sigh again. She loves mustangs. She's actually trained one from wild to saddle, if I am to believe her. She clearly needs a chance; and, I'm desperate. My visions of a lanky, sexy cowboy dissolve.

"Let's go look at the horses and I'll show you where you'll stay. I assume you'll want to live-in?"

Her jaw drops. She looks even more vapid than usual with her mouth hanging open. "Do you mean I git the job?" she whispers.

"On a trial basis," I say, equivocating quickly. "If in, say, two weeks, either of us is unhappy, we can forget it. How does that sound?"

"Perfect," she gushes. "Thank you, Jesus. You won't be sorry, ma'am. I promise. I'll work real, real hard. All I need's a chance."

* * *

She feels dizzy, but happy. Maybe it's the sugar rush from all that syrup. Destiny's head is buzzing, but in a pleasant way, as she follows Mrs. Corcoran outside and down to the big barn. It is Spanish style like the house, made out of matching yellow adobe-looking stuff. A blue tile roof. It is pretty. The whole place is pretty. There are stone walkways connecting everything. There are roses on the porch trellis and a garden and shiny-feathered red chickens all over the place. And there are other flower beds along the house and a Jacuzzi on the deck outside the kitchen. Inside is messy but the furniture and dishes and silverware all look expensive, and the rugs and books and stuff do too. Mrs. Corcoran has a lot of stuff, there are shelves everywhere crammed with books and framed pictures and weird stuff like bird's nests and plastic horse models, china dogs, and pottery. There is a layer of dust over everything. This doesn't look like "some housekeeping," it looks like major housecleaning, she thinks. But that's perfectly okay with Destiny.

Prince is here. She has actually found him. She'd clean the whole place with a toothbrush if it means she can stay.

Inside the barn are four stalls and a feed room and a tack room. The apartment is reached by wooden steps that run alongside the tack room. It takes a long time for Mrs. Corcoran to crutch up the steps but she refuses Destiny's offer of help. Mrs. Corcoran opens the door and precedes Destiny inside.

"God, it's hot in here," she says dramatically, stumping to a window and opening the wooden shutters and then the window. Light floods the little room.

It is perfect, so perfect! A log bed with a colorful quilt and pretty eyelet sheets and pillowcases. A pine dresser and nightstand. A plaid stuffed chair in the corner with a reading lamp next to it. There is even a little fridge and a hot plate, and a bathroom with a shower. It is all a little dusty but neat as a pin. Like no one has ever stayed here, ever.

Like she is a mind reader, Mrs. Corcoran says, "No one's ever used this room, everything's brand-new." She sounds sad when she says it.

"It's… lovely," Destiny says, trying for a word which would do justice. She steps to the window and looks out. Below, she can see Prince in his corral. He is looking up at her.

"Thank you," the old lady says, her eyes crinkling with a rare smile. "Do you think you could be happy here?"

It is such a strange question. Nobody ever worried about whether Destiny was happy or not. Maybe she just means, "will it do?"

Destiny assures her that it is perfect. She thinks about Hotel Cockroach. And Prince, right here, and says it again. "Yes ma'am. It's lovely! Just perfect."

Next they go down to the corrals and Sara introduces her to the stallions and tells her she'll be expected to clean all the corrals, twice a day. Destiny keeps glancing across to Prince's corral. He has his head over the rails, watching them. He nickers to her again and again.

"Chance is jealous of the new arrivals," Mrs. Corcoran says.

Destiny knows otherwise but keeps quiet about it. She tells her instead she has no problem with mucking manure.

"Can you drive my truck? It's automatic," Sara asks. Destiny is still afraid to tell her about the problem with her license, so she says, "Sure," and they get into the big new truck and Destiny drives slowly where Sara directs. They go through some gates into the big pasture where the mustangs are. Destiny gets out and opens and closes the gates so Mrs. Corcoran doesn't have to get out of the truck. There are dirt roads through the pasture and right away they come upon a big bunch of horses. They start running away and Mrs. Corcoran says, stop the truck, and the horses slow and circle back towards them, but not too close. Destiny is thrilled. Seeing wild mustangs, all running around together, is like one of her fantasies coming to life. They are so cute! Pintos and bays and black ones and brown ones. They have shaggy manes and long, bushy tails and they are all beautiful, and she says so.

Mrs. Corcoran looks at Destiny. Her smiling old lady face looks different, prettier. "Yeah. Aren't they great?" she says.

"Yes ma'am. They sure are."

"So you'll be feeding them twice a day, and doing a head count, checking to see them all each day, make sure everybody's okay. And we're going to pick a few to start training. We'll gather those up and move them to the upper corral. Okay?"

"Yes, ma'am!" Destiny says. She can hardly believe her good fortune. They continue to drive all around the big pasture, seeing more horses along the way.

"So, about your salary," Mrs. Corcoran says. "I'll provide food and the apartment plus two hundred dollars a week. I figure you'll be spending about thirty hours a week with the horses and twenty hours with basic housework. I can cook. Does that sound all right?"

Destiny says it sure does. She would pay to work here if she could. They drive up to the house, go back inside. Mrs. Corcoran says, "Wait here," and goes into what is probably her bedroom and comes back with a wallet. She gives Destiny five crisp twenty dollar bills.

She says, "Half of your first week's pay, in advance. So. You'll need to go get your things, and settle your affairs. I'll think I can manage to drive you back to town. Do you mind taking the bus back to Bakersfield?"

Destiny doesn't mind at all.

"How soon can you get back?"

"Today, if there's a bus," Destiny says.

"Oh! That soon! Great, even tomorrow will be fine. I'll have to get you; there is no taxi service in town, unfortunately. Call me when you get to the bus station."

"Okay, yes ma'am."

"You'd better come back," Mrs. Corcoran says sternly.

Destiny laughs, laughs in pure relief. "Don't worry. I'll come back," she says. In fact, she doesn't want to leave at all. It might look weird if she begged to stay, though. All she has to go back for is a few thrift store clothes, barely enough to fill a cardboard box. She can't wait to say goodbye to her crummy room, and Bakersfield, and Hotel Cockroach. And get back here, to her Prince.

THE HONEYMOONERS

I thought that perhaps I'd seen the last of Destiny Tubb. Nothing about her inspired my confidence... except her enthusiasm. With cash in her pocket she would probably call her dealer, go on a toot, and get busted and that would be that. Which is why I gave her the money. It's a test.

But the phone rings at seven thirty the next morning. It is her.

She is sitting on the bus stop bench with a cardboard box beside her. She jumps up as soon as I pull into the lot.

"Good morning, Destiny," I say.

"Good morning!" she chirps, grinning ear to ear.

I asked her if she minds driving. The grin fades.

"I would but, my license is, um, like, suspended," she mumbled, eyes on the pavement.

"Well, that's inconvenient," I snap. "My ankle's killing me. And you did say you could drive!"

"I'm sorry, I know how, but..." she moans.

"Well it's not a deal-breaker, for Christ's sake. Get in. You can drive once we're out of town." Her face explodes into a grin. She climbs in with the box on her lap.

"You can put that in the back seat."

"I'm sorry," she says again. Gets out to stow the box, then back in. She is hyper-ventilating.

"Put your seatbelt on," I say. I am annoyed at having to drive. I've hired her to help me, after all. But I should have figured she'd have had her license taken away, considering her felony for vehic-i-ler manslaughter.

"I'm sorry," she says again (third time's the charm, I guess). She adds, "Thanks so much for pickin' me up. I coulda walked. I'm sorry to be so much trouble."

I soften in the face of such groveling. "It's not that much trouble," I say. "Don't worry, I'm glad you're here."

She sighs and relaxes her shoulders. "Thank you," she says. "I'm real glad to git here. Praise God."

Oh, Jesus, I think. Not a religious fanatic. I fiddle with the radio. "Do you like music?" I ask.

"Oh, yes ma'am. I like both kinds, country and Western."

Had Destiny Tubb just made a joke, or was she really that dumb? I decided not to chuckle, just in case. I just say, "Me too. I play it when I work with my horse."

She smiles, staring ahead at the road. "Well, ain't that nice. I do like listenin' to music when I'm cleanin'."

"That's fine with me," I say. "I have a decent stereo. I'll show you how to use it. And, believe it or not, I have a collection of actual records, you know, vinyl."

"Oh, that's nice, I love that," Destiny says.

"Things are a pretty big mess right now," I say, after a few moments of silence. "I don't expect you to get everything clean all at once."

"All right," she says, straightening up in the seat.

"When we get home, you'll need to start feeding the horses right away."

"Yes ma'am."

"Feed two flakes to Chance and the stallions. Feed four bales out in the big pastures where I showed you. Don't forget to lock the gates behind you at all times."

"Yes ma'am."

"We're not in the army," I say. "You can call me Sara. But if you're more comfortable calling me ma'am or whatever, that's all right too."

She opens her mouth then shuts it. She nods.

"Relax, Destiny. We'll get along all right."

"Yes ma'am. "

Destiny Tubb went to work and didn't stop. She fed the horses with no trouble, and after some initial awkwardness, even handled the tractor, quad, and trailer better than I did. The girl could lift bale after bale of hay. I told her to concentrate on outside chores before any housework. First, muck the corrals and stalls. They needed it, having been neglected for days. (Lee's kindliness only went so far.)

I follow in case she needs help with the stallions or Chance. She heads to Chance's corral first. Even though he still has hay, he leaves it to follow her around like a puppy, until she retrieves his halter and ties him up. She is good with him, he bends his head into the halter like he'd been trained to do. She mucks the corral impeccably then pets him, talking to him quietly, then turns him loose. He trots after her as she leaves the corral.

"Looks like you two have made friends," I comment as she locks the gate.

"He's a fine horse," she says, her voice worshipful.

"Maybe you can find time to give him a good grooming," I suggest.

"Oh, yes ma'am! I sure will," she says with too much enthusiasm. I watch her with the stallions. Contrary to Chance, they shy away from her, letting her clean with no interference. But they seem to tolerate her presence well enough. She moves around them quietly but deliberately. I leave her to it.

After mucking, she sweeps the tack room and barn. She waters the garden and brings in the vegetables that needed picking. She feeds the hens and scrubs out their watering trough. She rakes the yard and flower borders. Except for a lunch break—she makes turkey sandwiches, not letting me lift a finger—she is a dervish, transforming chaos into order. I sit in the shade on the porch with my ankle propped up and a pitcher of iced tea within reach as she moves into the house. I hear her washing dishes in the kitchen and singing along to Tanya Tucker... and when I wake it is late afternoon. I rub my eyes and sit up, a little chilly. Reach for the crutches and get up, stump into the house. It smells of pine cleaner instead of dog. It is immaculate. The kitchen shines. The floors gleam. I go to use the bathroom which looks clean enough to operate in. I sigh happily as I pee. Maybe this is going to work out after all.

I call for her coming out of the bathroom. The dogs come, filing through the doggie door. I crutch into the kitchen but the empty bowls on the floor indicate they have already been fed.

I crutch out to the porch.

"Destiny!" I holler.

"Yes ma'am, down here," I hear her call back. "Comin'!"

She appears, hurrying up the path, breathing hard.

"How's it going?"

"Fine, I was just groomin Pr- Chance, like you asked."

"It's past time to feed," I say.

"I already done it at three, like you said."

"Oh! Really? Well, good. Great. The house looks fantastic. You've done a wonderful job."

She blushed. "Thank you, ma'am," she said.

"Well. Don't wear yourself out on the first day."

"No ma'am. I'm fine."

"All right then. I'll make us some dinner in a little bit. Is an omelette all right? "

"Like, aigs? Yes, ma'am, that sounds real good. I kin try cookin' it though. If you tell me how. You should be stayin' off that foot."

"I can manage."

"Is there anything I can git you?"

"No, I'm fine. You go ahead and finish up with Chance. Then why don't you call it a day. Have a shower if you'd like and we'll eat in about an hour."

"Yes ma'am!" She turns and hurries back down to the corral. As she disappears I hear Chance whinny in greeting.

* * *

"Hey, big fella. Hey, Prince." She runs her hands down his warm coat. She leans her face to his nose and breathes his grassy sweetness. She'd cried, earlier, in happiness, but now she just feels deeply at peace. The sun slants through the trees and the air is cooling down wonderfully. It is so peaceful here, so pretty. And she has a gorgeous apartment and everything. And Prince. She can't stop touching him, as if trying to convince herself it is all real. But he doesn't dissolve or anything. He is real, solid, all warm muscle and glittering, beautiful eyes with their cinnamon eyelashes and his striped legs and long, swishing mustang tail. On impulse she walks to the fence and climbs up a rail. He follows her and she taps him closer with her toe. He steps up alongside the fence. She slides down on his back. He is warm beneath her legs. His ears twitch. He curves his neck around and touches the toe of her boot with his nose. She strokes his mane, reaches around, and pats his rump. A door slams up at the house, and guiltily she slides off, her heart pounding. She'd better not push her luck. Ms. Corcoran—

Sara—said not to ride him. It is too much to hope for anyway. She should be happy just to have found him, to know he's okay; to be able to take care of him is a big bonus. She should be happy with that. And, she is. She really is.

She is so tired that she barely tastes the egg omelet and tomato salad but eats all that is put in front of her. She drinks a diet Coke while Mrs. Corcoran drinks almost a whole bottle of wine. It doesn't seem to affect her a bit though. Destiny gets up to do the dishes as soon as they are done eating.

"Destiny, when you finish those, please consider yourself done for the day. You must be exhausted."

Destiny says yes ma'am. Mrs. Corcoran asks if she needs anything, is the apartment comfortable enough. Destiny assures her it is very comfortable and she doesn't need anything.

"I'm sorry there's no television," Mrs. Corcoran says. We can pick you up one next time we go to town.

"That's okay," Destiny says. "I like readin' better anyway. Y'all don't mind if I read at night?"

"You like to read?" Mrs. Corcoran asks, like Destiny has just said she could fly or something.

"Yes ma'am, I sure do."

"Fiction or non-fiction?" Mrs. Corcoran asks.

Destiny has never thought about the difference, of preferring one over the other. Book were books. "Just about anything," she says, thinking it makes her sound ignorant.

"Well, you're welcome to borrow any of my books."

"Really?"

The old lady nods.

"Thank you, that's real nice," Destiny says. She looks at the overfull shelves with new emotion. Now they aren't just something to dust. It is like having a private library, no card needed. No return date. "That's awesome!" she adds.

"Well, rock on," Ms. Corcoran says, smiling. Destiny suddenly understands something about her employer. Ms. Corcoran loves horses and her dogs and books. She approves of other people who do too. The rest of life she doesn't seem to give a holler about. Ms. Corcoran gets up and limps over to the bookshelves. "Try this one," she says. "And this. Oh, McCullers! Yes…" She pulls down a half-dozen books and hands them to Destiny. "These will get you started," she says.

Destiny would rather have browsed and picked out ones herself. But she knows better than to look a gift horse in the mouth. She just thanks her employer again, and says good night.

She is so exhausted and muscle-sore from the day's marathon of labor that she uses the banister to haul her butt up the stairs to her apartment. Inside, she turns on the light, closes her door, locks it, and falls into the stuffed chair. It is beside the windows and she can look down, see part of Chance's corral. He is there, looking up at her window. Destiny puts her face up close to the screen and calls to him softly.

"I'm here, buddy." He whickers softly. He is so beautiful in the light of the nearly full moon. He is so at ease with the dark and the forest around him, the night and its breeze and the sounds of the creatures in it. Destiny feels like he will protect her from those unknown creatures; he'll let her know if a bear or something comes close.

She watches him watch her and thinks about starting to read one of the books. But instead she just leans her arms on the windowsill and watches her horse until she almost falls asleep right there. She rouses herself and pulls off her clothes and falls into the fresh, clean sheets and instantly sleeps. Later, she dreams she is riding Prince, riding free, almost floating, over the sage.

* * *

Later I thought back over those first weeks as the honeymoon period. Through a gauzy curtain of optimism the honeymooners gaze at each other. It is a time of overlooking any and all faults in one's new partner. Ignoring the flaws and quirks and mannerisms and incompatibilities that later—years and years later, or in Hollywood fashion, mere days later—will drive you insane. Destiny Tubb worked hard. My place would have fallen apart without her. She was inexhaustible and thorough. She lavished care on the horses, especially Chance. He'd never been so clean in his life, I was sure. She was polite and deferential to the extreme.

But in true Hollywood fashion, she began to drive me crazy almost right away. She was always around. I could hardly hobble out to the porch without her being there, industriously sweeping or pulling weeds in the flowerbeds. I could hardly head inside for a drink without finding her in the kitchen washing windows or dishes. I could barely write without looking out my window and there she'd be, in the orchard, picking apples. It was bizarre. I couldn't escape her. And I'd never realized how filthy my house must have always been. Because I surely never spent half the time that Destiny Tubb did, scrubbing, sweeping, dusting, polishing. At first I took to lurking in my bedroom and studio, but that quickly tired. I was conflicted about confronting her; she was, after all, simply doing what I'd told her to do.

It wouldn't have been so bad if the girl could speak decent English. Her voice scraped my sensibilities like fingernails on the proverbial blackboard. And her conversation was—how can I describe it? Boring, certainly, but dead-end might be a better description. She had limited topics of conversation that were repeated ad nauseam. Without another soul around, she began to talk to me at every opportunity, the moment I walked into a room she'd start in as if in the middle of a conversation. It was understandable, of course, considering the utter lack of anyone else around. Unfortunately she had fixated on her life in prison as her main topic. Every soliloquy was prefaced with, "back 'n Frontera…"

Example. We're having breakfast. Fresh peaches, the last of them.

Me: "Mmm, these peaches. So good."

Destiny Tubb: (mouth full) "Back 'n Frontera, they never heard of no fresh fruit, I'll tell you what. They had this fruit salad from a can and all the fruit was all mushy and you could taste the can."

Me: "Hm."

Destiny Tubb: "Back there, the food was nasty. But not all of it. Some of it was real good. But most of it was just nasty."

Me: "That must have been difficult."

Destiny Tubb: "Y'all ain't kidding. Even hot dogs. How do ya mess up a dang hot dog? I don't know, but they done it."

And so on. Back in Frontera, the food was nasty. Back in Frontera, you could hardly sleep because of all the noise all night long. Back in Frontera, Destiny Tubb read and watched TV. She regaled me with the plot of some soap opera she'd watched there every day. None of the stories were interesting; I tried to ask her about her fellow inmates, about her general treatment at the hands of the system. But her lack of observation and inductive skills made these inquiries bear no fruit, canned or otherwise.

In addition to all that, she ruined country music for me in short order; singing along under her breath in that off-key twang. It was like a parody of each song. I'd only come to like country music anyway through total immersion, up here on the radio it was either that or right-wing talk shows. But now I could barely tolerate any music, country or Western.

I know my attitude is harsh and judgmental; bigoted, even. I know that Destiny Tubb must possess positive qualities other than the ability to work as hard as a draft animal. And although it seems that she chatters constantly, she says nothing. After two weeks I know no more about her than I did the day I picked her up at the bus stop.

Me: "Do you have family, Destiny?"

Destiny Tubb: "Not much to speak of. Reckon I'll go on and finish up that laundry."

Me: "What did you do before your time at Frontera?"

Destiny Tubb: "Nothin' that added up to much, I'll tell you what."

Me: "So, did you grow up entirely in Bakersfield?"

Destiny Tubb: "Pretty much, yes ma'am."

Me: "And what did your father do?"

Destiny Tubb: "Ah don't remember much about him, ma'am, to tell ya God's honest truth."

I feel like a prisoner in my own house. The most unique, the absolute best thing about this place is its solitude. It is my place, where I can walk around naked in the garden or belt musical comedy songs at the top of my lungs in the kitchen or burst out crying any damn place I please. But that is gone. The one thing I treasure most about Hank's legacy to me is suddenly annihilated. My perfect privacy, my blessed solitude. Just like in the Joni Mitchell song, "You don't know what you've got till it's gone," I hadn't fully appreciated it. But now I surely, sorely miss it.

I resent Destiny Tubb for stealing my treasure.

TRAINING DAYS

Waking up in the barn apartment is a daily delicious shock. Finally her dreams are darker than real life. Each day Destiny got to realize anew that this is all real, she is really here with Prince. In this beautiful, peaceful place. Her luck has finally changed. Her prayers are finally being answered. She has a decent job at last. One that she actually enjoys. Not the housework; the housework is the price she pays to work with the horses. She'd clean a hundred houses to be able to do that, for free. But she's getting paid to work with horses, with mustangs. And getting paid to be with Prince. It is unbelievable, really. That is why she keeps expecting the dream to disappear.

It takes her two whole weeks to get that house clean. The more she cleans, the more dirty places she finds. Her employer is a really crummy housekeeper. And she is strange. Destiny is kind of afraid of her. She finds out Mrs. Corcoran is a doctor. Some of her mail—the mail that Destiny has to illegally drive the truck the three miles to the paved road to retrieve—reads "Dr. SB Corcoran." When Destiny asks her about it, Mrs. Corcoran laughs and says, "Yeah, I'm a witch doctor". She is always talking like that, Destiny never knows if she is kidding; she hardly ever laughs and her face is usually frowning. She most often sounds mad or at least irritated by something.

So Destiny is careful to work hard, to make sure Mrs. Corcoran sees her working hard. She tries being friendly, making conversation. But it never seems to go anywhere. Destiny feels stupid around Mrs.... Doctor Corcoran. Even though Destiny knows how to speak correctly, she falls into old bad habits around her employer for some reason. The smarter the doctor talks, the dumber Destiny becomes.

Except around the horses.

After the first week the doctor says they are going to start training the new mustangs. Destiny piles some hay into the holding corral and opens the gate to the big pasture. They don't have to wait too long, mustangs are completely aware of their surroundings and curious in the extreme. When Destiny checks a half hour later there are seven horses inside the corral attacking the hay. Destiny jogs up to the house.

The doctor follows her back down. Destiny is too excited to slow her walk to match the doctor's crutching limp.

The doctor stumps to the fence and leans her crutches on it with a big sigh. She holds on to the fence and stands on her good foot, the other cocked like a resting horse.

"Oh, nice, she says after a moment. "I like that roan gelding."

Destiny looks. The horse is the biggest one, with a big white head, dark eyes, silver mane. He looks red from a distance but up close he is like mashed potatoes speckled with a lot of paprika.

"That the one you want to start with?"

"What do you think?"

"Whichever one you want, I'll start 'em," Destiny says bravely.

"Then let's try him," the doctor says. "Let me have a rope. You man the gate. Just shoo him off. Let the rest back through."

So that's what they do. The doctor swings her rope, moving the horses. Destiny waves the roan off when he tries to go through with the others. She slams the gate as soon as he is alone. She is breathing hard, excited.

"Good job," says the doctor.

The paprika horse trots back and forth, whinnying. The rest of the horses are moving away down the road towards the pond.

"So, let's see what you can do with him," the doctor says.

It feels like being called to the blackboard at school. The doctor lets herself outside the corral.

The holding corral is twice as big as the round pen that Destiny knows how to use. Plus, this corral is rectangular; it has corners that the horse will use to avoid her. She'll have to be aggressive, keep him out of those corners, make sure she keeps him moving and not stop until she lets him. That's how you get the horse to bond up with you. If she does it halfway, all she'll accomplish will be teaching the horse he can get away from her.

She coils up the rope, makes sure the coils are smooth in her hand. She walks deliberately to the approximate center of the corral and stands quietly, letting the horse pace back and forth. He ignores her, looking down the road in the big pasture after his pals. Destiny waits until the other horses are out of sight, then waits some more. The horse continues to pace and whinny. His tail is up, his breathing loud.

As he passes her Destiny steps quickly forward, lunging at him and at the same time flinging out her rope. The rope leaps towards the horse's flanks and he bursts into motion. At the far end he begins to turn back as he'd been doing but Destiny is there and flings the rope again, forcing him around the perimeter of the corral. The roan explodes into a gallop. Destiny moves casually after him. When the horse begins to slow at the far corner, she throws the rope and the horse bucks but keeps going in the same direction. Destiny forces herself to breathe slow and regular. She forces herself not to run after the horse, to stand her ground and make the rope do the work. Back in Frontera she'd spent hours and hours practicing with the lasso. Now it's paying off, as she can urge the horse without moving too far from the center. She keeps moving the horse around and around, not daring to take her eyes off him although she wants to look over at the doctor, to see if she is pleased or not. But the horse demands her full attention. She is working hard, throwing and coiling the rope without taking her eyes off the horse, watching for the signs that he is getting ready to "negotiate," as Varney called it.

The horse is sweating hard and white foam flies from his mouth.

Destiny feels sorry for him and the urge to let up on him is strong. But this is her big test. She'll run this poor horse into the ground if she has to. But just then she realizes the horse's inside ear is on her. And then he drops his head and starts chewing. Destiny coils up her rope and holds it down at her side and backs up. Rewarding the horse's "try." Like she wears magnetic pants the horse turns in towards her, slows, stops; faces her. He's relaxed, and curious. Destiny waits until the horse takes cautious steps towards her. She stands still, breathing slow, as he comes up and she reaches out a hand and pats him on the forehead. He is hot and sweaty but his eyes are easy and quiet.

"Nice," calls the doctor. "Very nice."

Destiny rubs the horse some more, then steps back and sends him off in the opposite direction. He goes without too many hysterics. An hour later, Destiny has him haltered and is leading him.

"Do you think you can take him up?" the doctor says, meaning out through the gate and up the driveway to one of the upper corrals.

"Yes ma'am, I think so."

The doctor opens the gate and Destiny leads the roan horse through. They go up the drive, the doctor following. At the first corral Destiny stops, opens the gate, and leads the horse inside. He is calmly drinking from the trough by the time the doctor makes it up the hill.

"Well. That was impressive."

Destiny shrugs but she feels herself blush.

"I mean it, I'm impressed. You did that well. No fear. I like that. Tell you what. Let's concentrate less on the house and more on the horses. I can put up with a bit of dust. I think we can really do something with these guys."

"Yes ma'am."

"It's expensive feeding this many horses. The more we can train and move to good homes, the better."

"Yes ma'am. I get your point," Destiny says. She is thrilled. Concentrate more on the horses? There are sixty mustangs. Training even just the younger ones will take a long time. That there is some long-term job security. Destiny can't help but feel herself stand taller. She has a job. She is a horse trainer.

* * *

Destiny Tubb is actually a decent trainer. I was surprised; she seemed so passive. In the pen with the horse, she'd transformed. Her whipped dog posture straightened, her bland face became eager and fierce. I'm relieved. Because I have come to the conclusion that turning my horses onto a pasture, and making sure they had shelter and food and water, isn't enough. Every one of my mustangs that could carry a rider ought to be given the chance to do so, if only for a richer, more interesting life. I believe that horses and humans share a mysterious need to bond with the other. Even as the horse evolved from a tiny Eohippus to the modern horse, its destiny was to be domesticated. And the fact that it domesticated so well, so surpassingly excellently, proves to me that an individual horse has a longing to be with humans, to work with them, to carry them, eagerly, effortlessly. Why else would there be so many examples of horses loving their work, the work humans have given them? My horse Sapphire would gallop across the pasture when she saw me, and paw her hooves in readiness to ride. The milkman's or postman's or coal-man's horse of years ago knew its route and every stop so that their human never needed to even pick up the reins. The Pony Express horse, the racehorse, would run until its heart burst. Even the tragic warhorses, the destriers, would charge into the fearsome noise of battle and stench of death, carrying an idiot in iron armor. And die for that man.

God, I love horses. I love all my horses. I want each and every one to have the best possible life. I'm sure the very old and lame ones will be happy lounging around the big pasture for the rest of their lives. But the others. I want to let them be great if they can, or just fulfilled. A cow pony. A jumper. An old lady's trail horse; a young girl's dream. I don't want them to end up as lawn ornaments, overfed and bored; I want their lives to be interesting, full, happy. I think about that nice red roan, right now no doubt pondering his momentous day. I just know he's going to make a real nice horse for somebody.

And because of my stupid broken foot I have to rely on Miss Destiny Tubb to do it all. But it appears that maybe she can do it. And I'm relieved. But it is not a pure, nice feeling. It's tainted, polluted with a sick feeling, an old yet familiar feeling. It's jealousy.

Jealousy? I thought you pitied her.

Oh, Jesus. I thought I was done talking to myself.

Yoo-hoo. Oh, Doctor?

Well, I wanted to train those horses.

You hurt yourself. You needed help, you got help. You'll get a chance to train horses. But now you have exactly what you asked for.

I wish I were twenty-six. I'd show her some stuff about horses.

It's natural to feel frightened by this injury. As we age, medical issues can seem dire. Healing isn't taken as much for granted. But you have a fractured ankle. It is healing right now.

I just can't stand her, for some reason.

She's here because you need her.

Oh, sure. She's here because she needs me.

Maybe part of what you need is to be needed.

Oh, go away!

* * *

The red roan gelding learns quickly. Isolated from his herd, he instantly acclimates to human companionship. Within days Destiny can touch him all over, groom him, even pick up his feet. He lowers his head into the halter and is leading well. She works him every day in the round pen and then spends time with him in the evening while he munches his hay. Meanwhile, she and the doctor have isolated two more horses. A buckskin and a bay mare. The bay is old but still sturdy. Only looking at the hollows above her eyes or her teeth reveals her advanced age. Her teeth are yellow and brown and curved out long like a beaver's. It turns out that she has a temper, but Destiny finds that if she goes slowly, doesn't push her too hard, that the old horse will respond. She will take more time than the roan. But the doctor says that's okay. Whatever it takes, that's okay. The old mare has a sweet face and a lovely long full black tail. She has a white star centered on her forehead. Her name's Stella Vega. The red roan, they name Paprika. The buckskin, Willy.

The horses are all getting names: the doctor's friends had ridden up on their horses and out into the big pasture, they spent hours out there taking pictures. The one friend, Charlie, was the newspaper editor. His wife was Lee. Lee and the doctor were Best Friends. Destiny watched the two of them giggle and hug and wondered how it would feel to have a best friend. Anyway, the horse portraits are for the newspaper. They publish ten a week in a contest to name the horses. The person that nominates the most winning names will get one of the horses, one of the young ones, a Palomino mare. The doctor gets lists of names that get sent in and picks out the names she and Destiny like. The stallions get some of the first names: the gorgeous little golden dun is Wyatt; the white one, Cloud.

The rest of the paint horses all get named after artists, most of them ones Destiny has never heard of. There is Picasso's Muse, Matisse, Frieda, Georgia, and Pollock. Some of the names Destiny especially likes are Jasmine, Sage, and Scout. There is Misty and and Garth, Patsy and Lulu. Hopi and Ranger, Cody, and Deb.

The doctor and her friend Lee laugh a lot at names they make up: Butt Ugly. Gimpy. Scrawny and Psycho. Gramps and Two-Tooth. Clubfoot. Destiny is glad when they're just kidding and none of the horses end up with those names.

Destiny's days are full. First thing, she gets up before sunrise. She doesn't even bother with coffee anymore. She rushes down the stairs and outside to Prince's corral. Together they watch the sun peek over the mountains. Then she starts feeding the horses and checks the herds in the big pasture and then feeds the chickens and dogs. Then she makes breakfast for her and the doctor. Next she cleans house for about an hour: the kitchen, the bathrooms, makes the doctor's bed and picks up her clothes, strewn all around. Then she goes down to the corrals and after mucking, picks out a horse to work. Lately she'd work the roan, then the bay mare, then the buckskin. Then it is time for lunch. She goes back up to the house and makes sandwiches. The doctor loves sandwiches, cheese or tuna or turkey and Swiss. The doctor doesn't eat "red meat" and although Destiny misses hamburgers, she tells herself it doesn't matter. The doctor likes either root beer or real beer but sometimes lemonade. And Lay's potato chips, Classic. After cleaning up from lunch Destiny spends another two hours with the horses-in-training, then does yard work. Raking and weeding and stuff. Then it is time for the afternoon feed. After that, Destiny has free time until she is supposed to come eat dinner. The doctor cooks dinner.

Destiny is tired by late afternoon but it is her favorite time. The sun is going down and she hangs out with Prince. First she grooms him from head to tail. Then they play. Destiny teaches him to lead without a halter or rope. He walks right at her shoulder, as Destiny turns circles, backs up, paces complicated patterns. She gets him to lower his head all the way to the ground with the touch of her finger on his poll, the very top of his head. She even teaches him to "shake hands." But she is becoming worried about him. He isn't getting any exercise at all and he seems restless, bored. He's started to chew the wooden fence rails. And he pawed and stomped the bottom rails. She'd had to replace two rails just this week. The doctor had said Destiny was NOT supposed to work with him. But since the doctor broke her foot, she wasn't doing it. The more Destiny thinks about it, the stupider it seems. Prince needs to work; he needs his exercise, both physically and mentally. He'll get rusty with his training if nobody does anything with him. After all the blood, sweat, and tears she'd put in making him the great horse he is, it just isn't right to let him tarnish. So while the doctor is up at the house having her "cocktails," in the cover of the deepening dusk, Destiny starts to put Prince back to work. She gets out his halter and lead rope and at first just works right there in his corral. She lunges him, asks him to move at a walk, then trot, then lope, then stop, turn, repeat in the other direction. It is bliss. Prince responds right away. He is light on the rope and his transitions are quick, balanced. All Destiny has to do is ask and he gives. Prince seems to love it. His neck is arched in cooperation, his gaits are energetic but controlled. He is doing his best for her and it's a joy to behold. Prince in motion is like a song or a really good poem. His high stepping, floating trot. The way his nostrils flare and the bunch of his hindquarter muscles at the lope. His easy surging walk, ears pricked straight ahead.

One night, after she'd been working with him for over a week, Destiny halters Prince and makes reins from the lead rope. The doctor is inside with a bottle of wine and her nose stuck in a book. Destiny opens the gate and leads Prince out. To a tree stump that she climbs atop, and then slides onto his back. Destiny feels Prince's warmth under her legs. She feels his muscles, his spine like a flexible steel beam. She strokes his mane, smooths his flanks. Picks up the rope reins and at the instant she begins to push with her seat, he moves off. A steady, hypnotic walk. Destiny lets her back relax, her butt melt into his back. They move like one creature. They clop down the drive. After the drive curves and the house and barns are out of sight, Destiny clicks and squeezes her thighs and Prince leaps forward into a lope. They pound down the dirt road through the purple twilight. Her hands grasp his mane, wiry and soft at the same time. Her legs hold his sides lightly. She's never ridden bareback and it is scary without the saddle but it is different, too. She can feel Prince moving under her, she can marry her muscles to his.

What this is, is pure happiness. Better than ice cream with fudge and no calories. Better than a long hot bath or sleeping in on a day off used to be. Better than crystal, better than sex. Way better than sex. Destiny feels like she was born for this. God has placed Prince back in her life for a reason. So that Destiny can know she is good at something. She is good for something. She is good for this horse and he is good for her; together they make music from motion, they are beautiful.

* * *

"How's your helper working out?" It is Lee, on the phone. I am in my office, working on a story about a break-in at the thrift store in town. (Someone had taken coats, blankets, clothes, and fifty dollars in cash.)

I let loose a big sigh in answer. "Okay, mostly. She's good with the horses. She's got Paprika coming along, she's saddling him already."

"That's amazing. And how are you two getting along?"

"She's driving me crazy," I whisper. I roll my chair to the window, look out. I can't see Destiny Tubb. Probably down at the corrals. I add: "She's always fucking underfoot. I can't even hear myself think."

"Yeah. For a hermit like you it must really suck to have another human being around," Lee says.

"Your sarcasm is not lost," I say. "But, Lee, it's awful. We have absolutely nothing in common. Conversation is like pulling teeth."

"Poor Siggy. Come on, girl! I bet your house is clean for a change. Cut the kid some slack."

"It gets worse. I caught her scrubbing my cast-iron skillet. With soap! And I just know she's snooping when she does my bedroom."

"You're a real bitch sometimes, you know that?"

"Of course I do. Am I being too hard on her?"

"Well, are you?"

"Jesus. You sound like my Inner Therapist."

Lee giggles. "Your what now?"

"Never mind. Also, Lee, get this. She's practically fixated on Chance. Of all these horses. She spends way too much time down there. I don't want him bonding with her, you know? He's supposed to be mine."

"He's probably bored, but, you're right; you don't need him focused on her. He needs to focus on you."

"I feel bad I'm not able to work him right now. Should I be letting her do it?"

"I wouldn't. He's fine. It won't hurt him to have a few weeks off. Just start him slow when you do get back to him."

"I love that horse," I say.

"He is a handsome devil," Lee says. (A rare admission for a quarter-horse snob.)

I don't even tell Lee all the things Destiny does to drive me insane. She rearranges the drawers and cabinets in the kitchen. Now when I try to cook, I can't find anything. She tells me it is easier this way and that the shelves had been way too crowded. Of course they had been crowded, but at least I'd known where things were. Then she does the same to my spice rack... and then the entire pantry, linen closet, and bathroom! At least she is sufficiently intimidated by my office; she moves things to dust and then places them exactly where they'd been. If I leave a book or magazine on the side table, opened, pages splayed, spine bent, she'll replace it the same way, at the same angle. I can only tell she's been in there by the sparkling windows and ashtray, the lack of dust on my computer and shelves and file cabinets. But for the studio, it is like living in someone else's house, like being a guest. My sheets change with frightening frequency. My damp towels disappear and are magically replaced with newly laundered, fluffy ones, rolled up neatly, stacked in a big reed basket. The concierge treatment doesn't stop there. Destiny Tubb even cleans my old boots, and oils them. They look new. She sews on missing shirt buttons and cleanses my sock drawer of the ones with holes. These things make me nervous. Her attentions are too intimate. I can't wait for my ankle to heal so that I can ban her from my house.

So Sneaky

It is Halloween before summer lets loose its sweaty grip on the mountain. But this morning the yellowed grasses are stiff, glazed with frost. The juncos' advance guard arrives with the cold. I always mourn the passing of summer; to me, it's the real end of the year, it's when I reluctantly salute the passing of another year of my life. Birthdays are about celebration, and autumn, to me, is about loss. The trees let fly spiraling, dying leaves, the rains beat the earth into submission, a muddy death. It was November when Hank died. A dreary, cold month. Rainy, sodden, the ground squishy like rot. Soon it will be a year since he died. How have I survived a year without him?

The damned Inner Therapist turns out to be right, of course. It has been my "hobby" that has made survival bearable. If not for my sixty-one horses I would still be truly lost, deeply, darkly lost. Not that life's a picnic. I still move through most days an emotion-less zombie. Only Destiny Tubb arouses emotion. Annoyance, and occasional sincere, blood-purifying anger. There's something just so… sneaky about her.

I limp out to the garden to bid it farewell for another year. I get no further than the end of the porch before I stop in shock. There are horses in the garden. And in the orchard. Living lawn ornaments. The gimpy chestnut gelding, Cody, is gleaning apples from the lower branches. If I was not mistaken, there are Willa and Sugar and Lulu and Dolly P., partaking of dried cornstalks. My garden fence is collapsed, fence posts askew, chicken wire trampled in dangerous wrinkles. The horses look contented, pleased with their freedom. My heart is thudding, my adrenaline zinging, pricking my armpits. How many horses loose? Any of them hurt? How far have they gone?

I yell for that hulking incompetent. "Destiny!" I scream. Then I hear her coming in the tractor. She skids to a stop at the bottom of the steps, looking up at me, her face deep red.

"The horses are loose!" I scream the obvious. She has cut the motor and my voice is over-loud; I sound hysterical.

"I know, I left the gates open, I guess, but don't worry, ma'am, I'll get 'em all back," she says in one breath.

"You'd better," I snarl. "Where's Chance?"

"He's in his corral, pitching a fit," she says, and then I hear him whinny on cue. At the same instant I hear something else and it takes a second to identify the sound. But when I do, it is indisputably the sound of thundering hooves. They burst into view. Another bunch of horses comes galloping down the lane, across the flowerbeds, through the drive, into the orchard, scattering the first comers, and now twenty or more horses are galloping, wheeling, kicking, leaping over the lawn furniture, drunk on freedom but frightened of the unfamiliar.

"Jesus, shit!" I yell. "Get them rounded up right now!"

"Yes ma'am," Destiny says. She races to the barn. Returns with a bucket of oats, her lasso.

I seethe in fury and helplessness while she coaxes, prods, drives, and bribes the horses back into the holding corral. It takes almost two hours. I make my way down to check on the escapees for injury. There is one bloody fetlock and a newly swollen hock, but amazingly, no broken legs, nothing drastic. I think of all the hazards they avoided: not a horse fell into the septic field or crashed through the porch or was impaled on a post as they breached the garden. A few hours would tell if any of them developed symptoms of colic from the unfamiliar food: apples, cornstalks, flowers, and god knows what else. Meanwhile I send Destiny Tubb on the tractor to complete a head count in the pasture to make sure we have them all.

She comes back and announces that they are all accounted for.

"Are you sure?"

"Yes ma'am. I'm sure."

"Destiny. How did this happen?"

"I don't know, I mean, I must have left the gates unlocked, I mean I know I closed 'em and I thought I locked 'em, but I guess I didn't."

"Jesus Christ. How could you be so careless? This is just un-necessary! Needless. Avoidable! They could have gotten hurt, or lost and worse!" I whip her with my words, they are sharp-edged like barb wire.

"I know, I am so, so sorry," she moans, her moon face redder than ever.

"Pathetic!" I spit. "Go, just get out of here! I can't stand to look at you right now."

"Yes, ma'am, and I am so sorry."

"Get the hell out of here. Go!"

* * *

The newly cool air had felt wonderful. Destiny, up early as usual, and with her arm over Prince's warm neck, watches and listens to the sunrise. Then down to the barn. Climb the hay, heave bales, load them onto the trailer, down to the pasture, stop, open the gate, drive through. Stop to close the gate. As she is closing the gate, a movement draws her attention. She shades her eyes to the low rays of the sun and peers into the trees. There is a deer there, half in shadow. Then she sees the rest, there are seven of them. One has fuzzy, forked horns. Two are fawns, still small. They are close enough Destiny can see their wet noses and the gnats cir-cling their ears. She remembers to breathe and when she does, they startle and are off, bounding in cartoon leaps through the brush, and disappear. She smiles, feeling blessed with having seen such a thing. She gets in the tractor and drives off to feed the herd. Finishes her head count and circles back. When she gets back to the gate, a jolt—like grabbing onto the electric fence—stabs her core. Her heart almost stops, her vision blurs. It can't be true! The gate is wide open. And clear hoof-prints going out, fresh on the frost-shattered ground.

"Dear Lord make that didn't happen!" she prays, aloud, un-realistically, stupidly. Even her prayers are stupid. She is a total screw-up. Even when she's trying her hardest, she still messes up royally, disastrously. Inevitably. She is in shock, galvanized by fear chemicals. She slams the gate, locks it, and races down the lane and there are some of the escaped horses and the doctor, mad as a wet hen. Her faint hope that she could retrieve the horses without the doctor finding out is, of course, a joke. Destiny endures the doctor's rage and trying to calm her jumping stomach, runs to the barn for a bucket of oats. Once she gets old Dolly P. following her, the majority fall in line. But a bunch of them have run off beyond the orchard. Destiny leads the first bunch back through the gate and goes for the others. It takes a horribly long time; the horses are fractious and know that Destiny intends to lock them back up. They have other ideas. Finally though, the last two are coaxed back through the gate. The doctor sends her off to count them. As she drives the tractor through the big pasture, she tries to imagine a happy ending; none of the horses seem hurt too badly… Maybe the doctor will tell her it's no big deal. That she is forgiven.

But of course that doesn't happen. The doctor is still really mad. Tells her to go away! Destiny flees to the barn apartment. Does the doctor mean, go away from here? Is she fired?

Where is there to go? Nowhere. Nowhere but back to Hotel Cockroach, to stealing the day's newspaper, to more fruitless job interviews. To the cold streets, the traffic, everybody going somewhere important except her, the blowing plastic bags and crashing of winos' bottles onto splotched sidewalks.

Just when she imagines she could have a happy life. Just when she is getting good at something. Just when her body is getting really strong, and she is even losing weight, her skin healthy and pink. Just when she is beginning to dream about getting Justin back.

***

It was just like that with Mitch. Just when she thought she was finally getting to have a real life. A good-paying job, a nice apartment, a decent car, clothes, money, and a boyfriend too. It was like climbing to the top of a grand gilded staircase but when you get to the top, there's nothing at all but a horrible abyss to fall into. And you fall: down, down, and down.

So, life was really cool, except for a couple things. Justin was acting out his terrible twos. His favorite word was No, and he used it until Destiny thought he'd surely wear it out. He was cranky and just generally impossible. And it was really hard to take because Destiny's nerves were none too good these days. The drugs were taking a toll, she knew it, but she just wasn't ready to stop. These days the drugs were the thing that everything else revolved around.

And soon there were too many endless sleepless nights. And then finally sleeping, sleeping all day and most of the next. That was when Justin was a real pain. After a binge of three days or so and Destiny and Mitch were finally ready to sleep, Justin would start fretting, whining. It was torture. Destiny knew she had to do something. Once she put Justin in the back bedroom and closed the door and went into the living room on the couch and put a pillow over her head to block out his screams.

"We got to stop doing so many drugs," she said to Mitch. More than once.

"Yeah, you're right," he'd say. But when the crystal was gone, he'd ask Destiny for cash and he'd go score another couple of grams.

It wasn't squalor or anything like that. Destiny was still working and her apartment was clean and Justin was getting regular meals, always had clean diapers and he had toys and cute clothes. But Destiny wasn't eating right. She wasn't looking too good. Thin, yes, but her skin was breaking out and her hair looked crappy and her nails were all bitten off and she was always on edge. Things looked all right but nothing felt right. Like a dress that looks great on the hanger but like crap when you put it on.

Later, after the worst had happened, Destiny had plenty of time to wonder if it all could have been avoided. Which single bad decision, if changed, would have kept her on track? Which day was the fork in the road an inevitable one? How many wrong steps had she taken that she couldn't retrace her way back to where she had a chance to live a normal life?

Was it the moment she naively turned her back long enough for Val to fill her purse with stolen jewelry? Was it the day she walked in to Greg's and met the Bees? Was it that first bump? Or was it the day Mitch strolled into the recording studio?

Or did it all come down to that last day, that awful day, when they killed that poor man?

✳ ✳ ✳

I stomp noisily back into the house, slam the door behind, crutch to the pantry and pour a stiff shot of good whiskey. I down it at the sink then throw my stupid crutches across the room. I grip the counter to limp to the table holding the bottle and shot glass. Fall into a chair and pour another.

Stupid bitch. She is so lucky none of the horses were killed. How would she like to have to think of that for the rest of her life? I wondered if she thought about the man she'd killed. Did he have a wife, who missed him every second? Did Destiny Tubb ever spare any of her feeble thoughts for her?

Destiny Tubb didn't kill Hank.

But she just as well might have.

But she didn't.

She could have killed horses today.

But that didn't happen. It was an accident.

Accident, my ass. It was her stupidity.

People make mistakes. Shit happens. Remember Freddie?

Ouch. (I pour another shot. It's anesthetizing my emotions nicely.)

Well?

Well what? I'm drinking here.

Well, the girl apologized and she'll probably be religious about the gates from now on. So why not forgive her and move on?

Maybe she should suffer.

Maybe you should tell her she's not fired before she heads on down the highway.

Well, shit. (I know I'm right. I still need her.) Okay.

The Inner Therapist doesn't make a magical twinkling sound, or smoke, when disappearing. I hop over to retrieve the crutches, and jam them up into my sore armpits and head down to the barn.

"Destiny!" I holler at the bottom of the stairs. The door opens. Her red face peers down. "Come down here, please."

She clomps down. Her eyelids red, her eyes moist. She rubs at her nose with a twisted tissue. Stands before me with a hanging head like one condemned.

"I accept your apology for leaving the gate open."

She sniffs and gulps.

"I want you to promise me it will never happen again."

"Oh, yes ma'am. I promise. It won't never happen again."

"All right then. We're both going to move on, older and wiser. Don't you have some work to do?"

"I kin stay?" she said, her voice phlegmy.

"You'd better, there are a bunch of animals depending on you."

She is uncomfortably effusive, telling me how she'll do better, work harder, etc, etc. A whole little blubbery speech that makes me squirm.

I cut her off and send her on her way. She scurries off towards Chance's corral.

I sigh. If only there weren't something so sneaky about her.

CHRISTMAS SURPRISES

Grub-like, my leg without its cast is pale, hairy, repulsive. But I feel no pain, only weakness in my calf and thigh, and walking without that plaster shackle is buoyant, like the force of gravity has been decreased.

Cold winds, stabbing rain, hard, glittering frosts; early December. The horse's coats are fuzzy with winter growth. They abide the freezing rains, not dry in their expensive shelters, but under the pines, heads down, backs dark and shiny with wet. I worry about them and call Dave. He assures me they won't die of the cold. He advises if the temperature drops below twenty, and the herd is wet, and the wind is up, to give late afternoon feedings to the oldsters of warm bran mash with a little grain, maybe adding a little molasses. I rejoice at passing on this arduous task to Destiny. It takes her over an hour just to mix the feed in fifteen-gallon tubs and load them on the tractor trailer and then another hour and forty minutes to distribute it to all sixty mustangs. I am turning evil in my old age. It gives me joy to see her sweating and huffing in the bitter wind. It pleases me to see her grunt with exertion as she heaves the hay and hauls the buckets. I don't spend too long wondering if these feelings are detrimental. The Inner Therapist keeps trying to bring it up, but I am a new person released from the cast. I can keep busy again, too busy for self-analysis.

It occurs to me that Christmas might be an ideal time to try to sell our first horse and while writing a monstrous check for hay, I'm convinced. I lock my checkbook in the desk drawer deciding to look at the ones Destiny has been training.

She is in the round pen with Skye, one of the blue mares. Skye is saddled and moving smoothly around at a trot. Her black tail is flagged high; her blue coat—really, it's a mixture of white and gray—is striking; she's pretty.

Destiny sees me and stops the mare, pats her, then comes to the rail. Her cheeks are red and her lips are chapped, and she's just a little out of breath. She looks startled, guilty. But then she usually looks at me that way.

"She looks good," I say mildly. "Have you been on her?"

"Not yet. I been working a lot on the transitions, she's a little bumpy-"

"She looks ready to me," I say, on a sudden naughty impulse.

"Oh! Okay, yes, ma'am, I can give her a try," Destiny says. She stands dumbly for a few seconds then blinks and turns back to the mare. She ties the cotton lead on both sides of the halter and tosses the loop over the mare's neck. The mare stands, quietly chewing. Destiny fools with the saddle, checking the girth, slapping the stirrups, jiggling the cantle, for so long that I get restless. Finally, she sticks her boot in the stirrup and hops up, leaning over the saddle. The mare dances sideways, and Destiny guides her in a circle with the rope rein. Finally the mare stops moving and Destiny lowers herself to the ground. Then repeats the process, up and down, up and down. I'm getting bored, now, and just about to yell at her to get on with it when she swings her leg all the way over and is sitting on the mare. The horse's ears swivel wildly but she otherwise is still. Destiny reins the mare's head this way and that, then lifts the reins and jiggles her butt in the saddle and the mare turns in a tight circle. They circle at a walk, this way and that. Then Destiny moves the mare out, circling the pen's perimeter. She jiggles the horse into a trot, circles both ways.

I am no longer bored. The damn mare looks like she's been doing this forever. After about twenty minutes, Destiny halts the mare, backs her up, and dismounts. She pats the mare and croons to her. She even leans over and kisses her sweaty neck. Then Destiny turns to me.

"Pretty good," I say. "Not bad at all. I think she'll be ready by Christmas, don't you?"

"She did real good," Destiny says with an actual smile. Her cheeks are flushed, and I notice her face isn't as chubby, she looks quite pretty. And so young. "Ready for what?" she says.

"To sell, of course."

"Oh!" Like she's been slapped, her cheeks flame red. "Oh, sure, yes ma'am, I guess so," she mumbles.

"Good," I say. "I want you to ride her every day."

"Yes ma'am, I sure can," she says.

"Now. How many others will we have? We must have another, right?"

"That I been trainin'?"

"Yes, that you've been training."

"Oh, gosh, um, lemme see… (she counts on her fingers, mumbling under her breath) …that would be fourteen, ma'am."

"Fourteen?"

"Yes ma'am, but now, let's see, Charlie and Whisper and um, Lacey, they're still doin' ground work, and Picasso, shoot, he's a handful."

"How many have you ridden?"

"The rest. So, ten?"

"The rest? We have ten horses that are saddle trained?"

"Well, they ain't perfect," she said, her cheeks getting even redder. "And I ain't had all of 'em out on the trails."

"No shit!" I say. (I'm feeling suddenly quite happy.)

"I know you done told me to start four a month, but don't forget, that bay mare, we decided she was too old, gettin' stiff, remember? And last month Odie got himself kicked by somebody and was limpin' and we've been lettin' him heal up. So there was supposed to be sixteen. But there's only fourteen."

"Jesus Christ. That's fantastic! I want to see you ride them."

"All of 'em?'

"What's the matter, Miss Tubb? Too lazy to ride ten mustangs in a row?"

"Oh, no, ma'am!"

"Relax, Destiny, I was joking; you've done well. You don't have to ride them all right now!"

"Oh, but I can if you want me to."

"Well. I want to see some of them. Let's see… let's see the one you've been riding the most. Let me see the best one."

She looks at me like she's been asked a trick question, then says, uncertainly, "Oh, that's… Walker." (I nod, encouragingly and her expression changes, she's relieved; she's passed some test) "…wait till you see him, Doctor Corcoran! He's doing awesome." She's babbling happily as she drags the saddle off the mare and sets it in the dirt. "…then, you gotta see Paprika too, he's got such a sweet trot on him…" She leads off the blue mare and returns with a golden dun gelding. The horse yawns as she leads him into the pen like she's interrupted a nap. He's big for a three-year-old mustang and I remember I chose him for training because of that and because of his gorgeous, soft gray-brown color like caramel and his nice head with black points and big, soft dark eyes. I watch Destiny saddle and ride him. I am shocked but it's a happy jolt. If she really has even half the horses she says trained like this, I'm sitting on some serious income. I won't be too sad to lose the horses, they will go only to good homes, where they will have a chance to fulfill someone's dreams. This is my dream, coming true. Destiny has actually done it.

Holy shit.

* * *

Destiny isn't sure, but it feels like the Doctor had been trying to trick her into confessing. Had the Doctor seen her with Prince, or did she just suspect? Destiny had seen an old movie once on cable that was about a guilty man, so guilty that he confessed his crime even though if he'd just of shut up, he would have gotten away with it.

She feels good, though, about how all the horses performed for the doctor. It came as a shock that the doctor was thinking of selling them so soon. Sure, Destiny had known from the beginning that was the plan, but in the months of this solitary working with the horses, she's managed to put the goal from her mind for the most part. With each horse, she'd pretend that it was hers. That the blue mare Skye was hers; and good ol' Walker, who was her first success, and Ginger—with her shining red coat. And Lola, she sure was sweet. And Paprika, with his trot so smooth you could just set there. And Willa, black like a shadow at noon, so quick, so smart, but still a little scared of anything new. You just had to show it to her and let her take as much time as she needed to get used to it, whether it was a rope or a blanket or a currycomb.

Destiny feels like each of them was hers; so now she starts to get all choked up; a big old hard-as-a-rock lump swells up in her throat. But she fights it. It's okay, it is her job. She is a horse trainer. That the doctor thinks they can sell the horses should be a victory. It is a victory. Now pride doubles the lump in her throat. It has been a long, long time since Destiny has done anything worthwhile. The doctor said, "You've done well, Destiny." Sure, she said it like it was some kind of private joke, but Destiny knows it was a compliment none the less because the doctor said to be ready to show the horses to potential buyers and she was going to place an advertisement.

Maybe the doctor doesn't know about her riding Prince after all. Slowly, Destiny begins to feel relieved. It is time to feed. Mechanically, she starts the chore. Her mind is on Prince though. She is planning on riding him up the forest road tonight—the roads aren't too muddy and there is going to be a full moon.

* * *

SADDLE TRAINED MUSTANGS FOR SALE.
10 horses, mares and geldings. 60 to 140 days under saddle.
All tie, clip, trailer load. A variety of sizes and colors.
Experienced and approved buyers only. $1500 – $3500.
Call 760-417-2338.

I sold every horse before Christmas. Paprika, the red roan, brought his asking price of thirty-five hundred. Walker, the caramel dun, three thousand! As I made the deposit into the bank, I wondered if this horse thing might not be a money-losing proposition after all. This deposit alone could feed the herd for about three months. If we could step up the program and sell more horses, and pay the entire feed bill just by the sale of horses... I could easily afford to pay Destiny and the vets and so on. This mustang rescue could be self-supporting, almost. I knew Dave could always get more horses from the BLM. He had been thrilled to hear about our success in training the mustangs. He'd said the BLM was talking about cutting down the number of adoptions next year then added, "But you didn't hear it from me."

"Then there's nowhere for 'em to go, he said, except the long-term holding facilities. It'll be only people like you givin' some hope of a future for 'em."

Dave tried to give me credit for training the mustangs so well. I told him that Destiny had actually done it all.

"Then she's worth keepin'," he said.

"I think you might be right about that," I said, mellow with success.

The dogs are barking their heads off and Destiny is down in town at the feed store. The white diesel dually truck is unfamiliar. He drives too fast while my dogs circle his wheels. I yell at them to come and wince as Teddy almost gets squashed. Finally the asshole driving slows to a stop, with his stinky, loud engine still rumbling.

After a long moment the driver cuts the engine and steps down from the cab. My dogs are now barking frantically. I grab their collars. "Can I help you?" I yell. Something about "horses", so I drag my dogs into the front door and slam it shut. Immediately they trade barking for whining. I go back towards the truck, but the driver is already strolling around the property.

"So can I help you?" I call again. I catch up with him at Chance's corral. Chance is all the way in the far corner, his nostrils wide.

"Yeah, I saw your ad and was wondering if you wanted to sell any of them mustangs."

"Well, yes, eventually," I say, feeling uncomfortable. The guy is not tall or short. A bit stocky. No facial hair. A stiff hat brim shading his eyes, further hidden behind aviator sunglasses. Wranglers. Big belt buckle. Small hands. "So do you... do you train horses?" I ask.

He pulled out a round tin from a back pocket, opened it, and pinched tobacco. Stuck it under his lip. I squirmed inside. "Tell ya what, I'll give you two hundred apiece. I'll take twenty. That's a nice profit right there. I know what you paid for 'em. Winter comin' and all, you don't want to be feeding all these, right?"

"Take twenty? And do what with them?" I ask.

"I reckon that would be my business."

"No thanks," I say, the light dawning. "Not interested."

"Two-fifty, then."

"No, God, no, not at any price! And I suggest you leave, right now."

"Ain't no need to get snotty."

"There's no need for you to be here any longer. Goodbye." I plant my hands on my hips defensively, wishing I were wearing my gun. Wishing Destiny were here. I'm suddenly afraid of this creep.

He spits tobacco in my direction then spins and climbs up into his ridiculously huge truck. "Fucking bitch," I see his lips say after he revs the belching motor.

It's not until the diesel engine sound is completely diminished that I finally can breathe. Did that really happen? Was that guy trying to buy the horses for meat? No other explanation made sense. I shiver again. I'm certainly going to have a word with Destiny about locking the front drive gate, even for a quick run to town.

That night I thought about that as I wondered what to give Destiny for Christmas. I had mail-ordered a new pair of riding boots for her, her old ones had actual holes; her feet must always be wet. But after the success of the horse sales, I reconsidered. I decided she deserved a bonus as well. Tomorrow I was going to town; I'd stop at the bank. A thousand dollars in cash would be her other Christmas present. She deserved it.

If I were still alone, I'd have ignored Christmas, just like I did last year. Well, not quite; this year I wouldn't be drunk out of my mind, wandering the house in the dark, the cold dark, too uncaring to light the fire. If I weren't stuck with Destiny, I'd simply carry on as if it were just another day in early winter. Eat some oatmeal, work on a newspaper story, watch a little TV. But the fact is, she is here, and so I feel obligated to acknowledge the date with at least some celebration.

I buy a breast of turkey thinking that a whole bird is overkill for two people. I make mashed potatoes and gravy, a salad and warmed up a store-bought pumpkin pie. But as I bring the turkey breast to the table, nicely browned and fragrant as it is, it suddenly seems stingy. I feel stingy. It's not like I can't afford a whole damn turkey or a hundred for that matter. I am Scrooge, I am the Grinch. This piece of meat looks maimed. I am ashamed; though I smile and say, Merry Christmas.

That slab of meat is maybe appropriate after all. The old Andrews Sisters album of Christmas carols I'd put on the stereo is the only thing that makes it seem remotely like Christmas. There are no decorations; there is no tree; I don't believe in killing a tree just to hang some lights on it. There is no pile of wrapped presents, no rum balls or Christmas cookies. Certainly no crèche with baby Jesus and plastic camels and wise men. Most glaring of all, there are no kids running around, hyped up on greed and sugar, no grandmother dozing in a recliner. No sisters or brothers or cousins. No family. Just Destiny Tubb and me, a couple of maimed women, maimed as the stingy hunk of meat on my good platter; related only by our love for the mustangs, right now huddled under a pine grove, waiting out the wet snow falling listlessly from the colorless sky.

At least I have presents for Destiny after dinner. She gathers the plates and I change the album. Put on Elvis's Blue Christmas, to suit my mood. I wish she was a drinker so we could at least share a brandy. But I have mine and she has another diet cola.

"Leave those dishes," I say. "Come sit with me by the fire."

She wipes her hands on a dishtowel and perches on the edge of Hank's chair. I hand her the big box, unwrapped. She stares at it with an odd expression.

"I'm sorry I didn't wrap it," I say, again feeling stingy. I completely forgot to buy wrapping paper when I was in town.

She shakes her head, so hard that her ponytail slaps the sides of her face. It is then I realize she is crying.

"Go ahead, open it, it's not that big a deal," I say, misunderstanding her entirely. I think she is stunned and grateful to receive the boots. That maybe she is embarrassed that she hasn't gotten me anything.

Her hands are shaking as she opens the box. The boots are light brown, with lighter tan stitching along the tops. They aren't fancy boots, but nice serviceable ones. Real cowgirl boots.

"Thank you," she says with a big sob in the middle of the two words.

"You certainly deserve them," I reply. She just sits there and cries harder.

"Please, Destiny. It's nothing. Please don't carry on."

She just puts her hands over her eyes and really lets go.

"Please," I say, after listening to the mewling for a few minutes. "Stop now. You're making too big a deal about it."

"I'm sorry," she chokes, but still won't take her hands from her face. Tears drip through her fingers onto the knees of her jeans.

"It's perfectly okay if you didn't get me anything. That's not the point. You needed a new pair of boots."

"It ain't that," she finally croaks, voice thick. "It ain't that. I got you somethin'."

"What is it then, Destiny?" (Not really wanting to ask or know, but what else can I say?)

"It's… that," she says, closing the boot box and pointing to the brand name.

"Justin? They're the wrong kind?" (I am ready to be pissed. They aren't Tony Lamas, for God's sake?)

"Justin," she says. She caresses the printed letters. "Justin. It's my baby's name. I just miss him, is all."

I stare at her in shock, my mouth dropping open.

"You have a son?"

She nods. She is no longer sobbing but her eyes still leak tears. "He's eight," she elaborates.

"Where is he?"

"Foster care. I don't know for sure."

For the first time I see Destiny Tubb in a new light. She knows something about loss too. I pour myself another brandy. Bring Destiny a box of tissues. Start to gently ask questions.

Justin had been born in jail, the first time she'd been jailed, when she was eighteen. For stealing, but she had been set up. After a month, reunited with her baby, she struggled to bond with him, and to support him. I know nothing of what it must be like to have no skills, no money, and the responsibility of a child and as I listen, I begin to respect Destiny's courage, her determination to make a good life for herself and her little boy. She tells me about Mitch. About the drugs. About being seduced by money and good times and the hope of a future with a man. And about the accident. Prison. And while in prison, not attempting to contact her son. For his own good.

"What about now?" I finally ask when her tale reaches the present.

"What about now?" she repeats.

"Don't you want to try to get custody of Justin?"

"I don't think so."

"Can I ask why?"

"I don't want to mess up his life any more than I already done. I don't deserve him."

"Oh, Destiny. Of course you deserve him. He's your son. You're sober now. You're responsible, very responsible, I can attest to that. You have employment and a nice place to live. A perfect place to raise a little boy, if you ask me."

She shakes her head defeatedly.

"Destiny. Think about him. About Justin. Do you think he misses you? Needs you?"

Naturally this rebuttal brings fresh sobs and tears. I ignore the outburst and impulsively continue, "I'll help you, Destiny, if you want. I'll help you with the paperwork, to find him and get custody. You'll need a lawyer, but you're in luck, I happen to have an excellent lawyer. Now, her specialty is not family law but I'm sure she'll give us a great referral."

Destiny blows her nose and dabs furiously at her eyes. Blows again. Six tissues later, she reaches over and takes my hand in hers. Her palms are damp but they are not clammy. More like the green humid air of a greenhouse, full of growing things, of life.

"You mean Justin could live here?" she asks.

"Of course."

"You'll git me a lawyer?"

"Yes. I'll advance you his fees. You can pay me back over time. It shouldn't be that terribly expensive. Besides, here."

I hand her the envelope. She takes it and then it is her turn to stare with her mouth hanging open.

"How much is this?" she asks, fanning the crisp $100 bills.

"A thousand dollars. It's your bonus for the horse training. It should be more, really, but we'll work out something more formal for the next year. You should probably get a percentage of each sale."

"Oh, thank you, Doctor Corcoran. Thank you so much. I kin use this for the lawyer. Is it enough to git started with?"

"Probably. We'll work on it right after the holidays. But, Destiny, there is always a possibility that you'll be denied custody, you know that, correct?"

She nods.

"But I think that any judge will look at your current circumstances and think you deserve a break. Maybe it will just be visitation. Maybe you'll get full custody. But even at the worst I'm pretty sure you'll be able to have a relationship with him."

"I cain't thank you enough… But… I don't know… I just don't know if I kin be a good mother."

"No one does, Destiny. I've counseled enough mothers to know. But you are his mother and no one else can ever fully substitute that relationship for him. You're decent and kind, I've seen you with those horses. I think you'll be a fine mother."

Awkwardly, she hugs me. Awkwardly, I hug her back. Apparently neither of us are the hugging type. But afterwards, I feel warm and fuzzy. And I don't believe it is entirely due to the brandy.

* * *

Destiny looks around the loft apartment with new eyes. Where would Justin sleep? A little bed could fit near the window if she moves the striped chair. There is plenty of room in her big closet for his clothes and stuff. She could get a chest for his toys and a bookcase for his books. She looks at the envelope of money on her desk. The doctor said, in time, she'd get more bonuses. It might be enough to pay for clothes and food and toys and stuff for Justin. She'd have to figure out how to get him to the bus everyday for school. She still couldn't get a driver's license. On the tractor? Or maybe she'd just have to ride him down there on one of the mustangs. Or teach him to ride himself. She grins at the image of the two of them riding through the forest on their way to meet the bus. His lunch in a saddlebag: a Thermos of chocolate milk, an apple, a peanut butter sandwich. What if he likes it here? What if it turns out he likes horses as much as she does? Maybe he'd be okay here. Maybe he'd turn into the cutest little cowboy, the cutest little man, here. The doctor could teach him big words and manners and how to speak right. Maybe in time, he'd even come to love her, Destiny. His mama. She could hear his little baby voice saying it. Mama, mama. In a happy voice, demanding her attention, in one sad, and one bored. All his voices, the one word, said so many ways, meaning so many things, but always meaning the same one thing too. I'm his mama. The one and only.

Would he ever forgive her, though? Would he forgive her the years and years she hadn't been there? Could anyone ever really forgive their mother abandoning them? And what about the other thing. What about what she'd done to end up in prison and lose him in the first place? Did he remember that day?

* * *

Mitch's band hired a girl singer and Mitch talked about her far too much for Destiny's liking. Plus, he was gone a lot longer at rehearsals. Finally the stupid girl singer, Shandra, her name was, had to go to LA and so the band took a break from rehearsals and gigs and Mitch had some time to spend with Destiny. Naturally they got some crystal and had a little party, just the two of them. They got into bed for a while and messed around then had some beers and kissed and talked and played dice, Mitch loved to play dice. Justin was playing and napping like a good little guy; after Destiny fed him his lunch, he went right to sleep. After he woke up Mitch played the guitar for him and even played with him, building stuff with his plastic blocks. Destiny ordered pizza and raviolis for Justin but when it was delivered, Justin was the only one who ate. Mitch had opened a bottle of tequila and a new pack of cigarettes. "Let's play," he said, rolling the dice.

The party went on and eventually they came to the last of the drugs. The tequila bottle was almost empty. Mitch was out of smokes.

"Let's make a run, baby," Mitch said. "You gotta drive."

"I have to get Justin ready," she said, though the thought of it was daunting. He was playing happily in his playpen, crushing Cheerios with his truck. His diaper needed changing and his face was dirty and Destiny wasn't sure if she even had any clean diapers. She was twitchy and knew she couldn't stand to hear him start screaming right now. For sure he would scream if she tried to put him in the car.

"Leave him, we'll be back in a sec, "Mitch said.

"I can't do that, what if there's a fire?"

"There's ain't going to be a fire. C'mon, lessgo."

"I ain't leaving him!"

"Destiny. Look at him. He's fine. We'll be gone, like, five minutes, just to the corner and to Toby's. (Toby was their dealer). Come on, come on, I need a bump."

The thing was, so did Destiny. She looked desperately at the empty white packet on the table. She could feel herself getting strung out looking at it, wanting more, right now!

"Okay, okay," Destiny said. It didn't feel right but seriously, what could happen in ten minutes? Mitch was right, Justin would be fine.

They got in Mitch's red Firebird and Destiny drove. As soon as she started driving, she knew she was more messed up than she'd thought. She had to squint to keep the road from splitting in two. At the gas station on the corner, the kid behind the counter sneered at her as he took her money for the cigarettes. Y'all drive careful, he called in a snotty way as she staggered out.

Then Toby wasn't home.

"Dammit, shit!" Mitch screamed at the door, pounding on it fruitlessly. "Where's that motherfucker!" Lights went on next door so Destiny took Mitch's arm and pulled him back to the car, both of them weaving across Toby's dirt yard.

They held a none-too-calm discussion. Destiny wanted to go right home and Mitch wanted to go looking for Toby. He was pretty sure he knew which bar Toby frequented. Destiny was getting worried about Justin. But she needed a bump too, more so, the more Mitch yelled at her.

"How far is it?" she asked, giving in.

"Like five minutes!"

"Fine," Destiny said, starting up the car. A few blocks later she merged onto the highway, cutting the corner and just missing the guardrail.

She never saw the other car. Mitch was lighting a cigarette and then dropped it and she looked down to make sure it wasn't burning the floor carpet and suddenly there was a blaring horn and she looked up and she was in the wrong lane, headed right for another car—she could see the driver's scared face through the windshield, and then there was just enough time to scream and then the horrible crashing and then the darkness.

* * *

She'd left her son alone and gone out to buy drugs. And killed a man. She hadn't lived with her son since that day. Left him playing in a pile of Cheerios, with dirty hands and face and diaper. Everyday, since that day, when she thought of Justin, that's how she'd see him. Her abandoned little boy, all alone, in a pile of crushed Cheerios.

There is one remedy she knows to shake off those dark thoughts and how awful they make her feel. Destiny puts on her coat and goes down the steps. Puts on her gloves and hat and takes the gear, and goes out into the cold, to Prince's corral.

He hears her coming and is waiting, head over the rail. He nickers as soon as she comes out the door.

Hey Prince, she calls. He is so beautiful, his ears pricked and an interested look in his eye. His nostrils vibrate with another greeting. Destiny pets him and lets herself inside. He lowers his head for the bridle. She never bothers with a saddle now. Leads him out and moves him next to rail. Climbs up onto his warm back. Lifts the reins and he moves off. Right away the motion is soothing. They go down the driveway, frozen hard and slippery with old snow. But Prince's hard mustang hooves bite into the surface and they go slowly but easily. Turn at the gate up the dirt road and begin to climb.

The grade isn't steep but it goes steadily up and up. There are a few flatter spots and here Destiny lets Prince trot. He is powering up the mountain, his head curved to the task. His hooves beat a rhythmic pattern and his breath steams. Destiny leans slightly forward to keep herself balanced on his back, working with him. The reins are loose, her hands are on his withers, holding a handful of his russet mane.

She isn't thinking about much of anything, thankfully. Looking around at the trees and sage with their powdered sugar dusting of snow. Listening to the birds and the hidden creek, rushing over rocks.

Up to a plateau, high above everything. Looking all around, you couldn't see any sign of civilization at all. Just trees and rocks and canyons and mountains, like they are all alone in a private world.

After a while they head back down. Prince goes slower and even though some parts of the road are slippery, he places his hooves carefully, almost delicately. Destiny never for a minute feels nervous or unsafe. Prince has become an awesome trail horse. He is totally dependable and willing. Nerves of steel. Plus, she almost feels like he is always thinking about her, about keeping her safe—it's probably just her imagination, but it really seems like that.

At the gate Destiny feels a nervous twinge in her stomach. All of a sudden she doesn't want to go back to the doctor's ranch. But it's her home now. And it's Prince's home too.

* * *

I finish the dishes and put away the remains of the Christmas meal. Destiny had gone back to the barn and the house feels emptier than usual. I consider returning some phone calls but am not really in the mood to exchange holiday greetings. I miss Hank. If he were here I'd have bought him a dozen presents. A new truck and a truckload of tools; all that manly stuff he loved. I'd present him with a horse, one of the mustangs, trained just for him. I'd have baked him that damn cherry pie.

I am falling into a bad funk. My first thought is: more brandy. But then I know I'll have to battle that infernal Inner Therapist and I just am not up to another struggle for my soul. I know an easier way.

I put on my boots and coat and gloves and whistle up the dogs. Head down to see Chance. Breathing his sweet breath and rubbing his warm coat is like Valium. It chills me out, puts things in perspective, soothes the pain. Whoever said, "There's nothing better than the outside of a horse for the inside of a man" knew what he was talking about.

I'm already smiling as I approach Chance's corral. I don't see him, is he in the shelter? My smile drops and my steps quicken and then I'm running. He's not here! I look over the fencing, has he broken out? The rails are all okay. The gate is closed, the latch is down, but it's not locked. The chain and hook hanging open. But even if Destiny had left the gate open, would Chance really have let himself out then closed and latched the gate after himself? It seems highly doubtful.

How did he get out? Was he stolen?

"Destiny!" I yell but my voice shrinks in the cold wind.

I run to the barn, yelling the whole way. My voice echoes, my steps echo as I run up the steps to her apartment. She's not there. The boot box on her bed, the boots still inside, with tissue paper stuffing. The envelope of money on her dresser.

I run back down to Chance's corral, and am standing there, going nuts, when I hear hoof-steps and I look down the drive and here comes Chance, and Destiny riding him. She sees me at the same instant I see her. She startles and her mouth drops open.

"What do you think you're doing?" I shriek.

She immediately drops off Chance's back and begins leading him to me, holding out the reins like some kind of apology.

"I'm sorry, Doctor Corcoran, I really am," she gasps.

"I told you explicitly you were not to ride him!" I snap. My panic at having found Chance gone whips my anger into fury.

"I know," she moans.

"Then why did you? Have you done this before? How long has this been going on?" I scream like a banshee.

"I don't know," she moans, trying to hand me the reins.

Chance nuzzles her and for some reason it makes me even more furious.

"Don't know what? Answer me."

"I don't know, I don't know why."

I snort like a dangerous stallion. "How long? How long have you been riding my horse?"

"More than once," she admits, crying now, her nose red, snot dripping.

"Don't even fucking try to lie to me Destiny," I say, hard as a knife edge.

"I been riding him a while!"

"I thought so. It makes me wonder, Destiny, what other rules you've broken. What else you've been doing. I had a feeling I couldn't trust you. Do I need to check my silver, my bank book, my jewelry? Have you been going through my drawers, my papers?"

"No, no, of course not, no, nothing like that!" she sobs.

"How can I believe you?" I wait while she suffers, for the answer I know she doesn't have.

Finally, she shrugs. A sickeningly pathetic gesture.

"You're fired," I snap. "Pack your things. I can't have anyone living here who I can't trust. I'm sure you understand. Let that thousand dollars be your severance pay. I'd like you gone in the morning. Use my phone to arrange transportation if you need."

I take the reins and with a harder jerk than I mean to use, lead Chance back inside his corral.

"He's hot," I add. "If he founders because you worked him too hard in this cold, I'll have your ass. I'll sue. I'll call the police. Get me a blanket."

She does and I yank it out of her hands without speaking. She stands there dumbly, fighting tears and snot while I blanket the horse. My arthritic fingers can barely work the ice-cold buckles, which enrages me more.

"Go on," I say. "You're no longer welcome here." I brush past her and stomp up to the house, where I head immediately for the brandy.

Damn her! Just when it looked like she might be working out. But it was as I suspected all along. There was something sneaky about her and I just knew she was up to something, hiding something from me, lying to me, taking advantage. I should have known better than to involve myself with an ex-con. I briefly think of her little boy and feel a twinge of compassion for the little guy. Justin. But no wonder she's lost him, I think then. She's a total fuck-up and would betray her own mother to get whatever she wants. A sneaky, lying user.

Good riddance.

NOWHERE

Destiny's hands are shaking, and not from the cold. She can't believe what she's doing. She's horrified at what she is doing but she keeps on doing it. Stuffing clothes into the saddlebags. A case of energy bars, the perfect survival food. Water and a plastic tarp and matches and a flashlight. Rolling up the pretty quilt in the tarp and tying it with a lead rope. Bringing Prince into the barn so she won't have to make a bunch of conspicuous trips down to his corral with all the gear. In the barn Prince's steamy breath in the moonlight makes it look like a movie set. Destiny brushes him quick and checks his feet for stones. Puts on the thick saddle blanket and saddle. His bridle, over the halter. Makes sure she has extra ropes and a hoof-pick and brush and a big heavy bag of oats. She checks the saddle bags are even on his flanks. She is wearing two layers of clothes and makes sure she has her hat and two pairs of gloves.

She leads Prince out of the barn, wishing his clip-clopping wasn't so loud. Apprehensively she scrutinizes the dark house. She hasn't seen or heard from the doctor since being cast out with the words: "You're fired. You're no longer welcome here."

As she'd stumbled from the house, blind with tears, she first berated herself with the old refrain, Destiny, you are such a loser. The best deal you ever got in your whole crummy life and you blew it.

Inside her apartment—no longer hers!—she automatically looked out the window, down to Prince's corral. He was there, looking up at her. As she opened the window, he nickered. Thanks for the ride, he said. Prince knew the doctor was mad, but he thought she was mad at him. Prince liked the doctor okay, but she confused him, and as a result, he couldn't trust her, which meant he couldn't respect her. That was simply the way of the horse.

It wasn't even like she decided to take Prince. It was just that suddenly she was doing it. She waited for dark without once considering another option. As she waited she made a list of what she would take. And decided on a direction to go, and a hazy plan.

If she just rode far enough and got up high where it was still snowing, the snow would cover their tracks. And she'd just keep going until they found a nice little town somewhere and she'd get another job, if not training horses, then cleaning houses. She knew how to do that, at least. And she'd board Prince somewhere and as long as she could see him everyday and ride him, then maybe they'd have a chance.

Down the driveway, leading Prince, still glancing over her shoulder at the house. No alarm is sounded. At the curve in the drive, she stops and checks the girth, tightens it a little. He paws his front hoof. She ignores his impatience and sticks her foot in the stirrup, swings into the saddle. His muscles bunch, he is thinking of taking off before she asks him, and Destiny instantly just ever so lightly squeezes the reins. He relaxes, waiting like she's taught him, for her signal. Destiny gathers the reins, settles herself in the saddle, and clucks to him. Prince moves off at an energetic walk. Destiny doesn't slow him as she would have usually. It is a little slippery but she wants to get going, fast. Prince slides a little at the very bottom of the drive where it is the muddiest, but Destiny stays with him. It is a little scary, but now they are on the uphill road, where there has been no traffic and the snow is unbroken, squealing under Prince's hooves; it is good footing. Destiny urges him to a trot, sooner than she should. She should let him warm up more at a walk first. But her heart is pumping hard and the urge to get far away from the doctor's house is inescapable.

Up and up through the forest, through the cold, still, starry night. The farther they get the better Destiny feels. It is dang cold, though, and the idea of sleeping outside in the forest frightens her. But she's brought a lot of matches and hopes she can get away with making a fire, and try sleeping a few hours just before dawn; the doctor won't even know what has happened until tomorrow morning and by then Destiny and Prince will be so deep in the forest that they won't be found. And after a while the doctor will quit looking, and it will be safe to find a place to start over.

She can tell that Prince is wondering when they are turning back. Each time she stops him for a breather, he starts to turn facing back down the road. Each time Destiny corrects him, directs him back uphill, she knows that Prince thinks: Oh, not yet? But he happily keeps going. Destiny knows he'll keep going with her as long as she wants him to. She knows Prince is happy that Destiny is his leader. He trusts her and respects her. It was hard at first; he hadn't wanted to be led. In his herd, Prince had been the leader, Varney said. He had fought to become leader. But without his herd, in the round pen, she had showed him that she could lead. She made his defeat bearable by her clarity. She had shown him that there would never be pain. That she could insist on his submission, but honestly, without cruelty. That was the way of the horse.

For once Destiny feels like she knows what she's doing. For once she is prepared, she has gear, she has knowledge. She'd read a book in the doctor's library that was about a tracker. And Destiny learned about compasses and maps. She has both and knows she's headed in the right direction, into a vast stretch of BLM land. On the map, where Destiny is going, there are no roads. She hopes that with a probable eight-hour head start, Prince is capable of covering, say, twenty, maybe thirty miles. They would strike off into the forest soon; she has to get off the road. Every step on the road is one that they could follow in trucks.

Past the plateau where she liked to bring Prince, they turn down a little jeep track leading off from the main fire road. This is little more than a hiking path, overgrown with sage, branches low overhead. The road goes less than a mile and dead-ends at a little campsite. Destiny turns Prince north and they go into the trees.

It is slow going. The brush is thick and in places, she has to backtrack, sometimes a long way before there is an opening and then she'd recheck the compass and try to keep them headed north. Prince jumps over dead falls and splashes through a creek. He has to go under branches drooping with snow, and not flinch when the snow dumps on his flanks like a wet hand. But he's careful and steady because he is responsible for Destiny. He knows they are doing something important. It is exciting to be in this forest, far away from the rest of the herd. He is on alert but not apprehensive. There is no scent of lion or bear or wolf or dog. He trusts Destiny and will travel as far as she wishes.

It is a comfort to Destiny that she can hear Prince's thoughts. It makes her feel like she isn't alone. She isn't alone, and she never will be as long as they are together.

* * *

I am so furious I yell and curse and stomp around until my aching ankle makes me stop. I'm too incensed to light the lamps as the sky darkens and the fire dies in the fireplace; the house begins to grow cold.

That stupid bitch. I can't believe she's done this and ruined everything. Betrayed me just like everyone else.

What's that?

Well here I am, all alone again!

Again?

Everyone always leaves.

Who is everyone?

Misery loves company but I can't believe I'm talking to you.

Maybe you need to talk. Maybe it's time.

Time for what?

What do you think it is time for?

Oh, I know, time to be honest, let it all out, have a big psychological breakthrough.

Let's just clarify who "everyone" is. These people who keep leaving you.

Well, it's obvious. My parents. Hank. Now her.

Are you certain there is a connection? Your parents died of illnesses. That was not your fault.

And Hank?

Do you feel responsible for Hank's death?

Of course not. Even though…

Even though?

Even though we'd had that fight. And I never got a chance to make it up to him. To tell him it didn't matter. That I still loved him just as much.

Unresolved issues are difficult. But you can let go of the guilt.

I'm not guilty. It wasn't my fault. I told him he didn't have to go into town. The storm was bad. I told him to stay.

Then why did he go?

Because he was an asshole, I yell. He never listened!

Why did he say he was going?

You know. We needed some stuff from the store.

So he was just taking care of things. You depended upon him to take care of things.

Are you saying I should have gone? It should have been me in that truck?

What do you think?

I don't think he died for me! Do I? Did he?

Okay, fine. It's taken over a year to admit I feel guilty, that there must have been something I could have done to make Hank stay home that day. It wasn't our fight that drove him out into that storm, or anything so pat. But even if he had not gone, would that have saved him? Was it just chance that that drunk was coming the other way? Or was it his time; would he have keeled over anyway, with a heart attack, or a stroke? Or is it true that it was my fault?

It doesn't matter. The unanswerable questions don't matter. It's time to forgive him.

I thought you were going to say, it's time to forgive myself. I don't need to forgive Hank. He didn't die on purpose.

But he still left you.

Yes. He did. (I begin to cry, broken-heartedly.)

You're angry at him for leaving you.

Yes.

Forgive him. He loved you. Somebody had to die first.

I imagine Hank alone. If I'd died first. It's a brief and horribly vivid picture. I see him with his handsome head bowed. His erect posture crumbled. A sad old man, bewildered. It breaks my heart all over again and I know that I love him enough to have let him go first. To spare him this, this being alone. And I do, I do forgive him, for dying first.

✳ ✳ ✳

The next morning the rooster wakes me. I've slept like the proverbial baby, even without a half bottle of brandy. I feel light, cleansed. Emotionally cleansed and calm. Womb-calm. I get up and have a nice hot shower.

I'm in a forgiving mood. Destiny hasn't come to use the phone, to ask for a ride, so I assume she's still in the apartment. Probably waiting for me to come and forgive her.

Maybe I can understand why she was riding Chance. He's the best horse here. Maybe she was keeping up her courage and skills by working with him. Maybe it's not such a big deal. Why shouldn't she ride him? It's not as if I'm doing that well with him. Maybe I should have asked her to help me with him at least.

At any rate I decide it's not a firing offense after all. I need her, and God knows, she needs me. I dress and comb out my hair. Stuff my still wet braids into a hat and pick up my coat from the floor where, last night, I'd thrown it. Head out into the gray morning to forgive Destiny and ask her to stay.

The apartment's quiet, even though I call from the bottom of the stairs. I'm getting a funny feeling as I climb them. Her door's slightly open. I slowly push it wider.

What I see hits me like a jolt from an electric fence. Her bed's stripped, the quilt gone. Her drawers are open, mostly emptied. The envelope of money, her new boots (the box is here but empty) her clothes, are gone. So is Destiny.

She must be walking to town, I realize. But why take that heavy quilt? Just to spite me, to rip me off? But it's a lot to carry.

I decide to overtake her in the truck. Maybe she has just left. If I can catch her before she gets all the way to town, and the bus stop…

I jog to the truck and don't even warm it up. I go down the drive a little too fast. At the bottom I swing left towards town, fishtailing the truck in the snow. All the way down the mountain I keep expecting to see her, trudging along lugging that quilt. But the road is empty except for a knot of long-horned cattle and the occasional rabbit.

She's not in town either. I check the bus stop and the diner and the gas station-slash-convenience store. I check the market and I ask everyone I see. No one has seen Destiny. I use a pay phone to call the bus company in Bakersfield. Can I find out if she has come in on the bus? No. The answer is no, they don't keep those records.

Destiny has disappeared. She could be anywhere by now.

I drive slowly back to the ranch. I decide not to report her missing to the police or anything like that. I told her to leave, and she did. My only hope now was that she'd call or come back. Otherwise, I might have seen the last of Destiny Tubb. For so long that was what I wanted. But now the reality is different. I'm horrified at what I have done. She wasn't so bad. She tried hard. She had been a godsend, really. Destiny made everything happen. How could I keep the mustangs without her?

Poor kid. Where was she? What would she do? How would she ever get her son back now?

I am a terrible person.

Curving up the drive I hate myself. For someone with all this training in psychology, I sure fucked up good; and all because I hadn't understood my own issues. Quite the irony.

Something snags my attention as I top the drive. Something not right. I know what it is before I even turn my head to look. Chance always sticks his head over the rails to greet any vehicle coming up the drive. But not this time. I stop the truck and jump out leaving it running. He isn't in his corral. I check the round pen, the arena. The barn. Then I see it. Hoof-prints, partially obliterated by my truck tire tracks, but intermittently visible. Headed down the drive. I look around and the prints tell a story. From the corral to the barn. From the barn down the drive. His saddle and bridle are gone. And my saddlebags. Now I understand. She's taken Chance.

I run to the house and call the sheriff. It is Christmas morning; there is no one at the substation. I hang up on their answering machine and call 911. The dispatcher is a city girl who has no clue where my place is. I demand a deputy and give her directions and she says in a noncommittal way: We'll try and get someone out there sometime today, ma'am. Then I walk down the drive, following the hoof prints. At the bottom of the drive, they go right, up the mountain. I want to follow right away in my truck, but don't want to miss the deputy either. I wait, pacing, for an hour. Then two. I make several calls back to 911 until the girl loses her temper.

It is after noon before the deputy shows. He is a handsome young thing and very polite. I tell him what has happened; I try to be calm and rational but as I recount the tale, I am overcome with huge battering emotions: guilt, anger, fear, loss. I probably sound at least a bit hysterical.

He asks twice if Destiny has threatened me or has a weapon or threatened to use a weapon. Asks if there is anything else missing. If there was any way for Chance to have gotten loose on his own. I tell him no and no and no and we walk down to look at where the tracks headed up the mountain; then he gives me the bad news.

Since I'd paid $3500 for Chance, stealing him is grand theft. So the deputy's report will list that and a missing persons report. But, it is Christmas, they are short-staffed. Nevertheless, because it is possible that Destiny is lost, or in danger up in the forest, they will begin a search ASAP. But due to the holiday, it will take some time to call in the manpower and the day is already short. They will only have a few hours to search before dark.

Deputy King leaves and returns two hours later with only one other deputy.

No helicopter, no squads of trackers with bloodhounds, no teams of Search and Rescue experts, no hordes of volunteers with whistles and GPS devices. Just two young deputies, working out in the cold on Christmas. Probably mostly thinking of their double overtime pay.

I insist on following them. They shrug.

I follow the SUV up the mountain. We slide and spin on the melting snow. At a plateau, they stop and have a lengthy discussion about whether or not to put chains on the tires. I get out of my truck, impatient for them to decide. I wander off, smoking. Up the road a few steps. See the tracks going off the road, onto a small path through the trees. Chains or not, we aren't going to be driving through there. It is time for the helicopters and dogs and volunteers.

I yell to the deputies.

They come and look.

"We're not equipped to follow in there," King states the obvious, as cops are no doubt taught to do.

They hold a brief discussion partly in code. I wait for the translation.

To continue searching for Destiny and Chance the deputies will need authorization. It will require a multi-jurisdictional search. And there is a big snag. The other deputy, Sorenson, suggests that Destiny may have gone in a car, perhaps hitchhiking, or with a friend. And let Chance loose. In summary, maybe this was just a horse's trail. Not necessarily Destiny's. And there is no way a multi-jurisdictional search would be undertaken the day after Christmas for a horse.

"I'm sure she's riding him," I insist.

"That very well may be, but there's no way to really know," Deputy Smart Ass says.

The nice one, King, at least says they are sorry. They will take it up with the Commander and he will call me by tomorrow.

"Ma'am, I wouldn't hold out much hope for a search, King cautions. If Miss Tubb's still missing in three days maybe we can do more. Most likely, she'll come on home as soon as she gets cold enough."

* * *

It is so cold. Her hands are so stiff that it's hard to hold the match. She wastes three before she gets the flame going in the little pile of sticks. She shivers as the flames grow. She puts on too much wood too quickly and the flames almost die, but the second time she has more patience and at last she can feel some warmth. She puts her wettest pair of gloves on a stick near the flames to dry them. She'd torn some pine boughs from a tree and spread them on the ground and then put the folded tarp over that so she has a place to sit that's not wet. Prince's saddle rests at the head of the tarp so she can use it to lean back. But she's still too cold to lean back. Prince is tied to a young tree just a couple feet away. Just far enough so he can't step in the fire but close enough so he won't feel alone. He paws at the snow until he finds some grass. He's calm and concentrating on the gleanings of winter grass.

It is just past twilight. It will be the second night in the forest and now she knows how long and cold the night will be. Last night, they'd left the ranch at midnight, and ridden all night. She'd planned on stopping to sleep but was too afraid they'd find her if she did. And she was too scared of sleeping in the forest anyway. It had seemed like the darkness went on forever, like the sun had forgot to rise. It was incredible how much you could see in the dark, though, with the half moon and stars reflecting on the snow. But she had mostly relied on Prince to see the way. And finally the sky had lightened, slowly, so slowly. Gradually, she had been able to make out details in the trees and rocks and then the bunnies came out right before the sun actually peeped through the trees.

They'd kept going until about ten o'clock that morning. Ten hours riding. She knew she had to rest Prince, and find water. They'd gone a long time without water. She wanted to stop earlier but it wasn't until she finally heard a gurgle and found a little crick that they could stop. She unsaddled Prince and tried to rest.

She woke to find her nose so cold she couldn't feel it. Prince was shivering, standing with his head down. She struggled from the quilt and went to him, rubbed him vigorously with the saddle blanket, then draped the quilt over him. Fed him a few handfuls of oats, wishing she'd brought more. He stopped shivering almost as soon as he'd finished chewing the oats. She fed him an energy bar for good measure. She secured the quilt as best as she could with a rope then led Prince a little ways to the crick.

It was icy cold but he didn't mind. He was warming nicely in the quilt. He was ready to get moving. So was she.

Through the tall trees they go, so tall that there were only occasional patches of sun. Several times Destiny stops Prince in one of these little sunlit patches, just to feel the tepid warmth for a few minutes. All day, she is careful not to push Prince. The terrain is difficult and she'd realized almost at the beginning that this would become a real nightmare if Prince hurt himself. So she stays balanced in the saddle, no matter how tired she gets, or how sore her butt gets, and lets him have a loose rein, and lets him take his time, high-stepping through the tangled brush. Stops for a half hour at two in the afternoon, in a patch of sunlight where there is some nice grass for Prince. Then kept going until she found this place, just in time, before the dark dropped like sudden blindness.

There is a spring and a clearing and a big rock formation with smooth sides. Destiny builds the fire ten feet away from the rocks so she can sit up against the boulders and the fire would be between her and the forest. Prince is tethered at her side; there isn't a tree handy so she's tied his rope to a big boulder. Tonight there is a wind and the fire leaps like devils dancing in hell. Destiny is worried about Prince. She cusses herself because she hasn't brought a blanket for him. It would have been heavy but worth it.

Well, she has the fire. And her heavy sheepskin lined coat, one of the doctor's old ones, one of the first things the doctor had given Destiny. And she has herself a pair of dry gloves. And she can wrap the saddle blanket over her legs. So she gets out from under the quilt and as soon as she does, begins to shiver. The cold cuts through her jeans and long underwear like she's naked. She takes the quilt to Prince and doubles it then puts it over him. Ties it with two loose straps of rope. Knows she won't be able to sleep, she'll have to keep checking to make sure the quilt doesn't slip and end up hanging under him. As soon as Prince is blanketed, his head comes up. He curves his neck and puts his muzzle gently in her hand. Not looking for a treat, just saying thanks.

She huddles closer to the fire. It is too scary to build it up much, with the wind and all. But the embers are red hot and Destiny spends the night extending one body part after the other as close to the flames as she can stand. When that part is broiled, she defrosts another part. By the time the sky starts to lighten, she is exhausted and her eyes are dry and burning. But she waters Prince at the spring and gets all her stuff together and mounts him. Moaning at her sore muscles and bruises. Checks the map.

As best as she can figure, they have come more-or-less eighty miles. In a few miles they should cross a fire road. Once they are far enough past that, she plans to find a likely spot, make a camp and spend a few days there. They'd be just about in the middle of nowhere.

Prince carries her up and up, to the top of a ridge where the trees thin. Up there the wind is strong and Destiny has to dismount and weight the map to the ground with some stones to even read it. Something doesn't make sense. There is supposed to be a big mountain right to the east. They should have crossed that road by now. Where is that branch of that river? They never saw any river.

A sick feeling overwhelms her. She has no idea where they are. In the middle of nowhere, that is for sure. But it is the wrong nowhere.

She wants to rip up the map in frustration, she wants to kill herself. But she is too chicken to do either one. Her careful plan is a joke. Even if she found the little town where she planned to start over, did she really think she'd get away with it? She'd stolen Prince. Could she really ride into a town on a horse with no possessions and expect people not to ask questions? Probably the doctor already has the cops out looking for her in every town in the county. There are probably "Wanted: Horse Thief" posters with her picture on them. If she gets caught, and convicted of stealing Prince, it will be her third strike. Even Destiny knows about three strikes: three felonies and you were in prison for life.

She was stuck out here in the forest. At least Prince will help her; he'll show her things that will help her survive.

Found and Lost

She has been missing two days. Two days and three nights. The nighttime low temperature has been ten degrees, with a wind chill of minus five. Even as a seasoned country dweller, it is hard for me to imagine sleeping outside in that. Even with my nice down quilt. I worry about her freezing to death. And I worry about Chance. I worry about them getting injured, lost, hungry, thirsty, attacked by wild animals. I can't think of anything else but the fact that they are out there, in the wild; I can't do anything but try to find them.

The Sheriff's Commander called the day after Christmas. He said he was sorry but in his opinion the likelihood that Destiny had taken my horse and gone into the forest was remote. More likely, considering her "past," she'd managed to get to town and from there... who knew?

I ranted and railed to no avail. I was sure she was up in the forest, with Chance. But I couldn't convince the authorities. I threatened to use my "power of the press." I tried outright bribery. I claimed discrimination; Destiny's status as an ex-con shouldn't compromise her value as a human in need of rescue. I said I'd call my lawyer. I did call my lawyer. She backed up the cops, saying the same things. There was no way to know where Destiny had gone. She advised me to forget about Destiny and "the horse". I tried to explain what Chance meant to me.

You can write off the loss on your taxes, she said. I hung up, vowing to get a new lawyer.

Two days. Two days and three unimaginably cold nights. I vow to do something. Something Hank would do; something out of the box. I think until it comes to me. I call Lee who tells me who to call. An old guy, a guy whose politics and beliefs are a world away from mine; a retired trapper and hunter of bobcat, cougar, coyote, bear. I ask him who could search the forest with mules and horses and dogs. I mention a sum of money. He says he will contact his people and they will call me.

I wait. At seven that evening the phone rings. It is a guy named Al. He listens, then says they can search but "it will cost." To start tomorrow early, will cost even more. I ask and he names a price. I don't haggle but tell him I will be coming along, no argument.

It's your funeral, he says.

At four the next morning (if you can call it that—to me it is still the middle of the night), Al arrives with four other vehicles, two pulling trailers. I am already dressed and have coffee and muffins ready for them. There are six men and they all look like they might prefer raw meat to muffins. I am so anxious to get going that I don't catch all their names. They are large men, or look large, wrapped in their layers of GorTex and nylon camouflage. Their dogs cower in steel cages in the back of the trucks, shivering and whining to do their job. I am assured the dogs won't hurt Chance or Destiny, their job will be to track. The men and I will follow on the mules and horses. Al has brought a "reliable" mule for me to ride. I take Al into the kitchen and count out the four thousand dollars onto the table.

He scoops it up, nodding.

There will be a bonus if we find them within twenty-four hours, I say.

The whole thing feels like a clandestine drug deal or like paying off a kidnapper. I don't like Al or his companions. The men won't look me in the eye. I try not to think about the animals they've killed. How many hundreds? Are these the very guys that killed the last of the bears up here? The mountain lions are mostly gone too. Not to mention the deer and bobcat and squirrels and raccoons and birds… I hate hunting. That rattlesnake was the only thing I've ever killed with a gun. (I can barely stand to eat meat, because I always think about the fact it was a living thing. For one reason or another, turkey's my exception. And fish; a girl's gotta eat, after all….) These guys are professional animal killers. That's what they are. That's what they live for. I don't like anything about them and I don't think I can trust them farther than I can spit. I'm not even sure I will be safe. But they have tracked and packed all around these mountains. If anyone can find Destiny and Chance, it will be these skuzzy men with their guns and dirty horses and cowering hounds.

They get everything ready fast. No more than fifteen minutes after Al has pocketed my money, we are on our way. I had stayed up late not just baking muffins but gathering a first aid and emergency pack. I had socks and pants and sweaters. Boots and gloves and scarves. Two sleeping bags. A horse blanket and a camping stove and lots of food. The men have distributed it amongst themselves; all I have to carry on my mule are my saddle-bags, containing my personal gear. My mule is a tall, dark bay molly with a pretty head and delicate feet. She is quiet, yet I soon find out she walks fast and moves like a deer. I ask her name. Al tells me she doesn't have one.

As we start up the mountain road my no-name mule keeps a perfect distance from the horse ahead. There is no need for me to use either the reins or my legs, and soon I realize I am simply along for the ride.

As we climb, Al informs me in his hoarse smoker's voice that although the weather's been cold there has been no new snow, and that's to our advantage; if there are tracks, he will find them. It doesn't take too long, less than an hour, before we are at the plateau where Destiny and Chance turned off the main road. Al and two other guys get off and examine the prints, and then we continue down the narrow track. The hoof-marked path cut through the snow is clear. There are a few places where Destiny has backtracked to get around an impenetrable stand of brush. But Chance's tracks lead us like the Pied Piper, up into the tall trees, into the steep mountains, the wild forest.

* * *

She'd wanted to get away, away from the criticism, away from people who always made her feel inferior, away from the doctor, who she could never please, no matter how hard she tried. But now she longs for the least sight of civilization. Now it is almost as if civilization has never existed. Like she dreamed up things like houses with central heating, and cars and roads. Maybe she'd somehow gone through a time portal; she and Prince have been transported hundreds of years into the past. Or maybe she has somehow ended up on a different planet; or in a parallel universe. Or maybe, they are dead, and this is Heaven. Or Hell.

All the world is trees and trees. Rocks and one mountain ridge upon another.

She unsaddles him and removes his bridle and halter. He needs to be free to survive. He walks a few steps then lies down and rolls in the patchy snow, gets up and shakes himself. Stands there looking off to the horizon. Destiny gets to her knees then lies full length on the ground and rolls, kicking up her legs like he did, then gets up and tries to imitate his shake. Then she stands looking off to the horizon.

Chance grazes, nipping tiny mouthfuls of grass; pawing to uncover a green patch from underneath the snow. Destiny has made camp and sits by the blowing fire, eating another Nature's Nutty Energy bar, dreaming of a nice burger sizzling on a grill over that fire, or even a dang can of soup. Why didn't she at least bring enough food? She could've snuck all kinds of food from the doctor's pantry, and be here eating a real dinner, then having a cup of tea… she is hungry even after finishing the energy bar. She wishes she could eat grass like Chance. He even eats pine needles and acorns. She leans back on the saddle with the saddle blanket underneath her. But she can still feel the cold on her butt. She pulls the quilt over her. It is wet on the edges. Even when she tucks in like a mummy, even covering her head, she still can't get warm enough. If she hadn't had years of experience sleeping in horrible places, she would never have been able to sleep. But Destiny has been in prison. Finally her incarceration turns out to have been good for something.

When she wakes the fire is out. The mustang is lying next to her. She pulls the quilt over both of them and burrows under, lies down against his back, throws an arm over his neck, pulling him close. Immediately, it is warmer.

* * *

If only she could rewind her life like a videotape, like on the VCR they had when she was little. Destiny used to love rewinding the tapes, watching the movie characters run backwards. It had made her laugh to watch them do everything in reverse: fall up, take food out of their mouths, squeeze tears into their eyes. And she could rewind to her favorite parts. She wants to rewind her life to the good parts. To before she came back to herself on that highway, the cops already there. The red car smashed, glass everywhere and leaking fluids. Mitch already on a stretcher, being shoved into the ambulance like a pizza going into an oven. His clothes—his skin, his face, his hair—covered with blood like tomato sauce. The cop in her face asking questions but all she could do was watch as other cops and paramedics tried to extract the man she'd hit from his car. They were using a big cutting tool like a monster's can opener on the crumpled car. The windshield was all tiny, jagged broken pieces but Destiny could still see the man's bloody face. She could tell he was dead.

Go back, back, back, before. Before Mitch, before the drugs, before the Bees. Before, when Destiny had been poor and alone, but at least taking care of her baby. Back, back, back, to before, when Justin still loved her.

* * *

They were lying on a blanket on the floor, playing with a stuffed bunny. Destiny was making it hop, to make him laugh. He was lying on his tummy and when he laughed, he struck his fat fists on the floor as if the humor was just too much to take.

"Bunny hop, bunny hop," sang Destiny. "Hop, hop hop! Hop to the top!" She hopped the bunny up her knee, then hid it behind her leg, making it disappear.

"Oh, no, where'd bunny go? Oh, oh, oh!"

Justin's eyes opened wide. He stared at where the bunny had been then at Destiny's face. His expression was puzzled, comical.

"Ma?" said Justin. It was his first word.

"Mama! Yes, baby, that's me!" she exclaimed, her heart crumbling with happiness.

"Ma! Ma! Ma!" Justin yelled triumphantly.

"Yes, baby, I'm your mama," she said, grabbing him up in a squeeze. "I'm your mama. You're my big, good boy. And I love you so-so-so much."

Justin squirmed to get down and she let him go. He was impatient to get on with his fun. He would always have little patience for hugging and kissing; he was a boy, after all. And that was perfectly okay with Destiny. Just a little hugging and kissing was perfectly okay.

* * *

We didn't find them that day. It was an uncomfortable night, and not only due to the harsh cold and sleeping on the frozen ground. We had tents and pads and sleeping bags, food and even whisky, all hauled by the three pack mules. It was the company that made the night a trial. I had to be polite but it was difficult to listen to the hunting stories. They tracked and killed at the behest of ranchers, landowners, and even the government. They'd been hired by the Department of Fish and Wildlife upon occasion to track bears and lions that had strayed too near private property, frightening the owners, and those that had attacked livestock. They boasted the death of one bear that had mauled a man. That the man had been feeding the bear and probably deserved to be attacked just for his stupidity was not a factor they considered. I nodded a lot and made polite Hm! noises at the appropriate intervals. I was just happy they weren't raping me. Another consoling thought was that if these guys found Chance and Destiny, maybe it would effect a slight improvement on their dirty karma.

The next day was even colder, with a sharp wind. Dry snow swirled from a dead-looking sky just before dawn. The gear was stowed and we were under way before it was fully light. All day we followed their trail. There were places where the hoof prints became indistinct but that wasn't a problem, the dogs were on his scent and moved along quickly, noses waving over the ground, quivering-tipped tails pointed to the sky. Through the wet forest, mile after mile, the trail alternatively muddy underfoot, or covered in pock-marked frozen snow. The sun was obscured by a dense gray cloud bank, stern and unreadable, frowning like a malevolent nun. The trees and brush crowded us, wiping their cold wet branches on our last bit of dry clothing as we pushed our way along. No Name mule was sweating despite the cold, her body steaming, her wet mule smell poignant and pungent, the smell of resigned determination.

We camped in the late afternoon without finding Destiny and Chance.

* * *

The desert hills were an unearthly green, except where they were speckled with wildflowers, pink, purple, yellow, and yucca spikes, spearing the ridge tops with tall white blooms. It had been a wet spring but that day was sunny and warm, the sky an aching blue; it was too early for bugs, a balmy, sweet breeze wafted like ghost silk; as perfect a day as perfect gets.

We sat on the terrace of our newly finished porch on side by side wicker chairs. Holding hands. Watching the first humming-birds find the feeder and drink deeply, replenishing themselves after their miracle flight from distant jungles. Hank got up and led me to the hummingbird feeder and we stood motionless as the tiny birds whirled around our faces.

"Closer," Hank murmured, pulling me in so we were inches away from the birds. Their iridescent bodies flashed green, magenta, gold. Their tiny needle-like beaks dripped with sugar water. Their wings whirred and blurred. A female lit on the feeder's perch an inch from Hank's face. He leaned in, opened his mouth and gently closed his lips on the bird's tail. The bird extended from Hanks's mouth, unmoving, unafraid. It stared at me with tiny ink-drop eyes. I looked from them to Hank's blue-green, smiling ones. I leaned forward and accepted a kiss from the hummingbird. Touched the very tip of its needle beak, with my lips, tasting the faintest sweetness. Then I slowly took the bird from Hank's lips into my cupped hands. It sat a moment, heart beating a hundred times a minute, then lifted off, wings whirring, circled around our heads, then blew up like being tossed, flying a wide buzzing arc into the limitless blue. We watched it until it was a dot, until it was gone into the sky.

I looked back at Hank.

"My first hummingbird kiss," I said. He grinned and drew me close for a man kiss.

He said: "I'll kiss you with the whole world, just give me enough time."

* * *

I no longer feel the cold, or hear the hunting stories, or see Al and the trackers, I'm back with Hank; and I'm finally able to re-member him with a warm heart, with a secret smile.

You told me it would happen, and it has happened, I tell my Inner Therapist.

How do you feel about it?

Good. I feel good. I don't want to hurt remembering him. I don't want to forget him; I don't want to forget how good it was.

You won't forget him. And you will have new good times.

Maybe. Maybe I actually will. If I find Destiny and Chance, maybe I will.

Find them or not, you can still find peace.

That I very much doubt. If I don't find them, I think I will be haunted to the end of my days.

(There is quite a long moment in which I have no answer for myself.) Finally, my Inner Therapist says, in quite a parochial way: We'd better fucking find them, then.

***

The path is easier, the trees taller here and the underbrush thinner. We make good time climbing to the top of a ridge. Near the top, the dogs suddenly begin howling, first one then all of them. I kick my startled mule into a lope and catch up with Al.

"Have they found something?" I have to yell to be heard over the yowling.

"No doubt," he says.

"I don't want anyone hurt," I remind him. He nods and rides over to the dog handlers. They use their whistles and the dogs come flying. The handlers clip leads to the dog's collars. The dogs are all kinds, cattle dogs, German Shepherds, Labs, and and hounds. They leap and strain at the leads. It looks like they'll strangle themselves in their eagerness to overtake their prey, but I can't spare any sentimentalities for these poor dogs. We contin-ue up the ridge following the dog handlers, who are on foot. My teeth are clenched in anxiety as we approach the top. What if the worst has happened? If Destiny is hurt, or even dead? Or Chance. It is horrifying to consider but I have to face the possibility. They have been out here for five days. And if the worst has happened, it will be all my fault; at least partially my fault. I should have realized that Destiny had no options. When, in the indulgence of my anger, I fired her, sent her away, it must have been devastating.

I am so far beyond forgiving her. The last two nights, safe in my tent, on the high-tech pad and in the rated-fifty-below sleeping bag, I had still had a touch of what sleeping outside in the winter was like. Doing it without a tent, or sleeping bag, without proper clothing or food would be difficult if not torturous. She must have truly been at the end of her rope to stay out here. And I am the one who sent her down that rope.

At the ridge top the trees thin, then disappear. The ridge is bare and windswept. Just some rock outcroppings and some stunted live oak, patchy snow and dead grass bending away from the fierce wind. And an awesome view that goes on forever. But my eyes are not on the view. Just a few hundred yards from us is Chance, lying on the ground, up against a tumble of boulders, my quilt over him. He looks at us curiously and nickers a greeting. Lying against him, her arm over his neck, her face buried in his mane, is Destiny. I kick my mule into movement and as I get closer, Chance stands up. Destiny awakes when her "pillow" disappears. She looks at me in astonishment.

* * *

She wakes to her nightmare. Here they are, ready to take her away from Chance, back to prison—forever, this time. The doctor, and a bunch of huge, scary men on big dirty horses, with terrifying dogs, whining, snarling, straining for the chance to chase her and Chance, bite and rip.

She jumps up and lunges for Chance, to grab his mane, leap on him and race away—he is fast enough to outrun the fastest dog, and he'll kick them dead if he has to—but his head jerks up at the sight of the men and dogs and he whirls and dances off, snorting, eyes white, just far enough away, then stops and looks at Destiny and at the same time the doctor is dismounting a mule and coming towards her, and one of the men is right next to her, he is coming close, fast, holding a rope and a big rifle so Destiny runs to Chance and the man runs towards her and Destiny says, "whoa, whoa, boy"—Chance wants to gallop away but her voice holds him but that is a mistake because the man is there and throws a rope and the lasso spreads and is about to drop over Chance's head and he's captured. Chance rears, and bucks and screams. Destiny does the only thing she can, and spinning away, leaves Chance and runs for her life.

"Destiny! Wait! Stop!" I shriek, as she sprints away across the saddleback. The men are yelling, Al is barking at me, Destiny is running, running away, the howling and slavering of the dogs is deafening, the adrenaline-pumping chaos overwhelms me; Al keeps repeating himself and I finally focus on the words, "We'll get her!" as the hunters ride up with his mount and Al leaps on his horse, and they are about to give chase—"Wait, No!" I yell. I have to grab for the reins of Al's horse before anyone listens.

"No! I won't have her chased like that!" I holler in my no-nonsense voice and they pause, uncertainty in their eyes. They all begin arguing at once.

"Absolutely not," I repeat.

"But she's gittin' away," Al snaps.

I look, hauling back on Chance and he's right, she is, already getting small on the wind-punished plain, heading for the deep forest. I imagine being Destiny at this awful moment and what it would be like to be overtaken by these men and their killing dogs, to be pulled down by a pair of teeth or a rope around your body—no.

"No," I say. "I'll go. Alone. Help me on this horse. Now."

Chance is freaking. It is as if he has never seen me before, as if he's never seen a human before. He's become his former self, a wild stallion, untamed, free; he knows that flight is his weapon. He fights Al, but the man is as brute as my horse and his men manage to hold Chance, drag him close.

I am afraid, as scared as I've ever been, my heart ricocheting around my chest like a blood-filled rubber ball and I can't catch my breath and I surely can't imagine getting on Chance and riding him; all I can imagine is being thrown, trampled, his iron hooves bashing in my skull, trampling my spine… but I have to. I have to. I haven't ridden him since the beginning of summer and I don't want to now. I didn't want to even when we were back at the ranch, when he was safe in the round pen and relaxed, calm, with his big spotted horse dick dropped practically to the ground as proof of his composure.

My ankle throbs with ghost pain, though it hasn't hurt this much in months. As if my body is warning me of terrible hurts that are imminent. But I grasp the reins and the men hoist me up and I am on Chance's bare back.

"Let go," I say through gritted teeth. "Get back." They do, and step back.

I feel Chance's tense body quiver beneath my legs and I take a deep breath and will my muscles to relax.

"Good boy, let's go," I croak, and I cluck and tighten my heels against his sides and he shoots off like a bullet. I am almost left suspended in midair but an ancient, mostly forgotten reflex comes to the rescue and I grab a handful of his wiry mane and grip with my thighs and lean over his neck and we are tearing along, flying on staccato pounding hoofbeats, the wind pulling tears from my eyes, I can't see a fucking goddamn thing but at least I am holding on, I'm sticking to Chance like pine sap. I feel the rhythm, I lean into it, and I trust that Chance is going after Destiny and not towards some unseen, deadly cliff... I ride and Chance gallops and I know that even if I die today on this horse, that it will be a good death, because I am finally doing something for somebody else.

I don't need to guide Chance. He knows where he's going: he's racing right to Destiny. We catch up to her at the edge of the tree line. She hears us thundering up behind her and stops and turns, faces us. I pull up Chance but he's sliding to a stop on his own. Destiny's hands are in fists and her face is defiant, not fearful, her chest is heaving but her voice is strong.

"No!" she screams. "I ain't going back!"

I slide off Chance, ready to tackle her if necessary. We both breathe harshly, our chests going up and down in unison, not speaking. Staring at each other.

She breaks the silence. "I ain't goin back to no prison! Y'all better kill me instead."

"Destiny," I pant. "Nobody's sending you to prison."

She looks away, then slides her eyes back towards me.

"Please, Destiny. Let's go. Let's go home. I'm not pressing any charges."

Seconds pass. Slowly I can breathe again.

"Promise?" she finally says. Her wide eyes meet mine fully, for the first time. I never knew how pretty her eyes were. They are a mocha brown and through them I can feel her fear.

"I absolutely promise."

"I ain't going back to prison," she says, her voice and her face crumbling.

"No, dear. That's not going to happen. Let's get back to the campsite. We'll have something to eat then head home in the morning. Won't it be nice to sleep in your own bed? I'm sure Chance misses his herd too." (I am rambling nervously, it still feels like she might bolt for the forest at any second. She is caught, but still wild.)

She speaks in a hoarse croak.

"Prince."

(She said, prince?) "Prince?" I repeat. She might have hypothermia, I think, maybe hallucinating. Take it gently, I tell myself.

"His name's Prince," she says, nodding towards Chance.

"It is?" I ask, not understanding. Thinking, just keep her talking, she might make sense any second now. "Okay, sure, Destiny, we can call him Prince. Does he... does he remind you of a prince?"

She gives me a disgusted look, one that is completely sane.

"That was his name before," she whispers. "Back in Frontera." I get it. Like the proverbial slap upside the head. No wonder he responds to her. No wonder he never felt like mine. No wonder she is obsessed with him. And I see them again on the ridge top where we found them. The way they'd been lying together, her arms around him, her face in his mane, like lovers.

"He was yours," I say.

"Yes ma'am.."

"You trained him?" she nods. "He's always been your horse," I say, the rightness of what I am to say clicks like a key opening a lock. "He's still your horse. And he'll always be your horse. I might as well just accept that. You can train another one for me, right?"

I watch her face change as she understands my gift. That smile, it really does make her pretty. She says, "Yes, ma'am. I reckon so I can."

"Then we'd better get home, right?"

She nods. We aren't huggers but we do it anyway. And then we are both crying and laughing. And Chance snorts and dances, and begins to circle around us, in a fifty-foot circle. Like a round pen. We laugh more and shout encouragement at his beautiful display of training at liberty. But at once, everything is wrong. Riders bust out from the tree line, Chance's head jerks high, his nostrils flare red, and as the wranglers close in with lassoes twirling, Chance wheels and gallops for the tree line, his flying hooves sending up great plumes of snow.

THE BORDER

I let him go. That day, on the mountain, I let him go. Destiny was safe, but Chance was gone. The men frothed at the chance to chase him through the forest. I knew—as Destiny knew—that with even a few moments' head start, Chance could outrun the men and their horses forever. Even tracking him would be pointless, I thought; it was already snowing. It was possible to catch him, the men insisted, but I couldn't let them do it. Could not let Chance be chased down again, this time instead of a monster helicopter, monster dogs with flesh-tearing teeth.

I took Destiny straight to the hospital. She had hypothermia, and frostbite. She ended up losing the tips of three fingers. She was right on the edge, the doctor said. Another night out there may have been fatal.

We immediately began searching for Chance. I wrote a short article, and called everywhere; we printed posters and took out ads and drove, drove, drove, endlessly, in ever expanding squares and circles from the ranch, hoping to find a report of a loose mustang, possibly still dragging a purple lead rope.

Chance ran until he was sure he wasn't being followed. Then, he settled into a jog-trot that moved him efficiently through the forest. Instinctively his hooves avoided holes and sharp rocks, his head ducked under branches without effort. The forest, in its snow blanket, smelled terrific. He was a little drunk on the scents and the freedom of movement. The last few days had been stressful. The girl was herd leader there, but out here, he had to step up. Now, he was alone. Not a good thing, where herd animals were concerned. Not at all. He scented the air for equine scent. He smelled water. Good enough. He increased his pace down the mountainside.

An overnight storm dropped so much snow it was difficult to find grass, and leaves were long dried brown and non-nutritious. He kept downhill, even though the lower he went, the more signs of civilization he saw, and each bothered him; he was on high alert, but kept on. He needed food. Something else drew him down as well but he didn't bother to name it. Soon he found exactly what he was looking for. In a lovely big meadow, a small herd of mares. He easily leapt the fence and introduced himself. Of course the mares squealed and kicked; they galloped away; but immediately returned. Soon he had acquainted himself with each, and was enjoying the lush grass, spread out on the ground, even though it was man-smelling. After eating he ambled to a likely spot, not far from the mares, and his legs seemed to collapse as he finally laid down on the ground after his long ordeal. He rolled over onto his back, his belly seeming giant, his hooves flailing the air like a toddler's at a diaper change. Chance grunted in pleasure.

He was a mustang; he didn't bother with guilt, or regret, or sentiment. When Destiny was there, he loved her and he followed her lead because it felt right. Staying in his corral there, with the regular feedings and brushings and play in the circle and rides up the mountain at night… he had been content there. But he was a mustang, and as such had no plan to do other than live in the moment.

* * *

"Mom! Mom! When did we get a new horse?" Thirteen-year-old Ayla demanded. Another hectic morning in the Jacobs household, kids complaining, dogs scrabbling and panting, television news morons droning, cats yowling underfoot; meanwhile she was constructing four lunches and planning her week's shopping. Shannon Jacobs frowned at her daughter. "What?"

Ayla cried when her parents called Animal Control and they came and took away the horse that had magically appeared right after Christmas. She was used to presents being late. And that horse was perfect! So, so perfect. But her idiot parents couldn't see that.

No; all they saw was "mustang" which Dad said were "trash horses". Ayla couldn't believe how dense they were! Obvi, this horse was perfect, beautiful, regal, magical…

* * *

The Animal Services in Tule Creek (Pop. 3,101) served all neighboring hamlets within two hundred miles. The facility for cows, horses, camels, et cetera, consisted of a twenty-by-twenty foot steel pen attached to the shelter's trash shed. The pen occasionally housed, temporarily, a stray heifer or burro. Around here, people kept their livestock pretty close to home. So when a full-grown, mustang who-still-considered-himself-to-be-a-stallion, arrived, all hell broke loose. The horse would not stop whinnying—no, more like screaming, so loud and shrill—and he wouldn't stop kicking and striking with his hooves the iron bars of the pen, agitating the dogs at the rear of the kennels, which set off all the other dogs. Within two hours, the office manager was on the phone. Until they could figure out who he belonged to, they needed to find a better place for this crazy mustang.

* * *

"Well, hey there, Shawntelle, how are ya?" Randall couldn't imagine why his high school prom date was calling him. No booty call, however. Turned out she worked at an animal shelter and they had a stray horse. Mustang. If in ten days no one claimed it, it was adoptable for twenty-five bucks. "We gotta get him outa here, Randy," she wheedled. "He's tearin' down the pen out back. He's a gorgeous horse though. Thought ya might know someone who would want him."

Randall did want him. A quick trip with the trailer to the shelter; a few days feed. No big investment. If no one claims it in two weeks, and twenty-five bucks and it's his. It can join the others from the last auction. Actually, the timing couldn't be more perfect. He'd learned to feed up the nags a few weeks on free-as-hell pasture out back, have 'em all gain a few pounds, before the trip across the border. He just scored another five-six hundred profit on the next run with a practically free horse. He celebrated with another whiskey.

Chance allowed himself to be loaded and was relieved when circumstances changed for the better after the quick trip. A new herd, and mustangs! He quickly asserted himself. There was hay and water and room to gallop up the hill until there was a tall fence. Chance had no thought of jumping the fence. He was here with his kind. They slept under a waning moon, breaths syncopated in the night.

Chance barely had time to know his new herd when everything changed. One day, before sunrise: men and horses, and men on wheeled, sputtering objects, ropes, and dogs barking and yelling. They were herded into a chute into a corral and then onto a stock trailer. Too many of them, it was close, and fighting broke out immediately but soon enough they were united in fear as the trailer behind the huge, belching poisoned gas machine sped faster and faster through the dawn.

* * *

I was irritable. No, guilty, and sad. No, furious. On the phone again, making no progress. Apparently, Chance has disappeared. It has been three weeks. Destiny and I hope he's just gone feral. Maybe a miracle: he'll travel far enough to join the last wild herds in California. But we keep looking anyway.

I call the list of shelters again. You never know, with the holidays, maybe our notices weren't getting posted. I'll leave another round of messages.

"Well, yes, ma'am, we did have a horse like that but after the ten days we adopted him out as per the rules," a Shawntelle informed me. I stared at the map. Tule Creek wasn't that far! I asked for a better description. She sent me an e-mail with a photo attached. It was Chance.

"How do I contact the adopter?" I asked, my chest filling up with delicious hope.

"You found him?" Destiny was standing in to doorway. My phone was on speaker. She'd heard everything. And so as Shawntelle filled us in, she moved to my side and we clutched hands as we learned Chance had been "adopted." Eventually, it became clear: By a meat man.

"But he's a mustang," I sputtered. "They're protected!"

"No ma'am, he come in here a stray but we saw the brand so we contacted the BLM and we left a message but never got no call back, and we had to foster him out, ma'am, he was breaking down our corral here."

A government paperwork error? My adoption of Chance had never been registered with the Wild Horse and Burro program? Some phone calls later: Apparently. And as a result, Chance was on his was to Mexico to be slaughtered.

Destiny and I were on the road in twenty minutes. We figured we had to at least try. The most likely border crossing was Nogales. From Bakersfield, ten hours. I called Lee and told her what was up and she wished us luck. While in the truck I tried to contact the sheriffs, but cell signals were spotty.

We stopped in Bakersfield to pee and I used one of the last surviving pay phones; the receiver sticky with what I hoped was ancient ketchup. Charlie, bless him, said he'd try to contact the border police and the California brand inspector. Maybe Chance could be intercepted as they left California. We loaded up on fast food and kept driving through out the night.

"We're gettin' close," Destiny awoke me. A grayish pink dawn. Flat chaparral-studded desert. Cactus.

"I need coffee." I moan. My neck feels welded. I can barely turn my head. My mouth is nasty and spongy.

"But it's like, here," Destiny announced, pointing with her chin up the highway. I try to see. Sure enough, right ahead, a sign: Nogales, Mexico.

After a frustrating hour of finding ourselves in the wrong lane and having to circle around under suspicious stares of the border cops, we eventually locate the agricultural area. I knew from my research that horses bound for slaughter are unloaded at the border, inspected by a Mexican veterinarian who checks to see if the paperwork matches the horse and if the horse is fit for transport.

We have no way of knowing if this is the border the kill buyer is using; it's just the most common from California. We have no idea if the meat man wasn't so far ahead of us that the horses have already passed through. They might already be on their way to Zacatecas, to the slaughter plants. Once there, it happens quickly. The horses have already endured a twelve- to eighteen-hour journey without water of food or relief. Crossing the blazing Mexican desert, pressed against each other's quivering flesh.

"There! Here! Turn here," I cry, finally spotting not a sign but a parking area with too many stock trailers with semi's attached. There are fences behind. We pull in, my pickup dwarfed by the big trucks. As I slow, looking for an office, a human in charge, Destiny suddenly opens the door and jumps out. "I'll look," she yells, dodging a pickup with an old swearing cowboy. Fuck this. I park right there, and try to catch up to Destiny. I follow her pink sweatshirt as she threads her way through rumbling semi's. I lose her.

"Hey, lady, what the fuck?" yells a Latino man, slamming on his brakes. I see her. I hear her scream.

I run as best I can.

He is there. Destiny squeezes through the rails of the corral and is wrapping her arms around him and sobbing. The others horses have backed away, creating a roughly circular space for Destiny and Chance. I watch as the mustang gently lays his head on her shoulder, and half closes his eyes. I feel embarrassed, like surprising lovers in the act. I go to the office to buy back our horse.

Horses in Heaven

The rooster yodels before five in the morning and I don't wait for more crowing before I get up. It takes me a while to get going these days and I don't want to miss anything. Destiny used to help me with buttons and my boots, but now one of the other girls will do it.

Today we're having an auction. There are ten nicely started mustangs for sale, and another fifteen halter-trained colts. We decided last year to sell halter-trained colts too, because usually they sold easily and the new owners usually paid us extra to board them and continue their training. It cuts down on our capital outlay, and we can rescue more horses that way.

Destiny has recruited a dozen girls to help train the mustangs. Girls that need a chance. From Frontera Prison, of course, but also from broken homes and abusive ones, from the poorer communities and from the streets. We've only had one girl drop out, and none of them have ever broken the law again, or taken advantage of us. The first two girls moved out eventually, and they both are professional horse trainers. One works at a fancy riding camp for kids. Another got married and has two daughters and rehabilitates "problem horses" up in Tulare County.

Over the years we've sold over half the original mustang herd, leaving only the old, lame, and truly ornery. We've adopted a couple of hundred more. Trained them and sold most of them. Ironically, we got an award last year from the Department of the Interior for our efforts in saving the mustangs and helping "Preserve a part of America's Heritage." Guess they never read any of my articles; I'd never stopped writing about the travesty that the Wild Horse and Burro program had become.

I hired a new lawyer and started a non-profit company. We publish a newsletter and help to spread the word about what great horses the mustangs can be. We constantly campaign to end of the terrible business of horse slaughter and to help pass new laws ensuring continued protection for the wild horses.

Destiny and I even took a road trip to visit one of the herds. Way up to northern Nevada, to the Jackson Mountains, to see Chance's herd. When we finally found them, after two days of riding, we watched them through the binoculars all afternoon, until we had to leave. Destiny was sure there were some of Chance's colts in that bunch. I thought so too, although unless they were captured and DNA tested, there was no way to know. But I hoped they'd never be captured, even if they were to end up with us. They looked so right, there in that harsh valley, with its glittering, twisting creek and stunted pine trees. The mustangs' shaggy tails and their thick coats, dull with dust, seemed to be a part of the landscape, belonging there as much as the ground squirrels and scrub jays, as much as the wind and the thin clouds racing the ravens across the sky.

* * *

"Hey, buddy." Prince stands with his head over the rails as she approaches his corral. He whickers like he always does. She rubs his white-striped forehead and kisses his white-speckled muzzle. He's getting older but there are still plenty good years left for both of them.

She worries that's not true for Sara Beth. Even though she's always been interested in everything, lately it has seemed like her mind is really elsewhere. She's pretty crippled up and some days in a lot of pain. Destiny knows that the ranch and the non-profit are already legally hers to run as a full partner. But she still dreads the fact that Sara Beth won't be around for long. She can just feel it.

She refuses to move into the big house though, and won't, even after Sara is gone. It just wouldn't feel right. The apartment over the barn is her home, hers and Justin's. Sara Beth had built an additional bedroom when he came. It used to be full of toys and little boy clothes. Now it has sports trophies and posters of movie starlets, rock bands, and sports cars. He's going away to college next year.

It had been hard at first, reestablishing herself as Justin's mama. Eventually though, he warmed to her and the horses and to Sara Beth, whom he still called Gran. He hadn't been a perfect kid; he was always prone to bouts of anger and sulking. But he made friends and got fairly decent grades and played baseball and yes, learned to ride. Horse training isn't his calling though. Her little boy wants to help people. A fireman, or even a cop. He hasn't decided, but she knows he'll make the right choice; making good choices is one thing she'd made sure he understood. It wasn't toys or things that meant love, it was attention, guidance. It was Destiny's pride and privilege to be able, finally, do that for her boy.

Destiny woke before sunrise. This was the day! Justin was just as excited. She raced through chores in order to shower, wash her hair, and freshly braid it. Her favorite shirt, the sleeveless blue checked with pearl snaps. She regarded herself in the mirror. She no longer felt fat. She no longer felt like a loser. And today, she'd get to show Sergeant Varney.

He looked a lot older and his legs were more bowed than ever. His cabbage nose was even huger, somehow. But Destiny's heart overflowed the moment he stepped from his old pickup. They hugged and cried. Destiny introduced Sara Beth and Justin.

Justin asked, in that direct way of his, "Did you know my mom when she was in prison?"

"Yessir, I did," Varney said.

"She's better now," Justin asserted.

"She sure is," Varney agreed. "She doin' right fine. I'm real proud of her." Destiny's eyes blurred with tears as they walked slowly to visit the horses in the corrals. A lovely family, Destiny thought. An old man, an old woman, both wearing battered boots. Her young man, in his freshly waxed ones, college-bound! And herself: horse trainer, mentor. Mom. Doing right fine.

* * *

The auction goes well, we sell all the horses. Chance Ranch Mustangs has become known for sound and steady saddle horses. Destiny and I are in the office going over the accounts. The ranch pays for itself now and I've set up a trust to keep it going after I'm gone.

I remind her that she'll need to check the accountant's work. Make sure the taxes are always paid on time.

"I wish you wouldn't talk that way," she says as she always does.

"My dear, I'm older than the hills. I'm tired."

'You're probably just missing Hank again," she says.

"I always miss him. It's strange, isn't it? It never gets better. The pain just becomes the new normal."

"I wished I'd of met him," she says.

"Me too, Destiny. Me too."

"I don't want to lose you, Sara Beth," she says.

"I know, dear. But, you will. Not today though."

"I guess you're looking forward to seeing him."

I smile. "I don't have the faith you have, girl. Though sometimes I wish I did."

"You don't believe? In life hereafter?"

"I don't know what happens. But I'll tell you what. I hope you're right, I hope there is an afterlife. I'd love to see Hank," I laugh, then add, "And I hope I'm not still old and shriveled up, he wouldn't even recognize me."

She doesn't share my amusement. "Well, I do believe," she says seriously. "I do believe. I know you'll git to see him again."

"Here's hoping," I say, and raise my glass of wine. The ruby surface trembles slightly.

"You don't have to hope," she said. "I know it. I know something else, too."

"What's that?"

Destiny's smile at her friend and partner is tremulous. In it is regret, affection, gratitude; her whole heart.

"I know there's horses in Heaven," she says.

Chance
—Kelly McLane

Author's Note

I wrote the novel *Chance* in between 2009–2012. It took an additional seven years to publish it myself. In 2018 I formed the publishing imprint Mountain Mouth Press, publishing my first novel, *Venis*, and *A Journey With JJ* by Stephen Doorlag. When *The Mustang* movie appeared on social media in late 2018, I knew it was time to publish *Chance*.

The spark of an idea for the novel *Chance* occurred while I was interviewing a sheriff's commander in my new job as a newspaper reporter, but my obsession with wild mustangs began decades earlier.

As a child, I'd read about America's mustangs, and was part of the famous children's letter-writing campaign in the 1970's that influenced Congress to pass the first laws protecting the wild horse herds.

So when the officer mentioned a prison training program, with wild horses—mustangs—matched with prisoners, I was fascinated.

What I discovered while researching this book was deeply disturbing. A government agency charged with protecting the wild horses and burros was apparently systematically working to destroy them. Brutal, for-profit helicopter round-ups, back-room deals, fake statistics, and an indifferent public had created an inhumane perversion of the original *Wild and Free-Roaming Horse and Burro Protection Act of 1971*. Instead of finding sanctuary in their congressionally designated Herd Areas, the mustangs and burros were being fenced out from water and pasture, unscientifically culled, and rare and famous bloodlines being endangered as the herds became thinned beyond genetic sustainability.

A rounded-up horse's fate is far from secure (if they survive round-up, injuries and even fatalities are common, sometimes pregnant mares and foals are literally run to death). The government places the burden back on the public, by "offering" the captured horses at public auctions.

I adopted four wild mustangs while writing this book and even though I had ridden since I was small, and even won a ribbon for riding in high school, training a wild horse can be dangerous, frustrating, impossible, or quite magic. It's not for those without unlimited patience, time, resources, so naturally, there are never enough adopters for the horses that are captured. Many of the others end up in government-contracted pastures like those of the so-called "Pioneer Woman." "As part of the wild horse program, the government pays... per horse per day at the end of every month."—Pioneer Woman blog.* The landowners get richly compensated for homing the once-wild mustangs, part of the 70 million dollar budget for "managing" the wild horses and burros. "Pioneer Woman Ree Drummond is revealed as 23rd largest landowner in US with 433,000 acres—and the government paid her family $23.9 million in rent over the past decade," claims a November 2017 Daily News UK article. There are other sweetheart deals but Pioneer Woman is the most public example.

The public lands that comprise the horse's ranges are wild, rocky, and vast, and a wild horse herd a mere speck in a seemingly endless, empty landscape. But these same lands are legally designated "multi-use" and highly coveted by cattle and sheep ranchers and mineral and oil companies, who see the wild horse herds as a threat. Polluting the groundwater by fracking, mining and running livestock might go unnoticed except for the fact that horse carcasses are quite large and easy to spot from a plane that might fly overhead. As such they are the unwanted canaries in the coal mine of the American West. As rationale for their removal, the horses are scapegoated as destroyers of the rangelands, even though no science whatsoever supports this. The species Eqqus evolved on the American continent, making it a true native species. The horses' grazing patterns actually seed and fertilize the plains they travel on their daily rounds—as much as thirty miles a day—for forage and water, unlike cattle, which outnumber the wild horses on their own land by fifty cows to every horse.

Mustangs and wild burros have been credited with potentially reducing wildfire hazards, and used as an icon and tourist bait. But unfortunately none of these positives outweigh the big money interests and their Washington lobbyists. Even the wild horse and burro advocates are at war over donation dollars and differences in opinion on just about everything. There is no control group of wild mustangs: a herd that has been left alone for decades to live alongside their natural predators. The mountain lions and wolves have been decimated; today the only predator killing the mustangs is human.

The Bureau of Land Management's Wild Horse and Burro program of management, therefore, is an almost complete failure, with few exceptions like the prison training programs and the Extreme Wild Horse Challenge.

I visited the prison in Carson City Nevada was privileged to meet Hank Curry, the trainer there, and was able to observe the inmates working with the horses on a couple occasions. That is the stuff of magic. But only three programs like that exist, even though mustangs have been noted for their exceptional ability in many areas. They are used by Border Patrol agents and policemen, cowboys and children. They excel at endurance and are markedly more sensitive and aware than many domestic horses. The migration of pioneers, immigrants, early settlers, was facilitated by the wild horses they claimed and trained. The mustangs were recruited by the Army and fought war after war with legendary heart.

They deserve better; they deserve everything we can give them.

*https://thepioneerwoman.com/confessions/the-wild-horses/

ACKNOWLEDGMENTS

The legendary mustang trainer and man, Hank Curry, and prison administrator, Tim Bryant welcomed me to Silver City Correctional, Carson City, Nevada, where I met the inmates training wild horses, one of the coolest things I've ever seen

Jill Starr was an early reader and hosted me at Wild Horse Boot Camp in Lancaster, California and at Lifesaver's Sanctuary in Twin Oaks, where hundreds of mustangs, burros and domestic horses, rescued from slaughter and abuse, peacefully roam the mountainside.

Sonja Anne Roth was as exited as I when I adopted my first mustang, Jackson; and journeyed with me to see the wild horse herds and interview people on all sides of the issue in Los Vegas, Reno and Carson City, Nevada, and the BLM corrals in Ridgecrest, California.

My Dad and Mom, and Sue Jacobsen and Holly Jacobsen Steinmeyer, for nurturing my love of horses.

Stephen Doorlag, who encouraged me to finish.

Kelly McLane's detail from her WIP 2019 painting *War Room*, author's photo on the cover, and drawing of *Chance* on page 298.

Diane Spencer Hume for all the hand-holding and great book design, both times.

Gabriella West for editing and keeping me honest.

Sarah Aumann, for copyediting, cover design, and sisterhood.

Margurite Henry, for writing *Mustang, Wild Spirit of the West.*

Wild Horse Annie, aka Velma Johnston, for the horses.

This is a work of fiction. All characters and events are the work of the Author's imagination. The Author's opinion of the Bureau of Land Management's Wild Horse and Burro program, any facility matching wild horses and prisoners, or and any inmates or employees of the government or any prison, is entirely her own;

however there are many people whose knowledge and horse sense were valuable in the writing of this book which deserve mention, in no particular order:

Dennis Knipple, BLM; Laura Leigh, Wild Horse Education; Neda De Mayo, Return to Freedom; Joe and Nadia Lane, High Sierra Wild Horse Gentling Center; Craig Downer, *The Wild Horse Conspiracy*; Ginger Kathryns, The Cloud Foundation; Carol Walker, photographer and author, *Wild Hoofbeats*; Deanne Stillman, *Mustang*; James Anaquad Kleinert, *Wild Horses and Renegades*; Debbie MacDonald, Research Queen; Jetara Sethart and Shanti (RIP); Catherine Kindsfather, Terri Farley, and Cheyenne and Rachael and Cheyenne Waller.

I'm humbled and grateful to he writers who inspire and support me: Jane Smiley, Karen Karbo, Deanne Stillman, Jo-Ann Mason, Janet Fitch, Terri Farley, Carole Beers, and Pam Huston.

Also: Ron Gilbert, farrier to the stars, everyone at Rankin Ranch, Carol Hedges, Nancy "Longrider" Guzman, Dave "Davio" Pistone, Angie Skye Dawn Murray, Chris Nichols, Wendy-Tracey at Timber Winds Ranch; Susan Soderberg, mule whisperer; Dr. Chris Comeau, DVM; Jim Westin, for the frozen hoses, broken toes and mustang cookies, and El Dutche McLane.

And especially, to the mustangs: Jackson, Stella Vega, Gus and Captain Call, and Reno. May your families run forever free.